SOPHY FROZE, HER HEART BANGING HER RIBS

"You have no need to be frightened of me," Ives murmured. "I want very much to kiss you, Sophy, but only if you allow it."

Sophy took a shaken breath, Ives's words allaying her fear somewhat. Instinctively she knew that he was no brute like her husband, and that knowledge freed her. Ideas of what his kiss would be like had haunted her for days. Why not, she asked herself, find out what it would be like? Knowing she was a fool, she could not resist his blandishments, or her own curiosity. Throwing aside her doubts, she lifted her lips to his. "Please," she murmured, "please . . ."

Ives groaned and gathered her closer, his mouth finding hers. . . .

Also by Shirlee Busbee

Scandal Becomes Her

Surrender Becomes Her

Passion Becomes Her

Rapture Becomes Her

Whisper to Me of Love

Desire Becomes Her

Lovers Forever

Published by Kensington Publishing Corporation

SHIRLEE
BUSBEE

For Love Alone

ZEBRA BOOKS
KENSINGTON PUBLISHING CORP.
http://www.kensingtonbooks.com

First Zebra Books Mass-Market Paperback Printing: December 2013
First Warner Books Mass-Market Paperback Printing: May 2000
ISBN-13: 978-1-4201-2326-5
ISBN-10: 1-4201-2326-2

First Zebra Books Electronic Edition: December 2013
eISBN-13: 978-1-4201-3273-1
eISBN-10: 1-4201-3273-3

10 9 8 7 6 5 4 3 2 1

Printed in the United States of America

Prologue

❧

Marlowe House
Northumberland, England
February, 1805

Sophy, Lady Marlowe, never knew what woke her. One second she was asleep and the next wide-awake, heart thumping. She lay quietly in her bed listening to the sounds of the storm outside. Had it been merely the howl of the wind that had awakened her?

In the faint glow from the dying fire on the hearth, she could see the bulky shapes of the furniture scattered about the huge room. Nothing seemed out of place. Had she been having another nightmare?

A sudden burst of raucous laughter came drifting up from downstairs. Her fine mouth twisted. Her husband's guests. No doubt drunk and amusing themselves with any of the servant girls who had been unwise enough not to have locked themselves away in their quarters. Of course the Marquis, her husband, did not hire *virtuous* young women to work for him. Any female who came to work at Marlowe House knew precisely what she was letting

herself in for—the Marquis's excesses were legendary in
Northumberland. A faint expression of contempt crossed
her face. And in London. In fact the whole of England.

Deciding that dwelling on her husband's vices would
gain her little, Sophy was on the verge of drifting back to
sleep when she heard a sound: a faint scratching at her
door. *Someone was trying to enter her room.*

Wide-awake again, she sat up, instinctively seeking the
loaded pistol that was never far from her reach. Was it
Simon, her loathsome husband, thinking to exercise his
conjugal rights? Or one of his disreputable cronies—
Grimshaw or Marquette, perhaps—who were drunken
enough to try their luck at forcing their attentions on her?

Slipping from her bed, she shrugged into a dressing
gown and swiftly lit the small candelabra which sat
nearby. The pistol clutched in her hand, she stared at the
heavy door that opened onto the main hallway of the
house. The crystal handle of the door was being forced in
first one direction and then another. A mirthless smile
twisted her lips. It seemed that she had an uninvited visitor. It wouldn't be the first. In the nearly three years since
she had married Simon, the Marquis of Marlowe, Sophy
had learned well how to protect herself—not only from
him, but from his friends as well. She had traveled a
great, painful distance from the innocent, unsophisticated
young woman who at seventeen had been flattered by the
attentions of the much older man paying court to her. She
had been, she admitted savagely, a dreamy, silly little
goose!

Crossing to the door, she set down the candelabra on a
small table. The pistol primed and ready in her hand, she
took a deep breath. Unlocking the door, she flung it wide.

Without surprise she stared at the elegantly garbed

gentleman swaying drunkenly before her. Although the years of rampant dissipation were evident on his features, Simon Marlowe was still a fairly handsome man, his black hair thick and gleaming, his skin clear, his body hard and lean. But not yet forty-three, his bold features were already beginning to show the signs of his dissolute life. His eyes particularly, those cold blue orbs, so empty and lifeless, gave clear evidence of the decades of wanton debauchery.

Those same eyes were fixed on her now, a carnal gleam leaping in their depths as he gazed at her tall, willowy form standing in the doorway of her room. The gleam vanished the second she raised the pistol and aimed it at his heart.

"You do not listen, do you, dear husband?" Sophy asked softly, her golden eyes fixed dispassionately on his face. "I told you over a year ago that I would not suffer your abuses any longer. And nothing you have done since that time has changed my mind. You have beaten me and degraded me for the last time. Continue in your attempts to force your way into my bed, and I shall kill you."

Simon swore violently, his expression ugly. "You arrogant little bitch! You are my wife! You are not to deny me. How dare you threaten me?"

Sophy smiled thinly. "I dare because if I do not, I should have no choice but to kill myself rather than endure another night of your violent and distasteful rutting."

"Do not speak to me in that tone! I am your husband. You *shall* not deny me."

"I shall. You forfeited any rights to me on our wedding night, when you took an innocent girl, a girl who might have loved you, and raped her."

"I did not rape you!" he snarled, his eyes dark with fury. "You were my wife. It was my right."

"Ah, forgive me, perhaps I am mistaken. It was not precisely rape, but there was no kindness, no gentleness, no understanding for my virgin state. We had hardly left my mother's home before you fell upon me like a ravening beast, deflowering me on the seat of your coach, heedless of my cries or the pain you were inflicting. I cannot say that your methods have changed very much in the years that have followed." Her voice hardened, giving him no chance to interrupt. "Until I took matters into my own hands, you used me cruelly. You violated me, and, not content with that, you have struck me and treated me with contempt. You fill this house with blackguards and scoundrels—when you are here—and expect me to put up with their disgusting behavior. They insult me by their very presence in my home and you do not care if they subject me to the most repulsive type of action or distasteful speech." She looked at him, her contempt evident. "Do you really think that I wish to hear how many virgins they have initiated into prostitution? How many innocent maids they have seduced? Do you honestly think I enjoy seeing your friends drunk and openly fondling the slatterns they bring with them?"

Simon remained silent, his face darkening with rage as she spoke. "You are a prudish little bitch," he growled when she ceased speaking. "You think you are so high-and-mighty, so far above the rest of us mortals. You accuse me of having abused you. What about you? You owe me an heir. You have denied me my rights and broken your vows."

Sophy shook her head. "I owe you nothing, my lord. Whatever I may have owed you when we married has been paid to you a thousandfold. You have humiliated me by parading your mistresses before me. I endured your brutality for nearly a year before realizing that I would rather die than suffer your touch again."

Simon's fists clenched and unclenched spasmodically, and only the threat of the pistol she held aimed at his heart kept him from falling upon her. "Impudent jade," he snapped. "Someday you will regret this. I will see that you do. You will not always have a weapon to hide behind."

"You think not? I would not place any wagers on it, dear husband. This pistol and I have become fast friends. I am never without it. Even during your absences, which are thankfully frequent, it is always near my hand."

The vast hallway in which they confronted each other was in shadow. Only the occasional flashes of lightning from the storm illuminated its cavernous width and the chairs and tables lining one wall. A railing ran along the opposite wall and ended at the grand staircase leading downstairs. Beyond the staircase, the wide hallway continued in utter blackness. From the room behind Sophy, the wavering light of her candelabra shed a soft glow around her, intensifying the burnished gold of her tousled curls and faithfully outlining the gentle curves of her slender body.

With greedy hunger Simon's eyes fell on her breasts, remembering their silken firmness and her small, sweet nipples; his determination to taste those delights again became more urgent. Blind lust instantly consumed him, and his gaze narrowed as he assessed his chances of overpowering her. He eyed the pistol, then glanced at his wife's face.

Sophy read his thoughts as clearly as if he had spoken

them aloud and smiled grimly. "I would not try it, Simon. Killing you would not grieve me."

"I do not believe you," Simon blustered. "You will not shoot me."

"Won't I?"

In the blink of an eye, her aim shifted and she pulled the trigger. There was a loud explosion, the scent of black powder filled the air, and blue-gray smoke drifted all around them. Simon stared in horror at the neat hole that pierced the cloth of his jacket near his shoulder.

"You shot me," he gasped in disbelief.

"No. I shot your jacket. If I had wanted to hit *you,* I would have." She smiled again. "I have used your frequent and long absences well. I am very, *very* good with my pistol. Would you like another demonstration?"

Simon took a prudent step backward. There was still another bullet in her pistol. A sly gleam suddenly entered his eyes.

Sophy sighed in exasperation. "Simon, do not be a fool. I know I only have one bullet left. I will not waste it, so do not try to trick me into shooting wildly. The next time I fire at you it will be to kill you."

"Simon!" called a voice from below. "I say, Simon, are you there? We thought we heard a shot."

Throwing his wife a vicious glance, Simon leaned over the railing and looked down. Spying a tall, golden-haired gentleman below him, and a smaller, rotund man beside him, he said testily, "Your ears did not mislead you. Your bloody-minded niece just tried to kill me."

The blond gentleman, Edward, formally Baron Scoville and also Sophy's uncle, smiled beatifically. Half-foxed like Marlowe, he swayed slightly and glanced owlishly at his friend, Sir Arthur Bellingham, before murmuring. "Told you she was a right 'un, didn't I? Told you she had spirit."

"Spirit? You are a fool, Scoville," Marlowe spat. "She's a damned witch! I've a good mind to divorce her."

"Oh, please do," cooed Sophy. "You know I would like it above all things."

"Shut up! Not another word out of you," Simon said thickly, his eyes icy with rage. Looking down at Edward and Sir Arthur, he muttered, "Go away, the pair of you. Everything is fine. Tell the others that I shall be down in a minute." He flashed a venomous look at his wife. "*Especially* tell Annie that I will be down."

With a languid wave of his hand, Edward departed unsteadily, closely followed by an equally unsteady Sir Arthur. As they returned to the other merrymakers, Sir Arthur murmured, "Told you it was a shot, not lightning. I win the wager."

With the departure of the two men, the upper hallway was silent again as Sophy and Simon regarded each other. Simon was obviously still considering his chances. Sophy said tiredly, "Go away, Simon. Amuse yourself with Annie, whoever she may be, and your friends."

"Damn you! You are the only one who can give me what I want—an heir. You deny me the only thing I want from you." He took a step nearer and, forcing a pleasant expression on his dark face, said softly, "Give me an heir, Sophy, and I swear I will not ask anything else from you ever again."

Through cynical eyes Sophy regarded him. She had just turned twenty the previous October, but three years of marriage had left her with little belief in the promises of men. Particularly *this* man. She shook her head. "Never."

His face contorted with fury, and he raised a hand to strike her as he had done so often in the past. Sophy merely steadied her pistol and asked softly, "Shall I fire?"

Cursing, Simon spun on his heels and strode down the long hallway toward the staircase. In silence Sophy watched him go, hardly daring to believe that she had won—this time.

A crack of thunder rent the air, and almost immediately the hallway was lit by a brilliant flash of lightning. The very foundations of the house seemed to shake. Startled, Sophy froze and something at the end of the hall caught her eye. The gleam of a jewel? Reflected light from a mirror? Still blinking from the nearly blinding flash of only a second ago, she stared into the murky darkness. For one shaken moment she had the uneasy sensation that something—someone—was there. Was that the faint shadowy outline of a man pressed against the wall? Her eyes strained to pierce the blackness at the other end of the hall, but could see nothing. She hesitated a moment, then, deciding it had been her imagination, turned away.

All she wanted was to be safely locked within her room. She stepped back over the threshold and locked the door. Leaning weakly against the cool wood, she only now allowed herself to tremble. Her knees felt like pudding, and she wondered if she would be able to walk back to her bed. There had been other confrontations like this in the nearly year and a half since she had told her husband that she would not allow him to touch her, but tonight had been by far the worst. She had to find a way out of this horrible maze. She had to. Not only for her own sake but for Marcus and Phoebe, her younger brother and sister.

A shaft of anxiety went through her when she thought

of Marcus, only fourteen, and Phoebe, almost eleven, being left in the indifferent care of her uncle Edward. Simon had flatly refused to have them come live at Marlowe House when their mother, Jane, had died two years ago come September. Their father, the Earl of Grayson, had died in a hunting accident years ago, three weeks after Sophy's fourteenth birthday. Sophy had thought that her father's death was the most painful event she had ever suffered, but she had learned that there were other equally painful events to overcome. Her mother's death and her marriage both came to mind.

Placing the pistol within easy reach beneath her pillow, she threw off her dressing gown, blew out the candles, and slid back into bed. Staring blankly overhead, she wondered how she was going to endure years of exile at Marlowe House, virtually alone and friendless, forever fending off Simon's advances. Her own immediate problems lay heavily on her mind, and the fates of her brother and sister were never out of her thoughts. A dismal future seemed to stretch endlessly before her. Her only hope, she thought bitterly, would be for Simon to drink himself into an early grave.

Simon's thoughts of Sophy were far less kind as he half walked, half staggered toward the head of the stairs. Bloody bitch! I'd like to put my hands around her throat and choke the life out of her. Then I could go looking for another wife.

When he considered it, Simon was amazed at the fix he found himself in. Because of his reputation, he had not been viewed with pleasure by many of the ton, and as for marrying one of their daughters—absolutely not! He might have a title and a fortune, but no family of any substance had been willing to align itself with him. And he had wanted to marry. He had been forty years old and had needed an heir—damned if he'd allow some second cousin twice removed to inherit! When Edward had proposed a match with his niece in exchange for his gaming debts being cleared, Simon had nearly fallen on his neck with gratitude.

In the beginning, Sophy had seemed like perfection itself. She had been young, virginal, came from good breeding, even had a generous fortune that would be hers when she married. And she had been utterly lovely, one of the "Golden Scovilles." Like her uncle and her mother, she was tall, slim, fair-haired, exquisitely fashioned. Best of all, tucked away at the Grayson estate in Cornwall, she and her mother had heard little of the ugly gossip that followed him wherever he went.

He frowned. Well, that silly goose, Jane, had heard a thing or two, but Edward had been able to talk her round. Her brother had convinced Jane that Sophy's marriage to his dear friend, the Marquis, would be a great coup. There would be no need for Jane to tax her frail health with a London Season; an eligible party was standing right on her doorstep, eager to marry her eldest daughter. Simon knew that Jane's poor health—she had died before he and Sophy had been married a year—had influenced her decision to agree to the match.

How anything that had seemed so perfect could turn out so disastrous completely escaped him. Vixen! He would show her a thing or two. She had not bested *him*.

Intent upon his own thoughts, Simon was unaware of the dark, still figure watching his progress from the shadows beyond the staircase. The figure had been there for several minutes, and from his concealment at the far end of the hall he had watched and listened to most of the heated exchange between husband and wife.

As Simon reached the stairs, the man suddenly made himself visible with a slight movement out of the shadows. Staring uncertainly into the gloom at the other end of the hall, Simon demanded, "Who's there? Who is it?"

The man smiled, his right hand concealed behind him, and stepped partially into the light. "Why, it is only I, Simon."

"*You!* What the devil are you doing up here skulking around?"

"Ah, I thought that perhaps we could have that private conversation you requested."

"Now?" Simon asked incredulously. "Here?"

"Why not? It was one of the reasons you invited me to be your guest, was it not?" came the silky reply.

A sneer touched Simon's mouth. "Never doubted you were a clever fellow ... not after all the time Scoville and I have been feeding you those snippets of information you found useful to send to your master ... Napoléon."

"Why, what an outrageous notion," the gentleman returned easily. "If that were true, that would make me a spy—and you and your friend traitors."

Simon waved a dismissive hand. "You would have a difficult time proving it."

"Exactly." The other man clapped Simon amicably on the shoulder. "Now let us forget this unseemly conversation and return to your other guests."

Simon grinned nastily. "You are not putting me off that easily ... *Le Renard.*"

"Ah, you really have been poking about in my business, have you not?"

"I have indeed—and it is going to cost you a tidy sum to keep my mouth closed." Simon's eyes glowed with triumph. "I do not even have to expose you. All I have to do is whisper a word here or there that you are not what you seem and your reputation will be ruined. It would not take long for your ties to the French to become public."

"If I am unmasked, aren't you afraid that your part will come out?" the gentleman asked with an edge to his voice.

Simon laughed. "Do you really think anyone would believe that gentlemen like Edward and me would be supplying you with information? It is absurd. We are known to be wild and scandalous, but traitors? Piffle. Besides, for the pittance you have paid us, we only supplied you with gossip. I have discovered that you have other sources, better sources, here in England. Sources who have actually given you damaging information about troop movements and plans."

"You know all that, do you?"

"Yes, I do." Simon looked smug. "It took me a long time to finally uncover the identity of the Fox, but now that I have—I can crush you anytime I feel like it."

"Then why don't you?"

"Because I will find it much more amusing to keep you on a leash. And to make it even more entertaining, squeeze some gold out of you whenever I feel like it."

"You don't need the money—unlike Lord Scoville," the gentleman stated levelly. "I always wondered why you were willing to sell out your country."

"It amused me. And as for not needing the money, 'tis true, but every time you pay me, it will make you even more aware of the power I hold over you." Simon chortled. "I intend to get a great deal of pleasure out of watching you squirm."

"Do you really?" the other man asked softly, as Simon turned and prepared to descend the staircase.

"Yes, I really do," Simon said cheerfully over his shoulder.

"Then I am afraid that you *really* leave me no choice but to kill you . . ."

Before Simon could react, the other man struck him a savage, lethal blow on the head with the poker he had kept hidden by his side. Simon didn't even have a chance to cry out. He swayed, then tumbled headfirst down the long staircase.

When Simon lay unmoving in a crumpled heap at the base of the stairs his murderer carefully stepped back into the shadows. Slipping into his room a few doors down the hall, he casually wiped away the few specks of blood on the poker and replaced it in the stand at the edge of the hearth. Tossing the stained cloth onto the fire, he watched it wilt and blacken as the flames consumed it, the scent of scorched fabric briefly stinging his nostrils.

There was now nothing, he thought with satisfaction, to connect him, or anyone else for that matter, to Simon's unexpected death. There was nothing, in fact, to arouse suspicion that Simon's demise had been anything other than a tragic accident. The head wound could be explained away as having occurred in Simon's violent tumble down the stairs. When he had struck Simon, he reminded himself, he had not done so wildly. He had deliberately struck only one, well-placed blow—a blow that could have easily been caused by striking one's head against a step. He had no doubt that such would be the conclusion reached by everyone.

Taking a deep breath, he allowed a faint smile to cross his lips. All was well, although he admitted he'd had a nasty moment when Sophy had stared so piercingly in his direction. Had she seen him? He doubted it. She'd given no sign. But if she had, he considered slowly, he would simply have to silence her. Pity.

Putting the thought from him, he glanced complacently at himself in the mirror and gently patted his intricately tied cravat. His movements froze as he noticed with a chill that his cravat pin was missing. A very distinctive pin at that, the large bloodred ruby and ornate setting not commonly seen in the cravat pins usually worn by fashionable gentlemen. Telling himself that it meant nothing, that he could have lost it at any time, he hastily searched his room. It was not there. Where the devil had he lost it? In the hall? Nothing to fear from that. He took a steadying breath. Even if the ruby were found on the stairs, there was no harm in it. But if it were found underneath Simon's body. . . . He swallowed. Do not think of it. You are safe. You will not be undone by something so insignificant as a cravat pin! He had dallied long enough. It was time to slip down the servants' stairs and join the others, with no one the wiser that he had been gone. He smiled. Marlowe had been a fool to think that he could best *Le Renard*, the Fox. He hoped that sweet Sophy appreciated his efforts.

Lying awake in her rooms, still uneasy and unsettled by the scene with her husband, Sophy jerked bolt upright as the sound of a muffled thud met her ears, followed by the thud and thumping of a heavy object falling down the stairs. What was that? Simon?

Slipping on her robe once more, she hurried to the

door, unlocked it and stepped into the hall. Shadowy darkness met her eye; only the sounds of the storm could be heard. Something drew her on, however, and, taking just enough time to light a candle, she walked to the head of the stairs. She gasped as she stared at Simon's unmoving form on the floor below. Is he dead? Had he really been so drunk that he had stumbled and fallen?

Before she had time to consider her actions, instinct had her hurtling down the stairs to his side. Kneeling beside him, she nudged him gently, and called softly, "Simon? Are you hurt?"

There was no answer and never would be again. The flickering light of her candle clearly showed his head lying at an odd angle to his body and the matted blood in the thick black hair. Whether it had been the broken neck or his head striking one of the steps that had killed him, she had no idea, but Simon Marlowe was clearly dead. He would never pound on her door again. She would never have to face him down with a pistol again.

White-faced, Sophy rose shakily to her feet, her first thought to cry out, to alert the household, when a terrifying idea crossed her mind. Only moments ago she had shot at Simon. Everyone knew she hated him. And Simon, drunk or not, had gone up and down these same stairs for years. The question was sure to be asked: Why had it been tonight that he had fallen? Fallen almost immediately after she had shot at him and had threatened to shoot him again? She shivered. Would it be thought that she had pushed him? Murdered him?

As she stared at his crumpled body, she began to tremble with shock and an inexplicable fear. She must not, she thought dazedly, be found here. The urge to run, to hide, clutched her, and she swung away from the ghastly sight of Simon's body and stumbled to the stairs. Halfway up the staircase, she paused and, lifting her candle, looked backward, staring down at his still form, hardly able to comprehend what had occurred. He was dead, and if she were found here . . .

The very real fear that she would be suspected of pushing him to his death sent her scrambling up the remaining stairs. Trying to compose herself, to think coherently, she stopped at the top of the stairs and glanced helplessly around. As she did so, the jumping light of her candle suddenly ignited a bloodred spark near her feet. Mindlessly she stooped and picked it up. A cravat pin. One of the gentlemen must have lost it . . . tonight, she realized with a thrill of unease, else the servants would have found it and mentioned it.

A sound, half hysterical laugh, half sob broke from her. Her husband was dead, and she was concerned about a cravat pin? Trembling from shock, she took one last, frantic look at Simon's body and fled to her room. There she sank down weakly on a stool in front of her dressing table, the jeweled pin tumbling from her fingers. Dumbly she stared at the ruby as it winked at her in the candlelight. It was easier, safer, she admitted wretchedly, to think about the cravat pin than her husband lying dead at the base of the stairs. As she looked at the pin, she was aware that there was something oddly familiar about it. Where had she seen it before?

A sob burst from her. She was mad. What did it matter if she recognized the pin or not? *Simon was dead.*

Scared and shaken, she picked up the pin and buried it in the small jewelry box her mother had given her, then crawled into her bed and waited, dry-eyed and sleepless, for her husband's body to be found.

*   *   *

Two days later, on a cold, rainy February morning, Sophy stood staring at the newly turned earth marking her husband's grave in the Marlowe family graveyard. She still could hardly believe that Simon was dead.

She remembered little of the hours that had followed Edward's discovery of the body and crying of the alarm. Only gradually had she become aware of the stares of his friends and the whispers . . . whispers which even now, though his death had been declared an accident, were still being spread. They really believe that I killed him! she thought miserably. Her mouth twisted. Not that I wouldn't have if he had forced me to, she admitted honestly. But I did not kill him. It was an accident. It had to be.

The funeral was small. Edward, at Sophy's request, had asked most of Simon's friends to leave the morning his body had been discovered. And since Marlowe House was not precisely a lively place to be with its owner newly dead, they had eagerly complied. Only Edward, Sir Arthur, Sophy and Simon's heir, William Marlowe, a youth of eighteen accompanied by his widowed mother, were gathered around the gravesite to hear the vicar. When the last words had been said, the last wreath of flowers placed on the grave, Sophy turned back to the house with relief.

Edward had proved himself to be surprisingly kind, trying to lift some of the burdens of the funeral from her shoulders, but too much had passed between them for Sophy to soften toward him. After the vicar had a light repast and departed, Sophy requested a meeting with her uncle in what had been Simon's study.

Facing her uncle across the width of the desk that separated them, Sophy said coolly, "There is no reason for you and Sir Arthur to remain any longer. The house and property are William's now, and I am sure that he and his mother would like to begin settling in without strangers hovering about. I, myself, shall be leaving this afternoon for Cornwall."

"Uh, do you think that is wise, Sophy?" At her look, he muttered, "I mean your husband is hardly in the ground, and you take off for Cornwall—it don't look good."

"Since when have you cared for appearances?" Sophy demanded, her fingers tightly gripping the top of the desk.

"Since there are rumors about Simon's death." Edward returned unhappily. "I tell you, it don't look good. I will be blunt—some of Simon's friends think that you pushed him down the stairs. Think you should stay here 'til things quiet down a bit."

"Thank you for your advice, uncle, but I am determined to go live with Marcus and Phoebe . . ." A hard note entered her voice. "*Some*one should be seeing to their care."

Like Simon, Edward was forty-three, but the signs of his years of wild, careless dissipation rested lightly on his boyishly handsome features. He was not quite as youthful-looking as he had been a decade ago, but the creases that lined his face seemed to make him even more attractive. With his thick fair hair brushed back from his wide forehead, his starched cravat elegantly arranged, and his tall, fit body clothed in the most fashionable garments the most expensive tailors in London could sew, he was a commanding figure. But Sophy knew everything about him was false.

It was her father's fortune that paid for his lavish living. Edward had wasted his own not-inconsiderable fortune years ago gambling. He was weak. Vain. Unscrupulous. Selfish. But he'd had no say in her life since she'd married and, along with her fortune, had been passed like a parcel from her uncle's control to that of her husband. She smiled grimly. Edward had not liked seeing such a large chunk of the Grayson fortune escaping his hands and falling into Simon's, but he'd had no choice—her father's will had stated that her portion of the estate be disbursed when she wed. Of course, it had changed nothing for her, the law allowed her husband to hoard or squander her fortune as he saw fit. Fortunately, Simon had been wealthy enough in his own right and he had not dipped into her inheritance from her father. And as widow, she realized with shock, she had far more rights than a mere wife or daughter. She could do anything she wanted. She would finally come into full and total control of her own bountiful inheritance from her father. And the handsome jointure Simon had agreed to in a weak moment when they married. It, too, would be hers to command, with no one to gainsay her. Between the fortune from her father and the jointure from her husband, she was going to be an extremely rich young woman. More importantly, for the first time in her life, she was no longer under the domination of a man. Not a father. Not a guardian. Not a husband. Especially not a husband!

Edward's words confirmed her thoughts. Looking sulky, he muttered, "Well, there is nothing I can do to stop you. If you want people to think you murdered your husband, that is your affair."

"Thank you for your concern," she said dryly. "Now if you do not mind, I shall leave you—there are things I must see to before I go."

Two hours later, her belongings piled onto the Mar-

lowe coach that the new Lord Marlowe had graciously
lent her for her journey to Cornwall, Sophy rode away
from the place that had been her home for nearly three
long, miserable years. It was a place she never wanted to
see again. Her thoughts were focused on the future. Before many days, she would be home, home with Marcus
and Phoebe. And this time, no one would ever be able to
separate them again.

She grinned, her lovely golden eyes glinting with suppressed excitement. Her entire future lay in front of her,
and it was so *very* different today than it had been a mere
forty-eight hours ago. She was young. She was wealthy.
And she was *free*!

Chapter One

✦

*T*he elegant rooms were packed with gaily dressed ladies and gentlemen, the sound of their laughter and chatter almost overpowering. From the size of the glittering crowd, it appeared that Lord and Lady Denning's at home was going to receive the highest accolade possible from the members of the ton. It was indeed a dreadful squeeze.

Having found a small, quiet alcove in which to observe the activities, Viscount Harrington viewed the swirling mass with a jaundiced eye. To think that this was the height of ambition: to be packed into overheated rooms like raw recruits in the hold of a ship on their way to dreaded India; to see and be seen and to waste one's time prattling complete nonsense to vaguely familiar acquaintances, before departing and hurrying to the next social engagement. He shook his head. It was madness. Dashed if he wouldn't rather face a charge of Napoléon's finest cavalry than be subjected to another night like tonight.

So why was he here? Because I have to find myself a
bloody wife! Ives thought irritably, as he stared out at the
shifting crowd of women in their expensive high-waisted
gowns of pastel silks and spangled gauze. The gentlemen
were also garbed in the height of fashion; pristine white
cravats, formfitting coats, embroidered waistcoats and
black knee breeches.

It was almost incomprehensible to him that he found
himself in this position. Less than fifteen months ago, he
had been a carefree bachelor, marriage the farthest
thought from his mind. He had a position that he enjoyed—a major in the King's Cavalry—and with the war
against Napoléon still raging, there was every possibility
of rapid advancement. He had certainly never expected to
find himself inheriting his uncle's title and fortune and
being placed in the position of needing to beget an heir.

A shaft of pain went through him. Could it have been
just fourteen months ago that he had learned of the
tragedy that had overtaken the Harrington family? Fourteen months ago that he had found himself devastated by
the news that his father, uncle and two cousins had
drowned when his uncle's yacht had gone down in a sudden squall? In one fell swoop, Ives had found himself the
sole male survivor of the branch of the family which bore
the proud Harrington name. Aunt Barbara's two sons,
John and Charles, bore her husband's name, so that left
them out. Clearly it was his duty, he thought morosely, to
find a wife and replenish the Harrington blood. He owed
it to his dead father and uncle and cousins to make certain that the proud name of Harrington continued—to ensure that there *was* a twelfth Viscount Harrington to
inherit.

He sighed. I really *would* prefer to be fighting Bony,

he mused unhappily. Complex battle maneuvers he understood. Women were something else again entirely. Not that there had been no women in his life. There had been quite a few. But he'd had only one use for them. And certainly there had never been any gently reared virgins among them! His women had known what they were doing, why they were in his bed, and what he expected from them. He grimaced. It sounded bloody cold when he thought of it that way. But it hadn't been. He had also known what he was doing, having learned long ago that there was much pleasure to be gained from giving pleasure, even if he was paying for the woman's favors.

Ives glanced around the room. He wondered how some of the young ladies parading here tonight would react if he made a straightforward proposition: Marry me, give me an heir, and I shall see to it that you never want for anything again. You shall be a viscountess, live in a fine home, and have a tidy fortune at your dainty fingertips. Once you have given me my son, we shan't have to bother with each other very much. We shall live separately and what you do with your life will be your business—provided you are discreet and do not besmirch my name. So? Is it a bargain?

He scowled as he realized that what he proposed was not a great deal different than most of the marriages contracted in the ton. And he admitted sourly that he did not want a marriage like the one that had befallen his father. He definitely didn't want *his* wife running away with another man and leaving him with two sons to raise. Bloody hell, no!

A soft giggle interrupted his unpleasant thoughts, and his gaze fell upon a young lady, not more than eighteen, who had been angling for several minutes for his attention. The bleak expression on his bold-featured face and the dark emotion roiling in his devil green eyes made her blanch and scurry away. Viscount or not, she suddenly wanted nothing to do with him.

Ives was amused by her reaction, and a singularly attractive smile transformed his features. That it had often been compared to a brigand's smile did not detract from its impact. He knew that he was not *un*handsome, but he would freely admit that his nose was too large, his cheekbones too prominent, and his mouth too wide for true male beauty. But as several women had told him, there was something about him. . . . Whatever it was, when he flashed that smile, women responded—as did the young lady he had just sent into flight. She glanced back, and, seeing the change in his expression, her step slowed, and she dimpled and demurely lowered her eyes.

Ives nearly laughed aloud. Little minx. His thick black hair, coupled with heavily browed green eyes, skin far darker than was fashionable and a body of a Greek athlete had served him well with the opposite sex. The fact that he now came with a title and a fortune only made him that much more desirable. He grimaced, suddenly feeling rather vain.

"Charming though little Felice Alden may be, she is far too young for a dangerous rogue like you, my dear fellow," drawled a familiar voice. "I beg you, for her sake, do not raise her hopes."

Looking at the speaker who strolled up to stand beside him, Ives grinned. "Percival! What the devil are you doing here? I thought you never attended this sort of boring affair."

Percival Forrest, a willowy fop just a few years

younger than Ives, made a face. "M'father's sister. She came up to town for a few weeks and I was not quick enough to escape her clutches when she came to call. Insisted that I escort her here tonight." A sly smile crossed his sharp, attractive features. "No need to ask why you are here. How is the bride-hunting coming along?"

Ives shrugged. "Let us just say that the announcement of my nuptials is not in imminent danger of appearing in the *Times*." He jerked his head in the direction of the young damsel, who was still hovering in the vicinity. "And if the Alden chit is a sample of the majority of the prospects to bear my name, I fear that it will be a *very* long time before an announcement does appear."

The two men exchanged an amused glance. Percival had been a lieutenant under Ives's command until nearly five years ago, when he had unexpectedly inherited a comfortable fortune from his great-uncle and had sold out and returned to England. Ives had been sorry to see him go but pleased for his friend's good fortune. They had known each other all their lives—the Forrest estate lay near the Harrington family home, and they had been particular friends in the cavalry. Having grown up with him, Ives knew that beneath Percival's foppish exterior lay a fearless heart and a clever mind.

Ives had always enjoyed himself in Percival's company, and, upon his return to England last year, Percival had been one of the first people to call upon him. Their shared military background made a further bond between them. Unlike Ives, who would have preferred to bury himself in the country, Percival had taken to the ton like a duck to water. Since his arrival in London a month ago, Ives had relied increasingly on Percival's wickedly pierc-

ing insight into the antics of the ton to help him in his reluctant search for a wife.

They talked for a few minutes about a horse they had
both liked at Tattersall's but that neither had decided to
bid upon. From there the conversation drifted onto the
exciting news that had arrived in London only days ago
of Lord Cochrae's destruction of the French fleet at Aix.
From that victory, it was an easy jump to Sir Arthur
Wellesley's recent arrival in Portugal.

For the first time that evening, Ives was thoroughly enjoying himself. He was deeply immersed in conversation
with Percival, when something—a laugh?—caught his
attention.

Like a tiger scenting prey, his head lifted. The crowd
before him parted suddenly, and there she was.

Gripping Percival's arm, he demanded, "Who is she?"

Percival, in the midst of discussing a complicated military maneuver, looked nonplussed for a second. When
his gaze followed Ives's, he groaned.

"Oh, absolutely not! Of all the women here tonight,
she arouses your interest?"

When Ives remained unmoved, his gaze fixed intently
on the scintillating creature at the center of a circle of ad-
miring males, Percival sighed. "Oh, very well, if you
must know. She is Sophy, Lady Marlowe, the Marquise
Marlowe to be exact."

Ives was stunned by the sensation of dismay that filled
him. "She is married?"

Percival sighed again. "No. Widowed."

Ives's face brightened, and, with renewed intensity, his
eyes wandered over her. She was like a butterfly. A
lovely, golden butterfly. From the crown of her golden
curls to the tantalizing glimpse of her golden slippers be-

neath the hem of her golden gown. Her bare shoulders even gleamed like palest gold in the light from the many crystal candelabra gracing the high ceiling of the large room. And when she laughed . . . when she laughed, Ives was aware of an odd thrill going through him. She was, he thought dazedly, absolutely the most exquisite creature he had ever seen in his life. Tall and slender, she looked as if the slightest puff of wind would send her drifting away, and yet there was an air of strength about her. The profile turned his way was utterly enchanting.

"Introduce me," he commanded.

"Dash it all, Ives! Did you not hear a word I just said? She is a widow—a widow with a nasty past, believe me."

Ives glanced at his friend. "What do you mean?"

Percival grimaced. "Do you even know who Simon Marlowe was?"

"I seem to recall my father mentioning his name once when I was home on leave, but no, I do not know him."

"Which is just as well! He was by all accounts a nasty piece of work. *Not* a gentleman, despite his title—and certainly not a man any self-respecting family would wish one of their daughters to marry."

Ives frowned. "Are you saying that her family is not a respectable one?"

"Not exactly. Her father's family is exemplary." Percival looked uncomfortable. "It is her mother's family . . ." He cleared his throat and fumbled for words.

He had Ives's full attention now. "What about her mother's family?"

Knowing from long experience that Ives was not going to give up until all his questions were answered to his satisfaction, Percival muttered, "Damme, I had hoped your paths would not cross and that . . ." He took a deep breath, and blurted out, "Her mother was Jane Scoville."

Ives stiffened as a new, dangerous element added to the intensity of his gaze which was still fastened on Lady Marlowe's profile. "The same Jane Scoville that charmed my brother, Robert?" he asked in a deadly tone.

"The same," Percival admitted uneasily. "Now do you see why she is absolutely the last woman you would be interested in? And the identity of her mother is aside from the fact that there are rumors that Lady Marlowe murdered her husband."

A silence fell between the two men, Ives hardly hearing Percival's last sentence. Jane Scoville, he thought, his hands unconsciously clenching into fists. The heartless, silly jade who had beguiled Robert, until he had been mad with love for her. So besotted that he could not accept the news of her engagement to the Earl of Grayson. So very mad, so despondent, that on the day she had married the Earl, he had hanged himself in the main stables at Harrington Chase. Ives had just turned ten years old at the time, but it was as if it had all happened yesterday. He had adored his brother, twelve years his senior, and he had been the one to find Robert's body.

"And how is dear Jane these days?" Ives asked grimly. "I must pay her a call if she is in town."

"She's dead, Ives. She died several years ago." Percival looked thoughtful. "You could, I suppose, defile her grave if you think it would make you feel better."

A reluctant laugh was dragged from Ives, and he relaxed slightly. "No, I'll not stoop to that." He jerked his head in Lady Marlowe's direction. "But I might be tempted to extract a little revenge from her daughter."

Percival shook his head vehemently. "Did you not hear

what I said about her? *She murdered her husband.* She is not a lady, I, for one, would care to trifle with."

"I thought you said it was only rumors."

Percival looked annoyed. "So you were listening to me, after all! The official verdict is that he died in a fall down the stairs, but I was there that night—and I think she killed him." When Ives cocked an inquiring brow, Percival added, "I fell in with Marlowe's crowd when I first returned, which is how I know so much about his reputation. I do not want to make excuses for myself, but I had just come home after years of fighting in the wars and had seen and done things that were undoubtedly the substance of the most terrifying nightmares imaginable. Suddenly I had a great deal of time and money at my disposal. Marlowe and his friends were just the sort of wild and randy fellows to appeal to someone like me let loose in London, looking for adventure. It took me a while to realize that there is a great difference between wildness and wickedness. Marlowe was a downright nasty fellow, his friends not much better." Percival took a deep breath. "I am not proud of my actions that first year or two when I returned to England . . . but that is all behind me now."

"If the official verdict is accidental death, why do you still think she killed him?" Ives asked idly.

"Marlowe was drinking heavily that night, but I know that he was not *that* foxed. And, there had been a terrible argument between them only minutes before he fell to his death. It was well-known amongst us that he had been denied his wife's bed. He complained bitterly about it when in his cups. And it was equally well-known that his wife despised him *and* his friends."

"And that is the basis of your belief that she killed him?" Ives's incredulity was obvious.

"Of course that is not all!" Percival replied testily. "Not only had they just had an ugly row, but she had shot at him."

Ives's brow rose. "And naturally all this occurred in your presence?"

"No, it did not! But we all heard the shot, and Sir Arthur Bellingham and Lord Scoville—" At Ives's expression, Percival looked uncomfortable, and muttered unhappily, "Yes, Jane's brother was part of the same crowd. He and Bellingham, being Marlowe's closest friends, went to see what was amiss. Marlowe himself told them that his wife had just shot at him. Scoville wandered back and told the rest of us. He was quite proud of his niece's marksmanship. And that was not a half hour before Marlowe's body was found."

"She shot him?" Ives asked, more intrigued than scandalized.

"Yes—the bullet hole was in the shoulder of the jacket he was wearing when he died. Naturally the officials investigating his death wanted to know how it came to be there, and Lady Marlowe was quite open about it when they questioned her. She admitted that she had shot at him and she made no attempt to hide the fact that she utterly despised her husband. She was *not* a grieving widow."

"If her husband was the blackguard you claim him to have been, perhaps he deserved to be shot."

"Are you defending her?" Percival demanded, the expression in his blue eyes clearly aghast.

Ives smiled and shook his head. "No. I am just saying that there might have been a good reason for her to have taken a shot at the departed Marlowe."

"Well, that may be," Percival replied, slightly ruffled

by Ives's reaction to Lady Marlowe's sins, "but surely you see why she is not a woman that you would care to know more intimately."

At that moment, almost as if she sensed that she was the topic of the conversation taking place in the small alcove, Lady Marlowe glanced in their direction. As her clear, golden stare moved curiously over him, Ives felt as if he had been struck by a thunderbolt. Every nerve in his body tingled as their gazes met and held.

She was exquisite. Her features had been fashioned by a master hand, the tip-tilted nose, the high brow and delicately sculpted mouth blending perfectly with the determined little chin and stubborn jaw. No simpering damsel here, he decided, as he stared boldly back at her. Not with that jaw and chin. Yes, he could believe that she had shot at her husband. Might even have murdered him, if Percival was to be believed. And she was Jane's daughter.

His reasons for being in London, for being here tonight instantly vanished. He was after something else at the moment. Something that had waited a long time. Something that had eaten at him and fashioned him into the man he had become. Even after all these years, the hunger for revenge for Robert's suicide was not dead in his breast. It did not matter that she was merely the daughter of the woman who had caused the death of his brother. What suddenly mattered was that Jane was beyond his reach . . . but her daughter was not.

And if her past was anything to go by, she was not going to be the type of weak, innocent creature who might cause him guilt for what had just occurred to him. He was, he admitted unashamedly, going to thoroughly enjoy wreaking vengeance on the already infamous Lady Marlowe.

His fierce gaze never dropping from hers, Ives touched Percival's arm once more. "Introduce us," he said again, the note in his voice making Percival glance sharply at him.

"Oh, no," Percival said, "I am not going to be a part of seeing you make a fool of yourself. Find somebody else to help you make a cake of yourself."

Ives's eyes dropped to him. And he smiled, a smile that made Percival distinctly uneasy. "I have no intention of making Lady Marlowe my bride. But I suddenly have a yearning to meet this remarkable young woman . . . dear Jane's daughter."

Percival jerked and stared at him appalled. "You mean to punish her for what Jane did?" When Ives's dark head dipped arrogantly in assent, Percival said, "That is the most ridiculously idiotic idea you have had in a very long time. I hold no fondness for her or her mother, but *she* is not responsible for what happened to Robert."

Ives sent him a bland look. "Indeed not," he agreed, "but there is an interesting passage in the Bible, something about 'the sins of the fathers being visited upon the children'—or in this case, the sins of the mother. Now are you going to introduce me to her, or must I find someone else to do it?"

"Oh, damn and blast! I knew I never should have allowed Aunt Margaret to bully me into coming here. Come along then, if you are determined to make a fool of yourself." Percival shook a finger at Ives. "Just do not blame me for what happens."

Sophy was enjoying herself, or enjoying herself as much as she did at any of these gatherings. She had not wanted to come tonight, but Marcus, unexpectedly in the throes of his first calf love, had begged her to accompany him so that his attendance at such a stuffy event would not be so obvious. She smiled. At nineteen, Marcus had grown up into an extremely handsome and personable youth. His title and fortune only added to his appeal, and Sophy was just a little concerned about his current infatuation. She wanted to assure herself that the young lady was suitable. Not that she cared about fortune or breeding. What Sophy worried about was that the young lady's affections were for *Marcus*—not his title and wealth.

This was Sophy's first trip to London since her husband had died and she had gone to live with Marcus and Phoebe at Gatewood, the Grayson family estate in Cornwall. In the years since Marlowe's death, they had lived very quietly in the country, as much because it was their choice as the fact that their uncle continued to make inroads into the family's wealth. Despite the enormity of the Grayson fortune, funds had not been flowing with any regularity or generosity.

Fortunately, Sophy's monies were hers to command, and she had seen to it that they all three lived comfortably at Gatewood. A season in London was an expensive proposition, and she had not wanted to spend muchneeded gold on something so frivolous when there was still so much to be done at Gatewood. But this year, Lord Scoville had experienced a particularly good run of luck. Prompted as much by Sophy's increasingly angry demands for what was due her siblings, as by a sudden prickle of conscience, Baron Scoville had handed over a lavish amount of money for their use.

Marcus, restless and eager to see London, was determined to gain some "town bronze" and join his friends in the city. He had begged that they come to London.

Phoebe, only weeks away from turning fifteen, had unexpectedly added her entreaties. Her big golden brown eyes full of pleading, she had breathed, "Oh, please, Sophy. Do let us go! I would ever so much like to go to Hookham's Lending Library and Hatchard's bookstore. My friend, Amanda, says that they have a simply *vast* selection of books."

"Books!" Marcus had exclaimed with great disgust. "I swear, Phoebe, all you care about is books. I want to go to Weston's to buy some really fashionable garments. And to Manton's to shoot. And Tattersall's, to look at horses. And—"

"Yes, yes, I understand," Sophy had interrupted with a twinkle in her eyes. "You wish to make a dash." She smiled lovingly at Phoebe's young face. "And you wish to bury your nose in as many books as you can find. Very well, if you both want to go, we shall!"

"And you, Sophy? What will you do while we are in London?" asked Phoebe.

"I shall go to the British Museum and perhaps Westminster Abbey," Sophy stated calmly. The look Marcus and Phoebe exchanged made her laugh aloud.

The decision made, it did not take the siblings very long to set their plans in motion. They had arrived in London in March and had been settling very nicely into the Grayson town house on Berkeley Square. Marcus had already paid several visits to Weston's for his new wardrobe; Phoebe had been transported with delight over the number of books to be found at Hatchard's; and Sophy had found the British Museum positively fascinating. There were, of course, other entertainments that they had attended, either together or separately, and all three were feeling rather pleased with this first sojourn in London.

Despite her preference for quieter entertainment, Sophy had attended a few routs and balls during the past weeks and, to her astonishment, had thoroughly enjoyed herself. It was true that her path occasionally crossed that of her uncle and that there had been stiff, uncomfortable exchanges between them. There had also been unavoidable meetings with several of her late husband's friends, and the rumors about her part in Simon's death continued to be whispered about behind her back now and then. But all in all, she thought the trip to London had been a success; the ton had readily accepted them, and, though there were still a few raised eyebrows, most people had been surprisingly kind.

Edward's presence and the meetings with Simon's more disreputable friends were, at present, the only blights on her horizon. And since an "at home" was not the kind of entertainment which would normally appeal to Edward or Simon's other friends, she was fairly confident of enjoying the fifteen minutes allotted for this sort of entertainment without meeting any of them.

The circle of gentlemen presently surrounding her was mainly comprised of her brother and his friends. Two of them, Thomas Sutcliff and William Jarrett, she knew rather well—they lived in the vicinity of Gatewood and had grown up with Marcus. Since her return to Cornwall, she had become very used to them constantly being underfoot. At twenty-two, Thomas was the eldest and the acknowledged leader of the trio. Since this was his third London Season, he considered himself quite the man about town. Andrew, a year younger than Thomas, was affable and too easygoing for his own good. They were basically nice young men, and Sophy did not worry about Marcus when he was in their company.

Her gaze fell on another member of the group around her, and a faint ripple of unease dimmed her smile. Sir Alfred Caldwell was a new acquaintance of Marcus's, and Sophy could not say that she cared for him. At thirty-five, with a decided air of dissipation about him, he was much older than Marcus and his friends, and she worried that Sir Alfred's reasons for attaching himself to a green youth like her brother might not bode well for Marcus. Telling herself that she was being overly protective, she promptly put her concerns away. Thomas and William would keep Marcus from falling too deeply under Caldwell's influence.

There was one other member of the group surrounding Sophy, and she was not certain how she felt about him. One of Simon's more respectable acquaintances, Richard, Lord Coleman, had come to call at the Grayson town house within days of their arrival in London. He had been extremely polite and had proved himself to be very helpful. It had been Lord Coleman who had advised Sophy where to hire the extra servants they needed; Lord Coleman who had gone with Marcus to his first sale at Tattersalls; Lord Coleman who arranged a delightful outing at Astley's Royal Amphitheatre for the entire family; and it was Lord Coleman who frequently accompanied Sophy about town. He had never acted anything but polite and proper, yet Sophy could not forget that he had been part of Simon's cortege and that he had been at the house the night Simon had died.

She did not know why he had attached himself to her side, but she suspected that, like her first husband, he had reached an age where the production of an heir was beginning to prey upon his mind. He had not yet reached forty, but she guessed he was not very far from that age, and she rather thought that he was angling for a wife.

A distinctly cynical smile curved her mouth. No doubt he thought that having been married to one roué she might be agreeable to marrying another. Her fingers unconsciously tightened around her gold-spangled fan. She would die before she married again! And certainly never to a man of Coleman's stripe or one whose only use for her was that of broodmare! *If* she ever married again, and she sincerely doubted that she ever would, it would be for love alone.

Suddenly, she felt that she was being watched. When they had first arrived in London, there had been a lot of stares and whispers when she entered a room, but most of that had died away by now. This felt different. She felt almost as if she were the object of some large predator's assessment.

Casually, she looked around, her gaze locking almost instantaneously with that of a tall, hard-faced gentleman standing in the small alcove to her left. A jolt of something she could not define flashed through her as their eyes remained fixed on each other. Fear? Excitement? Anticipation? Or dread?

She could not look away from him, the impact of his bold stare so overwhelming that she simply stood there helpless, unaware of anything happening around her. It was only when his gaze dropped to the man standing next to him that she was able to jerk her eyes away and became aware of Marcus laughing at something Andrew had said.

Shaken, she forced a smile and tried to pretend the odd moment had never happened. It was only by the greatest effort that she kept herself from looking again in the stranger's vicinity.

"Oh, I say," Lord Coleman murmured from where he stood at her side, "here comes Percival Forrest. Did not expect to see him at this sort of affair."

"Who is that big, bruising-looking fellow with him?" asked Caldwell. "I do not believe that I have met him before."

Percival advanced upon them before Caldwell's question could be answered and, bowing gracefully before Sophy, said, "Lady Marlowe, how delightful to see you again. How have you been?"

Sophy made some reply, unbearably aware of the tall, intimidating stranger at Percival's side.

"Lady Marlowe, allow me to introduce my friend Viscount Harrington," Percival went on smoothly. "Like you, this is his first London Season."

Coolly acknowledging Lord Harrington, Sophy thought her heart would literally stop when her eyes plunged once again into the depths of his devil green stare. He smiled at her, a smile that made her heart kick into a mad gallop, and she did not know if that smile was the most exciting thing she had ever seen or the most terrifying.

Chapter Two

❧

*I*ntroductions were exchanged with the other members of the group around Sophy, but she was hardly aware of anything but the imposing man in front of her. He was definitely not handsome, she decided judiciously, as his features were too harsh and forbidding. But there was something about him . . . something dashingly attractive about his dark, craggy visage and those glinting green eyes.

Even when he turned away to acknowledge the other introductions and she was no longer the object of his forthright stare, she was tangibly aware of Lord Harrington. And she did not like it. The man was simply too arrogant by half! The way he had looked at her—as if she were a tempting morsel he might snatch up and consume at any moment. By the Devil's eyes! She would like him to just try it.

Lord Harrington's name was not unknown to her. There had been much gossip about him when he had arrived in London a few weeks ago, and Sophy had naturally heard the bare facts surrounding his unexpected ascension to his new title. That he was looking for a wife had also been mentioned, along with news that half the young ladies of the ton were sighing over him and eagerly setting their caps for him.

If he had flashed those same swooning young damsels the sort of look he had just sent her, she reflected wryly, their reactions were understandable. Of course, *she* was utterly indifferent to him. It would do him no good to waste his charms on her. In fact, she admitted with unaccustomed malice, she would take great delight in spurning him.

Sophy was appalled at her own thoughts. Under lowered lashes she studied him, wondering why he aroused so much antagonism in her breast. He was no threat to her, and had done nothing out of the ordinary. Well, he *had* stared. Still, she had no honest reason to feel as she did.

She had absolutely no interest in him whatsoever, she told herself stoutly. Not as a lover, if I were inclined to take a lover, which I am not, thank you very much. And as for a husband! She nearly snorted aloud. Viscount Harrington was certainly not the sort of man she would choose to wed *if* she were ever foolish enough to marry again.

Without warning, his eyes met hers, and Sophy was conscious of the way her stomach seemed to drop right down to her toes. She returned his stare squarely, unable to let him win even in this small skirmish. His dark head dipped almost imperceptibly, as if he were acknowledging the challenge she had thrown him.

A militant sparkle leaped to her eyes and a flush stained her cheeks. Suddenly she felt wonderfully alive, and the evening, which she had viewed with boredom, had become inexplicably exciting. With a toss of her golden head, she coolly looked away and murmured a quip to Lord Coleman that brought a smile to his face.

Despite telling herself that she was a fool, Sophy could not help listening with more than polite interest to the conversation between two gentlemen near her.

"Have you been in London long?" Lord Coleman asked Harrington politely.

"Since mid-March. And I must say that it has been a fascinating experience so far."

"Really?" drawled Sir Alfred in languid tones, a supercilious expression on his face. "My dear fellow, a word of advice—one should never *admit* to enjoying the London Season."

"I did not say that I was enjoying it," Ives returned lightly, a gleam in his green eyes, "merely that having spent my youth in the military and these past years fighting in the wars, I have been finding it . . . somewhat titillating."

Sir Alfred looked displeased, but it was Thomas Sutcliff who asked eagerly, "Have you fought against Bony himself?"

"His armies," Ives returned with a grin. "The majority of my service has been in India and Egypt. I cannot claim to have actually crossed swords with the Little Corporal himself."

The younger men looked impressed and embarked on endless questions about Ives's military exploits. Sophy was curious herself and though she had already decided that Viscount Harrington was not a gentleman she cared to know better, she thought Marcus and the others would do well to emulate someone of his stamp rather than of Sir Arthur Caldwell's or Lord Coleman's.

Harrington's relationship with Percival Forrest gave her pause, however. She had not forgotten that Forrest had been one of Simon's newest cronies before he had died. But for the moment, she saw no harm in allowing Marcus to embark upon a friendship with the viscount.

Shortly, Forrest and Lord Harrington took their leave and a few minutes later Marcus, having ascertained that the young lady who had captured his interest was not amongst the throng crowding the Denning house, declared the evening a devilish bore and suggested that they go on to more exciting entertainments. Since they had stayed their allotted time, everyone was in agreement.

Their stop at the Dennings' had been the last social engagement that Sophy had planned to attend that evening. She was quite happy when she was finally settled into Sir Alfred's carriage and it was heading toward the Grayson town house. It was past midnight, and though the comings and goings of the ton could last until after four in the morning, she was longing for bed.

Having seen Sophy to the door, Marcus and the others took their leave of her, eager to partake of more masculine entertainments. She was aware that Lord Coleman would have liked to linger, but she gave him no encouragement. After kissing her hand with more warmth than was polite, he had joined the others.

Once inside the house, Sophy smiled at the waiting butler. "Oh, Emerson," she said, as she delicately stifled a yawn, "I am so tired. I never knew that London could be so exhausting."

Emerson made a polite reply, his blue eyes twinkling in sympathy. Sophy had hired him, along with his wife,

an excellent housekeeper, on Lord Coleman's recom-
mendation, and she had liked them both the instant she
had laid eyes on them. Whether it was Emerson's exceedingly kind expression or Mrs. Emerson's bustling
cheerfulness that had won her over Sophy did not know.
Certainly, they had proved themselves to be hardwork-
ing, efficient, and pleasant to a fault.

After telling Emerson that he need not wait up for
Marcus, Sophy bid the butler good night and went upstairs. She had been positive that the moment her head
hit the pillow she would be sound asleep. Instead, to her
annoyance, she was rather restless and alert. Her annoyance grew when a dark face with mocking green eyes
and a brigand's smile kept hopping into her thoughts.

Blast the man! I am not the least bit interested in him.
He is just another stranger, a gentleman whose path I
happened to cross and, if I have anything to say about it,
will not cross again.

Having thoroughly convinced herself of this, she was
finally able to banish Harrington's disturbing presence
from her mind and drift off to sleep. Sleep, however, betrayed her. Harrington, his green eyes challenging, his
bold mouth laughing, relentlessly pursued her through
her dreams.

After Ives had departed from Sophy's presence, he
knew there was no reason for him to remain at the Dennings' house, having just left behind the only fascinating
creature present. His search for a wife, he admitted
glumly, was over for the night.

Although Sophy Marlowe was out of the question as a
prospective bride, Ives was astute enough to realize that
for the moment, hers was the only image he would judge

any other lady against. And he suspected—nay, was bitterly certain—they would all be found lamentably lacking.

Jane Scoville's daughter, he thought disgustedly as he and Percival left the Dennings' house behind and made for one of the St. James's Street clubs in Ives's comfortable coach. Of all the women there tonight, why did *she* have to take my fancy?

"You do not look very happy," Percival remarked, after a quick glance at Ives's face.

"I am not," Ives growled. "I am bloody furious! And I am thinking that it is palpably unfair for a heartless jade like Jane Scoville to have whelped that little golden butterfly we just left behind."

"Sophy? Need I remind you that you were the one who wanted to meet her?"

"Whether or not I wanted to meet her is beside the point! She is a complication I do not need. My sole purpose, before tonight, for being in London was to find a suitable wife. Suddenly, meeting Jane's brats has changed all that."

"You could just forget about them," Percival offered. "Let sleeping dogs lie and all that."

Ives speared him with a glance. "You expect me to forget what Jane did to Robert? Am I to forget that she drove him to suicide?"

Percival shrugged. As he had grown older and was able to consider Robert's suicide independently of Ives's oft-stated opinion, Percival had decided that Robert had been something of a weak, selfish fool. Of course, he would never say such a thing to Ives! And Percival had not been alone in his regard of Robert's feet of clay. Robert's own father had often stated that he had not been quite the golden young god his family believed him to be.

Be that as it may, Ives had idolized Robert and over the years had endowed his dead brother with many virtues and traits which had been utterly lacking in the live person. Robert's death, while tragic and senseless, had occurred at a particularly impressionable age for Ives. He had, unfortunately, never quite dealt with the reality of it. To do so, Percival thought slowly, would have forced Ives to see his brother as he really had been, a spoiled and self-centered young man who had been solely responsible for his own death.

Robert had made the choice. To hold some resentment against Jane for her treatment of Robert, Percival understood. To blame her entirely, as if Robert had had no say in the matter, was not the conclusion of an intelligent man—something he knew Ives to be.

There were few men Percival truly admired and respected, and Ives Harrington was one of them. Brave, honest, fair, and loyal; Ives was all of those things and more. It was only in this one area that Percival ever found fault with Ives: his blind, stubborn idolization of Robert.

When Percival remained silent, Ives demanded, "Well?"

Consideringly, Percival studied him. A thought occurred to him. "You know," he said neutrally, "there is a perfect way for you to extract your revenge if you are dead set on it . . . you could challenge young Grayson to a duel and kill him."

At the look of appalled outrage that crossed Ives's face, Percival almost smiled and glanced away quickly to hide his expression. Seemingly absorbed in the act of plucking an imaginary speck of lint off his jacket sleeve, he went on casually, "In fact, it is a rather clever scheme, if I do say so myself. You kill young Marcus, and Robert will truly be avenged. Jane brought about Robert's death; so it is only logical that you kill Jane's son."

"Of all the bubble-headed nonsense I have ever heard!" Ives burst out explosively. "If I were to face that young man on the dueling field, it would be tantamount to cold-blooded murder. He seems a likeable cub—I would have to be a black-hearted fiend to consider such a plan. What do you take me for, a killer of innocents?"

"It was just a suggestion," Percival said dulcetly. "I mean it would make just as much sense to use Marcus to gain your revenge as his older sister, would it not?"

Ives shot his friend a narrow-eyed glance. He was not a stupid man, and he realized immediately what his friend was doing. The guileless face Percival turned his way confirmed his suspicions. A reluctant laugh was dragged out of him.

"Damn you, Percival!" he said cheerfully. "Must you be so deucedly logical? Though it pains me to admit it, I see your point." Handsomely he added, "And of course, you are right—if revenge were my only motive, Marcus would make as much a target as his sister—perhaps easier. I am sure if I put my mind to it, I could find a way to insult him and create a reason for a duel. But you ignore the fact that it is not Marcus who arouses my, er, antagonism . . ." He smiled wolfishly at his friend. "And since you have unerringly put your finger on the flaw in my plans, shall we simply say that my interest in the young lady is not *entirely* devoted to thoughts of vengeance?"

"Ives," Percival began worriedly, his amusement having fled, "why must you have anything to do with Lady

Marlowe? Has it not occurred to you that to trifle with her may be dangerous? Her husband is dead. And there are some people who believe that she killed him. Does this not give you pause?"

"Nay, it does not," Ives returned blithely. "I like a good fight. I always have. Marcus would be no match for me, but the little butterfly . . . I suspect she will reveal wings of finely honed steel. And as for her reputation, it only adds spice to the situation and whets my appetite further. I think I am going to enjoy crossing swords with the formidable Marquise Marlowe."

"And I think you should be locked up in Bedlam!"

Ives merely cocked a brow and said lightly, "Come now, let us put the subject behind us and find our way to Boodle's. I feel exceptionally lucky tonight."

His words proved prophetic. He *was* extremely lucky, rising from the faro table around three-thirty that morning with an envious amount of winnings. After parting from Percival, he rode in his coach to the Harrington stables. Leaving the vehicle and horses in the care of his sleepy-eyed driver and groom, he quickly walked the short distance to Bedford Square, the site of the Harrington town house. He had already told his butler not to await his return and in a matter of seconds had unlocked the massive front door and stepped inside.

A frown marred his forehead at the sight of his butler, Sanderson, asleep on a chair near the door. The hall was in shadows. A pair of candles, burnt to almost nothing, spilled fitful light here and there.

Shaking Sanderson's beefy shoulder, Ives said, "Wake up, man. I thought I told you not to wait up for me?"

Sanderson came awake with a start and leaped to his

feet with such alacrity for a man of his bulk that Ives smiled.

"M'lord!" he cried, when he realized who had awakened him. "Forgive me, sir, I did not hear you enter."

"Obviously," Ives said dryly. "But why are you here? I thought I had dismissed you for the evening."

An uneasy look crossed Sanderson's plump face. "It was because of the gentleman, my lord. I did not think you would want me to go to bed and leave him alone in the house."

"What gentleman?" Ives demanded sharply, his frown returning. "I was expecting no company."

"It is the Duke, sir. The Duke of Roxbury. I explained to him that you were out and that you were not expected back until very late. He waved all my protestations aside and insisted upon waiting for you, my lord." Uncertainly, he added, "There was nothing I could do but put him in your study and see to it that he had refreshments. I apologize, my lord, for disobeying your orders, but he was impossible to turn away."

"Roxbury, eh? I wonder what that old devil wants." He smiled at Sanderson's worried expression, and said, "You are not to blame, old fellow. There are few people who can withstand Roxbury when he makes up his mind to do something. Do not fret over it. And now go to bed—I'll see to Roxbury."

A moment later, Ives threw open the door to his study and strolled into the center of the room. Roxbury, his silver hair glinting in the candlelight, was comfortably seated in a chair covered in wine-colored velvet. At his elbow was a silver tray with a half-full decanter of brandy and a pair of snifters. One of the snifters still held a trace of brandy.

Seeing Ives looming up before him, Roxbury sent him a singularly sweet smile. "Oh, my boy, it is good to see you! You are well, I trust?"

Ives grinned at him and refilled Roxbury's snifter as well as one for himself, while he murmured, "Do not try to bamboozle me, Your Grace! You did not force your way past my butler and wait up until this ungodly hour just to inquire about my health."

Roxbury laughed as he took the snifter Ives handed him. "Such a ciever youth! No wonder Wellesley's reports of you were so glowing."

Ives cocked a brow at him. "Kept track of me, did you?"

"Not surprising, since you are my godson—my favorite godson, in fact."

Ives snorted and, seating himself in a chair across from the older man, took an appreciative sip of his brandy. Looking at Roxbury, he said dryly, "Since I seem to recall that I am your *only* godson, I should hope I would be your favorite!"

Roxbury smiled. "What you say is true, but let me assure you, dear boy, that if I had any other godsons, you would still be my favorite."

Ives chuckled. "Have done, sir. You did not seek me out tonight simply to let me know of your esteem, gratifying though it is." Ives's expression sobered. "Why are you here, Your Grace? What may I do for you?"

Roxbury sighed, his smile fading. Staring at his snifter, he said softly, "I am sorry about your father, my boy. Your father, Richard, was one of my best friends. I miss him. And his brother." He glanced at Ives. "Did you know that your father and I were only months apart in age?" As Ives shook his head, Roxbury went on meditatively, "He would have turned seventy-one this coming July . . . I will be seventy-one in November." He sighed again. "We grew up together, your father and I. Your uncle Guy, too, but it was Richard and I who were the best of friends."

Gently Ives said, "I know the two of you were close. I appreciated your help last year. Going through my father's effects was no easy task for either one of us, and it did not help that there was also my uncle Guy's estate as well as the final affairs of my two cousins to handle." Ives's face grew pensive. "It is hard for me sometimes to believe that they are all gone. My cousins, Adrian and Thomas, were younger than I am."

Roxbury nodded. "Guy married late in life. He was almost forty when he married Elizabeth." He smiled faintly. "Unlike your father, who had not been even twenty-two when he married. I think Richard's early marriage and his production of a son almost immediately allowed Guy to put off thoughts of marriage. He had two heirs and did not have to give up his rakish life in order to provide them. And of course, your birth so many years later gave him a third."

"True enough, but I must say again, sir, that I do not think your presence here is to discuss my family history. What may I do for you?"

"I was not just reminiscing, you know," Roxbury said reprovingly. "There is a point to my conversation."

Ives smiled faintly and nodded. "I never doubted it for a moment, sir, and I have to confess that I am eaten alive with curiosity."

"Impatient is more like it. You young people are always in such a hurry. But I will not keep you in suspense any longer." Roxbury took a fortifying sip of his brandy and, staring intently at Ives, asked, "What do you know of your father's life during the past few years before he died? Adrian's, too, for that matter."

Ives frowned. "Very little. I assume that my father was busy helping my uncle run the estate. After his retirement from the vicarage a few years ago, his letters were always full of events at Harrington Chase. And as for Adrian, we were not close, even though he was only about three years younger than I. I was away at school, then in the military, and have not been home very often since, so I really had no opportunity to know either of my cousins very well."

"Would it surprise you to learn that Adrian had been doing a bit of sleuthing for me? Feeding me bits of information that he thought I might find interesting? He became quite adept at it." At Ives's look of astonishment, Roxbury nodded. "Yes, he was proving himself to be a very able spy. He had many friends amongst the French émigrés and was able to help me ferret out those whose loyalties might not have been as . . . ah . . . profound as they should have been." Slowly, Roxbury added, "Adrian was not the only member of your family who developed into a keen spy either. About eighteen months before his death, your father began to help. He was bored with life in the country and had stumbled onto what Adrian was doing for me." A smile crossed Roxbury's lined features. "He came calling on me and demanded to be allowed to help. Said that he saw no reason why the young should have all the fun."

Ives nodded, a bittersweet smile curving his mouth. "That sounds like Father. He always thought it was palpably unfair that while I was off fighting in the wars and having all the adventures, he had to remain home, safe and protected in England. If he had been even a few years younger, I believe he would have offered his services to fight against Napoléon."

"In his own way he *was* fighting against Napoléon. Together, he and Adrian became my two best men. Your father was perfect—who would ever suspect a retired vicar of spying?"

Ives shook his head. "It is rather hard to believe—my father, a spy? And my cousin, too? If anyone other than you had told me this, I would have called him a liar."

"Which is why they made such wonderful spies, no one suspected them, until . . ." Roxbury took a long gulp of his brandy. "Does the name *Le Renard* mean anything to you?"

"The Fox? I assume you are not talking about the little red-coated creature?"

Roxbury smiled grimly. "Indeed not! The particular fox I am speaking of I have been chasing for several years and am no closer to catching now than when I started." His gray eyes met Ives's. "*Le Renard*, as he calls himself, has been a painful thorn in my side for longer than I care to admit." Roxbury looked thoughtful. "In the beginning," he admitted, "his depredations were not very serious or dangerous, and there were other matters I felt were more important than putting a stop to his pilfering of mostly useless information. In recent years, however, he has managed to extract quite a few nuggets of damaging information—information we would have preferred the French had not learned. From beginning as a mere nuisance, the Fox has become a major problem."

"And Adrian and my father were helping you catch him before they died?"

Roxbury nodded. "The bastard is well named, I'll give

him that! Just about the time we think we have him trapped, he manages to slip away." Roxbury's hand closed into a fist. "No matter how close we come, his identity is still secret. I do not even know if he is a member of the French émigré society, or if, God forbid, he is an Englishman won over by Napoléon's gold. I fear the latter. But I have no proof of either. He could just as easily turn out to be the son of a French aristocrat who has attached his future to Napoléon's star."

"What opinion did my father and Adrian have? They must have learned something?"

"Indeed, I believe they had." Roxbury looked uncomfortable. "And that was one of the reasons I offered to help you with your father's papers . . . and Adrian's as well. I was hoping I would find something that would prove enlightening. I did not."

"But if you found nothing, why do you think either one had made a new discovery?"

"Because your father had sent me a message. He stated that he and Adrian hoped to have exciting news for me within a very few days. There was just one thing they needed to confirm before they revealed their discovery." Roxbury stared hard at Ives. "The *Elizabeth,* as seaworthy a vessel as I have ever known, with Adrian and Richard aboard her, went down the very day I received that message. The storm that supposedly sank her was really no more than a blustery breeze with a smattering of rain. Both Richard and Guy were experienced seamen. Adrian and Thomas were not unfamiliar with the yacht. They had often sailed on her themselves with a minimum of crew. They were all competent, able seamen on a sound, seaworthy vessel, sailing into a minor weather disturbance. Yet the vessel went down . . . with all hands on board."

Heavily, Ives said, "You've never said so before, but do you think that the sinking of the *Elizabeth* was no accident?"

Roxbury nodded. "I firmly believe that the Fox knew they were close on his trail and he sabotaged the yacht."

"How could he have been so certain that they had not already discovered his identity and notified you? And how could he have been so sure that my father and Adrian would both go sailing that day? Sinking a boat is no easy task, especially if one wants no suspicions aroused. And don't forget, the yacht sank in December, not exactly a month one would choose to put to sea for amusement or any but the most pressing reason. It seems to me he left a great deal to chance."

"You were abroad when the *Elizabeth* went down, and since you have returned to England, most of your time has been spent in the country, so you would not be aware of the fact that there was a wager," Roxbury said quietly. He made a face. "A wager that even the most tactless fool would be unlikely to mention in view of the tragic results. But there *was* a wager, a wager that had been written in the betting book at White's several weeks prior to the tragedy. It clearly stated that on December 10, 1807, Lord Harrington would set sail on the *Elizabeth* and no matter what the weather, would make the run from Weymouth to Worthing in a specific time. The time was known only to Lord Harrington and Lord Grimshaw, the other man involved in the wager. Your uncle had claimed that he had done it before in the same amount of time, and Grimshaw had declared that he did not believe it." Roxbury flashed a wintry smile. "They almost met on the dueling field over it, before the wager was decided upon. Everyone knew of the wager. It was common knowledge that your father and Adrian and Thomas were going to be on board that day—Harrington honor was at stake. Not surprisingly, the wager had drawn quite a bit of interest. For a week before the race, talk in the clubs was of little else."

"So the Fox could be certain his prey would be on board," Ives said flatly.

"That is my belief. And it also shows you the caliber of man we are dealing with. It did not matter to him how many men died, as long as the ones who were dangerous to him did. Remember, not only were members of your family lost, but your uncle's entire crew as well. Six men in all went down with the *Elizabeth*."

Ives frowned. "If the race aroused such interest, weren't there other yachts and boats in the area? Didn't anyone see what happened?"

Roxbury studied the contents of his snifter. "Yes, there were several vessels scattered about when your uncle's yacht left Weymouth. Some had intended to race alongside the *Elizabeth*, but the weather, while not dangerous, was unpleasant, and, in the end, there were only two within sight of the *Elizabeth* when she went down. Strangely, all the men on those boats agree that for some time prior to her sinking it was obvious something was not quite right. The *Elizabeth* was sitting lower and lower in the water, and her tacking and direction were most erratic . . . almost as if she were drifting . . . almost as if no one was minding the sails and helm."

"And when she sank? Neither of the two boats was close enough to rescue anyone who had been on board the *Elizabeth*?"

"Rather interesting that you should mention that . . ." Roxbury met Ives's hard gaze. "There was never a sign of any survivors—the vessel went down with everyone on board."

"I have always found that impossible to believe," Ives growled, rising impatiently to his feet. Pacing back and forth in the room, he said, "Even if the ship sank, all the men were experienced enough to swim free. There should have been *someone* in the water near the sinking."

Roxbury tipped up his snifter. "There was no one," he said softly. "No one at all."

"You have a theory." It wasn't a question, and the dangerous glitter in Ives's green eyes would have given a lesser man pause.

Roxbury nodded. "Indeed I have. I have not said anything before now because I wanted you to have time to deal with the deaths of your family. I wanted you to be firmly settled into your new estates. I wanted you to have no distractions. I would have preferred to give you more time. In fact, I'd as lief not involve you at all, but the situation is such that you are the only man I feel I can trust fully with the truth."

He hesitated a moment, then said bluntly, "It is my belief that not only did the Fox sabotage the *Elizabeth* so she would sink well away from land, but that he also took out, er, insurance. I think he drugged the barrel of grog which he knew all the men on board would be drinking. If they were all drugged, it would explain the yawing and erratic movements of the vessel just before she went down. There was literally *no one* at the helm. And when she sank, the crew and the others were already unconscious. They sank right along with her." Roxbury met Ives's eyes. "The Fox," he said grimly, "killed them all."

There was a long pause as this sank in.

"And you want me to catch him," Ives said softly.

Roxbury lifted his snifter, clinking it against the one held in Ives's hand. "And I want you to catch him."

Chapter Three

✌

*F*or a long time after Roxbury had departed, Ives roamed the confines of the study, his thoughts dark and deadly. His father had been murdered. Murdered by a traitor.

A cold implacable rage filled him. In the lonely silence of his study, Ives made a vow. The Fox would die.

Dawn was sending delicate pink-and-gold fingers of light over the city when Ives eventually made his way up the stairs to his room. His valet, his former batman, Ashby, had long ago sought out his own bed, and so Ives was alone in his bedchamber as he quickly stripped and crawled beneath the crisp linen sheets.

For a brief moment, the sensation of the cool, clean material caressing his body made him smile. Thinking of the many nights over the years that he had slept in places he would not wish on the worst felon made him appreciate the fine feather bed and the sheer comfort of his surroundings.

But his enjoyment of the physical pleasures faded immediately, and sorrow at his father's death washed over him once again. This time it was deeper and almost more

painful than it was when he first heard of the tragedy
which took his father's life, along with those of his uncle
and cousins. But now! To suspect that it had not been just
an act of fate but that it was very likely—nay, almost certain—that they had been murdered, was to rip open the
wound anew.

Ives did not allow himself to dwell on the tragedy.
During his time in the military, he had seen much death
and suffering and had learned quickly to assimilate it,
then put it aside. A man could not think clearly, method-
ically, if his emotions were involved. Now more than
ever he needed to be able to keep a cool head.

Roxbury's information tonight had been stunning. Not
in his wildest fantasies would he have conceived that not
only Adrian, but his own father as well, had been working secretly for his godfather. A grim smile crossed Ives's
features. He shouldn't have been surprised. He had
known that Adrian was ripe and ready for mischief, and
that his father, despite being nearly forty years older than
Adrian, had not been much better.

And as for Roxbury's part . . . Ives shook his head.
Roxbury was every bit as secretive and conniving as the
man known as *Le Renard.* Perhaps more so, since he was
a well-known member of the aristocracy and welcomed
everywhere.

While there were those who knew or suspected Roxbury's other side, the general public had no idea of how
far his tentacles reached; the shadowy figures who wandered in and out of his life as he collected information,
like a spider in the center of a web; the cold-blooded
schemes he would boldly concoct for England's benefit.
It was whispered that few major decisions were made at
Whitehall without Roxbury's advice, or approval.

Because of his relationship to Roxbury, Ives had been aware that his godfather was not quite the dilettante he appeared to be. During his years in the military, there had been one or two odd activities he had been asked to undertake that had come at the direct behest of his godfather. He had always been puzzled by the apparent control Roxbury exerted over his various commanding officers, but he had not thought too deeply about it. He had been, he admitted with a wolfish grin, too busy trying to stay alive. Tonight, however, Ives had discovered that the hints and whispers he had heard since childhood, all his suspicions about his godfather, were true.

The prospect of tangling with this fellow known as the Fox could not have given Ives more pleasure. He was used to action and danger, and aside from his grieving, these past months in England had been boring and all too predictable. Even if there had been no connection between the Fox and his father's demise, Ives would have leaped at the chance to track him down. That the Fox had no doubt murdered his family made it fiercely personal. A smile that would have made even Percival's blood run cold curved his mouth. Oh, but he was going to enjoy hunting the Fox to his lair.

It was well past five o'clock the next afternoon when Ives descended the main staircase of his town house. He was freshly bathed and barbered and looking forward to a quiet evening at home. The hunt for a suitable wife had been temporarily put aside, with no little relief. But that was not to say that he was no longer hunting—he was, for a far different prey.

Vengeance was a great tonic, Ives thought sardon-

ically, as he sat down in the dining room and heartily ate
the meal waiting for him.

Since his was a bachelor household and he had only
himself to please, he ate at hours that suited him, whether
it was fashionable or not. Fortunately, his cook, Ogden,
was also a former military man, much to the dismay of
several of the London staff, and knew precisely what his
employer liked to eat and when. Consequently, it was a
rare sirloin, spring peas, and roasted potatoes upon which
Ives feasted, with none of those fancy sauces to disguise
the clean taste of the food.

Ogden and Ashby were not the only former comrades
on Ives's staff. Upon leaving the military, he had raided
the ranks for those men who had proved themselves useful to him under a variety of conditions. In addition to
Ogden and Ashby, Cecil Sanderson, the butler, John
Carnes, his coachman, and William Williams, his head
groom, were also in his employ. His colonel had accused
him of taking half his company with him, but Ives had
only laughed. His family had been nearly wiped out and,
facing the unknown in England, he had wanted men he
could trust around him, men he had come to view almost
as family.

Pushing away from the table, Ives said to Sanderson,
who was serving him, "Will you get the others and tell
them that I need to speak to them in the library? Shall we
say ten minutes?"

Sanderson knew precisely who the others were, and,
ten minutes later, the five military comrades were standing respectfully in front of their former commanding officer. Ives waved them to seats around his desk and
quickly, succinctly revealed all that Roxbury had told
him last night.

There was a moment of stunned silence, then William Williams, who had grown up near Harrington Chase, burst out, "Are you saying that the guvnor was murdered? By this Fox fellow?"

Ives nodded.

"And we are to catch him?" asked Sanderson, his usually merry eyes cold and determined.

Again Ives nodded.

Another moment of silence as they considered the situation. It was Ashby who asked quietly, "How much do we know about him, sir? Did Roxbury tell you anything else? Or do we simply start sifting dirt in the dark?"

Ives flashed an icy smile. "Roxbury has little to go on, but he did give me a list of three names for us to start with. Be aware that none of the men on the list may be our quarry. But they were all frequently seen in my father's or my cousin's company during the weeks just prior to their deaths. Which could mean nothing at all, just mere coincidence, but it seems likely to both Roxbury and me that one of them is our man, or may lead us to our man, else my father and Adrian would not have been so interested in them. They were not, according to Roxbury," he finished dryly, "the type of gentlemen my father or Adrian would normally have found convivial. Each one has a questionable reputation. Roxbury has had his own men watching them for the past several months, but so far they have turned up nothing overtly suspicious." Ives grinned like a tiger. "We, of course, shall do much better." He handed the list to Ashby, who was seated nearest to him.

Ives did not have to read the list to know the names on it. They were burned on his brain, and mentally he ticked them off as the list was passed around to his men:

William, Lord Grimshaw; Richard, Lord Coleman; and Etienne Marquette.

Two Englishmen and one Frenchman.

"Are we the only ones who know about this, sir?" asked Sanderson.

"Yes, and I want it to stay that way. That, incidentally, is an order."

"So," began Ogden, uneasily rubbing his bald head, "how do you want to proceed, sir? Begging your pardon, but seems to me that you should be the one doing the investigating. It is not very likely that any of us could walk smash up to any of these gentlemen and just start a casual conversation. We ain't exactly born to the manor." He grinned, revealing his broken and missing teeth.

There was a general laugh and Ives said, "Your point is well taken, Ogden. I will deal with the gentlemen themselves. That is one of the reasons Roxbury laid the problem before me—his men could only watch from the fringes. Your part will be to discover everything that you can from their servants and tradesmen and the like. You will probably be duplicating Roxbury's efforts, but I prefer to start afresh. Once we have gathered the general information, you will proceed to make friends with the servants, and former servants." He sent them a cynical look. "It is common knowledge that if you want to know anything disreputable about a gentleman, all you have to do is ask his servants, especially those who have left his employ."

"What about the lieutenant, sir? Is he going to help you with the others?" Ashby asked worriedly. "Seems to me you need some help. Three to one is not odds that I like."

"Forrest? More than likely I shall bring him in on this, but until I tell you differently, assume that we are the only

ones who know about our friend, the Fox, and this list.
You may decide amongst yourselves who is going to in-
filtrate which household. And do not forget to watch your
backs."

The men nodded and started to rise, but Ives stopped
them. "Remember, we must arouse no suspicions. On the
surface, keep up your daily routines and carry on as
usual." Ives smiled faintly. "I will, of course, understand
the occasional dereliction of duty—provided you have
some useful information for me when you return."

Alone in his study once more, Ives sat back down and
studied the list. Lord Grimshaw's inclusion had not been
so surprising. After all, he had been the instigator of the
wager that had sent the Harrington men to sea in the first
place.

It was interesting to note, Ives thought, as his gaze slid
down the paper, that he had just met Lord Coleman last
night . . . and in the company of the fascinating little
golden butterfly. Was she involved? he wondered. Might
she know something? He doubted it, but it would be enjoyable to combine a little pleasure with the business at
hand. Very soon, he decided with an odd twist in his gut,
he would make certain his path crossed that of Lady Marlowe.

Sophy did not know whether to be pleased or disappointed when the day following the Dennings' at home
brought no sign of Lord Harrington. She had half expected that he would call, and she told herself firmly she
was very glad that he had not.

All in all, she had spent an enjoyable day. One of her
few favorites amongst Simon's friends, Henry Dewhurst,
had taken her and Phoebe for a drive in the park. Phoebe

had thoroughly enjoyed it, her big golden eyes glowing with delight at the sights of all the fashionably dressed ladies and gentlemen, the gleaming carriages and spirited horses.

"Oh, Sophy, do look!" Phoebe suddenly cried excitedly, her cheeks flushed and her soft golden curls bouncing near her temples. "Is that not Brummell himself? The Beau?"

Glancing at the neatly garbed young man, impeccably attired in shining Hessians and a dark blue, elegantly fitting coat, Sophy smiled in his direction, and murmured, "Indeed it is."

At that moment, the Beau looked at them and, recognizing Sophy, tipped his hat to her and bowed grandly. As Dewhurst's carriage swept by, Phoebe, her expression blissful, sank back against the cushions. "Beau Brummell actually acknowledged us!"

Sophy and Henry exchanged a comfortable look. It was one of the many things that she liked about him. He seemed to share her opinion in most things, and they dealt very well together, which surprised her since his cousin was Lord Grimshaw, whom she absolutely detested. The two men were always together and Sophy knew of their deplorable reputations. Yet there was something so very disarming and utterly charming about Henry that she tended to forget his relationship to Grimshaw.

Last year Henry had gently indicated that he would not mind having a deeper relationship with her, and Sophy supposed that if she wanted a lover, she could do worse than Henry Dewhurst.

Nearly forty, Henry was a handsome man, with laughing blue eyes and wavy chestnut hair. His manners were impeccable, and he was rumored to be *very* wealthy. Gossip claimed that if it were not for Henry, his older brother, the Baron Dewhurst, would be bankrupt.

Everyone liked Henry. He was extremely affable. Gentlemen thoroughly enjoyed his company, and, despite his raffish pursuits, many a society matron's bosom swelled with pride to have him attend one of her entertainments. In fact, the only thing Sophy held against him was his relationship with Grimshaw, which he couldn't help, and his friendship with Simon. He did not seem the type of decadent rogue who made up the majority of Simon's friends.

Thinking of his association with Simon, Sophy frowned slightly. Abruptly she said, "You know it has always puzzled me, your friendship with Simon." She glanced at him. "You've never acted like the others. I've never seen you foxed or chasing any of the maids. You've never made indecent suggestions to me. Actually, you were always very kind and polite to me."

Henry glanced uneasily at Phoebe and, to his dismay, found her intelligent gaze fixed on him. Acutely aware of the younger girl's stare, he cleared his throat, and muttered, "Um. Simon was a, er, good sort." At the outraged expression on both ladies' faces, he added hastily, "At least he was when I was with him. I know his reputation was, ah, deplorable, but he, uh, never did anything untoward that I ever saw."

"How can you defend him?" Phoebe demanded hotly, all her sympathies with her sister. "He was a blackhearted monster! He was mean to Sophy and would not even let her visit us after Mama died!"

Henry looked stricken. "Oh, I agree. In his treatment of dear Sophy, he was indeed cruel." He should have stopped there, but foolishly he rattled on. "Amongst the gentlemen," he said thoughtlessly, "Simon could be, er, quite jovial."

It was obvious that neither lady cared for his opinion, and poor Henry spent the remainder of the drive home redeeming his blunder. By the time they reached the Grayson town house, both ladies were laughing at his sallies, and he left them knowing he had been forgiven.

Upstairs in Sophy's bedroom, the two sisters had put aside their bonnets and pelisses and were discussing the afternoon's entertainment.

"It was so exciting to see the Beau himself," Phoebe said for perhaps the tenth time since they had arrived home. "And to think that he acknowledged us! Marcus will turn green."

"I thought," Sophy answered teasingly, "that you had decided London society was boring and you wanted nothing to do with it?"

A thoughtful expression crossed Phoebe's face. "It *is* boring most of the time, but I must confess there are parts of it that are very, very interesting." She looked at Sophy. "Don't you find it boring? To be forever dressing and undressing and rushing around to one grand affair after another? Constantly mingling with strangers and forced into the company of people you hardly know? Don't you grow weary of it? I know I would! If it were not for the bookstores and libraries, I would hate every minute of our stay—and I am too young to attend even half the functions that you do! Thank goodness!"

Sophy made a face. "It is not so very bad," she began slowly, "but I cannot deny that I shall be happy when we return home." She sent Phoebe an affectionate look. "It will be pleasant, will it not, to be comfortably settled at Gatewood once more?"

Phoebe studied her older sister, thinking she was the most beautiful, kindest, *dearest* creature in the world. "Do you intend *always* to live at Gatewood with us?" she asked suddenly. "Are you certain you will never remarry and go away again?"

There was a note in Phoebe's voice that made Sophy look at her closely. "What is it, sweetheart?" she questioned. "Do you think that I am going to leave you?"

Phoebe glanced away, her lower lip betraying the faintest trace of a wobble. "You do not know how awful it was," she muttered, "after Mama died, and Marcus and I were all alone at Gatewood."

Phoebe had been lying on Sophy's bed, Sophy sitting in a chair nearby, and at Phoebe's words she sprang up to clasp her sister in her arms. Brushing a kiss across Phoebe's brow, she said fiercely, "I will never leave you alone again. *If* I were to ever marry again, and that is highly unlikely, it would be with the clear understanding that you, and Marcus, too, if he wished, would live with me." She hugged Phoebe's skinny little body next to hers. "I would never even consider an offer for my hand from a man you did not like, nor from someone who did not want you with us."

Phoebe let out a huge sigh. She smiled, and said shyly, "I like Mister Dewhurst."

"Oh, do you?" Sophy replied with a laugh. "Are you matchmaking?"

Phoebe shook her small golden head. "Oh, no. I would never do that, but he is very nice, is he not?"

"Indeed he is, but I have no intention of marrying him," Sophy said lightly. "As a matter of fact, I cannot even think of one gentlemen whose wife I would like to be." To her horror, the dark, barbaric features of Lord Harrington suddenly filled her mind. Shaken by the force of emotion his mere memory could conjure up, Sophy pulled away from Phoebe.

Getting to her feet, she avoided looking at her sister, and murmured, "Shall we go downstairs and see if Marcus is home? You can boast about the Beau bowing to us and make him positively envious."

Irritated with herself for allowing thoughts of Lord Harrington to enter her mind, Sophy was somewhat preoccupied during the remainder of the day. A quiet evening for the two ladies had been planned, each one declaring her desire to curl up with a book. Marcus, of course, was going out for the evening and would not be home until very late.

With an effort, Sophy refrained from asking where he was going and with whom. He was very much the young gentleman about town these days, and she tried not to hover. It was not easy for her. Marcus might be all of nineteen, but he was still her younger brother, and London could be a dangerous place.

Her restraint was rewarded when, on the point of leaving, Marcus turned, grinned at her, and said, "Sutcliff and Jarrett and I are going to Vauxhall Gardens and perhaps later to one of the gaming clubs. I promise not to lose the family fortune."

"I should hope not!" Phoebe responded tartly. "Uncle Edward's habits are bad enough."

Marcus's face darkened, and he shot his young sister an unkind look. "I am not," he said stiffly, "Uncle Edward!"

Bowing jerkily to Sophy he stalked from the room.

Sophy turned to Phoebe. "Did you have to say that? He is nothing like Uncle Edward, and you know it."

Phoebe hunched a shoulder and fixed her gaze on the book in front of her. "He needs reminding every now and then," Phoebe said gruffly.

Sophy thought the comment unfair. Marcus, for all his ardent desire to cut a swath through London society, displayed no signs of the determined rake and gambler. His amusements so far had been perfectly normal and acceptable: shooting at Manton's Shooting Gallery; boxing at Gentleman Jackson's; attending cockfights, bearbaitings and horse sales at Tattersall's. Evenings were often spent in the company of his two boon companions, attending various social functions with the occasional foray, like tonight, to the many gambling houses and clubs with which London abounded.

She was uneasy about his friendship with Sir Alfred Caldwell, but so far Marcus had shown no desire to be a seducer of innocents, nor to dedicate his days and nights to the pursuit of drink and gaming. Sophy was proud of him. And as for Uncle Edward . . .

Her brow wrinkled, and she was bitterly conscious that Edward's eager embrace of every vice imaginable made life exceedingly difficult for them all. Not only was he depressingly irregular with the monies legally due Phoebe and Marcus, Sophy was also gallingly aware that he was going through her father's fortune at an alarming rate. And until Marcus turned twenty-one, there was nothing that they could do about it.

When she had arrived at Gatewood after Simon's death, one of the first things she had done was to visit the family solicitor, Mister Thomas Brownell. He had been overjoyed to see her, his concern for the family obvious, and the news he gave her was disturbing indeed. Baron Scoville had no control or say in *her* affairs, but with her siblings it was an entirely different matter.

Her father's will clearly gave his brother-in-law a free hand and dangerous access to all of the family fortune. Fortunately, and it was the only good news she had received, a huge portion of the estate was entailed, which prevented Edward from selling their home out from under their feet, and the vast tracts of land that went with Gatewood. On the other hand, there was nothing to prevent him from bleeding the estate dry, as he was doing. The most Sophy could do was badger and cajole her uncle to do the right thing: renounce his rights and allow her to see to the care of her brother and sister *and* the stewardship of their remaining fortune.

Gazing blankly at the opened book before her, Sophy snorted. He was certainly willing to allow her to care for Marcus and Phoebe. What he would *not* do was release control of the family fortune, or what remained of it.

Rage surged through her when she thought of shifts she had been forced to undertake to keep Marcus and Phoebe in the manner which was their right. She had spent huge sums of her own money on Gatewood, trying to restore it to its previous grandeur. And, of course, since *dear* Uncle Edward was so wayward with paying the quarterly allowances which would have seen to all that, it was Sophy who frequently paid the day-to-day living expenses for her brother and sister.

She glanced across at Phoebe's bent golden head and thought of Marcus's delight at being in London. She regretted none of it. She would do it all again in a flash, but she *did* resent her uncle's blatant abuse of the trust her father had given him.

She did not blame her father. There was no way he could have known he would die so unexpectedly, or that his wife would not live to see her children reach their majority. Sophy's bottom lip drooped. Not that her mother would have been much of a brake on Edward's spending habits, but as his sister, Jane certainly would have been able to exert more influence over him than a mere niece could.

With a sigh, Sophy forced her thoughts in another direction. Dwelling on the perfidy of Baron Scoville's actions only infuriated and depressed her. Determinedly burying her nose in the book before her, Sophy put all thoughts of her uncle from her mind, and she and Phoebe enjoyed their quiet evening together.

Her sleep was not quite so tranquil—she dreamed again of Lord Harrington. Upon awakening she could not fully remember the details of the dream, only the memory of his green eyes, mocking and daring her. Cursing him roundly and herself as well—having lived with Simon, she knew an astonishing variety of oaths—Sophy faced the day wishing fervently that she could depart immediately for Gatewood and leave Lord Harrington and her uncle far behind.

Grimly resolved to enjoy herself, Sophy promptly agreed the next day to an evening at Vauxhall in the company of Lord Coleman and Sir Alfred Caldwell, along with another couple, Mr. and Mrs. Randal Offington, neighbors from Cornwall who were visiting for a few weeks.

The outing went well. The group enjoyed a fine meal in one of the supper boxes, watched the Cascade and fireworks, and listened to the fine voice of the well-known

Mrs. Bland. The Offingtons, married only a year, were near to Sophy in age and were particular favorites of hers. She liked their easy company enormously.

It had been decided to end the evening with a stroll along the tree-lined Grand Cross Walk, which traversed the gardens, and Sophy was relaxed and cheerful as she set out with her friends. Gaily lit lanterns marked the way, and Sophy was enjoying herself, occasionally stopping to talk or wave to a few people she had recently met in London. All in all the evening had been lovely, even if Lord Coleman and Sir Alfred persisted in paying court to her.

The sight of a tall, commanding figure striding purposefully toward her was the first blight on the evening. It was bad enough, Sophy thought waspishly, that he boldly invaded her dreams—must he also show up in reality?

Harrington was accompanied once again by Percival Forrest, and to Sophy's dismay, they seemed perfectly happy to merge with her group once greetings and introductions were exchanged. She was not quite certain how he accomplished it, but in a matter of minutes, Lord Coleman and Sir Alfred had been displaced from her side, and it was Lord Harrington's hand on her elbow politely guiding her down the graveled walkway.

There was silence between them as they walked, although Sophy was dizzingly aware of him, the strength and size of him, and the seductive, almost caressing, warmth of his hand on her arm. She sought desperately for the light repartee that usually came so easily to her tongue, but her mind was blank. Utterly.

Like a mechanical doll she walked with him, conscious only of the man beside her, the soft, night air, and the suddenly sinister forest crowding near. The rest of the group had disappeared, and Lord Harrington deftly turned her down the notorious Dark Walk.

Outrage churning in her bosom, she stopped abruptly and glared at him. "I do not know quite what you think you are doing, but I demand that you return me to the others *immediately*!"

Ives glanced down at her, seeing the angry flush on her cheeks and the molten gold of her eyes, and decided that temper became the lady. His lips curled briefly. And wouldn't she just delight in separating his head from his shoulders if he dared to tell her so!

"What are you smiling at?" Sophy demanded suspiciously, not at all pleased that her request seemed to amuse him.

"Is one forbidden to smile in your company, Lady Marlowe?"

"Of course not! You may smile all you wish," Sophy replied grandly, "once you have returned me to my friends."

A gleam entered in his eyes. "And if I do not?"

Sophy's bosom swelled. "If you do not," she said coolly, "I shall know you for a blackguard." Her chin lifted. "And I do not acknowledge blackguards. Ever."

Ives laughed. "Dear Butterfly, is this how you keep such rogues as Coleman and Caldwell in line? By threatening to refuse to acknowledge them?"

A blistering retort was on the tip of her tongue, when a fearful cry stilled it.

"Oh, *pray* do not! I beg you. Oh, please let me go!"

The voice was female, young, obviously terrified, and on the point of tears. Her infuriating companion forgotten, Sophy picked up her skirts and sprinted down the dark path in the direction of the voice.

It had come from a secluded nook just a short distance from where she and Ives had been standing. As Sophy reached it, another cry came, even more frightened than the first. "Oh, sir, do not! Let me go!"

Despite the shadows, Sophy took in the scene in an instant. Two people were seated on a rustic bench in the center of the nook. The girl, who had just cried out, was not more than fifteen. Her gown was ripped, baring one slim shoulder, and she was desperately struggling in the arms of a man—a man much larger than the small, slim figure which fought so vainly to be free.

"You monster! Unhand her this moment!" Sophy snapped, her slender body braced for battle.

Having come up behind her, Ives put his hands on her shoulders, and murmured. "Ah, I think I had better handle this, Lady Marlowe."

Sophy shot him a look. "Oh really? Is this not precisely what you planned with me?"

Ives smiled down lazily at her. "I rather doubt it. If I were trying to seduce you, sweetheart, I would be getting far more cooperation than this clumsy fellow."

A bellow from the gentleman in the nook prevented Sophy from further speech. "Clumsy!" he roared, letting the terrified girl go and lurching to his feet. "By Satan's balls! Who are you to speak so of me? And who, I might ask, are you to be meddling in another man's affairs? I've a good mind to run you through." He took an unsteady step forward, peering at Ives and Sophy. His gaze fastened on Sophy and he seemed to become even more enraged. "Damn it to hell! I might have known it would be you, Sophy, always ruining a fellow's fun."

Seemingly oblivious to the drunken gentleman and the frightened girl, Ives cocked a brow at Sophy. "You know this, er, gentleman?"

Sophy's lip curled. Sending a scathing look at the gentleman in the nook, she said grimly, "Allow me, Lord Harrington, to introduce you to my *dear* uncle Edward, Baron Scoville. Since you both seem to have the same disgusting propensities, I am certain you will, no doubt, become fast friends!"

Chapter Four

❧

*I*ves glanced thoughtfully at Edward, who stood there glaring balefully at them. The girl was sobbing quietly in the background, forgotten for the moment. Baron Scoville was elegantly attired, his intricately tied cravat gleamed whitely in the shadows and his dark blue coat fit him superbly. Despite the signs of dissipation and overindulgence beginning to blur his face and form, he was a handsome man. Ives could discern a slight resemblance to Sophy: the slender build, the golden hair and eyes. The similarity ended there.

The lack of adequate light made it hard to see him fully, but Ives had seen and heard enough to know precisely the sort of man standing before him. Lord Scoville was obviously just the type of depraved bounder that most people of good breeding avoided like the plague. And he was the Butterfly's uncle?

Ives rubbed his jaw and looked down at Sophy. "Your uncle, you say?" And at Sophy's curt nod, he added casually, "Pity."

Unaccountably his comment made her want to laugh,

that and the offended expression on her uncle's face. Stifling her amusement and ignoring both men, Sophy stepped around her uncle and sank down on the bench beside the girl. "Do not cry," she said softly. "He cannot hurt you now. Come along with me, and I shall see that you are driven safely home."

"Now see here, Sophy," Edward said, blustering, "this is none of your affair."

"That is not exactly true," Ives said calmly. "Rescuing innocents from the grip of scoundrels is everyone's affair."

Sophy gaped at him, her eyes round with astonishment. Lord Harrington was taking her side in this ugly situation?

"By Jove!" Edward protested. "No one dares to call me a scoundrel!"

"Perhaps not to your face," Ives replied coolly. "But if I read this unpleasant little scene right, only a scoundrel would have attempted to force his attentions on a female this young. And only a double-damned scoundrel would have persisted with a female of *any* age when she had clearly made her wishes to the contrary known."

Edward's face grew purple with rage and his entire body shook with fury. "By Satan's balls! No one speaks to *me* in that fashion. Name your seconds!"

Ives shook his head. "Not tonight. Tomorrow morning when you have had time to consider the situation and you are not so obviously foxed, if you feel the same, I shall be happy to oblige you. Until then, I suggest you take yourself off and allow your niece and me to escort the young lady to her home."

Sophy could hardly believe it when, a second later, Edward, glaring furiously at Ives, spun on his heel and staggered off down the path, muttering and swearing under his breath. He collided with a small group of people coming in the opposite direction and cursed them roundly before disappearing into the darkness.

As the group approached, Sophy thankfully recognized the Offingtons and Forrest and her other companions. Stopping in the center of the path, Caldwell asked, "Wasn't that Scoville?"

Sophy made a face. "Yes, it was."

It was Sara Offington who first noticed the young girl clinging pathetically to Sophy. "Oh, and who is this charming child? A friend of yours?" she asked politely, pretending not to have had a very good idea of what had occurred. Sara's tact and good sense was one of the reasons Sophy liked her so much.

Looking down into the tear-drenched, pansy brown eyes of the girl before her, Sophy asked, "What is your name, dear?"

"A-a-nne Richmond," she stammered.

"Not old 'Lucky' Richmond's heiress?" gasped Lord Coleman.

Shyly Anne nodded. "He was my father."

Silence descended. "Lucky" Richmond had been a legendary gamester a decade or so ago, a gentleman notorious for the vast sums he had lost gambling. The sobriquet "Lucky" had been given in jest of his phenomenally bad luck. He had swiftly gone through his own respectable fortune and, shortly thereafter, to no one's very great surprise, had married the daughter of a wealthy merchant and retired to his country estate.

Within ten months, Richmond's wife had presented him with a child, dying not six months afterward. Left with a fortune and a baby daughter to raise, Richmond had promptly put his infant child in the care of a competent staff of servants and returned to his profligate ways.

He happily spent his days and nights gambling and wagering unbelievable amounts on any type of contest that took his fancy. To everyone's astonishment, including his own, he seemed unable to lose no matter how ridiculous the wager. He became "Lucky" Richmond in the truest sense of the word. When Richmond had died little more than a year ago, his sole heir had been the young girl sitting beside Sophy.

In the dim light of the few lanterns, Sophy could see that Anne was an attractive child. Neatly formed, she had enormous speaking eyes that spoke volumes, a tip-tilted little nose, and masses of dusky ringlets. Sophy suspected, however, that Edward's interest had been in Anne's fortune as much as her physical beauty.

Thinking about the unlikelihood of such an innocent being left alone in the company of a man with a reputation like Edward's, Sophy frowned. Something was amiss here, and she intended to find out what it was. But not right now. Right now she needed to get Anne safely home.

She was on the point of rising when Henry Dewhurst, his cousin Lord Grimshaw at his side, and Etienne Marquette following closely behind, wandered up. It must have been obvious that something had happened. His kind face full of concern, Dewhurst said, "Oh, I say, Lady Marlowe, is something amiss? May we be of service to you?"

Sophy shook her golden head and murmured, "Thank you, no. Nothing of any import transpired. Just another one of my uncle's little escapades."

"I thought I saw Scoville just a moment ago," said

Lord Grimshaw. "He did not look a bit pleased." He gave an ugly bark of laughter. "But then he seldom looks pleased after crossing swords with you."

Etienne Marquette, his glossy black curls gleaming in the faint light, laughed. "It is common knowledge that *la belle* Marlowe is by far the better the swordsman. You should take pity on him, *madame.*"

Sophy stiffened. "I will take pity on him," she said in a hard little voice, "when he displays some pity for someone other than himself."

"Ah, *madame,*" Etienne sighed dramatically, "during all the years that I have known you, I have always thought that you were far too harsh on your poor *oncle.* He means no harm by his—what is it you English say— his pranks."

Grimshaw gave another bark of laughter. "Pranks! Indeed, yes! You are far too stuffy in your manner, gel," he said with rude familiarity. "It is no wonder that you and Simon were such a poor match. He was full of ginger and beans, while you . . ."

Watching intently from the sidelines, Ives decided that he did not like Lord Grimshaw very much. His manner toward Lady Marlowe bordered on the insulting, and his hard gray eyes and saturnine features were a definite hint that he was not a particularly pleasant fellow. Knowing that Grimshaw's name was on the list of suspects and that he had been the instigator of the wager that led to his father's death, Ives was aware of an instant antipathy rising within him. As for Etienne Marquette, Ives could not envision the willowy fop in front of him being the clever man the Fox was purported to be. But then appearances were deceiving.

Ives shot Percival a look, and, correctly interpreting it,

Percival stepped forward and said smoothly, "I do not believe that any of you have met Viscount Harrington or Lady Marlowe's good friends, the Offingtons. Allow me to introduce you."

Introductions were exchanged, and Ives continued to study the three newcomers. Henry Dewhurst was a slim, dandified gentleman, his affection and intimacy with Lady Marlowe obvious.

Marquette appeared to share Dewhurst's bent toward dandyism, his cravat so high and starched that he could hardly turn his head, and his lilac coat so tight Ives wondered in passing how he could move at all. Marquette was an attractive man, though, with liquid dark eyes and a light, pleasant manner.

Lord Grimshaw was a different matter entirely. The expression on Lady Marlowe's face as she looked at Grimshaw suddenly caught his attention and Ives's gaze narrowed. It was apparent that Grimshaw was also well-known to her and not a particular favorite.

He glanced consideringly at Coleman. His name was on the list, too, and again Lady Marlowe seemed to know him well. Ives's mouth tightened. From what he had learned recently, none of the men suspected of being *Le Renard* were the type of gentlemen he would have associated with someone like Lady Marlowe.

It had not taken his men very long to discover the reputations of the men on the list or to report that they were a trio of generally unsavory, nasty fellows. The lady, Ives thought sourly, seemed to have exceedingly poor taste in her companions. More of interest to him, however, was the fact that she appeared to be quite familiar with all three of the men suspected of being the Fox. Could it be mere coincidence?

Aware of Anne's increasing agitation and the curiosity of the others, Sophy stood up, and said forthrightly, "We have lingered here long enough. If you will excuse us?"

Not waiting for a reply, she glanced down kindly at Anne, and murmured, "I think that your father's luck must have been with you tonight when Lord Harrington and I came upon you. Now, if you like, I shall see that you reach home safely."

"And I," said Ives promptly, "shall be delighted to drive you there. Ladies?"

It was very smoothly done, and in what seemed a blink of an eye to Sophy, despite the protests of some of the other gentlemen, Ives bid the others good night and bundled her and Anne into his carriage. A moment later they were bowling down the cobbled streets toward Anne's residence on Russell Square.

Sending Ives a severe look as he sat across from her, Sophy asked, "How did you do that? You just whisked us away from the others and into your coach as if by magic."

Ives smiled that lazy smile she was beginning to know too well. "In the military they teach us all manner of maneuvers."

Sophy snorted. Turning her attention to Anne, she asked quietly, "How is it, my dear, that you were placed in such an invidious position tonight? The outcome could have been far different. Where was your chaperon? Didn't you have anyone to oversee your welfare?"

Anne looked away. "My aunt is my guardian," she said haltingly. "She is a great friend of your uncle's."

"Oh, dear," Sophy muttered. "Any friend of Edward's, I am sorry to say, is no one to have the care of a child like yourself. What was she thinking of, to let you out at night, alone in the company of a man like Edward?"

"She wants me to m-m-marry him."

"*Marry* him!" Sophy exclaimed, outraged. "How utterly wicked! I shall not allow it!"

Anne looked at her with suddenly hopeful eyes. "Oh, Lady Marlowe! Will you help me? I have been so frightened since Aunt Agnes insisted that Miss Wilson, my governess, and I come up to London." Wistfully she added, "We were very happy at home in the country and Miss Wilson was so very kind to me. I-I-I miss her terribly."

"What happened to her?" Ives asked quietly.

Anne glanced shyly at him. "Miss Wilson objected to Aunt Agnes's plans for me. She said that I was far too young to be out and that I should still be in the schoolroom. Aunt Agnes dismissed her on the spot."

"But why," Sophy demanded, "does your aunt want you to marry so very young and to a creature as depraved as my uncle?"

In a voice far too adult for her age, Anne said, "It is because of the money. Besides my father's wealth, Grandfather Weatherby left me the bulk of his fortune. He and Aunt Agnes fought all the time, and he cut her out of his will. She has very little money of her own, and I think Lord Scoville has promised her some money, once we are safely wed." Anne sighed. "She would want the marriage in any event. She can never forget that Grandfather was a merchant, and she thinks that by marrying a member of the peerage I shall improve my position and hers, too."

"Oh, good gad!" Sophy burst out, thoroughly revolted. "Of all the utter twaddle." She glanced at Anne. "Do you particularly want to return to your aunt's care?"

"W-what do you mean? I have no choice, do I?"

"Indeed you do!" Sophy replied spiritedly. "I would be most pleased to have you come and live with me."

Ives sat up, as if jabbed with a sword. The Butterfly was far too impetuous for her own good. "Shouldn't you think about this a little more?" he said carefully. "Don't you think that you are being rather hasty?"

He suddenly found himself the object of two pairs of decidedly hostile eyes. Drawing herself up grandly, Sophy said stiffly, "I really do not see how it is any concern of yours, Lord Harrington. It is a perfect solution." She glanced over at Anne. "Don't you agree?"

"Oh, yes," Anne breathed ecstatically.

Sophy smiled warmly at her, the smile dying as she looked toward Ives. "Please have the driver change directions," she commanded coolly, "and take us to Berkeley Square."

Ives shrugged, rapped on the panel behind his head, and gave the change in destination to the driver. Thoughtfully he stared across at Sophy as the carriage swayed and bounced upon its way. It seemed that in addition to being imprudent and impetuous, the lady also had a mind of her own. It was something he would do well to remember in the future when dealing with her. He grinned. He had always enjoyed a lively tussle and was rather certain that Lady Marlowe was going to provide him with one.

Sophy glanced at him suspiciously. "Why are you smiling?"

Ives looked as innocent as someone with his marauder's features could. "At the happy ending of tonight's events?" he offered angelically.

Sophy stared hard at him. What was the man up to? Except for having swept her rather unwillingly down the Dark Walk, he had been all that was polite, and she had to admit that he had done nothing improper during their walk. He had even taken her side against Edward. Even now, he was behaving in an exemplary manner. So why didn't she trust him?

Le Renard had watched Ives escort the two ladies away with a speculative eye. Did the dolt actually believe that he stood a chance with sweet Sophy? He smiled nastily.

After being married to Simon, it was unlikely that Sophy would ever chance the hallowed state of marriage again. Certainly not with someone like Harrington, a former military man, whose air and manner gave clear evidence of a man well used to command. Sophy, he admitted with a great deal of ambivalence, was not a woman who took kindly to being ordered to do anything. And Harrington? He had been what? A nobody, a major in the cavalry who had been fortunate enough to exchange a military career for a title. Thinking of Ives's inheritance, he chuckled suddenly. *I wonder if the fellow is grateful to me? He should be. After all, he owes his sudden rise in the aristocracy to me.*

But he was not chuckling a few hours later when he had finally detached himself from the others and made his way home. It occurred to him that he had dismissed Harrington too swiftly. It was possible that the new viscount might bear watching. He had almost underestimated the Harringtons once before, and he was not about to do it again.

He did not think there was any real danger from Harrington's direction, but he was an extremely crafty, careful creature—one of the reasons he had not been caught all these years. Because of his success, he conceded reluctantly, he had perhaps grown too confident in his ability to throw pursuers off his trail.

The brush with Adrian and Richard Harrington had changed all that. They had not been as close to discovering his identity as they had assumed, but just the fact that they had been casting about for his scent a little too near to home alerted him to the dangers of overconfidence. And so, he thought with a malicious smile, he had taken care of them.

Dismissing his hovering servant, he poured himself a brandy and settled comfortably into a chair in his study. At the moment, he was rather pleased with life, although Sir Arthur Wellesley's arrival in Portugal did give him pause.

Napoléon had done very well on the Continent, but placing Wellesley in command of the British troops might change all that. He sighed. If Napoléon were to be defeated, his long run as *Le Renard* would be over and all that lovely French gold would stop pouring into his hands. He sighed again. Ah, well, he had made fortune enough to keep him in ease for the rest of his life.

He smiled. He would retire in glory, his identity unknown. There was, after all, very little to connect him to the Fox. He frowned. That damned ruby cravat pin, he thought irritably. Where had it gone?

He had worn it frequently. The size and brilliance of

the ruby had been remarkable. Dozens of people could identify the pin as his.

Worse, he knew he had been wearing it when Simon had drunkenly announced his intention of letting his wife know who was master in *his* house. He clearly remembered stroking it as he considered Simon's actions. It had been at that very moment that the plan to waylay Simon had sprung into his mind, and it had taken but a moment to slip away from the drunken crowd and lie in wait for his prey. And upon confirming his worst suspicions, that Simon had identified him, why, he'd had no choice but to kill the bounder.

Simon had been his first kill, and he admitted that he had been rather nervous about it. The thunderous raging of the storm that night had not helped his nerves in the least. And that one frighteningly illuminating flash of lightning! He had been almost certain Sophy had seen him lurking against the wall. But she had not.

His frown deepened. Mayhap, she had, and had kept quiet all these years for her own purposes.

He snorted. How illogical! He was, he decided, being rather melodramatic this evening. He took a sip of his fine, smuggled French brandy.

If Sophy had seen him, she would have given some sign by now, and as for the cravat pin . . . He had considered briefly having a duplicate made, but there was the fear that the duplication would become known.

No, he had concluded he was better off letting sleeping dogs lie. The pin was probably resting in some crevice in Marlowe House. After all this time, who would remember when he had lost it? Or connect it with Simon's death? He needn't worry about its loss coming back to haunt him. As for Harrington, if the viscount proved troublesome, why he would simply have to dispose of him.

Harrington was in Sophy's thoughts that night also, but she did not come to any firm conclusions about him. She was wary of him, but could not deny he had been very helpful. She told herself she was grateful, but she admitted she was also suspicious and not a little mistrustful of him, too. She made a face as she lay sleepless in her bed. Being married to a beast like Simon could do that to a woman.

Not only was she wary of Harrington's motives, but there was also the fact that since Simon's death, she had run her own affairs and those of her siblings with no help from anyone else, and she was not certain how she felt about Harrington's intervention. Ruefully she admitted that mixed in with her gratitude was just a bit of resentment at the way he had coolly whisked her down the Dark Walk, then been amused at her reaction.

A yawn overtook her, and she snuggled down into her bed, feeling rather satisfied with the night's doings. Anne was safe from Edward's clutches and sleeping soundly just two doors down the hall. Phoebe and Marcus had been slightly taken aback when Sophy presented them with an utter stranger and blithely informed them Anne would be staying with them indefinitely. After their initial shock, they had taken it well. Phoebe had been her usual sweet self, shyly welcoming the other girl and making Anne feel instantly at ease. Marcus had been almost indifferent to Sophy's stray, but he had bowed politely and murmured that he hoped she would enjoy her stay with them.

It was not until the next morning that the ramifications

of what she had done were brought home to Sophy. After the stress of the previous evening, she had slept in. She had just finished a leisurely morning tea, Phoebe and Anne sprawled indecorously on her bed, when the unpleasant message was brought to her that her uncle and an unidentified lady were waiting for her in the blue saloon.

Anne gasped and jerked upright. "It is my aunt. I know it is. She has come to drag me back to Russell Square." Brown eyes imploring, she had gazed beseechingly at Sophy. "Oh, please! I beg of you, do not let her take me away!"

"Nonsense," said Phoebe stoutly, despite the faint shadow of unease in her gaze. "Sophy will not let anyone wrest you away from here. You are safe. Sophy will protect you."

"You do not know my aunt," Anne replied piteously. "She is most determined, and she has brought *him* with her." A sob came from her. "If I am returned to her, I am lost! No one will be able to save me from the horrid fate that was almost mine last night. I am doomed."

It was not too dramatic a reading of the situation, as Sophy knew full well. It occurred uneasily to her that she might have acted hastily. She had brought Anne into her house, but she had no legal right to keep her there. If her aunt demanded Anne's return, and it was very probable that she would, legally Sophy would have to comply or find herself on the wrong side of the law.

Her thoughts jumbled and unpleasant, Sophy reassured Anne as best she was able and, once both girls had been shooed from her room, hastily scrambled into her clothes. Feeling decidedly apprehensive about how to proceed, she descended the stairs not half an hour later.

One thing was very clear in her mind. She would not desert Anne.

The memory of her own desperately unhappy marriage came back to her. Law or no, she could not stand helplessly by and allow Anne's aunt to thrust her into the arms of a blackguard like Edward. A militant gleam entered the gold eyes. There had been no one to save her from Simon, but Anne was not without protectors. *She* would see to it that no one forced the girl to suffer the same ugly fate she had endured at Simon's hands.

Her color high, her back rigid, she marched toward the blue saloon. Righteous determination carried her into the room. Spying Edward lounging in sartorial elegance against the marble fireplace mantel in a plum-colored coat of superfine and buff breeches, she plunged into battle.

Boldly she said, "Strange, I distinctly remember telling Emerson that persons with a certain lack of morals were not allowed entrance to my house. What are you doing here? And how did you manage to force your way past my butler?"

Edward sent her a look of pure dislike. "That is a rather nasty tongue you have, my dear. Someday someone is likely to clip it for you. I only pray I live to see the day."

"Well, it will not be you, will it? You only prey on the weak and defenseless," she said sweetly.

Edward's face mottled with rage, and he actually took a threatening step toward her, when he was brought to a standstill by the other occupant of the room. Rising to her feet from the sofa where she had been sitting, the woman said calmly, "My lord Scoville, do not, I pray you, allow this poor, misguided creature to deter you from the reason we are here."

Meeting Sophy's unfriendly gaze, she said coolly, "I am Agnes Weatherby. I understand that my niece is here. I wish to have her brought to me immediately." In a scolding tone, she added, "You have interfered in matters that are no concern of yours, and it is only because of my kind heart that I have not laid charges against you for kidnapping. If you prove obstructive, you may be assured that I certainly will see a magistrate immediately. Now where is my niece?"

Agnes Weatherby was a handsome woman. And hard, Sophy thought grimly, as she stared at the chiseled features before her. She had the same color of eyes as her niece, but while Anne's eyes were warm and gentle, Agnes's resembled nothing so much as stones. She looked to be a well-cared for thirtyish. Her dark hair gleamed with health and vitality, and the figure beneath the striped gown was lush and full, but there was no sign about her of concern for her niece's well-being.

Sophy was not certain how to approach Agnes Weatherby. The law was on Agnes's side, and, from the set expression on her face, it was apparent that appealing to her better nature would not suffice. But did she understand the true situation? Perhaps Agnes was not as bad as Anne had indicated. There was, Sophy reminded herself hopefully, every possibility that Edward had poured out only his part of the story, greatly embellished to cast him in the best light possible.

"Did my uncle tell you what happened last night?" Sophy asked.

"Indeed he did! I cannot imagine what you thought

you were about barging in on a private moment between an affianced couple."

"Affianced? Is that what he told you? Well, let me tell you what really transpired," Sophy began sharply. "When I found them—after your niece had screamed for help—there was no sign of an engaged couple about them. Anne's gown was torn from her shoulder. She was sobbing and obviously terrified. My uncle, it pains me to admit, was drunk and forcing his attentions on her in a most vulgar and brutal way. I shudder to think what he would have done to her if I had not happened along when I did. There is no other way to put it. He was in the midst of attempting to rape a mere child. A child, I might add, almost young enough to have been his granddaughter. It was a disgusting scene, and I did what any responsible person would have done—rescued her from a dangerous and unpleasant situation."

"I think you misread what you saw, Lady Marlowe," said Miss Weatherby stiffly. "Lord Scoville may have been a trifle, er, blunt in his attentions, but he is, after all, a mature man deeply in love with my niece."

"With her money," Sophy snapped.

"It does not matter," Miss Weatherby replied tightly, "whether it is her fortune or her face which inflames him. The point is, she is my niece. I am her guardian. And if I give him leave to address her, it is none of your business. Now send for Anne immediately!"

"No," Sophy said baldly, hanging on to her temper by a thread. "I will not. Anne will stay here with me until I am convinced that you will not force her into an abominable alliance with a dissipated old roué like my uncle."

Edward let loose with a string of oaths that would have made a pirate blush, but neither Sophy nor Miss

Weatherby turned a hair. Nor did any of them notice the door and the soft-footed entrance of a fourth person. A fourth person who, after closing the door, stood there observing the scene.

"I told you," Lord Scoville said furiously, having vented the worst of his spleen, "that she is a stubborn, spiteful, wicked, interfering bitch! Did I not? Didn't I tell you she would do anything to thwart me?"

"Yes, you did warn me, my dear Lord Scoville, but I did not believe you." Miss Weatherby fairly purred, looking warmly in his direction. "I see now that you spoke only the truth." She sent Sophy an icy look. "Since you are proving yourself to be so spiteful and utterly unreasonable, you leave me no choice but to apply to the law. You may expect a visit from the authorities within the hour. Make certain that Anne is ready to accompany them."

"I would think twice about what you mean to do, madam," Ives said coolly, making his presence known. "The law might also find itself interested in *your* behavior and *your* motives for entrusting the care of a delicate child like Anne to a less than sterling character like Baron Scoville." He smiled, not nicely. "Have you considered that it might be you appearing before the court to defend your actions?"

Chapter Five

⁓

Sophy gasped and spun round to stare in Ives's direction. She was so delighted, so relieved to have an ally, that any resentment of his high-handed actions during the previous evening were forgotten. Even his brash intrusion into what was an extremely private matter was forgiven. He looked, she thought happily, very menacing and implacable as he stood there by the door. Just exactly the sort of ally she needed at the moment.

Her features alight with pleasure, she said, just as if he had not barged into the midst of an ugly scene, "Lord Harrington, how kind of you to call. We were just discussing Anne's stay with me. Miss Weatherby is Anne's aunt."

His green eyes twinkling, Ives approached her and bowed low over her outstretched hand. "After our adventures last night, it seemed appropriate that I call upon you this morning." Casually tucking her hand under his arm, he turned to face the others.

"I am Viscount Harrington," he announced with deliberate hauteur.

"I do not care who the bloody hell you are," growled Edward. "You are interfering in a personal matter that is of no interest to you."

"Hmm, I had hoped," murmured Ives, "that after a night's sleep your nasty temperament would have improved, but I see that I am doomed to disappointment." He glanced down at Sophy, who was trying discreetly to free her hand. "I know that you have told me that this dundering rake is your uncle, but surely there is some mistake?"

The words were said with such innocent bewilderment, that Sophy nearly choked on the amusement bubbling up within her. The encouraging gleam in Ives's green eyes was her undoing, and, unable to help herself, she burst out laughing.

"There is no mistake. And you, my lord, are incorrigible!"

Ives smiled lazily at her. "And you should laugh more."

Looking across at Lord Scoville and Miss Weatherby, he said, "I think that it is time that you were leaving, don't you? Let me assure you that your niece will be safe enough with Lady Marlowe. In fact, I venture to say that she will be safer here than she ever was in your hands. And as for you"—he glanced at Edward—"I would suggest that you give up your pursuit of ladies of such a tender age. The next time I find you abusing an innocent, I will do more than knock you down."

"It was you!" Edward howled, just now realizing precisely who the big man at Sophy's side was. "You hit me! Refused my challenge."

"Yes, I believe that I had that honor," Ives drawled, "and I suggest that unless you really want to find out just how good I am on the dueling field that you take yourself off. And Miss Weatherby with you. You have inflicted your company on Lady Marlowe long enough."

"Well!" huffed Miss Weatherby. "I am shocked! Yes, shocked by such rude, overbearing manners."

It was clear that she did not quite know what to make of Lord Harrington's entry into the battle. His confident manner had aroused the uneasy suspicion within her that it might be prudent to withdraw from the lists for the time being. Further argument today could only prove to be unproductive, and there was every possibility that Anne's stay with Lady Marlowe might turn out to be a very good thing.

After all, Lady Marlowe was the daughter of an earl, the niece of a baron and the widow of a marquess. To think that her niece was hobnobbing with such blue blood was a very heady thing for Miss Weatherby. There was also, Miss Weatherby admitted, the unfortunate fact that Lady Marlowe, ably abetted by Lord Harrington, was not going to release Anne without a fight. This could lead to embarrassing questions about her guardianship of the Richmond heiress, something Miss Weatherby wished to avoid at all costs.

While Edward continued to bluster, Miss Weatherby put as good a face on it as she could, and said, "I see that you will not be swayed, and since you seem to have only Anne's good wishes at heart, I will agree to let Anne stay with you . . . for the time being." She bent a stern look upon Sophy. "I shall hold you accountable, Lady Marlowe, for any harm that might come to my dear, *dear* niece while she is under your roof."

Sophy bowed as haughtily as a queen. "Let me assure

you that Anne will certainly not be subjected to the type of treatment she has suffered at *your* hands!"

Miss Weatherby stiffened, her eyes narrowing. Clearly half tempted to wade in and continue the fight, she glared at Sophy.

It was Ives who broke the deadlock, saying calmly, "I am sure that your niece will be well taken care of. Lady Marlowe has already shown herself extremely expert in that area. She has had the sole care of her younger brother and sister for a few years now."

When Edward started to object, Ives bent a deceptively bland eye upon him. "The *sole* care," Ives repeated softly. The expression deep in those devil green eyes gave Edward pause and his grumblings prudently subsided.

"Very well, then," Miss Weatherby said. "There is nothing further for us to discuss today."

"Oh, there is one other thing," Sophy contradicted smoothly. "There is the matter of Miss Richmond's clothing and personal effects. I would suggest that you have them brought here as soon as possible." She smiled at Miss Weatherby. "The poor child has only the gown she was wearing last night, and that is badly torn. I am sure that you would not want it gossiped about the ton that you sent her to visit me with hardly a stitch of her own clothing, now would you?"

Miss Weatherby's bosom swelled. But with a curt nod, she bid them good day and—with Edward trailing angrily behind her—swept from the room.

Sophy looked admiringly at Ives. "I must say that was well done of you, my lord! For once, you have my sincere thanks for your timely intervention."

Ives lifted her hand to his lips. "Ah, but I have no

doubt you would have vanquished them all on your own, my dear Lady Marlowe."

Oddly breathless at the touch of his lips on her skin, Sophy jerked her hand from his and moved quickly to put several feet between them.

"What brought you here at so opportune a moment this morning?" she asked bluntly when she felt she was in command of herself.

"A polite call?" he offered, his eyes gleaming.

Her gaze flew to his. "Is that all it was? Just a polite call?"

"What do you want it to be, sweetheart?" Ives inquired with a smile that turned her bones to honey.

With an effort, she kept herself from smiling back at him. Flashing him a dark look, she said, "You are too forward, my lord. I am *not* your sweetheart!"

"Well, not yet, anyway," Ives returned imperturbably.

Sophy took in an outraged breath, and her lovely eyes filled with gold fire. "Not only are you far too forward, my lord, but you are arrogant as well."

Ives tried to look chastened. "You are no doubt correct, my lady. I pray you forgive me and put it down to my having been a mere soldier until a short time ago. Having lived rough for a number of years, I confess that the fine manners of the aristocracy are a great puzzle to me."

"You are also," Sophy retorted, trying very hard not to smile at his feigned wretchedness, "a great fraud!"

Ives sighed heavily. " 'Tis all too true, I fear." He shot her a hopeful look. "Mayhap you would take me under your wing and teach me how to go on?"

"Perhaps you could stop trying to bamboozle me and tell me why you came to call this morning?"

"*Bamboozle!* As if I would do such a thing! Nay, nay, sweetheart, you have me all wrong!"

"I am *not* your sweetheart!"

His eyes crinkled attractively at the corners and even before he opened his mouth, she knew what he was going to say. Her own eyes glinting, she warned, "And don't you dare say 'not yet!' "

He laughed and, closing the distance between them, took her hand in his once more and murmured, "Sweetheart, you wouldn't have me tell you an untruth, now would you?"

Sophy muttered something rude under her breath and, after futilely struggling to free her hand from his, glared up at him.

"My lord, I do not know what maggot has gotten into your brain, but I assure you that I am not some easy light-skirt you can overawe with your charm. I will speak frankly to you: I am not casting about for either a husband or a lover. If you think to pursue such a relationship with me, I will tell you to your face that you are wasting your time. Now, dash it, let go of my hand before I box your ears!"

"Such talk and from a lady of your breeding!" he gasped, his green eyes mocking her. "I vow I am shocked."

Since he looked anything but shocked, Sophy snorted and demanded, "My hand, my lord?"

"Ah, such a pretty hand it is, too. Do you really object to my holding it?" He brushed a kiss across the back of it.

Managing to jerk it free from his grasp once more and ignoring the tingle that raced up her arm, she said sternly,

"My lord, I must ask you to leave if you are not going to behave in a proper manner."

Edging toward the door, she added, "I do appreciate your help, not only last night, but this morning also." She glanced back at him. "But while your intervention was appreciated, it was unneeded and does not give you the right to take liberties with me or to force yourself upon me. If you wish to keep in my good graces, I suggest that you leave . . . *now*."

"That is certainly telling me, isn't it? Is that how you have kept the gentlemen at bay all these years since your husband's death?" he asked interestedly, not moving an inch.

Sophy gritted her teeth. The dolt was impossible! "Since they *were* gentlemen, I did not have to speak so plainly," she replied sweetly.

Ives threw back his head and laughed. "Ah, sweetheart, *that* is certainly telling me."

"By the Devil's bones!" Sophy swore, forgetting herself by using one of Simon's favorite oaths. "Will you leave, my lord, or must I have my butler throw you from the house?"

Chuckling to himself, Ives walked toward her. "Now don't get yourself all twitterpated, my lady. If you really want me to leave, I shall." Ives smiled down at her, then dropped a kiss on the tip of her nose. "Whatever pleases you, sweetheart."

Leaving her staring after him, Ives strolled out of the room. It was several seconds before Sophy's heart resumed its normal pace and her chaotic thoughts untangled themselves.

She told herself it was anger that prompted the rapid heartbeat; but the odd thing was, she didn't feel angry at all. In fact, a bubble of laughter threatened to escape from her. The man, she thought helplessly, was impossible! And arrogant! And, she admitted uneasily, there was the possibility that he was very, very dangerous to females with susceptible hearts. . . . Which of course, she did not possess!

During the following days, Sophy's opinion of Lord Harrington did not change. Torn between vexation and amusement, she grew to expect him to appear magically at her side at whatever function she happened to be attending. In fact, she began to realize that she was growing rather used to having the rather large and alarming Lord Harrington hovering at her side whenever she appeared in public.

Worse, he had craftily insinuated himself into her household, coming to call frequently and outrageously wooing Phoebe, Anne, and Marcus to his side. *They,* she thought darkly, thought him a great gun. As well they should, since he always seemed to be arranging outings for their amusement.

In the days since Lord Harrington had foisted himself on her, he had arranged to take everyone to Astley's Royal Amphitheatre one evening and had thrilled Anne and Phoebe by giving them a ride through Hyde Park in his dashing high-perch phaeton.

Not content with enslaving Anne and Phoebe, he had introduced Marcus to Gentleman Jackson himself at the former boxer's boxing saloon on Bond Street, much to Marcus's gratification. He had even hosted a meal at Offley's for Marcus and his two boon companions, feasting on the hotel's excellent beefsteak and enjoying themselves hugely.

Why, only yesterday, Sophy remembered almost indignantly, he had swept aside her objections, something he did with infuriating regularity, and cheerfully escorted the three ladies to a tour of Madame Tussaud's Wax Museum and afterward, to a scrumptious tea at Grillon's Hotel. The younger ladies were clearly enamored of him and his easy, teasing manner kept them both giggling. He had become an integral part of Sophy's life and to her great dismay she was growing to like it.

But Lord Harrington seemed to be her only concern these days. She and her siblings were happily partaking of the pleasures London had to offer. Anne Richmond had settled into life at the Grayson town house as if she had been born to it, and Lord Scoville had not intruded further into their affairs. Anne and Phoebe were fast friends, and Anne clearly looked upon Sophy as her savior. There was nothing, she swore passionately to Phoebe, that she would not do for dearest Lady Marlowe. Nothing.

Anne's relationship with Marcus, however, could only be termed tepid. He politely tolerated her, and she viewed him with a wary forbearance.

While things were going rather well at the moment, Sophy was vaguely aware that something of a more permanent arrangement would have to be made for Anne. As requested, Miss Weatherby had promptly sent over Anne's effects and made no push to change the situation.

Anne's drain upon Sophy's purse, at present, was slight, and Sophy begrudged her not a penny, but she could see that there were going to be problems down the road. What would happen when the Season ended and the Grayson family returned to Cornwall? Of course, they would take Anne with them, but what sort of a dustup would ensue with Miss Weatherby? Sophy would not even let herself think of what might happen in a few years if the situation remained unresolved and it was time for Anne to make her London debut and young men were to come courting, as was certain to happen given Anne's beauty and great fortune.

The state of Anne's affairs worried Sophy and one afternoon about ten days after the interview with Miss Weatherby and Edward, Sophy asked her explicitly about it.

The three ladies were sitting in the small conservatory at the rear of the house, enjoying the spring sunshine as it beamed through the many windows. Phoebe and Anne had been halfheartedly plying their needles on some edifying samplers, and Sophy had been idly leafing through a pattern book sent to her by her favorite modiste.

Sophy had not really been paying attention to the book in front of her. Her mind had been on Anne's situation. Looking across at Anne's industriously bent head, she asked abruptly, "Why is your aunt so set on your marriage to my uncle? What does she gain by it?"

Anne was startled by the question, and for a moment her pansy brown eyes were blank. As comprehension set in, she put aside her sampler, and answered simply, "As I told you that first night, she wants me aligned with the aristocracy and your uncle was going to settle a substantial sum of money on her after we married. She doesn't have any money of her own. My grandfather disinherited her."

"I know all that, but doesn't she have the ability to draw on your fortune?" Sophy asked, thinking of the way her uncle was raiding her siblings' fortune.

"Only for my upkeep and for that she has to apply to

the trustees of my father's and grandfather's estates. Any sums for my care are generally disbursed directly to the creditors themselves, once the trustees determine they are legitimate. Aunt Agnes is given a household allowance for the day-to-day running of my establishment, and I understand that they pay her a sum of her own because she is taking care of me. Since she lives wherever I do, she has no actual living expenses. But the trustees are very strict. She is always complaining that they go over the household accounts rigorously, questioning all her expenditures. They are not stingy. They simply make certain that the money is spent on *me* or for my welfare."

A frown furrowed Sophy's forehead. "Isn't she your legal guardian? Or are the trustees?"

"She is. The trustees watch over my fortune, but Aunt Agnes supposedly watches over me. My father named her my guardian after Grandfather died. She was my only living relative and he thought, if something were to happen to him, it would be better for me to be in the care of a relative than an utter stranger. He was aware of the safeguards my Grandfather had put in place to protect his estate from her grasp, and he took similar precautions."

"And when you marry?"

"When I marry I suppose that my fortune will naturally be in the hands of my husband. The trusteeship would be ended." Anne looked very adult as she said thoughtfully, "I believe what Aunt Agnes and your uncle planned is that once he and I were married, and he came into control of my fortune, he would settle a large portion of my money on her for having helped him marry me."

"Why, that is utterly Gothic!" exclaimed Phoebe, who had been listening avidly. "It is a good thing that Sophy came along when she did! And I think that my uncle must be a dashed loose screw!"

"Phoebe!" Sophy scolded, choking back a laugh. "You must not talk that way. It is most unbecoming."

"Marcus says it all the time," Phoebe countered stubbornly. "And you do, too, so why can't I?"

"Because you are being raised a lady. I am beyond redemption, and your brother is a gentleman—they do as they please."

"But you are a lady," ventured Anne, "and you say whatever you want."

"You forget," Sophy answered with a dancing smile, "I may be a lady, but I am also a widow, and widows have far more freedom than mere ladies!"

"I wish I were a widow," sighed Anne, and both Phoebe and Sophy burst out laughing.

"For shame," Sophy said teasingly. "Not even a bride yet, and you are already wishing your poor husband in his grave."

Having heard Sophy's history from Phoebe, Anne glanced at her through her lashes. "And did you never wish your husband dead?"

The laughter left Sophy's face, and in a hard little voice she admitted, "My husband's death was something I devotedly prayed for nearly every waking moment of my marriage. When he died I felt that my prayers had been answered."

About to enter the conservatory to which he had been directed by Emerson, Ives paused in the doorway. For a gentleman contemplating a closer, more intimate relationship with the lady, hearing those sentiments fall from her lips was not precisely encouraging.

A little frown appeared between his eyes. He knew all

about the death of Lady Marlowe's husband and the speculation that she might have murdered him, but he had
dismissed it. Sophy's words, however, gave him pause.
He'd not heard that note in her voice before, and, for the
first time, he wondered about the circumstances surrounding her husband's death.

Sophy spied him just then, and cried, "Lord Harrington! Whatever is Emerson thinking of, to set you loose in
the house unescorted."

Ives grinned at her and stepped into the room, bowing
to the three women. Looking at Sophy, he murmured,
"You must not blame your butler. He attempted most
earnestly to do his duties, but I convinced him that you
would not take it amiss if I showed myself in."

Sophy's eyes kindled at this further example of his
high-handed ways.

"But what if I *do* take it amiss?"

"Ah, sweetheart, you would not punish the man for
something not his own fault, would you?"

Having been on the losing end of several tussles lately
once Lord Harrington had determined upon a course,
Sophy gave Emerson her complete sympathy.

Warily eyeing her guest, she muttered, "Not only are
you rude and overbearing, but I see that you have now
added intimidation to your many crimes."

Ives looked injured. "Nay, nay, sweetheart, you are all
wrong. I did not intimidate him. I convinced him it was
wisest to let me have my way."

Well used to Lord Harrington's bantering ways, the
two younger ladies giggled, and he grinned at them and
winked.

Accepting the inevitable, Sophy asked, "Was there a
reason for your call? Or have you just come to vex me?"

"Vex you, sweetheart? How can you speak so cruelly to me when you know that your slightest whim is my command?"

His dancing eyes invited her to enjoy the jest, and she gave a reluctant laugh. "I wish that I may live to see the day that you pay attention to any whims of mine!" she retorted tartly. "Now was there a particular reason for your call?"

"Actually there was. I was going to ask you if I might escort you to dinner with your friends, the Offingtons, on Thursday evening at Stephens's."

Sophy snorted. "I suppose it would do me little good to refuse?"

He smiled. "It would seem a bit silly for you to do so, wouldn't it?"

"Are you ever at a loss?" Sophy asked regretfully, tamping down a strong desire to meet his smile. "Does nothing deter you?"

Oblivious to the wide-eyed stares of Phoebe and Anne, he took Sophy's hand in his and brushed a kiss across the back of it. "Not from something that I want."

The laughter had faded from his face, and the searching look he gave her made her mouth grow dry, but before she could recover her wits, he took his leave.

He had hardly disappeared from view, before Anne sighed. "Oh, Lady Marlowe, how can you resist him? He is so handsome and so amusing. It is obvious that he finds himself vastly attracted to you. Why do you repulse his advances? I know *I* would not!"

Absently rubbing her hand where his lips had lingered Sophy muttered, "At your age, I doubt that you are an infallible judge of character. Do not be fooled by him. I learned at my own cost that gentlemen are always at their most charming when they are hunting."

The conversation was dropped, but her own words would not leave Sophy's mind. Hunted was precisely how she felt. Ives Harrington was very definitely, despite her warning to the contrary, pursuing her. And none of her rebuffs, not scathing replies or cool glances, put him off his stride. He appeared to be unstoppable. And the question facing her was, did she truly want to stop him?

Sitting alone in her bedroom that evening after dinner, Sophy stared sightlessly into space, considering the problem. Her decision never to marry again had not changed, and to be honest, she was not certain it was her hand that Ives was seeking. Her eyes narrowed. Knowing the gentleman, a mistress was more than likely his goal.

That aside, however, she could not deny that she found Viscount Harrington too attractive by half. More attractive than any man she had ever met, even Simon, before he had shattered her illusions. In her idle moments she had considered what it would be like to have an affair with Ives. A very, very discreet affair, of course. The fact that she was even considering such an idea stunned her and made her decidedly uneasy.

But the idea did have merit. Once she had allowed him the intimacies that Simon had taken, she would be able to view Ives with disinterest, even revulsion, as she had her husband. More importantly, it was likely that she would no longer be plagued by indecent dreams of Ives kissing her, touching her . . .

A tap on the door distracted her unsettled thoughts and, at her command, Phoebe and Anne came into the room. They were both dressed for bed and, following their rou-

tine on the evenings Sophy was at home, they had come
to spend some time with her before retiring.

Conversation was light and desultory, the girls teasing
her a little more about Ives and discussing plans for the
following week. Phoebe was sitting at Sophy's dressing
table, idly fiddling with the various brushes and combs
and bottles of scent scattered across the top of it. Anne
was curled up at Sophy's feet, her head resting on
Sophy's knee as they talked.

The small, ornate jewelry box that always remained on
Sophy's dressing table eventually caught Phoebe's attention, and, glancing across at her sister, she asked, "Is that
the jewelry box that Mother gave you?"

Sophy nodded, a sad little smile on her face. "Indeed it
is. You may look at it, if you like."

Reverently, Phoebe picked it up and promptly dropped
it, spilling a sparkling array of bracelets, rings, and pins
across the floor.

"Oh! I am sorry, Sophy. It just slipped from my hand."

"Do not worry," Sophy replied as she and Anne began
to help Phoebe retrieve the scattered trinkets. "There is
nothing of any great value in it, anyway."

In a few moments all had been set to rights and Phoebe
was about to put the box back in its place when Anne exclaimed, "Oh, wait, I see something shining under that
chair."

Crossing the room, she bent down and retrieved the
object. Holding it up to the light, she gasped. "Never tell
me that this is paste, Lady Marlowe! It is the most gor-
geous ruby I have ever seen in my life. Surely it is real."

Sophy's face drained of all color as she stared at the
glittering ruby cravat pin in Anne's hand. All the ugly
memories of the night Simon died rushed back: the fight

with Simon, the flashes of lightning, the booming thunder and the half-seen—half-imagined—figure of a man pressed against the wall near the head of the stairs. Reliving the terrifying moments of seeing Simon's body lying so still on the floor below her, she was not aware of the passing seconds or the look on her face.

"Sophy!" cried Phoebe, alarmed. "Are you all right?"

Sophy gave herself a shake and managed a weak smile. "Sorry. I do not know what came over me. And to answer Anne's question, I have no idea whether the stone is real or paste. I found it at Marlowe House. I'd forgotten that I even had it."

"Forgotten!" exclaimed Phoebe. "How could you forget about it?"

Sophy shrugged. "It was right after Simon died, and I was very busy. I simply thrust it into the jewelry box and never gave it another thought. It must have slipped beneath the other jewelry, and since I seldom wear anything from this box, I never noticed it."

"You found it?" asked Anne. "If it is not real, it is a very good paste. I would have thought the owner would miss it and ask after it. Did no one ever inquire about it?"

"No," said Sophy slowly, realizing disturbingly that Anne was correct. She took the ruby pin from Anne's hand and examined it closely. Holding it up to the crystal chandelier overhead, it flashed and sparkled with a deep bloodred glow. Surely paste would not be so vivid? And if it was real, why had no one ever mentioned that it had gone missing?

Long after the girls had departed for bed, Sophy sat staring at the ruby pin. Tomorrow she would take it to her jeweler and have him examine it. Perhaps then, at least, one question about the ruby would be answered.

*   *   *

Not certain why, she told no one of her decision, and early the next morning she left the house and directed her coachman to take her to the fashionable jeweler she used on Ludgate Hill. He confirmed her suspicions that the stone was real. The entire pin was unique and very, very costly. Easily worth a small fortune, he informed her. Thanking him, she hurriedly left the shop.

Reaching her rooms, she again took the cravat pin from her reticule. No one would simply overlook or forget about a jewel like this. Unless there was some reason. But what reason? Sophy asked herself in puzzlement. If it had been simply lost, what could be simpler than asking if it had been found? Unless, she thought with a chill, there was something about its loss that someone did not want revealed?

She swallowed. Did the location in which it had been found have anything to do with why no one had come seeking it? Again she remembered the illusion of the shadowy figure and the ruby gleaming like a drop of blood at the top of the staircase—the staircase at the base of which her husband lay dead. She swallowed again, telling herself she was being silly and imaginative. There was probably a perfectly logical reason why no one had asked after it, she told herself stoutly.

A thought occurred to her. Perhaps someone *had* asked after it, but the inquiry never reached her. Edward had overseen the departure of Simon's guests during that terrible time. Had one of them asked after the pin and her notably unreliable uncle merely forgotten to mention it to her?

She took a deep breath. She would ask Edward.

Chapter Six

❧

*A*rranging an interview with Edward had not been easy, but on Thursday afternoon, at Sophy's request, he came to call. She was alone in the room when Edward arrived, and she had given Emerson instructions to show him immediately into the green saloon on the first floor.

She had seen to it that the girls were gone to Hookham's Lending Library and that Marcus was out with his friends for the afternoon. For reasons she could not explain, she did not want anyone else to know about her interview with Edward. Which was, she knew, perfectly ridiculous.

Edward was nattily dressed in a formfitting coat of blue superfine and pale yellow breeches. The brilliant gloss of his Hessians was a tribute to his valet, and his linen was dazzling white. Bowing over Sophy's hand, he said, "I am glad to see that you have come to your senses, my gel. Miss Richmond's affairs are none of your business, and you were fair and far off poking your nose where it wasn't wanted."

"I did not ask you here to discuss Miss Richmond. And

I would remind you, you may have not wanted me to interfere, but *she* did!"

Edward flashed her a dark look. "Think you have the
upper hand, hey? Puffed up with yourself, ain't you? Well
let me tell you something, if you and that feisty young
cub of a brother of yours don't start treating me more respectfully, you'll find out swift enough who is really
driving this rig!"

Sophy frowned. "What do you mean?"

Edward smiled nastily. "I mean that if I decided to
make a push to have the care of Phoebe, there would be
nothing either you or Marcus could do about it! I am her
guardian, and it is only through my generous nature that
I have allowed you a free hand. I can take her to live with
me whenever I want!"

At Sophy's stunned look, he crowed, "Thought you
had me at a standstill, didn't you? Well, think again! I'll
make certain you never see Phoebe again until she is married off to the man of my choosing. How do you like
that?"

"You would not dare!" Sophy spat, her golden eyes
fierce. "Make no mistake, I will never allow you the care
of Phoebe's person. You will *not* do to her what you did
to me. I will not allow it. *I will kill you first.*"

The unmistakable fury in Sophy's face caused Edward
to step backward. "Now, now, it don't have to come to
that," he protested. "I have no intention of poking my
nose where it ain't wanted if you do the same."

Controlling herself with an effort, Sophy asked tightly,
"Precisely why do you want to marry Miss Richmond so
badly? Doesn't raiding Marcus and Phoebe's fortune provide enough for you?"

"A man has to look ahead," Edward returned easily,

not the least discomfited by Sophy's attitude. "In less than two years, Marcus will be twenty-one, and my trusteeship will end. I will have to turn everything over to him, even Phoebe's care and fortune. Leaves me in a devil of a fix. Been thinking about it a lot." He smiled charmingly at Sophy. "Thing is, without their fortune I won't have a feather to fly with. Thought I ought to start looking about for a way to recoup my losses. Gambling ain't the answer, too risky, but marriage to an heiress! That would fix me up right and tight. Been hanging out for a rich wife these past several months, but most of 'em got a pack of starchy relatives to watch out for fortune hunters like m'self. I wouldn't even get a nod, much less an opportunity to pay court. Couldn't believe my luck when I discovered that Agnes had the care of the Richmond heiress."

"And exactly how did that come about?" Sophy asked, her disgust obvious.

Edward had the grace to look embarrassed. "Er. Miss Weatherby ain't precisely up to snuff, if you know what I mean. We were rather, uh, good friends, and she mentioned her niece to me."

Sophy gasped with outrage. "Miss Weatherby is your *mistress*?"

"Was!" exclaimed Edward feebly, seeing that he had put his foot into it. "I may be a blackguard of the worst kind," he admitted, "but even *I* wouldn't keep my wife's aunt as my lightskirt. Very bad ton!"

His shameless candor left Sophy speechless. He saw absolutely nothing wrong with his actions. He even, if the expression on his face was anything to go by, thought she would applaud his plans for ensuring his financial stability.

When Sophy remained silent, Edward took it as an encouraging sign. "Now you see why it is important for you to send Anne back to her aunt. Be to your benefit, too," he added shrewdly.

Sophy arched a brow.

"Stands to reason," he said, "if I have the Richmond fortune at my fingertips, I won't need to dip into Marcus and Phoebe's funds."

Shaking her head, Sophy said, "You are too despicable for words! I do not know what you planned to accomplish by coming here, but let me assure you that I have no intention of changing my mind about Anne's stay with me."

"If that don't beat all!" he exclaimed. "You were the one who requested I come to call. Thought it all a hum, but then I decided, my niece and all, so I came. If you didn't want to see me, why the devil did you invite me here in the first place?"

Reminded of her reasons for this interview, Sophy started. Taking a deep breath, she said slowly, "I have a question to ask you. Do you remember the night Simon died?"

"Do I remember? Good gad, how could I forget? Man was a good friend of mine."

"You took care of everything, seeing to the departure of his friends and whatnot. Did anyone mention to you that they had lost something?"

Edward frowned. "Lost something? What?"

"A cravat pin."

Obviously puzzled by her question after so many years, Edward shook his head. "Not that I recall."

Bringing forth the pin from the drawer of a small satinwood table, she showed it to him.

"I found this at the top of the staircase on the night Simon died. Do you recognize it?"

His eyes narrowed as he stared at the pin, and an odd expression crossed his face, part astonishment and something else Sophy could not name—craftiness, perhaps?

"No, I can't say that I do recognize it," he said finally. "But let me look at it more closely."

Taking the pin from her, he examined it carefully, and though his face revealed nothing, Sophy was positive he recognized the pin. Looking over at her, he commented, "Found it the night Simon died, hey? At the top of the staircase where he fell?"

Sophy nodded, but after a moment or two, he returned it to her and shrugged. "Pretty piece of work. Can't see why you had me come here on such a sleeveless errand. Wasted my time. Busy man."

Sophy's lip curled. "Indeed you are, frittering away money that is not yours."

"Nasty tongue you have, gel. Always thought so. Too bad Simon didn't teach you better," Edward said, his golden eyes, so like hers, bright with dislike.

Sophy made no reply. Edward sketched her a scant bow and stalked from the room.

For several minutes, Sophy stared speculatively at the ruby pin she still held in the palm of her hand. Her uncle had recognized it, she was positive. But he had denied it. Why?

She left the green saloon and thoughtfully made her way upstairs to her bedroom, putting away the pin in her jewelry box. Her uncle really was despicable, she observed, not for the first time. He honestly thought that she would approve of his plans for Anne. And he blatantly

admitted that without the fortune her father had so un-
wisely placed in his hands he would be all to pieces.

His threat concerning Phoebe disturbed her the most. It
was something she could never allow to happen, and she
hoped that he had merely been blustering in his usual
manner. But just the fact that he had even mentioned it
worried her immensely.

Marcus was understandably furious when Sophy told
him about Edward's threat. His young face taut, he
swore, "By Jove! Just let him try to take Phoebe from us!
Just let him try. I will run him through before I will let
him lay one hand on her."

Sophy gradually calmed him, convincing him all that
was needed for the present was a vigilant eye.

With Phoebe it was a trifle more delicate. Sophy did
not want to terrify the child, and so she merely warned
her never to go anywhere with her uncle, no matter what
the circumstances.

"As if I would!" Phoebe returned heatedly. Her gaze
sharpened. "Why are you warning me against him now?
What has he done?"

Sophy shook her head. "He has done nothing, my pet.
I just do not know what sort of maggot he may get in his
brain. I am only taking precautions."

"Is it because of me?" asked Anne, her brown eyes
huge in her little face.

The two girls were sprawled across Phoebe's bed,
where they had been scanning some of the books they
had just brought home from the library. Seeing the anxiety in Anne's face, Sophy smiled at her and gently patted
her cheek.

"This has nothing to do with you. Our uncle has always been a disagreeable beast, and I only wanted to remind Phoebe always to be on her guard around him."

The girls seemed to take her words at face value, and, feeling that she had done all she could for the moment, Sophy returned to her own rooms, where she began to prepare for dinner that evening with the Offingtons and Viscount Harrington.

After the interview with Edward, Sophy was not in any mood to join friends for what would undoubtedly be, under normal circumstances, a most convivial evening. If it were not such a small party and her absence would not be greatly missed, she would have come up with an excuse to remain home. But it would have been the height of rudeness to abandon the Offingtons, and even the vexing Lord Harrington, at the last minute if there was no pressing need for it.

By the time Lord Harrington came to escort her to Stephens's Hotel on Bond Street that evening, Sophy's mood had improved somewhat. Pushing her troubling thoughts aside, she went down the stairs to greet Lord Harrington. To her annoyance, just the mere sight of him, standing so tall and handsome in the grand foyer, unfairly caused a wave of breathlessness to sweep over her. Damn him, too!

Bending gallantly over her hand, Ives murmured, "May I say that you are enchanting this evening, my lady?"

"I doubt that anyone could stop you from saying or doing precisely what you please, my lord. Certainly to date I have seen no one do so," she returned tartly, allowing him to drape a cream-colored Spanish cloak over her elegant gown of apricot shot silk.

"You wrong me, my lady. Why, only the slightest hint

from your sweet self would make me instantly change my ways."

Unable to resist the twinkle in his eyes, Sophy laughed. Satisfied with her reaction, Ives escorted her out of the house and into his carriage.

Sophy was startled to find that the Offingtons were not already in the coach waiting for them, and she cast an inquiring eye toward her escort.

As the horses leaped into action and the carriage rolled smoothly down the street, Ives said, "The Offingtons will be a trifle tardy joining us at Stephens's. It seems they were delayed returning home from a tour of the royal menagerie this afternoon by an accident between the driver of their coach and that of some cow-handed young blood trying to drive to an inch. I received a note from Offington just as I was leaving stating that they would join us within the hour."

Seated beside her, Ives grinned down at her in the dim light of the carriage. "I am afraid that you shall have to endure my undiluted company until they arrive."

"You could have let me know of the delay," Sophy said coolly, not certain she was comfortable with the change in plans.

Ives took one of her hands and lifted it to his lips. "I could have," he murmured, "but then I would have been denied your very charming company."

She shot him a look. "Perhaps I would have preferred it that way. Did you think of that, my lord?"

"The thought did cross my mind," he confessed brazenly, keeping a firm hold on the hand she was trying discreetly to free from his grasp, "but upon reflection, I decided that perhaps it was a good thing." He smiled angelically. "It provides us with an opportunity to get to know each other better, does it not?"

"Perhaps," Sophy said bluntly, "I do not want to know you better."

"Sweetheart! How can you say such a thing? After all that we have shared together."

Giving up the fight for her hand, she glared at him. "Do you know," she said finally, "that I would very much like to box your ears?"

"And I," he said softly, as he pulled her into his arms, "would very much like to kiss you. Shall we agree upon a trade? You may box my ears, if I may find out if your lips are as sweet as I believe they are."

Sophy froze, her heart banging against her ribs. One part of her was amused by his audacity and curious about his kiss. Another part was vaguely frightened, as the memory of Simon's cruel consummation of their marriage in a vehicle much like this one drifted painfully through her mind.

The two men were nothing alike, she told herself worriedly. And she was no terrified virgin. Ives Harrington was *not* her husband—he had no power over her. Surely he would not attempt to force himself upon her. Wordlessly she stared up at Ives's dark, rough-hewn features, fright and indecision on her face.

"What is it?" he asked quietly. The expression on her face and the stiffness of her body warned him that something other than feminine reluctance was at work here.

When Sophy did not answer him, he murmured, "You have no need to be frightened of me, sweetheart. I want very much to kiss you, Sophy, but only if you allow it."

Sophy took a shaken breath, his words allaying her fears somewhat. Instinctively she knew that he was no brute like her husband, and that knowledge freed her. Ideas of what his kiss would be like had haunted her for days. Why not, she asked herself, find out what it would be like? Knowing she was a fool, she could not resist his blandishments, or her own curiosity. Throwing aside her doubts, she lifted her lips to his. "Please," she murmured, "please . . ."

Ives groaned and gathered her closer, his mouth finding hers. Half-prepared to be repulsed by his kiss as she had been by her husband's, Sophy was dazed by the storm of emotion that exploded through her as his lips gently, expertly explored her own. His mouth was warm and compelling, his lips firm and knowing, and she shuddered under the onslaught of the sweet sensations his embrace evoked.

His arms were iron bands around her, and she leaned into him, pressing herself against his hard length, oddly enough feeling, for the first time in her life, protected and cherished—and, oh, so, vibrantly alive. It was a novel experience, and she reveled in it, unaware that her actions were nearly Ives's undoing.

He had told himself he would not rush her, that he would give her time, but having her slim warmth pressed so ardently against him, having her sweet mouth pliant and obedient under his own was almost more than flesh and blood could bear. Her response was more than he had hoped for, more than he had dreamed of during all the restless nights since meeting her. Muttering an imprecation against her lips, he deepened the kiss, his tongue surging into her mouth.

Shamelessly, Sophy allowed him his way, her head falling back over his arm as he plundered her mouth. Her body seemed not to be her own, the most elemental sensations springing to life within her. She suddenly ached with a need she had never imagined, her very flesh unbearably sensitive to his lightest touch.

With shock, she realized that not only was he kissing her in the most blatantly intimate way possible but that one of his hands was lightly cupping her breast, his thumb rubbing rhythmically over the swollen nub of her nipple.

Aghast at her own actions, she struggled to escape him, and when he did not immediately release her, an atavistic fear shot up through her, dispelling all her pleasure and clouding rational thought with the memory of Simon's brutal ruttings. She fought like a wild thing, her fists beating against his chest, her body straining desperately away from him.

Lost in the magic of Sophy's sweetness, it took Ives a moment to realize that the lady was no longer agreeable to his embrace. Not only *not* agreeable, but absolutely frantic to escape. Instantly his head lifted, and his arms fell harmlessly to his sides.

Like a terrified, feral creature, Sophy shot off the seat and threw herself into the far corner of the coach. "D-don't touch me!" she stammered, her breathing labored, her face pale and strained in the uncertain light filtering into the coach from the flickering streetlamps outside.

Astonished, Ives eyed her. Something, he realized, was very wrong. This was certainly not the reaction of a sophisticated, worldly woman to a passionate embrace. More like a terrified virgin, he thought with a frown.

Gently, he said, "Sweetheart, I told you that your slightest whim is my command. If you do not want me to kiss you, I shall not." He smiled whimsically at her. "I will not deny that I hope most fervently to change your mind, but you have no reason to fear me."

His words calmed her, and, feeling like a perfect fool, Sophy tried to regain her composure. Sitting more naturally, she straightened her gown and pushed back a curl that had tumbled free from the artless knot on the top of her head.

When her breathing returned to normal and she felt in command of her voice, she muttered, "I warned you, my lord, that I do not want either a husband or a lover. If you wish for a lady of a more . . . accommodating nature, I suggest you set your sights elsewhere."

He sighed dramatically. "Nay, sweetheart. I'm afraid that only you will do for me."

Temper sparking, she sat up even straighter in her corner. "And I have told you that I am not interested in any sort of relationship with you other than that of acquaintance! Are you a dolt? A dunce? Do you not understand simple English? I do not want to become your mistress!"

A crooked grin that did odd things to her heart crossed his craggy face. "That's certainly speaking plain. Mayhap I shall just have to change your mind, hmm?"

Torn between amusement and vexation at his audacity, Sophy snorted. "You shall not. My resolve is firm, and you are a conceited fool if you think you shall change my mind!"

"Ah, a challenge. I always liked a challenge," he observed confidingly. "Yes, a challenge is just the thing to put me on my mettle. Makes life more interesting, don't you agree?"

Sophy shook her head in despair. He was impervious to insult! Worse, even when she was her angriest at him, she was always conscious of an absurd desire to laugh at his impudent actions.

Deciding it would not do at all for him to know the indecision that bedeviled her, and heaven knew he needed no encouraging, she said frostily, "You have been warned, m'lord. I shall say no more about it."

Thankfully they had arrived at their destination, and there was no more conversation.

Stephens's was a haunt favored by the military, especially the army, and Sophy was not surprised to discover that there were several gentlemen there with whom Ives seemed to be well acquainted. During the time that they waited for the arrival of the Offingtons, Ives introduced her to a bewildering array of men still in service, as well as several who, like him, had recently become civilians.

Ives proved himself to be an exemplary host, his behavior elegantly solicitous on her behalf. He showed no sign of the passionate man who had crushed her against him such a short time previously. There was nothing in his manner she could find fault with and, utterly absorbed by his lively tales of his activities in the cavalry, she was almost disappointed when the Offingtons arrived and she was no longer the sole object of his attention. Her thoughts were completely contradictory, and Sophy was uncomfortably aware of it.

Their meal was delightful, the conversation gay, and Sophy was able, for the most part, to relax and enjoy herself. By the time the evening had nearly ended, she was shocked to discover she had not thought of the troubles with her uncle once and that she was finding Ives's company far too amusing for her own good.

It was only when they were preparing to leave that the mood of the evening changed. Laughing at some quip

Ives tossed her way, Sophy happened to catch sight of a group of men just arriving for a late meal. Recognizing her uncle amongst them, she frowned. What, she wondered, was he doing here?

Edward was with a largely familiar group: Lord Grimshaw, Henry Dewhurst, Etienne Marquette, Sir Alfred Caldwell, Lord Coleman, and several other military men, as well as Edward's favorite crony, Sir Arthur Bellingham. She was slightly puzzled to see Edward here; Stephens's and its clientele were not the usual sort her uncle found amusing. Stephens's was, in its own way, respectable and exclusive, traits one did not normally associate with Baron Scoville.

Ives noticed their arrival also, and his gaze sharpened. He quickly scanned past Edward and his cronies, Bellingham and Dewhurst, to view Grimshaw and the others on his list of suspects. He was not surprised to see them here. It was logical that if one of the three on his list was the Fox, he would have many contacts and friends amongst the military and inhabitants of the Horse Guards. How else could he supply his master, Napoléon, with information?

Seeing his suspects with a group of men he knew to be officers in the army, Ives realized again the enormity of the task in front of him. In the past several days, his own men had discovered nothing very striking about the three men on the list—except for their shockingly licentious ways—and any one of them could be the Fox. Or not.

Spying Sophy sitting with Ives and the Offingtons, Henry Dewhurst immediately made his way to their table. Bowing and smiling, he made himself agreeable, his admiration for Sophy blatant and, to Ives's mind, annoying. Naturally the other gentlemen drifted over and general introductions were made.

Ives noticed at once the stiffness between Sophy and her uncle, but it was a foxed Sir Arthur Bellingham who blurted out, "I say, Sophy, did you really threaten to kill Edward this afternoon? Thought he was foxed when he told me. Niece and all. You wouldn't kill your own uncle, would you?"

Sophy froze. If it wasn't just like Edward to go about telling all and sundry the contents of what had been an extremely private conversation. The man had the taste and tact of a blind ferret. Embarrassed at suddenly being the cynosure of all eyes, Sophy tried to make light of the situation.

"You know my uncle, Sir Arthur," she said quietly. "Exaggeration is part and parcel of his personality."

"*Exaggeration!*" exclaimed Edward, who was not in much better condition than Sir Arthur. All of the gentlemen had obviously been imbibing heavily throughout the evening, though no one as yet was clearly drunk. "By Jove! Are you denying that only this afternoon you stated plain as a pikestaff that you would kill me before you would let me undertake my duties as guardian to Phoebe?"

"I may have allowed my temper to prompt me to speak hastily," Sophy said tightly, her eyes sparkling angrily.

Edward sneered, well aware of the discomfort he was causing her. "So you wouldn't kill me, if I took over the care of Phoebe, hey? Changed your mind about my character, have you?"

In the face of such open provocation, Sophy could not control herself. "I will never change my mind about ei-

ther your character or your morals," she ground out.
"You are a disgraceful roué who should have no part in
the raising of an innocent young woman."

"Ha!" shouted Edward gleefully. "You may think
what you like, gel, but *I* am Phoebe's guardian, and I can
do whatever I please." His eyes full of malice, he murmured, "Think I will see my solicitor tomorrow morning
and start proceedings to claim my rights to the brat. Best
prepare yourself to give her up to me."

"I will kill you first!" Sophy spat, responding to his
barbs exactly as Edward knew she would.

Edward looked at Bellingham. "Told you," he said
with satisfaction.

It was an unpleasant end to the evening, and Sophy
was furious with herself for letting Edward goad her into
hot speech, especially in public.

Having accomplished his task, Edward wandered off
taking Bellingham and several others with him. Deftly
smoothing over the unfortunate incident, Dewhurst, Sir
Alfred Caldwell, and the Frenchman, Etienne Marquette,
remained to chat with Ives, Sophy, and the Offingtons
for several moments longer.

Sophy was not mortified by the scene with her uncle.
Their dislike for one another was well-known, and it was
pretty well understood that if one put Lord Scoville and
Lady Marlowe in each other's vicinity, a heated exchange was certain to occur. Still Sophy was sorry it
happened and, glancing at Ives once Dewhurst, Caldwell, and Marquette had rejoined their original group,
murmured, "I apologize for letting my wretched tongue
ruin your party. I should never have let him make me
lose my temper." She smiled at the Offingtons. "I apolo-

gize to both of you, too, but at least you were prepared for what happened."

Sara nodded, a twinkle in her eyes. "If I were a lady inclined to games of chance, I would have wagered a decent sum on the likelihood of a similar outcome at *any* meeting between you and your uncle." She patted Sophy's hand. "Do not let it distress you, dear. We know how Edward is, and I am sure that Viscount Harrington has seen far worse confrontations than that little exchange between you and your uncle."

Ives took a sip of his hock. "Mrs. Offington is correct. My only regret is that I did not intervene sooner and send him on his way." He smiled at Sophy. "It is I who should be apologizing to you. I should not have allowed him to accost you."

Sophy smiled saucily. "While you are nothing like my uncle, you *do* share one unfortunate trait," she purred. "Once determined upon a course, I doubt anyone could stop either one of you."

"A hit! A definite hit!" crowed Randal, by now used to the constant sparring of the other two.

Ives nodded, his green eyes appreciative. "I agree. The lady is becoming quite adept at slipping under my guard."

Something in his tone of voice made Sophy look away, her cheeks faintly pink. Drat the man! He was far too dangerous for her peace of mind, and if anyone was slipping under anyone's guard, it certainly was not she. More likely, he was slipping under hers!

Once Ives had seen his guests to their homes and he was alone in his carriage, he considered the nasty scene between Baron Scoville and his niece. Something, he decided judiciously, was going to have to be done about Lord Scoville.

Even as Ives pondered the situation, the Fox, with a far deadlier solution, was thinking much the same thing: Something was *definitely* going to have to be done about Edward Scoville.

Chapter Seven

❧

*W*atching Edward from across the table where they were sitting, the Fox was annoyed. Who would have thought that after all these years that blasted ruby pin would come back to haunt him? And that of all people, it would be Edward Scoville who brought that disagreeable news to him!

The two men were seated in a quiet corner at the latest hell that had caught the fancy of the hardened gamblers Edward considered some of his dearest friends. The Fox had already been irritated by the scene Edward had created with Sophy at Stephens's earlier that evening, and now to find out that Edward knew about the cravat pin was enough to make him curse his luck.

The pin, even the location of its discovery, did not prove anything, but it was damned unfortunate that Edward should have come into that information. Damned unfortunate.

Despite having imbibed freely throughout the evening, Edward was still in fairly good control of himself and, staring into his friend's face, he murmured, "Wager you thought you were clean out of it, didn't you? Thought no one would ever guess the significance of that pin, didn't you?"

The Fox cocked a brow. "I am afraid that I do not follow your reasoning, dear fellow. I am very happy that the pin has finally come to light. It is worth a small fortune, and I have often wondered what had become of it."

"Then why didn't you ask me about it before you left Marlowe House when Simon died?"

"My dear man, surely there were more important things to be concerned about than the loss of a cravat pin!"

Edward's eyes narrowed. "Ain't just the loss of the pin I'm talking about. . . ."

He fidgeted and wouldn't meet the other man's gaze. "Simon told me he'd finally identified the gentleman who had been buying our information," he said at last. "You were clever with your disguises, I'll grant you that. If it weren't for the pin and knowing what I learned from Marlowe, I'd never have suspicioned it was you. Of course, he never told me who you were—very close-mouthed was Simon."

Edward took a gulp of his port. "Could have knocked me over with a feather when he told me he'd been trying for months to discover who you were. He was very pleased with himself, I can tell you that! I never knew that he was even curious about our mutual benefactor. *I* wasn't—the gold was the only thing that interested me. But Simon always played his cards very close to his chest, and he liked to have power over people. The night he died, he said he was going to confront you, let you know you weren't as clever as you thought." Edward frowned. "Didn't matter to me at the time. No pie of my making! You'd always been generous with the ready when I had something for you—best to let sleeping dogs lie."

He leaned forward confidentially. "Thing is, my position is a trifle uncertain at the moment. Marcus and Sophy are kicking up such a dust about the way I'm handling his and Phoebe's fortune that I have to be a bit circumspect, you know. Been thinking of ways to bring myself about. The Richmond heiress would do nicely, but since Sophy has me boxed for the moment, it seemed to me that you would be willing to pay me a nice sum for the return of your pin—and for me to forget what I know about it."

"And why do you think that?"

Edward looked startled. "I recognized the pin! And I could name dozens of others who know that it is yours."

"I fail to see why you think that would matter to me," the Fox said coolly. "I have already admitted that the pin is mine. Just because I never mentioned losing it means nothing." He smiled wolfishly. "You have nothing, my friend."

"The devil I don't!" burst out Edward. "I know that Simon was going to confront you that night—said he was going to make you dance to the tune of his piping. Only he died. Fell down his own stairs that he had climbed up and down for years without an accident—and at times when he was far more foxed than he was that night! And your pin was found in a very incriminating place. You never asked for it. Stands to reason you must have had a good reason for simply abandoning a piece of expensive jewelry like that. Like perhaps you know more about Simon's death than anybody ever guessed, eh?"

The Fox yawned delicately. "My dear fellow, you

yourself said that our dear friend Simon did not tell you
the name of the man he'd identified as your, er, benefactor. So you have nothing but the merest conjecture to
back up your claims. Just because my pin was found in
Simon's house—where I was a guest, I might add—
proves nothing." He smiled gently at Edward. "Go home,
my friend, and sleep it off. You are letting your imagination run away with you."

"Imagination!" Edward exclaimed, incensed. "Ain't
my imagination. Don't know why you threw your lot in
with the French, and I don't care, but you cannot convince me that you are not the fellow who used to slip
around and buy information from Marlowe and me." His
gaze sharpened. "For all I know you still do."

"Edward, Edward, my friend, you are not making any
sense. Do you really want your past indiscretions made
public?" the Fox asked with polite interest. "Do you really want all and sundry to know you were willing to sell
out your own country for mere gold?" He shook his head
sadly. "I am shocked by what you have just disclosed to
me. But we are good friends, and I shall put your ram-
blings down to your having had too much to drink this
evening. We shall not speak of it again."

"Won't we?" Edward demanded with an ugly gleam in
his eyes. "Think again!"

The Fox shrugged. "Whatever you say, my friend. And
now, if you will excuse me, I shall be on my way. I see
that Bellingham is trying to get your attention. I shall
leave you to his tender mercies. Good night."

He rose from the table and strolled away. No one seeing his benign expression would ever guess the murderous thoughts chasing through his mind.

The conversation with Edward had annoyed him far

more than it had disturbed him. Scoville had nothing but the fact that a cravat pin identified as belonging to him had been found at the top of the staircase where Simon had fallen. Everything else was pure conjecture, but it was conjecture that the Fox had no intention of allowing to become public. Once suspicions, *any* suspicions, were aroused, his usefulness would be over. While it was unlikely that he would ever be unmasked, the gossip and speculation alone would ruin him and leave him in total disgrace.

Edward, he decided as he left the hell and walked toward his residence, had just become a very big problem, and there was only one effective way to deal with problems of that sort. . . .

Lying sleepless in his bed that night, Ives mulled over the events of the evening. He would have preferred to dwell on Sophy's charms, but having seen the three men on his list together with several military men reminded him again of the difficulties that faced him in unmasking the Fox, *and* the man who murdered his father.

Ives's men had been most diligent in their investigations, but what they had discovered added little to what they already knew. The Fox was undoubtedly a scrupulously careful, clever man, having operated for years right under the nose of Roxbury and the like. In fact, Ives decided grimly, it was likely the man would remain undetected if they continued going about the affair as they were.

They needed, he realized suddenly, something to draw the man out. The Fox obviously covered his tracks well, and he was hardly fool enough to lead them directly to his

den. So a way of making him break cover had to be
found.

Ives considered the problem until sleep overtook him,
but when he woke the next morning, as often happened to
him, a possible way of trapping the wily Fox had occurred to him. Not waiting even to dress, he demanded
writing materials and swiftly scratched out a note to be
delivered at once to the Duke of Roxbury.

That afternoon, Ives met Roxbury in the out-of-the-
way tavern the Duke had recommended in his return message to Ives. They had a private room, and Ives had
barely entered before Roxbury said impatiently, "Tell me
of this idea of yours."

Ives grinned. "What? No social observances first?"

Roxbury's sleepy gray eyes met his. "Of course, my
dear boy. I am afraid that curiosity overcame my manners." Languidly waving one hand, he said, "There is port
and hock on the table over there if you would like some
refreshments. You may pour me a glass of hock."

Once libations were taken care of, Ives settled himself
in a chair across from his godfather and said bluntly, "My
attempt to discover the identity of the Fox is only going
to end in failure if we continue in the manner we have so
far." When Roxbury started to protest, Ives commanded,
"Hear me out, sir. When I am through, I think you will
agree with me."

Roxbury sighed and subsided back into his chair.

Regarding his wineglass, Ives said, "I do not know
how my father and Adrian stumbled across his identity, if
they did. Whatever they discovered was over a year ago,
and I am sure by now our friend has covered whatever
tracks the others may have come upon." He glanced at

Roxbury. "You yourself admitted that this is an extremely clever man who has operated brazenly right under your nose for years. I do not think that there is going to be very much, if anything, that will directly link him to being the Fox. He is far too smart for that."

Ives leaned forward. "What we need is to approach the problem from the opposite end: Instead of trying to find where he has gone to earth, we need to have him break cover and come out into the open."

"And how do you propose we do that?" his godfather asked caustically. "Place an advertisement in the *Times*?"

Ives smiled faintly. "Not quite. What is the one thing we know conclusively about the man?" Ives asked rhetorically, and then answered the question himself, "He is a seller of information, a purveyor of military secrets."

His gaze locked with Roxbury's. "So why don't we arrange for some vital information—perhaps the plans for the summer deployment of Wellesley's troops on the Peninsula—to fall into the hands of someone suspected of dealing with the Fox? I am sure you already have several fellows that you suspect of passing along military secrets to our elusive Mr. Renard. Why not see to it that one of them has access to, say, an extremely important memorandum—a memorandum the Fox would not be able to resist?"

Roxbury sat up, his eyes narrowing. "Lure him out . . ."

"Precisely, sir. Present him with a rather large, nearly irresistible bone and set our trap accordingly."

Roxbury sat back in his chair, frowning slightly, as he turned the idea over in his mind. As the minutes passed, and Ives waited tensely for reaction to his plan, Roxbury's frown gradually disappeared, and a sly smile began to curve his lips.

"My dear, *dear* boy, what an excellent plan! And I know just the fellow at the Horse Guards we can use as our dupe."

"The memorandum must appear legitimate," Ives warned. "The Fox is too wily to be taken in by anything smelling even faintly of a trap."

"Oh, I agree completely," Roxbury said, nodding. "But it so happens that just the sort of document you have suggested does exist. In order to make certain—if the worst happens and the Fox *were* somehow to slip through our noose—that the information would not do any harm, the existing memorandum will have to be altered to reflect erroneous information. I agree that it must be information that appears valid. Of course, it will have to be arranged that our pawn has access to the memorandum, access that makes it far too tempting for him to resist."

A look of intense satisfaction crossed Roxbury's lined features. "I think it can all be arranged most satisfactorily. Our dupe, closely followed by us, will take the bait directly to the Fox, and that will be the end of *Le Renard*!"

"I only hope it all goes as smoothly as you think it will," Ives returned cautiously.

Roxbury shrugged. "It is better than simply trusting to a piece of luck to bring us about." He stood up. "Now if you will excuse me, I shall be on my way. I must set events into motion. In the meantime, I suggest that you become very friendly with a Lieutenant Colonel Meade. He is seen frequently in the company of the men on the list that I gave you." Roxbury grimaced. "We have long suspected him of pilfering information, but have not been able to prove anything."

He smiled sleepily. "Just think, we may not only catch the Fox, but close up a leak at the Horse Guards as well!"

Ives frowned. "Meade, you say? I believe that I met the fellow just last evening at Stephens's. He was with Grimshaw and the others. Burly man? Blond hair and blue eyes? A face like a pouting cherub?"

Roxbury beamed at him. "I could not have described the man better myself!" Clapping his godson on the back, he urged, "Now go and become one of our dear colonel's most cherished friends."

Ives made a wry face. "Thank you, sir. Just what I always wanted, to consort intimately with suspected spies and traitors."

Returning to his town house, Ives immediately called a meeting of his men and gave them a recital of the facts. The men seemed heartened by Ives's plan, and it was decided, since one of them would be tailing their quarry at all times, that they would work in relays watching Meade. Ashby, Ives's valet, drew the first watch.

"I want to know everyone he meets and everywhere he goes," Ives said grimly to his former batman. "At no time do I want him *un*observed. I want you on his heels like a hound on a hare."

Ives grinned at him. "However, I would prefer that you not bring attention to yourself. The same goes for the rest of you," he added as he glanced around the room. "Remember, all is secrecy. We must not let him know that we are shadowing him." He frowned slightly. "And be on the lookout for others watching him—my godfather may set his own dogs on him, and I do not want us tripping over one another. If you suspect that others are interested in him also, let me know instantly."

The men nodded. William Williams asked, "And you, sir? What are you going to do?"

Ives grimaced. "I have the pleasant duty of becoming the blasted fellow's bosom friend."

Becoming Meade's friend was not arduous. They had the military as common ground as well as several mutual acquaintances. Dining with Lieutenant Colonel Meade that evening and later accompanying him to one of the more popular hells, Ives was astonished at how easily he managed to ingratiate himself with the other man. But then Meade, despite being a suspected spy, was a rather likable fellow, a trifle simple but with an easygoing, undemanding personality. By the time Ives returned home that evening in the early hours of the morning, after a night of gambling, drinking, and whoring, there was little doubt that Meade considered them brothers under the skin.

Cultivating a friendship with Meade entailed many nights that were a boring and predictable repetition of the previous evening's entertainment. It also, to Ives's growing disgust, entailed becoming very friendly with the suspects on his list as well as several other gentlemen who had formed the nucleus of Simon Marlowe's set.

His nocturnal activities left Ives with little time in which to pursue the fascinating and elusive Lady Marlowe, but he did manage to call several times during the following weeks at the Grayson town house, and twice he managed to coax Sophy into driving in Hyde Park with him.

The fact that Ives was no longer frequently seen in her company at the various balls and routs she attended did not pass unnoticed, and Henry Dewhurst twitted her on it.

Approaching her one evening at a ball, after they had exchanged warm greetings, Henry did a discreet double take, and murmured, "Is it my imagination, or has the rather large gentleman who has been taking up so much of your time lately vanished from the lists?"

If anyone else had made that comment, Sophy would have been deeply chagrined, but her relationship with Dewhurst enabled her to see his words for the gentle teasing they were. She smiled faintly at him. "Alas, you see that he has abandoned me—thank goodness!"

Dewhurst laughed. "I wondered how long you were going to put up with his commanding manners." He flashed her a keen look. "You were seen so often in his company that I began to speculate that perhaps you changed your mind about never marrying again. Have you?"

"Good heavens, no!" Sophy said gaily, although the smile that accompanied her statement was a trifle forced. Despite her light words, Ives's defection hurt. Not a great deal, she told herself quickly; but she could not deny that she missed his company—far more than she liked to admit.

Lord Grimshaw wandered up just then, his gray eyes appreciative as they roamed over Sophy's slender form. She was clad this evening in a gown of palest gold silk, which left her shoulders bare and displayed a generous amount of her breasts. As always, just Grimshaw's look made her flesh creep. Of all Simon's friends, she disliked him the most.

The rakish manners and coarse activities of Marquette and Lord Coleman—in fact, most of Simon's friends— had repelled her when she first met them, but the moment she laid eyes on Grimshaw, she had been aware of an instinctive revulsion for him.

The others had flirted scandalously with her, had even attempted the occasional stolen kiss, but there was nothing frightening about them. They were simply hardened rakes reacting to the proximity of a pretty female. With Grimshaw it was different.

Sophy had swiftly learned how to repulse the others, and they took it in good stride, but Grimshaw . . . Grimshaw had been appallingly persistent. Nothing seemed to deter him, and after a particularly ugly scene when she had to fight her way free of his lascivious embrace, Sophy had taken to making certain she was never alone with him and kept to her rooms when he was a guest at Marlowe House. Telling Simon would have been useless; he would have thought it a great jest and chastised her for being such a little prude. Grimshaw frightened and repelled her, and in the ensuing years he did nothing to change her initial feelings about him.

Almost as if he guessed her thoughts, Grimshaw smiled. Not a nice smile. "How is it," he asked carelessly, "that you are out and about these days without the hulking viscount lurking in the background? Does he allow you to run tame, or did you freeze him out?"

Sophy stiffened, and Dewhurst sent Grimshaw a pained look. Putting a restraining hand on Dewhurst's arm, she said levelly, "I am afraid that my relationship with Viscount Harrington is none of your business, and I would remind you, that these days, no man *allows* me to do anything!"

"Which is unfortunate," Grimshaw returned with a gleam in his gray eyes. "I have always thought that you needed the hand of a strong man. Since Simon died, you've developed into quite a shrew, my sweet. If you don't watch that sharp tongue of yours, you may find that you have driven off every member of the male species."

Controlling her temper with an effort and reminding herself that she did not have to put up with his presence if she did not wish to, she said bluntly, "You are entitled to your own opinion. Now if you will excuse me, I intend to go in search of more congenial company."

She was on the point of turning away, when Grimshaw murmured, "Like the viscount? I see that he has arrived and is fast making his way to your side."

Sophy spun around to see that Grimshaw spoke the truth, and a tingle of delight shot through her at the sight of Ives's tall form striding determinedly across the floor in her direction. The evening, which had seemed oddly flat, suddenly became dazzlingly vibrant, and the smile Sophy gave Ives when he finally reached her side brought a dazed expression to his craggy face.

Bowing low over her hand, he murmured, "Can it be that you are actually pleased to see me, sweetheart?"

A flush stained her cheeks at his public endearment, and her fingers trembled unaccountably in his warm grasp, as she muttered, "Viscount Harrington! If you would only learn to keep a civil tongue in your head, I am certain that our acquaintance would proceed more smoothly."

"But tediously, do you not agree?" he returned with a twinkle.

Sophy snatched away her hand, which he was all too inclined to retain, from his, and said politely, "You remember Mr. Dewhurst and Lord Grimshaw?"

Ives bowed to both men. "Of course. Lately I have

been seeing a great deal of them. They need no further introduction. Good evening, gentlemen."

Sophy looked puzzled. "You have become friends?" she asked uncertainly. Dewhurst might be a favorite of hers, but she knew that he was as reckless a gambler and hardened a rake as all the others. And of course, Grimshaw . . . The thought of Ives becoming friends with a man whose mere glance filled her with revulsion was disquieting.

Grimshaw laughed. "Ah, yes, the viscount has been joining your beloved uncle and me and several other friends for some enjoyable evenings lately." He looked at Ives. "How much did you drop last night playing with Meade and Caldwell? Five thousand? Ten?"

"Enough," Ives replied lightly, "to make me wonder if I am a gambler, after all."

Ives was very aware of Sophy's dismay that he should be losing such vast sums as well as the fact that he was apparently on such easy terms with a fellow like Grimshaw, *and* her uncle. He sighed inwardly. The lady was elusive enough, but if she thought he had turned into a reckless gambler and enjoyed the company of men like Grimshaw and Scoville . . .

Dewhurst spoke up. "Did you receive the Allentons' invitation for the weekend house party planned for mid-May?" he asked. "Allenton said he intended to invite you. It should be amusing. There will be some deep drinking and heavy gambling if I know Thomas Allenton and his lady. You should find it enjoyable."

"The Allentons' house party?" Sophy inquired sharply. "You have been invited to stay at Crestview?"

Ives flicked a brow upward at her tone of voice. "Yes,

I have, but I have not yet made up my mind whether to attend or not."

"Oh, you will find it most amusing," Grimshaw said. "Sally Allenton puts on a fine house party." He cast a sly look at Sophy. "Unlike some hostesses, she is very easygoing and does not cast a rub in a fellow's way." He winked. "She also has some of the most . . . accommodating . . . female servants."

It was a most improper conversation to be having in front of Sophy, but she did not appear shocked by it, Ives thought. But then if everything he had heard of her husband was true, she would not be. In fact, she had probably been exposed to far worse.

For a moment Ives was conscious of a great burst of rage within him at what Sophy must have endured. Simon Marlowe, he thought savagely, should have been drawn and quartered!

Hiding his distaste for Grimshaw and the entire episode, Ives murmured, "Hmm, so I have heard. But I have also heard that there are many members of the ton who do not approve of either Allenton or his dashing wife. They are considered far too fast and careless of convention to suit many people."

"Only by stiff-rumped old harridans," Grimshaw drawled. "I tell you, the Allentons are most amusing. You should accept the invitation. The company will be uncommonly gay."

Henry glanced at Sophy, who had been listening to the conversation with growing dismay. "And you, Lady Marlowe? Are you attending the house party?"

Her refusal of the invitation was sitting on her writing table at home. She knew *exactly* the type of party it would be—she had survived too many similar orgies at Marlowe House while her husband was alive—and had thought that there was nothing on earth that would compel her to willingly attend such a wretched affair again.

Allenton had been a frequent guest at Marlowe House, and he was of the same ilk as Grimshaw. The unsettling news that Ives appeared to be firmly clasped to the bosom of the most depraved of Simon's friends gave her pause. She could not credit that he was as immoral a fellow as this conversation would lead one to believe, yet what else could she think? Perhaps, she thought unhappily, she should attend the Allenton party and see for herself.

Sophy smiled weakly and admitted, "I have not yet made up my mind. I have heard that Crestview is very beautiful, and May is a lovely month. It might be pleasant to leave London briefly for a weekend in the country."

"I would not have thought that such a party would be to your liking," Ives said slowly, a slight frown growing between his brows.

"Oh, and what gave you that idea?" Sophy asked lightly. "I assure you that I have attended many parties of this sort."

Ives shrugged and let the subject drop. This was not the time to convince her that the last place she wanted to be was at Allenton's house party. If he understood it right, it was going to be nothing short of a drunken bacchanalia and an excuse for the others to commit any sort of depraved excess which crossed their minds. For all her fashionable ways, Sophy was not *that* sophisticated, and he did not want her subjected to any unpleasantness. More importantly, he thought grimly, he did not want her to see him in his current guise of flagrant degenerate!

* * *

The chance for private conversation between them did not occur until the next day, when Ives came to call. To Sophy's annoyance, he showed himself into the conservatory where she had been reading a new novel from the Minerva Press. Ignoring the flutter in her chest, she told herself that he was too arrogant by half and that he was in desperate need of a sharp set-down. Show himself in, indeed!

After greetings were exchanged, Ives immediately brought up the subject of the Allenton house party. "I wondered," he began carefully, "if you had made up your mind about the Allentons' invitation?"

"Why?" she demanded, her eyes narrowing. "Why do you care whether or not I have decided to attend their party?"

Normally he would have handled her more carefully, but the late nights he was keeping, not to mention the heavy drinking and the urgent need to keep her as far away from that sordid part of his life as possible, made him clumsy.

Ives smiled, a smile that made her bones feel like sun-warmed honey, and promptly shot himself in the foot as he said, "Because, sweetheart, I do not think that it is the type of party you would enjoy. It would not be wise for you to attend."

Sophy gasped with outrage. He was telling her what to do! The utter gall of the man. It was perfectly acceptable for *him* to attend the wretched affair, but he had the audacity to tell her that she should not. How dare he!

"And you are a fool if you think that you can dictate to me where I should go! You have overstepped yourself, my lord. What I do is none of your affair, and I would remind you to remember that in the future," she said icily, her lovely eyes brilliant.

Cursing himself for taking his fences too fast, Ives groaned. Damn and blast! There would be no stopping her now, and it was his own bloody fault. Trying to undo the damage, he murmured, "You mistake my intention, Lady Marlowe. I only thought to warn you that the party may not be what you are used to."

Sophy's lip curled. "I think *you* forget, my lord, that I was once married to one of the most debauched men in England. Believe me, there is nothing that will happen at the Allentons' house party that will surprise me. Nothing will occur that I have not seen previously."

"Then you are determined to accept the invitation?" he asked grimly.

"You may lay money on it!" Sophy retorted with great relish.

Chapter Eight

❧

*T*he weather for the Allenton house party was particularly fine. The sun was warm and golden, the sky a soft spring blue, and the air fragrant with the scent of roses and lilacs. Staring glumly out of the windows of her room at the Allenton estate of Crestview, Sophy was not consoled by either the charming setting or the wonderful May day.

She had been, and she was the first to admit it, a fool for having allowed her temper to rule her. And she had no one but herself to blame for the predicament in which she found herself.

Having met most of the guests the previous night when she arrived from London at the Allenton home in Surrey, it was appallingly clear that the house party was going to be every bit as vulgar and debauched as she had feared. Worse was the news confirming that Edward would definitely be in attendance. But far worse than that, it was obvious from his actions last evening that Ives Harrington was not the man she had first thought him; he was, it appeared, every bit as lewdly inclined as Simon had been.

There was an unhappy droop to Sophy's mouth as she stared out of the window of her second-floor room. She thought that she had begun to know Ives Harrington, but recalling his conduct last night her spirits sank. He had been right in the thick of it all, laughing coarsely and drinking wildly, his boon companions Grimshaw and a military man named Meade. Even more depressing, she had actually caught him ogling and pinching the bottom of one of the pretty housemaids. She sighed heavily. She had no doubt that the same housemaid had shared his bed last night.

The idea of leaving crossed her mind more than once. Many of the guests were old friends of Simon's, and they were definitely not the sort of people she wished to become reacquainted with. A shudder went through her.

Last night's raucous activities were a clear indication that events were not going to improve. The mere fact that Edward, Grimshaw, and all the others from Simon's past were in attendance only confirmed her dismal opinion. She was in danger. By being in this very house, she was leaving herself open to the advances of men she detested and she was bitterly aware that she ran the risk of finding herself in a very precarious position. Crestview, this particular weekend, was no place for anyone who wished to hang on to even a shred of virtue. She should leave. Now. There was nothing here for her. Except Ives.

A pang went through her and she wondered bleakly when he had come to mean so much to her. She could pretend no longer that the only emotions she experienced in his company were irritation and annoyance. She cared for him. Damn him!

She did not know how it happened or when he had gone from amusing irritant to someone whose very presence was vital to her happiness, but it had happened. By infinitesimal degrees he had breached her defenses and deftly insinuated himself into her heart. Her problem now was how to get him out of that vulnerable space before he did more damage.

Sophy frowned. The only way that she saw to accomplish her goal was to grasp the nettle and bear the sting. She would have to see him at his worst and let disgust and contempt fill her heart in place of the softer emotion that had come to dominate it. And the one sure way of doing that, she conceded grimly, was to remain at Crestview.

Waking with an aching head and a mouth that felt like the floor of a henhouse, Ives was wishing violently that he was anywhere but at Crestview. The look of hurt and shock on Sophy's face when she had caught him fondling the housemaid had been one of the lowest moments of his life. It was bad enough that she saw him cavorting familiarly with men he freely stigmatized as scoundrels and blackguards, but to observe him acting like a damn-all rake of the worst kind . . .

The expression on her lovely face, the disbelief and bleak disappointment that had flashed across her features had been like a knife blade in his heart. And there was not one damn thing he could do about it! Not unless he wanted to undo everything he had done so far and frighten off his quarry.

The Fox was near, Ives could swear to it. There was no doubt in his mind that he was probably already on very good terms with his quarry. More importantly, events seemed to be moving in the direction he wanted.

Last night, appearing far more drunk than he actually

had been, he had played hand after hand of whist with Grimshaw, Meade, and Coleman. Marquette, Dewhurst, and a few others had been looking on, and to his intense satisfaction, the subject of the planted memorandum had been mentioned.

It had been Meade, of course, who brought it up. He had been completely foxed and could not help bragging a little about what he knew. Marquette—or had it been Dewhurst?—had made some comment about the progress of Wellesley's troops on the Peninsula, and Meade could not help referring to a very important memorandum that had just crossed his desk that very day.

When pressed by Grimshaw and Coleman and the others to reveal its contents, he had grown sly and, beyond throwing out tantalizing hints, had revealed little. Ives was certain the Fox had been present and his quarry now knew that a very important document existed and that his tool, Meade, could lay his hands on it. The question remained: Would he take the bait?

Ashby entered the room just then with a silver tray containing a tall, lidded pot, various condiments, and china and utensils. Watching blearily as his manservant placed the tray on a nearby table, Ives asked, "Tell me that you have brought me very black, very hot coffee and a great deal of it."

Ashby grinned. "Deep doings last night, were there, my lord?" Ives sat up and promptly groaned as his head exploded into a thousand shards of pain. "Indeed there were. Too deep for me, I am afraid. Many more nights of this sort of activity, and I shall be a withered old man before my time." He glanced at Ashby. "Anything interesting to report?"

Ashby shook his head. "No, except that this is a curst

rum household, I can tell you. Too many young and pretty female servants about and most of them gigglers with greased heels, if you catch my meaning. As for William and John, they have discovered nothing either, other than there is some mighty fine horseflesh driven by your friends."

Taking the cup of coffee Ashby handed him, Ives took a wary sip. It was bloody-damn hot and strong enough to melt teeth—just the way he liked it on a morning like today.

Several cups later, Ives felt enough in control of himself to attempt to rise and dress. The room spun, and for one awful moment he thought he would lose the contents of his stomach. But the room finally slowed and he was able cautiously to wash and groom himself.

Garbed for the day and feeling a trifle more in control of himself, he said, "There is something the three of you can do for me. Keep your eye on Meade, but keep an eye on Lady Marlowe, too." His mouth twisted. "I can offer her little protection since I shall be involved with Meade. None of the gentlemen here seem above forcing their attentions on anything female, and a few of them would not stop at rape. I do not want her in any danger."

Ashby nodded, his face somber. "I see you had your room changed. Is Lady Marlowe next door?"

Ives started to nod, but then thought better of it. "Yes. Lady Allenton simpered and looked arch when I requested the change, but she made no comment."

"What are you going to do today?" Ashby asked as he gathered up things and prepared to leave the room.

"I would like to hide out and nurse my head, but I am afraid that option is not open to me. Fortunately, I doubt that many of the guests will be up and about until late in the afternoon, so I may be able to please myself for much of the day."

Ives looked thoughtful. "I shall probably try to redeem myself somewhat with the lady, but I suspect that endeavor will end in futility. And this evening when she sees me acting as depraved and salacious as Grimshaw and the others, all my efforts will be for naught." His expression was grim as he finished speaking.

Ives's observations proved correct. Most of the guests did sleep the day away, and his plans to ingratiate himself into Sophy's good graces came to naught. Unlike nearly everyone else, she was certainly up and about, but she had nothing for him but stiff replies. The contemptuous glances she flashed him from those great golden eyes of hers sent his heart right down to the bottom of his highly polished Hessians. He went up to change for dinner in a thoroughly foul mood.

Despite her cool reception to his overtures, Sophy felt herself half-hoping she had been mistaken in him. Perhaps last night had been an aberration? She made a face in the mirror as she watched her maid arrange the masses of golden hair in a charming knot of curls on the top of her head. Was she so desperate to believe well of him, she wondered, that she was now willing utterly to delude herself? She snorted. Suddenly disgusted with herself for being such a weak-willed ninny, she determined to take action.

Unhappily she faced the fact that the man who had charmed her and broken down her defenses had been merely playing a role in order to slip beneath her guard and that his true character had only recently been revealed. Her mouth tightened. Well, she wasn't going to waste any more heartache on Ives Harrington, she decided fiercely. She would endure tonight, but in the morning she was leaving for London.

And she was retreating to the relative safety of her room immediately following dinner. And locking the door.

To Sophy's surprise the evening meal was almost pleasant. She was spared Edward's presence; a coaching accident detained him, and he arrived too late to join them for dinner. The food was excellent and the service exemplary. That Henry Dewhurst was seated on one side of her, and Ives on the opposite side of the long table and as far away as possible, helped enormously to make the meal enjoyable. At least until Henry mentioned Ives's name.

The sweet course had just been served, and Dewhurst, his gaze resting thoughtfully on Ives, murmured, "I am amazed at the change in Harrington these days, aren't you?" Dewhurst laughed slightly. "Lately, he has become as wild a rake and compulsive a gambler as dear Simon once was, don't you think?"

The strawberry tartlet she had been eating turned to mud in her mouth, and Sophy replied stiffly, "I am afraid that Lord Harrington's activities do not interest me."

Henry cocked a brow. "No? Then why are you here? This is not your sort of affair either, my sweet."

Sophy shot him a miserable glance. "Is it that obvious?"

His blue eyes were kind as they rested on her face, and beneath the table he gave her hand a comforting squeeze. "Only to someone who has known you a long time. It is apparent that *something* brought you here, and since it was not myself, I didn't have to look very far for my rival."

She managed a smile. "You needn't worry that I have lost my heart to him. I am only here because I was foolish enough to let my temper goad me into reckless action. I intend to leave in the morning."

Henry nodded. "Which news makes me happy." He sent her a chiding look. "You *really* should not be here. It is going to be a wild romp, unless I miss my guess."

A teasing gleam suddenly lit Sophy's eyes. "This from *you*? How many times did I preside over just such an affair as Simon's wife?"

"Too many, my dear, far too many," he returned, and began to talk of other things. But Etienne Marquette, who was to her left and had been discreetly listening to her conversation with Henry, said softly, "What *Henri* says is true. This Harrington seemed such a *dull,* plodding sort of fellow when first we met, but now! *Mon Dieu!* I certainly never thought to see him at an affair like this." His black eyes glittering with a slyness she had never noted before, he murmured, "It is like watching a leopard change his spots, *non*?"

He glanced down the long table in Ives's direction. "I wonder," he speculated, "which is the real Viscount Harrington. The dullard? Or the rake?"

Since Sophy had no answer for him, she was very glad when Lady Allenton signaled that the ladies were to leave the gentlemen to their port and cigars and follow her into one of the large saloons for coffee. Sophy planned to drink one cup of coffee, then politely take her leave, but an interruption put that thought from her mind.

The ladies had just been served when the butler entered the room, and announced, "Miss Weatherby, madam."

To Sophy's astonishment, in sailed Agnes Weatherby, her gown a dashing confection of rose silk and lace, the bodice cut daringly low, revealing an impressive amount of soft, white flesh. It was apparent from the way the two women greeted each other that she was expected and on good terms with Lady Allenton.

"My dear Agnes, I am so sorry that you arrived too late to join us for dinner. Did the servants see to your needs?"

"Oh, yes, a wonderful dinner was immediately sent up to me, and I enjoyed it immensely. I am only sorry that our coach was so tardy in delivering us. A thrown wheel, you know."

"But you are here now, and that is all that matters," Lady Allenton said with a smile. Waving her hand around the room at the assembled ladies, she added, "You know everyone?"

Agnes glanced around, her stunned gaze meeting Sophy's. "Oh yes, I know everyone."

Lady Allenton touched her arm, and asked archly, "Your room is satisfactory? Dear Edward requested it for you particularly."

"Yes, it is most satisfactory," Agnes replied, almost simpering.

Bile rose in Sophy's throat. Edward had claimed that Agnes Weatherby was no longer his mistress, but it appeared that he had lied. The man, Sophy thought furiously, had simply no morals at all. Attempting to force Anne into marriage with him was bad enough, but setting up her aunt as his mistress was outrageous.

It appeared that Agnes Weatherby was every bit as

brazen as her lover, for a few minutes later she came up to Sophy and stated coolly, "I am surprised to see you here. From what Edward has said, I would not have thought you would find this sort of affair acceptable."

"Yes, I am quite sure he will be very surprised to find me here," Sophy replied grimly, all ideas of an early retreat banished from her mind.

Agnes eyed her uncertainly. "I suppose," she muttered, "that you will use my . . . relationship . . . with your uncle against me?"

"Only if you are so foolish as to try to take Anne away from me and force her into marriage with Edward," Sophy replied sweetly.

"Oh, Edward has quite gone off that notion," Agnes answered airily. "He has another plan to lay his hands on the ready."

"Really? And what might that be?" Sophy asked in spite of herself.

A crafty look crossed Agnes's face. "I cannot tell you, but he has explained all to me." She paused, a vexed cast to her mouth. "At least he has told me much of it. If everything goes as Edward plans, we will never have need of Anne's money." A definite simper appeared on her face. "We may even marry."

Frowning, Sophy regarded her. "I would warn you that my uncle is not a man to be trusted. He often makes false promises."

Agnes sniffed and took a sip of her coffee.

It was obvious that Edward was unpleasantly surprised to see Sophy when the gentlemen entered the room shortly. He had joined the others at their port, and from his flushed features and bleary eyes it was clear that he had already partaken freely of the bottle. He was relaxed and laughing at something Grimshaw said when they entered the room.

Seeing his niece standing next to his mistress, he faltered. His eyes bugged, and his smile disappeared instantly. Aggrievedly, he burst out, "Oh, good gad! What the devil are *you* doing here?"

Sophy smiled mirthlessly. "Certainly not enjoying myself!"

Coming to a stop in front of her, he replied, "Well, stands to reason! This ain't your sort of doing. 'Pon my soul, never thought to see you at one of these rough-and-ready romps."

Oblivious to the interested stares of the rest of the room, Sophy snapped, "So I gather, else you would not have brought your mistress with you—a mistress you told me you had put aside. Another lie, dear uncle?"

"Ain't a lie!" he protested. "Aggie and I were parted when I spoke to you."

"No doubt simply for that one particular day," Sophy retorted, her long-simmering resentment against her uncle beginning to bubble up.

"Well, what if it was? None of your business."

Carefully putting down her cup and saucer on a nearby table, she said, "I am afraid that as long as you hold the reins to my brother and sister's fortune, everything you do is of interest to me."

"Ha! Needn't worry about that much longer. Got a plan that won't fail! If all goes well, won't need their money. That should please you."

"The only thing," Sophy said in a hard tone, "that would please me would be to see the last of you."

Edward grinned at her. "The only way that will happen, my gel, is when I die. Don't plan on doing that for a long time."

"Perhaps," Sophy purred, her eyes a bright angry gold between her long lashes, "if you continue as you are, you might just suffer an untimely end."

Edward laughed smugly. "Don't threaten me, gel. And you might start praying that I do live a long life. Something happens to me and there are those who will remember that you swore to kill me." Edward was now enjoying himself, and tauntingly he added, "Think of that the next time you are wishing me to the Devil."

Sophy's hands clenched into fists, and it was obvious to everyone that only by the greatest of effort was she controlling an urge to fly at her uncle. Ives, who had been watching the nasty interplay, decided to put an end to it before Sophy's control broke.

Strolling up to them, he took Sophy's hand in his and said, "Have you seen the gardens in the moonlight? They are very beautiful. Allow me to show you."

"Oh, I say," protested Grimshaw, who had also observed the byplay between Sophy and Edward, "I must insist that you allow *me* that pleasure." He smiled thinly at Ives. "I claim the right as one of her most enduring admirers. Isn't that so, sweet Sophy?"

"Non, non!" Etienne Marquette exclaimed, his glossy black curls gleaming in the candlelight, "I insist that you give me the honor. Permit me, Lady Marlowe, to escort you outside."

Lord Coleman and Sir Alfred Caldwell immediately added their own invitations, and Sophy glanced in dismay from one face to the next. She trusted none of them, not even Ives, and the last place she would go with any of them was somewhere dark and private! Grimshaw, especially. The way he was looking at her made her flesh creep.

Forcing a smile, she said politely, "I thank you for your kind invitations, but I am afraid I must refuse all. Now if you will excuse me?"

She slipped her hand from Ives's and quickly made her way to her hostess. Claiming a headache, Sophy took her leave and swiftly retired to her room. Remembering the look on Grimshaw's face, she locked the door and for safety lodged a chair under the doorknob. Not for the first time, she was glad she'd had the foresight to bring her pistol with her.

She sighed as she slipped out of her gown, having dismissed her maid for the evening. She had thought she was long past the days when she needed a pistol, but it seemed she was wrong. All it would take now was for Grimshaw or one of the others to try to force his way into her room to make her every fear real.

Downstairs, as the evening progressed, the party became as lascivious and lewd as could be expected, and Ives was damned glad that Sophy was out of it. Surrounded by Grimshaw, Dewhurst, Marquette, Meade, and Caldwell, he watched as Edward lurched after Agnes Weatherby, attempting to remove her garter. The lady was shrieking with laughter as she made halfhearted attempts to escape, and Edward was being loudly urged on by Dewhurst and Grimshaw and the others who stood near Ives. Many of the other guests were already so drunk they could not stand, and from the sounds and occasional glimpses into the various darkened corners of the room, it was obvious that more than just garters were being removed. Disgust rose within him, but outwardly

Ives kept a slightly drunken smile firmly affixed to his face.

Once Lady Allenton had withdrawn, leaving her husband boldly pawing a dashing young widow, the evening became even wilder and more debauched than Ives had imagined, one man and woman almost openly coupling on the satin couch, uncaring that others were watching. Ives suspected that before too long, more would join them, and he decided that—Fox hunting be damned—he was not going to subject himself to this sort of sordid behavior. Affecting a stagger, he made his way toward the opened doors to the garden, and muttered, "Need some fresh air. 'Fraid I'm going to cast up my accounts."

Once outside in the cool night air, he took in a deep breath. How many more evenings must I spend in this fashion? he wondered bleakly. And how long would it be before someone noticed that he did not partake as freely of the various entertainments as did the others? Certainly he had no intention of rutting publicly. And sooner or later, he was going to be caught dumping the contents of his glass into some handy receptacle.

The randy pursuits of Grimshaw, Coleman, and the others offended him, and he honestly did not know how much longer he could continue playing their game. And as for Sophy . . . He sighed. Deeply.

Toying with the notion of discovering if the Viscount was quite as drunk as he appeared to be, the Fox had watched Ives leave through narrowed eyes. Before he could put that plan into motion, Edward stumbled up to him where he stood with the others. Having greeted everyone, Edward sidled up to the Fox. Swaying in front of him, a witless grin on his face, he leaned forward, and whispered, "Can't talk here. Someone might hear. Wrote it down." His face almost touching the Fox's, he clumsily shoved a creased piece of paper into the other man's waistcoat pocket. "Thought it only sporting to give you fair warning."

Having delivered his ultimatum, Edward staggered off. A look of distaste on his face, the Fox waited a few minutes before making some excuse and left the room for the privacy of the hall.

What was the cretin up to now? Grimly he read Edward's note. There was no salutation, but it was signed.

Urgent that we talk privately.
And no tricks. I hold the winning hand. Meet me in Allenton's library to discuss things at three o'clock this morning. We should have privacy at that hour. Be there or it will go ill for you.

Frowning blackly, the Fox stared down at Edward's flamboyant signature. The simpleton obviously thought he was being very clever, but the very manner in which he was handling his attempted blackmail only pointed out how dangerous he had become. The Fox looked thoughtful. He would meet Edward, damn the fool! His expression pensive, he went back inside to join the others.

Sophy woke with a start, her heart pounding. Something had disturbed her sleep and she lay there listening intently. She stiffened as she heard the stealthy scratching at her door. In a flash, she was out of bed, and with shaking fingers lit the candle on her bed table. Calmed somewhat by the comforting flickering light of her candle, she cautiously approached the door and put her ear against the wood. Nothing. She looked to be certain that the chair was holding and it was then that she noticed the slip of folded paper on the floor at her feet. Putting the candle down, she picked up the note and read it.

Her first thought was that Edward had gone thoroughly mad if he thought that she was going to meet him anywhere at the ungodly hour of three in the morning. As she considered it though, she wondered if his idea wasn't plausible. When else could they meet with no one around? And she had to admit to a certain amount of curiosity. Perhaps he would tell her about the scheme Agnes Weatherby had alluded to this evening?

She glanced at the ormolu clock on the small mantel of the fireplace. It was nearly three now. She reread the note. Why was it urgent? she wondered. And why now? Why couldn't it wait until they returned to London? She didn't like the threat either. But remembering his vow to take Phoebe away from her, she considered the idea.

Still undecided, she slipped into her robe, a filmy thing of gossamer silk and lace, and thought about the situation. The house was quiet, and the hour was late. Everyone would have gone to bed or would be too drunk to do her any harm.

She looked at the note again. That was definitely Edward's handwriting and signature. She would recognize it anywhere. A chill went through her. But had he written it for someone else, thinking it a fine jest to lure her away from the safety of her room by sending her this note? Her lip curled. It would not be beyond him to accommodate Grimshaw or even Marquette, who was nearly as bad, but she did not want to believe that he had sunk quite that low.

There was a ring of truth about the note, and after several more seconds had passed and the hands of the clock had edged closer to the hour of three, she made up her mind. She would meet him.

The pistol weighing heavily in the dainty pocket of her robe, the candle in one hand, she cautiously eased the door open. The hall was bathed in darkness except for the circle of light from her candle. Silence met her ears.

Taking a deep breath, she sidled from her room, closing the door behind her with an audible click, and edged toward the staircase. Having reached the main floor, where only silence and pitch-black darkness greeted her, she was reassured that everyone had retired for the night. She found the library without effort, guided by the light spilling from the half-open door.

Stopping outside the library, she considered again the wisdom of what she was doing. Was it a trap? Would she enter the room and be fallen upon Grimshaw or one of the others with rape on his mind? Her fingers grasped the comforting handle of her pistol. Well, she wasn't the only one who would be surprised, she thought grimly.

She pushed the door wider, and called softly, "Uncle? Are you here?"

There was no answer and she frowned. Half-stepping into the doorway, she called again. "Edward? It is Sophy. Are you there?"

When only silence followed her words, she edged farther into the room, her every sense alert for danger. The room seemed deserted, the light coming from a single candle which sat guttering on the corner of a large table to her left. Most of the room was in shadows, but from her position in the doorway, she saw nothing to alarm her. Then she heard it. A groan. Coming from behind the table.

It came again, louder this time, the sound of someone in pain. Forgetting for the moment her own danger, Sophy rushed over to the table and stared in shock at the body of her uncle lying on the floor. He was moaning and attempting to sit up as he muttered, "My bloody head. Oh, my bloody head."

Contempt flashed across her face. He was drunk. That was her last thought. A stunning blow crashed into the back of her head, and she fell soundlessly to the floor almost at Edward's feet.

Edward stared at her crumpled shape, stupefied, and then at the dark figure who appeared out of the darkness. "I say," said Edward, perplexed, "what is Sophy doing here? And what happened to her? Never say she is foxed?"

The other man smiled. "No, my dear fellow, she is not foxed." He daintily stepped around Sophy's sprawled form and gently took the pistol from her limp hand. Leveling it at Edward, he murmured, "Her presence, however, was most necessary."

Edward frowned, too drunk and dazed from having suffered Sophy's fate a short while ago, to understand his own peril. "What are you doing with that pistol?" he asked idiotically.

The Fox smiled more broadly. Aiming at Edward's head, he said softly, "Simply tying up some loose ends, my friend." And calmly shot Edward between the eyes.

The sound of the shot echoed throughout the house, but moving with unruffled haste, the Fox made certain that Edward was truly dead, then placed the pistol back in Sophy's hand before swiftly leaving the library.

As he stepped into the hall, he could hear the noises of the roused house and smiled to himself. Right on time.

Carefully smoothing the lapel of his black-silk robe, he disappeared into the shadows at the end of the hall and waited coolly to melt into the crowd when they came tumbling down the stairs to find the results of his work. A yawn escaped him. Murder was such an arduous business.

Chapter Nine

The stealthy opening of Sophy's door brought Ives instantly awake, and, barely taking time to fling on a robe to cover his nakedness, he sprang across the room. The click of the closing of her door made him stiffen. Had someone entered her room?

The faint gleam of light peeping under his own door, told him that such was not the case. Someone was standing in the hallway right outside her door. When the light receded, disappearing in the direction of the main staircase, a terrible fear struck him. Was he too late? Had someone already entered her room and ravished her while he slept? Was it the *departure* of the villain which had roused him?

His face grim, Ives warily opened his door. The hall was in darkness except for the faint light drifting down the stairs. Concern for Sophy overrode his instinct to follow the predator, and Ives slipped into Sophy's room, calling softly, "Sophy, do not be fearful. It is Ives. I heard a sound. Is all well with you?"

Complete silence followed his words. He swiftly

crossed the room and discovered that Sophy's bed was empty. It had been *Sophy* descending the stairs?

Utterly perplexed and not a little worried, Ives stepped back into the hallway. What the devil was she up to? The unwelcome thought occurred to him that she might be meeting a lover. It did not seem likely, and he banished the idea almost as quickly as it had occurred. So what was she doing?

The light from her candle had already vanished when he reached the top of the stairs. He hesitated a moment, debating the wisdom of his next actions. The lady already believed the worst of him, and he doubted that if she discovered him creeping after her in the darkness that she would readily believe that he had only her best interests at heart.

Yet, he simply could not go back to bed and forget about her. There could be some innocent reason for her to be wandering about the house at this ungodly hour, although he could not imagine what it could be. If this were the case, she could find herself in a rather vulnerable position if she were to stumble across one of the drunken revelers.

He grimaced. It seemed he had no choice but to follow her and make certain that she was unmolested. He suddenly grinned. Except, of course, by himself.

Ives had almost reached the bottom of the staircase, when the sound of a shot exploded throughout the house. Leaping down the remaining stairs, he hesitated, trying to get his bearings in the blackness and attempting to get a fix on the direction from which the shot had come.

As the seconds passed and he stood there indecisively, he heard the sounds of the first doors opening and apprehensive exclamations from the floor above. He had to find Sophy.

After one false start, he caught a glimpse of the faint glow of light from beneath a door midway down one of the long halls that snaked through the house. Only moments ahead of the others, Ives plunged into the library to find a dazed Sophy half-standing, half-leaning on a table . . . a very dead Edward nearby.

The ugly hole in the center of Edward's forehead and the pistol clasped in Sophy's hand told the story, but Ives could not credit his eyes. Sophy, a cold-blooded murderess? Even enraged, she would not shoot a defenseless man. He would stake his life on it.

He smiled grimly. It looked as if he was going to have to do just that.

The progress of the other inhabitants cautiously coming down the stairs could be heard, and Ives knew he had only seconds in which to act. He snatched the pistol from Sophy's slack fingers and concealed it in the deep pocket of his brocade robe. Pulling Sophy into his arms, he shook her slightly and gave her a smart tap on the cheek.

"Look sharp, sweetheart! We haven't a moment to lose."

Sophy groaned and put a trembling hand to her head. She stared uncomprehendingly at Ives's dark, tense face. "My head," she muttered. "Someone struck me." She blinked. "Edward," she said weakly. "My uncle. He was here. Drunk."

"Well, he is dead now," Ives said coolly. "Very dead. And if we are to brush through the next few minutes without you ending up on the scaffold, you will have to trust me and hold your tongue. Let me do the talking."

"Dead!" Sophy gasped, horrified, as she gazed up at

him. "But he cannot be. He was alive, I tell you, only a moment ago. I spoke with him."

"Let me assure you, you will not be speaking with him again," he retorted bluntly, uneasily aware that they were on the point of being discovered. He swung her around and pointed to Edward's corpse. "As you can see, he is quite dead. And *you* were lying beside him with a pistol in your hand. Now keep your mouth shut and follow my lead."

At his words and the sight of her uncle's lifeless body, Sophy instinctively shrank back against Ives. "But what happened?" she asked, shocked and shaken by the scene. "Who shot him?" An urgent look on her lovely face, she said, "I swear to you that I did not!"

His features softened, and he gripped her shoulders reassuringly. "I never doubted it, but I am afraid, dear Butterfly, that someone arranged it to look as though *you* had." It was the only explanation that fit the scene, Ives thought grimly. Sophy had a very bad enemy.

There was no time for further speech. The door to the library was slowly pushed wide, and Allenton, followed by several of the other gentlemen garbed in hastily thrown-on robes and carrying candles, came into the room.

"Good gad!" exclaimed Allenton as he took in the scene before him. "Someone has shot poor Scoville. Murdered him."

All eyes went from Edward's body on the floor to Sophy firmly clasped in Ives's protective embrace. "It would appear so," Ives said levelly. "We heard the shot and found him like this."

"Together?" drawled Grimshaw, a decidedly unpleasant look on his saturnine features.

Ives nodded curtly.

"But how is it," inquired Lord Coleman, his eyes full of suspicion, "that you happened to arrive here ahead of all of us? Hmm?"

Ives grinned at him and dropped a kiss on the top of Sophy's head. "The lady," he said smoothly, "had a notion for a moonlight walk." His smile fading and his gaze boring into Coleman's, he added, "We were already downstairs when we heard the shot."

"Now why," asked Grimshaw, "do I have trouble believing you? It is just a little *too* convenient."

Sophy felt Ives stiffen. "Are you implying that I am lying?" he asked very softly.

Realizing his danger, Grimshaw said hastily, "Ah, no. Not at all." He cleared his throat and muttered, "But what was Edward doing here? And who killed him? And why?"

"Do you think it might have been a robbery?" asked Allenton, glancing nervously around the room.

"It could have been," Ives answered slowly. "But we have no idea what occurred. We are as puzzled as the rest of you."

Etienne Marquette, who had entered the room a few minutes behind Henry Dewhurst, said bluntly, "*Mon Dieu!* But this is all very odd. Lady Marlowe's animosity toward Edward was well-known, *oui*? Recently many of us have heard her threaten to kill him. Even this very evening there was that scene between them in the saloon. If I had to choose someone who might have murdered Scoville, my first choice would be, I regret to say, Lady Marlowe." He bent a hard eye on Ives. "Are you saying that Lady Marlowe has been with you the *entire* evening? That she has never been out of your sight?"

Ives's clasp tightened around Sophy when he felt her stir in what he suspected was vehement denial. "Not only with me," he replied levelly, "but hardly out of my arms."

Still half-stunned from the blow to the head and the shock of finding her uncle dead, Sophy had been following the exchanges with difficulty, but she already realized precisely how precarious her position was. If Ives had not reached her first, the scene that would have greeted the others would have, without question, condemned her to the scaffold. She would have been found swaying over the body, a pistol clasped in her hand. All her protests of innocence, of being struck on the head, would have been for naught. She would have hanged.

Gratitude for Ives's quick thinking flooded her, but as the minutes passed she perceived that in trying to shield her, he was digging a trap for both of them, a trap she greatly feared would prove impossible to escape.

Henry Dewhurst approached them. A peculiar expression on his face, he demanded, "Are you telling us that you are *lovers*?"

Dewhurst's incredulity was obvious, and Sophy felt a pang. In his fashion, Henry had been one of her most persistent suitors, and she knew that Ives's words hurt him. But without placing herself in grave danger and publicly proving Ives a liar, she could not refute any of the tale. Miserably she stared back at Henry

"Yes," she said in a low tone, "we are lovers."

She was aware that Ives relaxed slightly at her statement. Aware, too, that she had thoroughly ruined herself, she turned her head aside, unconsciously resting her cheek against Ives's broad chest. She supposed a ruined reputation was better than hanging, but at the moment that thought brought little comfort.

"Not only are we lovers," Ives added boldly, "but the lady and I intend to marry by special license, just as soon as I can arrange it."

Sophy gasped and stared up at him in horrified disbelief. Fierce protest hovered on her lips, but Ives silenced her by the simple expedient of kissing her, hard and possessively. Lifting his head a brief moment later, he surveyed the startled gentlemen, and murmured, "Our walk in the moonlight was to celebrate our decision to marry."

"I see," said Dewhurst tightly, his hands clenched into fists at his sides. "If that is the case, even under the sad circumstances, I suppose that congratulations are in order."

"Most unusual," murmured Lord Coleman, who looked unconvinced by Ives's story. "Man dead on the floor. No time to be thinking of congratulations."

Since Ives held firm to his story, and no one could contradict his words, attention turned to Edward's corpse. Eyeing the body uncomfortably, Allenton said, "The authorities must be notified. Sir John Matthews is a neighbor and a justice of the peace. He will know what to do."

He looked around at the others, and muttered, "It is difficult to believe, but someone murdered Scoville, perhaps even someone in this house. We are all going to be under suspicion, and it is going to be damned unpleasant until the guilty party is discovered. In the meantime, I suggest that the library be locked and we retire to our rooms to dress. I shall wake the servants and have one of my men ride to Sir John's place." He sighed. "There will be no more sleep tonight for any of us."

Everyone agreed, and, after watching him lock the door to the library, they all returned upstairs to their various rooms. Ives kept a firm hand on Sophy's arm, and when she would have sought out her own room, he gently but inexorably guided her into his chamber.

The door had hardly shut behind him when Sophy freed herself from his grasp and swung round to face him. "I cannot marry you!" she said forcefully. "Whatever made you say such an outrageous thing?" She frowned. "I understand why you had to indicate that we were lovers, but to declare that we are to wed! Are you mad?"

Despite the lateness of the hour and the terrible events of the evening, Ives thought that she had never looked lovelier. It was true that there were purple smudges under her eyes and that her hair tumbled wildly in great golden masses around her shoulders, but those signs of her ordeal only increased her ethereal beauty. Her features were pale and strained, her eyes huge as she stared at him in the dancing candlelight, increasing her look of vulnerability, and Ives was suddenly aware that he would move heaven and earth to see that she never had to undergo a night like this one again. He would keep his little golden butterfly safe from harm, if she would allow it. And from the expression on her face, he thought ruefully, it appeared that he was going to have a fight on his hands.

Smiling faintly, he murmured, "It is true that I am mad, sweetheart. Quite mad. For you."

Sophy glared at him, her hands on her hips. "Will you cease? This is no time for frivolity. What are we going to do?"

"What we are going to do, dear heart," Ives said slowly and determinedly, "is precisely as I told the others. I will obtain a special license and we shall marry."

"I will not marry you!" Sophy said through gritted teeth, her earlier gratitude evaporating, the memory of his deplorable actions during the preceding several hours rushing to the fore.

The man had recently shown himself to be a drunken, hardened rake, every bit as bad as Simon had been. And he thought she would *marry* him?

It was common knowledge, too, that he was hanging out for a wife simply to sire an heir. She had been married once for that reason and had no intention of finding herself in that deplorable position again.

Something else had been niggling at the back of her mind, and, scowling, she asked suddenly, "How was it that you arrived so timely to the library?"

Ives shrugged. "I heard you leave your room. I followed you."

"You followed me!" exclaimed Sophy, perplexed. "Why?"

"Because I was afraid that you might come to harm wandering about unprotected in a place filled with the wickedest sort of rascals I have ever seen in my life," he said simply.

Her confusion evident, Sophy stared back at him. "You were trying to guard me?" she asked incredulously.

A crooked smile curved his mouth and he bowed. "That was my intention."

Sophy put a hand to her head and turned away from him. "I do not understand you," she muttered. "I do not understand why you are here or why you act one way and then another, or why you came so readily to my defense this evening. I do not know why Edward was murdered, nor why someone tried to implicate me in his death. I do not understand any of it."

Gently Ives pulled her to him. His warm, broad body at her back, her arms wrapped around her and his chin resting on the top of her head, he murmured, "There is only one thing that you need to understand right now; I will never allow you to come to harm, and I will never do anything to make you hate me." He hesitated, then asked, "Sophy, why were you in the library?"

Dully she returned, "Edward sent me a note requesting that I meet him there." She frowned. "It was an odd sort of note, even for him. He threatened me and told me not to play any tricks, as if I would!"

"Was it signed?"

"Yes. I would recognize Edward's signature anywhere."

"Do you still have the note?" he asked sharply.

She nodded. "It is in my room, on my dressing table."

"When you go back to your room, I will go with you. I want that note."

She stiffened, and would have turned around except that Ives held her where she was. "Do you think the note is important?"

"Very. I suspect that the note was originally intended for the murderer and that he used it to lure you downstairs to the library."

Sophy shuddered. "Someone must hate me very much."

"I doubt it, sweetheart," Ives said softly. "I think our murderer was simply looking for a handy scapegoat, and you were available. Your feelings about your uncle were well-known. Do not worry about it. I have every intention of keeping you safe. And," he added in a hard voice, "finding out who put my future wife's very pretty neck in danger."

"*Must* we marry?" she asked in a small voice, the cold reality of her situation sinking in.

Ives sighed. "I am afraid so, sweetheart. Your reputation will be in shreds after tonight. You have a dangerous enemy, one I do not want you to fight alone. I can protect you far better as my wife than if you were merely a lady I was courting."

Sophy stirred in his embrace and turned around to stare up into his dark, brigand's face. "Have you been courting me?" she asked uncertainly.

He smiled gently. "To the best of my poor ability."

"I thought you wanted me to be your mistress," she returned honestly.

"That, too," he answered wryly. He looked at her, the expression in his devil green eyes hard to define. "I was willing to take whatever you were willing to give me."

With trembling fingers she brushed the lapel of his robe. "Ives . . . my first marriage was . . . terrible . . . and when Simon died, I swore that no man would have me at his mercy again."

"You would rather hang than marry me?" he asked bluntly, his expression enigmatic.

Sophy hesitated. "I do not look forward to death any more eagerly than the next person, but there are some things that are *un*endurable."

"And you think that marriage to me will be unendurable?" he demanded.

She searched his craggy features, her heart aching. Just a few weeks ago she could have answered that question with a resounding no, but because of his actions lately, she was no longer certain. She had, after all, seen him half-drunk and ogling one of the housemaids just the other night.

When she remained silent, Ives's lips thinned and he said flatly, "You really do not have any choice. You *will* marry me, else you are ruined. And then there is the problem of Edward's death. And who murdered him. At the moment, my story has carried the day, but if you spurn me, if we do *not* marry, don't you think that suspicions are going to be roused? Don't you think that people are going to wonder why we did not marry?"

He shook her slightly. "You little fool! I am your only hope to brush through this ugly affair with a minimum of scandal. Marry me, and I can protect you. Refuse me, and you leave yourself vulnerable to the worst sort of ignominy."

Gently he added, "People might speculate that I lied and claimed you as my lover to protect you, but no one is going to believe that I married you for that reason."

Sophy looked away. Everything he said was true. Her reputation was in shreds, had already suffered simply by being in this very house, and there was no possibility that the inhabitants would keep their mouths shut about Ives's declaration that they were lovers. All of London would know. She shuddered.

It was not for herself that she dreaded the gossip and innuendo, but she knew her reputation would reflect on both Marcus and Phoebe. They had weathered the storm of Simon's death, but could they weather this one as well?

No matter what she did, marry Ives or not, there was going to be rampant speculation and gossip about Edward's death. But if she were to marry Ives, there was no denying that much of the scandal would be blunted. She would be the wife of an aristocrat with powerful connections, the bride of a man respected and liked by others of high rank and standing. Few people would be willing to risk offending Harrington. As his wife, that mantle of protection would extend to her and also to Marcus and Phoebe. They would be safe from the majority of the stigma.

But if she and Ives parted, it would open the door for even more ugly gossip and scandal. And not just for herself. Marcus and Phoebe would share in the shame.

Indecision churning in her breast, she glanced up at him. "Why are you willing to marry me?" she asked quietly, her lovely eyes fixed intently on his face.

His mouth twisted. "Because I need a wife. An heir." He drew her nearer. "And quite frankly, my dear, because I find you utterly irresistible."

He kissed her. A long, lingering kiss, his lips warm and compelling, his hunger kept fiercely leashed.

Sophy's mouth quivered beneath his. Uncertainty, fear, and another stronger, more elemental emotion sprang cautiously to life within her. His embrace awakened all her old demons, Simon's brutal kisses never far from her mind. And yet with Ives she was aware of a vast difference, a difference she could not explain or understand, but it was there and it comforted her.

Conscious of the fragile ground on which he trod, Ives did not force the pace, but with great reluctance, eventually broke the embrace and set her slightly away from him. "Well?" he inquired coolly. "Are you going to marry me?"

Sophy stared blindly at the open V of his robe, trying to sort through all the contradictory emotions roiling within her. "Yes," she said finally. "I do not see that I have any choice in the matter."

"I could have wished for a trifle more enthusiasm," Ives said dryly, "but I see that I shall have to content myself with simply the knowledge that you have agreed to be my wife."

Turning away from her, he added briskly, "And now I suppose we should dress and see about meeting with the others."

In a daze, Sophy allowed Ives to escort her to her room and handed the note over to him. What had happened seemed almost incomprehensible to her, and for several minutes after he had left, she stood in the center of the room unable to think clearly. Edward was dead. Murdered! And she was going to marry Ives Harrington!

His expression thoughtful, the Fox climbed the stairs with everyone else. His plan had not gone as he envisioned, and he was furious. Murderously so. The look he flashed Ives before he continued on down the hall to his own room was *not* kind.

In the safety of his room, he shed his robe and quickly dressed, his mind on the events of the evening. Everything had gone just as he had planned until that bastard Harrington had shown up. Now, because of Harrington's unwarranted intervention, there was going to be a lot of speculation about who had murdered Edward. And why.

With Sophy out of the picture, he was still certain that there was nothing to point to him; but he was anxious—anxious and infuriated as he had not been since he had sent Harrington's relatives to the bottom of the sea. Though he had been scrupulously careful tonight, there was always the possibility that he had overlooked some tiny element, that someone had seen some trifling event, remembered something that would tie him to Edward's murder. His face darkened. Damn Harrington to hell!

Even now he experienced a thrill of fright as he remembered his shock at the sight of Ives's broad form appearing so unexpectedly out of the darkness. A few seconds earlier and he might have been caught. As it was, he had barely stepped out of the room and into the concealing shadows when Ives had come striding down the hall. He frowned. The fellow was proving to be quite meddlesome.

In the meantime, however, he had other things to think about. Such as providing another convenient scapegoat, even if only temporarily. Frowning, he paced his room seeking some way to find an additional measure of safety from tonight's debacle. Recalling that someone had mentioned robbery, a glimmer of an idea occurred to him. A robbery. He smiled. Of course. But his satisfaction vanished almost immediately and his smile faded as another thought came to him. A robbery would solve one difficulty, he admitted sourly, but there was still the infuriating problem of Harrington.

Harrington's coming onto the scene troubled him in many ways. He was suspicious of the man already and for him to have thwarted a perfect solution to a vexing problem . . .

Did the man know something? Suspect something? Had it just been luck that Harrington had followed Sophy? From his concealment in the shadows, it was obvious that Harrington had been trailing Sophy without her knowledge. Why? The obvious conclusion occurred to him, and his lips thinned.

To think he had nearly been caught because of another man's lust for a woman. Not that Sophy was not worthy of such lust, but the Fox, while having all the normal appetites of the flesh in abundance, never let his carnal inclinations interfere with business. Taking care of Edward and framing Sophy had been strictly business.

Hearing the sounds of the others gathering in the hall, he put the problem from him for the time being and went out to join everybody else. It was several hours later before he had time to consider the problem of Ives Harrington and the possible implications of his marriage to Sophy.

Sir John Matthews had been and gone after pronouncing his shock at the murder of Baron Scoville and promising to notify the proper authorities. While he said nothing himself, the Fox had seen to it that robbery was touted as a motive for the shameful deed. Edward's body had been removed.

The ladies, of course, now knew of the murder and were frightened by the news of such a terrible event occurring while they had slept such a short distance away. Lady Allenton had been aghast. Agnes Weatherby had fainted when the news of her lover's murder had been broken to her.

But none of that bothered the Fox. Beyond his concern about Ives Harrington, the whereabouts of Edward's note had taken on paramount importance in his mind, and he cursed Harrington again. If all had gone well, he had planned during the ensuing furor to nip up to Sophy's room and retrieve Edward's note, but now . . . His lips thinned into a rigid, ugly line. Now that damned note might prove dangerous to him.

A thought occurred to him, and he relaxed slightly. The existence of the note, he suddenly realized, was probably not going to come to light. Because of Harrington, Sophy was safely out of it and it was highly unlikely that she would admit to having a reason to meet Edward in the library. But Sophy knew of the note. And no doubt, Harrington.

All his problems, he thought grimly, seemed to go back to Harrington. He did not trust the man, did not trust his sudden and inexplicable conversion to vice-prone pursuits, did not trust his instant friendship with Meade; and especially did not trust him since Meade seemed to have conveniently come across such interesting news, if Meade's drunken hints could be believed. In the meantime, the Fox had much to consider and plan.

Ives, too, had much to plan and consider, not the least of which was his nuptials. After Sir John had given his pronouncements and departed, Ives climbed the stairs and knocked on Sophy's door.

When he entered her room, Sophy was dressed and packed, her valise resting on the bed. Her features pale and set, she asked, "May we leave?"

Ives nodded. "Yes. I have given Sir John our direction and he saw no point in our remaining here. I believe that several other of the guests are going to be leaving shortly also."

Sophy glanced away. "And our marriage. You are still determined upon it?"

He approached her and, taking one of her cold little hands in his, dropped a warm kiss upon it. "I was never more determined about anything in my life, sweetheart."

She flashed him a look. "You may come to regret it," she warned. "I am not a malleable creature, nor one noted for her docility."

Ives grinned, his devil green eyes dancing. "Which should only make our life together most interesting, don't you agree?"

Chapter Ten

❧

*I*ves moved with military precision and a little more than twenty-four hours later on that Monday, May 22, 1809, at one o'clock in the afternoon, with only her siblings and Anne Richmond to support her, Sophy found herself becoming his wife.

Ives's guests were equally sparse. His godfather, the Duke of Roxbury, and Percival Forrest had been in attendance at the brief ceremony, as well as Lady Beckworth, a pleasant-looking woman some sixty years of age whom Ives introduced as his aunt.

Sophy moved through the ceremony in a fog, aware and yet not aware of what was going on around her. As she entered the small, private chapel Ives had chosen for their wedding, she was vaguely conscious of the fact that someone had seen to it that there were two enormous baskets of yellow roses and white lilies flanking the area where they would say their vows. At the last moment, just before she had gone down the aisle to stand by Ives, a laughing Phoebe had thrust a small bouquet of rosebuds into her hands. And then she was aware of nothing but

Ives himself. Ives, the tall stranger with the brigand's smile who would become her husband.

As she joined him in front of the official who would marry them, her eyes met his and she could not look away from that intent green gaze. They stared at each other, something fierce and powerful springing to life in Ives's green eyes that sent a shudder of half panic, half delight through her. She might have run then, but as if sensing her intentions, Ives reached out and possessively covered her hands with one of his. Glancing down at his strong hand lying on hers, a bubble of hysterical laughter rose up through her. There was no need of marriage vows—he had already laid claim to her.

And then it was over, and Ives was taking her into his arms and kissing her. His mouth, warm and mesmerizing, lingered for a long, sweet moment on hers; then he was lifting his head and smiling down at her dazed, flushed features. Lightly caressing her bottom lip with one finger, he said for her ears alone, "I think, madame wife, that we shall deal very well together. Very well, indeed."

Almost immediately, everyone retired to the Grayson town house, where a small buffet was laid out for the delectation of the wedding party. Sophy was certain the food was delicious, but she was too stunned and, quite frankly, too nervous to eat. She was Ives's wife!

Uneasily she looked across the room to where Ives stood surrounded by the gentlemen, laughing at something Marcus had said. She was pleased that Marcus and Phoebe had taken the stunning news of Edward's death and her immediate marriage to Ives so well. Anne had taken the news with almost as much aplomb as the others, for she no longer had to fear Edward's advances.

Lady Beckworth bustled up to her just then, diverting

her attention. Forcing a smile, Sophy murmured, "This must all seem very strange to you."

Barbara Beckworth smiled and shook her head. "No, my dear, it does not. Ives was never one to do the expected."

Sophy nodded, trying to think of something else to say. She knew little of the Beckworths, had not even known that Ives had any other relatives until this afternoon. Only this morning, Ives had explained that his aunt was a respectable widow, a doting grandmother, who did not go out in society very much anymore.

Fortunately for him, he had said with a twinkle, his aunt had been visiting in London with an old friend and had been quite thrilled to be invited to their wedding. She had also agreed, he had gone on smoothly, to stay at the Grayson house and chaperone the younger members of the family while he and Sophy enjoyed a few days of privacy at his country estate, Harrington Chase, before returning to London. Having cut the ground away beneath her feet and left her with no room in which to argue, Sophy had been forced to agree with his plans. Sophy had met Lady Beckworth and discovered for herself that she was as practical as she was kindhearted and grudgingly concluded that the lady was indeed capable of overseeing the household at Berkeley Square for a few days.

Apparently not expecting any reply, Lady Beckworth went on comfortably, "I thought that I was quite used to his fits and starts, but I must confess that this sudden marriage to *you* has surprised me."

Sophy stiffened. "My reputation, you mean?" she asked in a tight little voice.

Lady Beckworth looked shocked. "Oh, no! Of course, I have heard the gossip . . . and there is no denying that

Lord Marlowe was a well-known—But that was not what
I was referring to," she added hastily. She hesitated, an
uncertain expression crossing her plump features. "It
probably is not important," she finally said, "but you *do*
know about his older brother, Robert?"

"His brother?" Sophy exclaimed, startled. "I never
even knew about *you* until today."

"Oh, dear! Me and my prattling tongue. Ives will be
most vexed with me," Lady Beckworth said, looking
guilty.

"Why should he be? I am married to him. As his wife,
it is only right that I know about his family," Sophy returned reasonably, despite the sudden knot in her chest.
"What is there about the mention of his brother that
should make him angry?"

Lady Beckworth sighed heavily. "I am not surprised
that he has said nothing to you. It was so very tragic.
Robert committed suicide. Years ago," she said confidingly, "before you were even born. He was much older
than Ives, and Ives simply idolized him. He took Robert's
death hard. He swore to be avenged on the woman who
had caused it. The family was quite distressed by his
thirst for revenge. After all," she added artlessly, "it was
not *her* fault that Robert took her rejection of him so trag-
ically. Who could have guessed that he would hang himself on her wedding day?" She gave a delicate shudder.
"So terrible for Ives. He found him, you know. Absolutely shattered the boy."

Sophy's heart ached for Ives's tragedy, but she was
puzzled why he would be angry with his aunt for mentioning his brother's suicide. Was he ashamed of the manner of Robert's death?

"I see," murmured Sophy, not really seeing at all. "It must have been quite painful for him."

Lady Beckworth nodded vigorously. "Oh, it was. After his mother had deserted the family—she ran away with a military man—when Ives was a mere boy," she said candidly, apparently seeing nothing wrong in revealing the family skeletons to a new bride. "Left on their own, the three of them—Ives, Robert, and his father—were very close. My dear brother never looked at another woman. His heart was quite broken. In their own way each one of them was very bitter and wounded by Joan's desertion. Quite frankly, I was surprised when Robert fell for—"

She stopped and laughed deprecatingly. "My wretched tongue! My children are always pleading with me to think before I speak, but I am afraid that their pleas are useless. I am," she admitted, almost with pride, "perfectly incapable of minding my tongue. I always have been."

Taken aback by Lady Beckworth's indiscreet volubility, Sophy could only smile weakly. She was fascinated by this glimpse into Ives's early life, but she suspected that her new husband would prefer to reveal any family scandal to her himself.

Sophy would have given much to have heard more, but even if his aunt was not conscious of treading carelessly over sensitive subjects, she was. Somewhat hastily, she said, "Will you excuse me? I simply *must* speak to the butler."

Lady Beckworth smiled complacently. "You run along, my dear. I am sure that you are quite rushed. Now that we are family, we shall have other times for cozy conversations."

"Yes, of course," Sophy muttered as she hurried off,

telling herself that cozy conversation with Lady Beckworth was a fate to be avoided at all costs.

Ives had watched Sophy's conversing with his aunt,
and her hurried exit. A little frown creased his forehead.
Introducing Sophy to his aunt had been a calculated risk
but one he felt he had no choice in running. He needed a
respectable woman to stay with Marcus, Phoebe, and
Anne at the Grayson town house during the first few days
of his marriage.

He was not an unreasonable man. He was quite fond of
Marcus, Phoebe, and Anne, and had every intention of
keeping Sophy's little family together. But dash it all! He
was *not* going to start his married life with Marcus,
Phoebe, and Anne underfoot! Things were fragile enough
between him and Sophy as it was and he had decided that
a few days spent, just the two of them, at Harrington
Chase would allow them a little breathing room before
they plunged into the complications of merging their two
households. He wanted, nay, *needed* some time alone
with his reluctant bride.

Roxbury murmured something to him at that moment
and he had no time to speculate further on what embarrassing facts his aunt might have cheerfully dropped into
Sophy's ear. By the time they had bidden their wedding
guests good-bye, installed Lady Beckworth in the
Grayson town house, and were finally on their way to
Harrington Chase, Ives had completely forgotten the incident.

At present the newlyweds were comfortably settled in
Ives's well-sprung coach and were bowling along the
road several miles from London on their way to Harrington Chase situated near the county town of Chelmsford in

Essex. Ashby and Sophy's personal maid, Peggy, along with a few trunks, had been sent ahead.

As they had left London, Sophy kept up a lively monologue, chattering gaily about the wedding and the guests and how kind it had been of Lady Beckworth to agree to stay at the Grayson town house for a few days. It was obvious that she was nervous and Ives decided to let her prattle on, leaning comfortably back against the maroon velvet squabs of the coach and adding a comment now and then when she seemed to run out of steam.

Sophy *was* nervous. Memories of Simon's brutal rape in a coach such as this one within hours of their marriage filled her mind with the most terrifying images. She sat bolt upright as far from Ives as she could get, her gaze flickering restlessly about and certainly never straying in the direction of her very new, very large husband. She wished desperately that she still had her pistol. What she said she had no idea, the compulsion to keep talking driving her to utter the most inane comments.

Ives let her run on for quite some time, thinking eventually she would wind down; but when it became apparent that was not going to happen, he leaned across the narrow space that separated them, and said quietly, "Sophy, stop it. I do not know what you fear, but let me reassure you I have no intention of falling upon you like a ravening beast."

She jumped at his touch, but hearing his measured tones and seeing his expression, some of her nervousness disappeared. Risking a glance in his direction, she said softly, "You must think me very silly."

In the fading light he smiled. "No. I think that you are adorable."

Sophy blushed. Simon had never paid her any compliments, and she was not quite certain how to react. Casting about for a safe subject, she said, "Tell me about Harrington Chase."

He shrugged. "There is not much to tell. It is an Elizabethan manor house that has been in my family for many generations. The park that surrounds it is noted for its beauty. I hope that you will like it."

"Did you grow up there?" she asked curiously.

Ives shook his head. "No. My father was the second son, and I grew up at the vicarage."

A teasing smile crossed Sophy's face. "Never tell me you are the son of a *vicar*?"

Ives laughed and proceeded to change the subject, distracting her with stories of his days in the cavalry. It was not many hours later that the coach slowed and began to travel down the smooth carriageway leading to Harrington Chase.

Sophy had relaxed with Ives as the time had passed and he had made no overt moves toward her. At least, she told herself, she would not suffer the degrading experience of having her second marriage consummated on the seat of a coach! But as they neared their destination, she could feel her tension increase.

Simon's lovemaking had filled her with revulsion, and while there was little about Ives that bore a resemblance to her first husband, she could not help being uneasy about the coming hours. She swallowed painfully, aware of the dampness on her hands and the churning in her stomach. In a short time, Ives would come to her and make her his wife in the fullest sense of the word, and she was dreading it. Dear God, please, don't let it be *too* awful.

Despite the lateness of the hour, the house was ablaze

with light, but Sophy had little time for first impressions. Ives hustled her out of the coach and escorted her up the broad steps and into the house. They were met by a smiling butler and an efficient-looking lady of indeterminate age who was introduced as the housekeeper, Mrs. Chandler. A moment later, Ives still at her elbow, Sophy was whisked up the stairs and into her suite of rooms.

His arm resting on the pretty pink-marble fireplace mantel, Ives watched her as she wandered around the spacious sitting room adjoining her bedchamber. Her traveling gown just happened to be in a deep shade of rose, and it complemented the rose-and-cream furnishings of the room. Standing in the middle of the lovely Aubusson carpet, woven in the same shades, Sophy looked over at him, her hands clasped tightly in front of her.

"It is a very nice room," she said politely, her eyes everywhere but on him, her tenseness almost palpable.

"Yes, it is," Ives agreed, a teasing glint in his eyes. "And you will find that it is a very nice house and that you have a very nice bedroom, too. The morning room is considered very nice also."

She glanced at him. "Are you mocking me?" she asked suspiciously.

He smiled, a slow, warm smile that did odd things to her heart. "Perhaps a trifle, sweetheart."

Crossing to her, he took one of her hands and dropped a kiss on the back of it. Steadily meeting her gaze, he said quietly, "Sophy, I know that your first husband was a brute. I am not, despite what you may have observed lately, the same sort of man. You have nothing to fear from me. I only want you to be happy."

She regarded him warily. "And if I told you," she finally said, "that the only thing that would make me happy would be to sleep alone in my own bed, you would heed my words?"

He sighed. "Don't be a fool, my dear. I intend for you to be my wife in every sense of the word." Again he hesitated, his eyes searching hers. Reluctantly he said, "Considering the circumstances surrounding our marriage, I would understand if you wished for a few days before I come to your bed."

Sophy gaped at him, hardly daring to believe what she was hearing, but he seemed sincere. She almost fell on his neck with gratitude, but then she reminded herself that it was only a few days' grace, not forever.

She had always faced her demons head-on, and there was no use postponing the evil moment. She would just as soon know how bad it was going to be as soon as possible. She turned away and muttered, "No. I will not put you off." With paralyzing honesty, she added, "I would prefer to get it over with."

Ives burst out laughing, his green eyes dancing with genuine amusement. "Oh, sweetheart! 'Get it over with'? Could you not garner a bit more enthusiasm?"

Ruffled, Sophy glared at him. "I never found the act pleasurable. I believe that it is much overrated," she admitted gruffly, her cheeks stinging. "S-simon claimed that I was not very good, that he would as soon lie with a board as with me."

His expression gentle, Ives pulled her into his arms. "I am not Simon, Sophy." He kissed her sweetly, his mouth soft and coaxing.

Helplessly Sophy felt herself responding, a galaxy of bewildering sensations and emotions exploding through her. When he finally lifted his mouth from hers, her lips unconsciously clung to his, and there was a dazed look in her eyes.

"You are no board, my dear," he said thickly. "But even if you were, I think perhaps that Simon was a very poor carpenter."

Regretfully, he put her from him and, pushing her toward the door which led to her bedchamber, murmured, "Now go. Your maid awaits you. I shall have a tray prepared for us and join you shortly."

Sophy obeyed him, walking like a zombie through the doorway and into her bedchamber. Greeted by a shyly smiling Peggy, with great difficulty Sophy forced herself to concentrate on the present and not the incredible sweetness of Ives's kiss.

In the large dressing room, just off the bedroom, a bath had been prepared for her. A filmy gown and a gossamer silk robe lay across one of a pair of ivory-damask-covered chairs. Only half aware of what was happening, she allowed Peggy to help bathe and perfume her, the spicy scent of carnations and lilies filling the air. After slipping into the amber-hued gown and bronze-colored robe, she loosed her hair from its crown of curls and Peggy brushed until it shone like newly minted gold in the candlelight. With a whispered wish for her mistress's happiness, the maid disappeared.

Seated before the satinwood dressing table, Sophy stared blindly into the mirror, her mind in chaos. I am married, she thought dazedly. To Ives.

As if she had conjured him up, his image suddenly appeared in the mirror. He was wearing a heavy, deep purple silk robe, loosely belted at the waist, and Sophy was painfully conscious that he was naked beneath it.

For a long time they regarded each other in the mirror,

then Ives smiled crookedly, and murmured, "Well, sweetheart? Are you ready to 'get it over with'?"

She nodded, moving like a dreamer when Ives helped her from the stool, obligingly allowing him to guide her into her bedchamber.

It was a lovely room, with soaring ceilings and gleaming crystal chandeliers; a bank of tall, wide windows were against one wall. Another Aubusson carpet in the same shades of rose, cream, and green lay on the floor. The imposing canopied bed was draped in a beautiful shade of palest turquoise silk. Despite the season, a small fire leaped merrily on the hearth of a fireplace with a green-marble mantel. Several chairs and a sofa upholstered in the same pale turquoise silk as the bed were arranged cozily around the fireplace. There were delicate satinwood tables scattered about the grand room, and silver candelabras had been placed here and there, the soft glow of candlelight enhancing the beauty of their surroundings.

But the sight of such elegance did not still the sudden terror in Sophy's breast, and, almost desperately, she seized upon the mundane sight of a silver tray heaped with food and drink.

"Oh! How wonderful! Food. I am simply starved!" she said breathlessly, hurrying over to the table where the tray was situated.

His eyes on her slender form, Ives murmured, "Yes, so am I. Absolutely famished."

She flashed him a meaningless smile and busily piled her plate with sliver-thin slices of roast chicken and veal, tiny buttered spring potatoes and peas, stewed mushrooms, and potted lamprey. There was also an array of sweets and biscuits, as well as wine, brandy, and she allowed Ives to pour her a glass of sherry.

They ate in front of the fireplace, Sophy's fears and nervousness having returned unabated. It was not an *un*comfortable meal, but both of them were almost relieved when the last morsel had been consumed, the last sip of wine swallowed, and the plates and glasses placed on the table.

Sitting like a little girl, her back ramrod straight, her knees pressed tightly together, and her hands folded in her lap, Sophy stared blankly at the fire.

Seated in a chair across from her, Ives sighed, his thoughts of Lord Marlowe vicious. He considered again the idea of allowing her a few days in which to become more resigned to their marriage—and him in her bed—but finally discarded the idea. He had offered her that option and she had declined it. And he was not *that* altruistic. He wanted her. She was his wife.

Standing up, Ives approached her. Putting out a hand, he said, "Bed, sweetheart?"

Sophy jumped and stared up at him resignedly. Cursing Simon a thousand times, he gently pulled her to her feet. His hands moving slowly to her shoulders, he kissed her, softly and warmly.

"I am not," he said against her quivering mouth, "Simon. Will you please trust me to bring us both pleasure?"

Sophy bent her head, her curls tickling his chin. "Why should I trust you?" she asked painfully.

Ives sighed. "I can offer you no reason, sweetheart. But I would ask you this—have I ever done anything to hurt you so far?"

Sophy shook her head, realizing with astonishment

that it was rather enjoyable standing here in his arms, his
warm, broad body pressed next to hers, his breath gently
stirring the curls at the nape of her neck. When he suddenly bent and kissed her there, a shiver that had nothing
to do with fear snaked down her spine. His hands moved
over her slowly, kneading her stiff shoulders and stroking
her back, and as the minutes passed and he did nothing
more than lightly explore her shoulders and back, some
of her tenseness lessened.

Resigned to the consummation of their marriage,
Sophy offered no objection when Ives's lips found hers
once more, and he began to kiss her. There was nothing
brutal or displeasing about his kiss, his mouth sliding
softly, teasingly over hers, his tongue tantalizing her as it
dipped and then receded.

An odd sensation began to build within her, a feeling
she had never experienced before; sun-heated wine
seemed to flow in her veins, and, low in her belly, a
shockingly sweet fire seemed to have burst into being.
She was distinctly startled to discover that she found
nothing but pleasure in his embrace and that she wanted
to touch him, to run her hands over him as he was doing
to her.

She had never willingly embraced Simon, and, tentatively, she put her arms around Ives, finding that she liked
the feel of his hard muscles beneath her hands, liked her
breasts nudging his chest. Instinctively she pressed
closer, marveling at the solid width of him and the enormous, seductive heat radiating from his big body.

Taking her uncertain embrace as encouragement, Ives
allowed a little of his tightly leashed hunger to show, his
mouth hardening with passion, his hands cupping her
bottom, pulling her against his aching, swollen shaft.

She did not move away from him, but he felt a slight tension invade her body, felt the resistance that had not been there a moment ago. Suppressing a groan, wondering how he was going to survive the night, he moved his hands back to her shoulders and, reluctantly lifting his mouth from hers, stared down into her wary features.

"I want you, Sophy," he said huskily. "I will not always be able to be gentle with you. I will try to be, but there is such a hunger within me that I fear once unleashed . . ." He swallowed, his hands tightening on her slender shoulders. "Do you understand me?"

Sophy searched his taut, dark features. He would not, she suddenly realized, deliberately inflict pain on her, but it was clear that he had his limits. Her eyes never leaving his, she said pitifully, "Please, just do not hurt me."

"Never, sweetheart. Never," he muttered, and pulled her into his arms once more.

There was no going back for either of them after that, and in her heart, Sophy admitted that she would not have turned aside if she could have. She wanted the unexpected magic he wove around them to continue. She desperately needed to find out if all men were as brutal as her first husband.

Ives kissed her a long time, standing there before the fire, his hands almost floating over her body, his touch so light, so gentle that Sophy had no cause to fear him. His kisses were warm and coaxing, his mouth seductively sipping at hers, his teeth, oh so teasingly nibbling at her soft bottom lip. Like a bee seeking honey, Sophy unconsciously pressed closer, her back arching as his warm hand slid downward to her hips, her breasts full and aching as they pushed against his broad chest. His lips continued to torment her, his tongue teasing hers, just as his touch teased her, the slow brush of his fingers up and down her spine making her tingle and yearn for more.

When one of his hands suddenly cupped her breast and his thumb moving burningly across her nipple, she gasped and unconsciously surged closer, almost begging him to continue his caress. She felt the smile on his lips and, stunning both of them, bit him in frustration.

His hand tightened around her breast and against her mouth, he muttered, "Be careful, sweetheart. I give as good as I get."

Sophy trembled but not with fear, and, daringly, her tongue slipped into his mouth. Oh, but he tasted sweet. And dangerous. And so *very* exciting.

A shudder went through her. This was sorcery, she thought giddily, emotions she had hardly dreamed of springing up through her. Sorcery and black magic. As her tongue probed and slid along his, nothing had ever prepared her for the pleasure, the intensely primitive sensations such actions could give, and another, stronger shudder shook her. Ives's groan, the rapid increase of his breathing, and the increasingly frantic motions of his hands as they roamed over her revealed that he, too, shared in this dark sorcery. That the emotions roiling within her were raging within him. It was thrilling knowledge.

When Ives suddenly crushed her to him, and his tongue boldly followed hers back into her mouth, Sophy was stunned at the burst of pleasure that exploded deep within her. His erotic probings inflamed her further, pulling her deeper into the spell that had overtaken them.

She was hardly aware that he had slipped her robe off and dragged her silken gown down to free one breast, hardly aware that it was her naked flesh his clever fingers shaped and caressed. She only knew that she had never felt anything like it before in her life, and that she wanted it to continue.

Slowly, tenderly, Ives lured her deeper into desire, his hands and mouth moving voluptuously over her, showing her that there was indeed much pleasure to be gained by another's touch. Even when he carefully lowered her to the rug before the fire and tossed aside his robe, she barely protested, too enthralled by all that she was feeling.

Not even when his lips left hers and slid tormentingly down to her breast did she object. The hot, sweet sensation of his mouth closing over her breast made her sigh and arch up against his nuzzling lips. As he pulled and nibbled on her swollen nipple, pure heat streaked from her breast to her womb, and she became aware of an ache between her thighs, an ache that seemed to encompass her entire body, leaving her conscious of nothing *but* the ache and the increasing need to assuage it.

Ah, Jesu, but she was sweet, Ives thought fleetingly, his own passion inflaming him almost to the point of madness. The need to seek relief from the relentless demands of his own body warred with the longing to move slowly, to tease and tantalize his reluctant bride into sharing the same hunger that consumed him.

His hand bunched up her gown, sliding it upward over her hip. Her thigh was warm and firm beneath his touch, and his fingers wandered, brazenly exploring the smooth flesh he had laid bare. Fondling her buttock, he pulled her to him, helplessly pressing himself against her, letting her feel the heated, solid length of him, letting her know how hungry he was for her.

Sophy stiffened at the insistent touch of his rigid member against her thigh, memories of Simon battering her, *hurting* her with just such a weapon, darting through her mind. Instinctively she pushed against Ives, terror driving her. "No," she panted. "No. Let me go! You will *not* hurt me again!"

Groaning, Ives fell back, lying on the floor beside her, staring up at the ceiling. Several rather savage fates for Simon Marlowe flashed through his mind, and, suppressing an urge to curse long and with great vehemence, he finally turned and looked at Sophy.

She had not moved far from him. Seated on the floor just a foot from him, the fire casting shadows on her face, she stared at him as he gazed steadily back at her. Her breathing was rapid, the breast he had freed from her gown rising and falling rhythmically, the rosy nipples hard and swollen from his passionate caresses. The gown was still bunched up around her hips, her long legs bare to his gaze. Ives closed his eyes in despair as a keen blade of desire knifed down his spine at the glimpse of several dark golden curls peeking from between her thighs. Ah Jesu. What was he to do?

Fear and desire churned within Sophy as she stared at him. Naked, he looked very large and dangerous lying there on the floor beside her. He had made no overt movement toward her; there was no fury or anger on his face.

Warily regarding him, realizing that he had no intention of forcing her, some of her fear lessened, her initial terror fleeing. Simon, she admitted almost hysterically, would have beaten her into submission for daring to repulse him in this manner, but Ives . . .

She swallowed painfully. "You must think me very foolish," she finally said in a small voice.

Ives smiled with an effort. "Not foolish, just badly scarred by a bastard I would give much to have alone for five minutes . . ."

Only half-aware of what he said, against her will her gaze traveled over him as she unconsciously noted the smooth, hard chest, the flat belly and . . . She swallowed, her eyes suddenly riveted by the sight of his shamelessly erect manhood between his thighs.

Her breath quickened; the ache between her thighs suddenly intensified. She could not tear her gaze away from him, could not stop looking at that impressive rod of hard, male flesh. She had never seen a naked man before, had never, she realized giddily, *wanted* to. . . .

Ives froze beneath her stare, his own breathing shallow and constricted, helpless to control the surge of heat that went through him, helpless to control the increased swelling of his unruly member. It seemed to have the lady's undivided attention, if her rapt, intense expression was anything to go by. He waited, afraid to break her concentration, afraid to do anything but lie there and let her look. . . .

As if compelled, she touched him, her hand closing warmly and firmly around him, and Ives jerked and groaned beneath her touch.

"Sweetheart," he managed thickly, "if you touch me, it is only fair that I be allowed the same pleasures."

Sophy nodded dazedly, completely absorbed by the sensation of the silky hard flesh in her hand. So smooth, she thought. So powerful. . . .

Ives's hand slid warmly over her hip, and Sophy gasped when his gently probing fingers slipped between her thighs and rubbed there where the ache was most incessant. Blind, urgent desire erupted through her as he continued to stroke and fondle the soft, damp flesh. Simon had never touched her so. His touch had been grasping, greedy, cruel.

Gently Ives inserted one finger within her satiny heat, and Sophy smothered a moan of sheer pleasure, pushing down against his invasion. She wanted, she was stunned to realize, more. Much more.

Several passionate minutes later, when her body was trembling and begging for release from his increasingly demanding caresses, Ives slowly laid her back on the floor once more and fitted himself between her legs. And when he filled her, when he moved on her, slow and sure and oh, so sweet, Sophy did not think once of pain or Simon.

Chapter Eleven

✒

*W*aking in the early-morning hours of darkness, the fire now just a glowing heap on the hearth, Ives stared at the ceiling overhead, thinking about the evening and the sweetness of their joining. It was an easy thing to do; they were still lying on the floor, and Sophy's warm weight cradled next to him was a potent reminder.

What had happened between them had been incredible, and Ives had the satisfaction of knowing that in the end Sophy had taken as much pleasure from the consummation of their marriage as he had.

He did not, however, delude himself into believing that one coupling had banished all of his wife's demons. Her life with Simon Marlowe must have been hellish. Certainly Simon's careless brutality had left scars, scars that he was going to have to heal, if Sophy would let him. He was extremely hopeful that the next time he made love to his very beautiful and desirable wife, she would trust him just a trifle more than she had tonight.

His mouth twisted. Teaching her to trust him was going

to be well-nigh impossible until he had finished this blasted business of *Le Renard.*

He did not look forward to the next several weeks. On one hand he would be trying to convince his mistrustful wife that he really was an exemplary fellow, and on the other, he would be abandoning her much of the time as he continued his charade and went about acting the part of a lecherous, drunken libertine. Deserting a new bride, he thought wryly, would certainly give his portrayal of a heartless cad a certain cachet.

He and Roxbury had discussed the situation at length the previous night. His godfather had not been at all pleased at the unexpected turn of events. Neither the news of Scoville's murder nor Ives's imminent marriage had sat well with him.

"By Jove! Did you have to be quite so gallant?" he had demanded as they had sat sipping brandy in the library of Ives's town house. "And did it ever occur to you that you might very well be marrying a woman who has killed both her husband and her uncle?"

Ives smiled lazily across at his incensed godfather. "The thought has briefly crossed my mind. And I suppose, in so far as Scoville's death is concerned, I could have simply ruined her reputation and let it go at that. . . ."

His lazy smile vanished, and his green eyes steadily meeting Roxbury's, he said softly, "I could not let her hang. You see, I have been of a mind to marry the lady for some time. It has been my most ardent wish for several weeks now, but she had proven to be rather unencouraging. The baron's murder only gave me the advantage I was looking for."

Roxbury snorted and took a sip of his brandy. "I suppose you know what you are doing. But damn and blast! I don't like you leaving London right now. And your marriage makes the situation a trifle ticklish, wouldn't you say?"

"Indeed it does," Ives admitted. "And while I would very much like to explain matters to Sophy, I think that, for the present at least, the fewer people who know what we are about, the better. Though it goes against the grain, I shall say nothing to her."

Roxbury sent him a fulminating glance. "I should bloody well hope so! I absolutely forbid you to say anything about this matter to your bride! Not one word!"

Ives nodded slowly, seeing a great many pitfalls in front of him, but generally agreeing with Roxbury. "It is not going to be easy for me to continue the charade," he conceded honestly, "but I have little doubt in my ability to carry it through." He smiled ruefully. "The situation with Sophy, of course, will be quite, ah, interesting until we have finally captured the Fox. Once he has been safely dealt with, I can confess all to my justifiably furious bride and proceed to show her how fortunate she was in marrying me. Until that time . . ." He shook his head. "Until that time, she is going to believe that she has married as thoroughly bad a man as Simon Marlowe was reputed to be."

Roxbury snorted again. "Not reputed. Fact. He *was* a bad man."

Ives shrugged and, changing the subject slightly, asked, "What did you think of the note?"

Roxbury looked thoughtful. "I believe that you are right; it was not originally written to Lady Marlowe, but to someone else whom Lord Scoville intended to blackmail."

"The Fox, do you think?"

"I don't know. I suspect yes, but only because I dislike coincidence. There is the added fact that we know that at one time, Scoville and Marlowe dabbled in selling secrets to the Fox. It was relatively innocuous stuff and because we had other, more serious leaks at that time, we paid them little heed. And, of course, after a few months, the pair of them grew weary of playing their little game of gentleman spy—although Scoville did continue, off and on, until control of the Grayson fortune fell into his lap."

Roxbury grimaced. "Knowing the gentlemen involved, I am sure that Marlowe and Scoville wondered who it was that was buying their information. I've often wondered about the circumstances of Marlowe's death. I don't doubt that he would have thought it a great jest to have someone like the Fox under his thumb. As for Scoville, in view of the note and what it implies, I would wager a small fortune that Scoville recently stumbled somehow across the man's identity."

Rubbing his chin, he said slowly, "Scoville's murder was reckless and swift. The framing of Lady Marlowe both clever and ruthless in both cases. All four of those attributes could be applied to our friend, and we are fairly certain that he was probably at that house party. Given past history, I find it hard to believe that someone else just happened to murder Scoville. And it would have to have been a terrible secret that Scoville threatened to reveal to drive a person to murder. Most people would pay, and pay handsomely, to keep an embarrassing indiscretion from becoming public, and God knows that nearly everyone at Allenton's party had much they would prefer not see the light of day.

"On the other hand, most of them are so brazen in their

vices, so indifferent to public opinion, that many of them would have laughed in Edward's face at the idea of being blackmailed. Depraved as Allenton's guests were, I doubt that even they would select murder as a way of eliminating an embarrassing problem. But if, and it is a big if, Scoville *did* stumble across a clue to the Fox's identity, well, then his murder makes perfect sense."

Ives nodded, having already come to the same conclusions. "What about Meade?"

"What about Meade?" Roxbury asked testily. "You said that he let it be known Friday night that he has access to some vital information. We have to hope that the Fox now knows this fact, too, and that he will make contact with Meade. So far, the men who are watching Meade have indicated that he has made no effort to steal the memorandum. What worries me is that he will simply copy it right under our noses or memorize it." Roxbury sighed heavily. "And unfortunately, we can do nothing about him until he leads us to the Fox, if he ever does. The recent news that Vienna has been attacked by the French makes it all the more urgent that we flush out our quarry."

Ives frowned. "I do not think that our clever friend would simply take Meade's word for the contents of the memorandum. I think he would want to see the actual document before he paid him."

"I agree. Which is why we are watching the bait almost as closely as we are watching Meade."

"Assuming that Scoville *had* unmasked the Fox, I wonder," Ives said slowly, "what it was he discovered. If he was murdered because of it, it had to have been something he came across not very long ago. . . ."

Roxbury took another sip of his brandy. "I agree," he

said as he set his snifter on the table. "Once you return to London, you can sniff around and see what you find out about Scoville's latest dealings. Who knows, murdering Scoville might turn out to have been a mistake for our crafty friend."

Lying on the floor at Harrington Chase, Ives was inclined to agree with Roxbury's previous assessment. It might not be the memorandum that traps the wily Fox, but Scoville's murder.

Despite the carpet, the hardness of the floor was making itself felt, and, ruefully, Ives admitted that he had grown used to sleeping in a comfortable bed these past several months since his return to civilian life. Shifting slightly, he freed his arm from beneath Sophy's head and a second later carefully lifted her from the floor and carried her over to where the bed awaited them.

Gently sliding her under the covers, Ives considered joining her; but the sudden surge of heat in his loins made him decide against it. It would be too tempting to make love to her again, and he was convinced that pushing her too fast would prove detrimental in the long run. They had consummated their marriage and for now that would have to satisfy him.

He would, he told himself consolingly as he quietly left her room, have years in which to enjoy the marriage bed and Sophy's sweet body. A little restraint now, he thought with a grin, would no doubt be very good for his character. And it might be easier on Sophy if she woke alone in her own bed. She would have, he mused as he slipped into his own bed, much to think about the night which had just passed.

*　　*　　*

Ives was correct, on all counts. Waking to a room full of sunlight, Sophy lay in the big bed blinking sleepily for several moments. It took a while for reality to sink in, but a slight discomfort between her legs and a twinge here and there recalled her instantly to where she was and what had happened the previous evening.

Vividly the memory of last night's stunning intimacy spun through her mind, and she sat bolt upright, glancing warily around the room. To her intense relief there was no sign of her very large, too-attractive-by-half husband. A little frown creased her forehead. Manipulative husband, too.

Sophy might have allowed herself to be manipulated into her current position, but she was very aware of the fact that she *had* been manipulated, and she did not like it.

On several counts, for although she did not discount the fact that she had not fought very hard to escape her fate, Ives Harrington was simply too used to having his own way. And *far* too used to arranging things to his own liking. The way he had so expertly maneuvered her into his arms last night was a perfect example.

Her lower lip suddenly curved into an unconsciously dreamy smile. He was also, she admitted with a sigh, quite the most fascinating man she had ever met, and she did not trust him one bit.

Everything else aside, she simply did not like the way that he had so quickly and expertly cut the ground from beneath her feet on several important occasions lately. Like a wounded gazelle, she had been isolated from the herd and swiftly snapped up by a green-eyed predator. And yet he had been kind, she thought slowly, and considerate in many ways. But the fact remained, she did not trust him. Neither his motives, nor his glib words.

But what, she asked herself soberly, as she sat up and swung her legs from the bed, was she going to do about it? The man was now her husband. And as her husband, he held almost total sway over nearly every aspect of her life. He even, she thought sourly, still had her pistol. Her eyes narrowed. He had requested that she trust him; it would be most interesting to see how he reacted when the shoe was on the other foot!

Putting the problem from her for the time being while she tended to more practical matters, Sophy rang for her maid. An hour later, bathed and gowned in a charming confection of jonquil muslin and pale green silk ribbons, her hair caught up in a cunning arrangement on the top of her head, a spangled green ribbon threaded through the golden curls, she left her rooms.

Descending the magnificent floating staircase, she eventually found herself on the main floor of the house. For a moment, she stood there undecided, trying to get her bearings. Spying a black velvet pull rope in one corner, she was on the point of ringing for a servant when a door to her left opened and Ives strolled out.

Annoyed at the leap of her heart at the mere sight of him, she said coolly, "Good morning. I was just about to ring for one of the servants."

"That won't be necessary," Ives said, a smile on his handsome mouth. "I was on the point of coming upstairs to see if you were awake and ready for your tour of the house and introduction to the rest of the staff."

"May I be allowed to eat first?" she asked tartly.

Ives grinned at her, a devilish gleam in his eyes. "Developed an appetite, have you?" he murmured, his gaze wandering with frank sensuality over her face and form. "I shall have to see that I keep you quite satisfied."

"You can keep me satisfied," she retorted swiftly, a flush staining her cheeks, "by taking me to the breakfast room *now*."

He laughed and, putting her hand on his arm, promptly led her down the hall to a large, airy room overlooking a meticulously kept rose garden.

The mouth-watering scent of bacon, ham, and kippers assaulted her nostrils. Heedless of the view, Sophy headed right to the long buffet against the far wall, where several silver warming trays were arranged. It was only after she had enjoyed her meal and several cups of coffee that she was finally ready for the tour of her new home and introductions to the remainder of the staff.

Ives set out to charm his bride, and by the time they had toured most of the important rooms of the house, met the staff, and strolled in the spring sunlight through the extensive gardens that surrounded the house, Sophy was quite relaxed and comfortable with him. It was obvious that Harrington Chase was a well-maintained and excellently staffed country home. And not, she thought with a shudder, anything like the shoddy, poorly run house that Marlowe had brought her to as a bride. But then, she admitted, perplexed, her second husband was not *exactly* like her first—though he had displayed recently distressing tendencies in that direction.

It was clear that the servants respected and liked their employer and that Ives treated them fairly. Again very different from the relationship between Marlowe and his staff. With an effort Sophy jerked her thoughts away from those unpleasant days. It would never do to be constantly comparing the two men, and yet it was very hard not to contrast this morning with her first miserable days at Marlowe House.

Catching sight of the slight droop to her mouth, Ives guided her to a small shady bench and, seating her, sat down himself. Keeping her hand in his, he asked, "What is it, sweetheart? Is something not to your liking?"

Sophy swallowed and flashed him a small smile. "Oh, no. There is nothing *not* to like. The house and grounds are very beautiful and the staff is most kind. I am sure that I shall be quite . . . contented here."

Deciding not to press, Ives nodded, and murmured, "I always thought that it was a magical place whenever I came to visit as a boy. I certainly never thought to own it."

"It must have been very hard to lose so many of your family in such a tragic fashion. A boating accident, wasn't it?"

A muscle bunched in Ives's jaw. "Yes. The result of a wager."

Sophy's heart sank. If she needed confirmation that reckless gambling ran in Ives's blood and that his recent actions were not just a passing whim, his words had given it to her. A wager. Every male of his family, except for Ives himself, lost because of a silly wager. How often had she heard Simon and Edward boasting of the ridiculous wagers they had made? The huge sums of money lost on the turn of a card, the speed of a horse, or the flight of a fly had caused her many a sleepless night. Was she doomed to repeat that experience?

Just when the silence would have become uncomfortable, Ives said, "You have had your share of tragedies, too, haven't you?"

She glanced at him, questions in her eyes.

"Your father's death. Your husband's sudden death. Edward's murder." Very deliberately he added, "The men in your life all seem to suffer untimely ends."

"What do you mean by that?" she demanded, snatching her hand from his.

"Why, nothing. I was only commenting on a curious fact."

Eyes blazing, she stood up. "I had nothing to do with Simon's death and I did *not* murder my uncle!"

Ives smiled crookedly. "I believe you, sweetheart. I would not have married you otherwise."

"Thank you very much for that!" she spat, not a bit appeased. Her eyes narrowed. "Why *did* you marry me? Besides your need for an heir, that is. Why did you so gallantly provide me with an alibi? Could it be that *you* had something to hide? How do I know that it wasn't you who hit me on the head and murdered my uncle?"

Ives scowled. "Don't be a fool!" he snapped. "I had no reason to murder your uncle."

"And how do I know that?" she asked angelically. "Am I to take only your word for it?"

"Dash it all, Sophy! I am no murderer. You cannot believe such a thing of me," Ives protested angrily.

"Being thought capable of murder is not very pleasant, is it?" she said quietly.

"No, it is not," Ives growled. "I should not have spoken as I did. It was a stupid comment to have made. Forgive me?"

Sophy sighed. "There is nothing to forgive. Simon's death was an accident, but there have always been those that believed I pushed him down the stairs. And why not? I had fired a pistol at him only moments before. For those that believe I have murdered once and gotten away with it, Edward's death is just another example of what a clever murderess I am." She smiled sadly. "I am quite certain that there are already wagers being laid in the clubs on the length of your life now that you have married me."

Standing up, Ives pulled her into his arms. His cheek resting on her hair, he said softly, "Then I shall just have to live a very long time. And we shall just have to discover who murdered Edward ourselves, won't we? And prove them all wrong."

Hope suddenly flickering across her features, she glanced up at him. "Can we actually do that? Find the murderer?"

He smiled down at her. "Together," he said softly as his mouth caught hers, "we can do anything."

It was several minutes later before Sophy emerged flushed and breathless from his embrace. With trembling fingers she patted the spangled ribbon in her hair and said with little indication of the rioting emotions within her, "I hope that you are right. Finding the person who murdered Edward will not be easy."

"Hmm. I dare say. But do not forget, we have a clue that no one else does," Ives replied easily, his mind more on the sweetness of Sophy's kiss than on what he was saying.

"The note?"

Ives nodded. "That tells us that Edward was clearly attempting to blackmail someone." He grinned at her. "We just have to discover who."

A little frown creased Sophy's forehead. "The night Edward was murdered, Agnes Weatherby mentioned to me that he had some scheme he had concocted to shore up his finances. She told me quite openly that he no longer intended to pursue Anne's fortune, that he had come up with something else."

It was Ives's turn to frown. "That's a bit of information you never mentioned before, and I find it rather illuminating. I think," he said quietly, "that upon our return to town, a private conversation with Miss Agnes Weatherby might be our first order of business."

Sophy nodded. "I agree. Edward's murder aside, something of a more permanent nature must be done about Anne." She glanced at him from beneath her lashes. "You *are* going to let me continue to act as her guardian, are you not?"

He grinned. "I would not dare attempt to stand in your way. In fact, I already had every intention of speaking to my own solicitor about the pair of us becoming her legal guardians. You might," he drawled, "even find that being married to me has some advantages when we confront Miss Weatherby about Anne's future."

Sophy made a face at him, and he laughed out loud as they continued their stroll. The stables came into view, and the subject was dropped.

Stopping to admire a pasture full of sleek, long-limbed horses near one of the main buildings, Sophy asked, "Do you raise your own stock?"

"I plan to," Ives replied. "My cousin, Adrian, was an expert horseman. As I understand it, in the months just prior to his death, he had convinced my uncle that starting their own stud farm would be both practical and profitable." His gaze suddenly bleak and his voice heavy, he added, "Along with everything else, I found that I had inherited a sizable band of broodmares and several exceptional stallions. None of the mares were bred last year because of the deaths and the uncertainty about what I planned to do."

His eyes on the grazing horses, he said softly, "I have always enjoyed horses myself and while I am not the horseman my cousin was, I feel that he left me an excellent start. I owe it to him to at least see if his dream is attainable." He smiled down at Sophy. "And so, madam wife, unless we come a cropper, we are going to be in the business of raising horses. You see before you the start of the Harrington Stud, and Adrian's dream."

"That's very kind of you," Sophy said, her eyes soft as she gazed at his hard profile.

Ives shrugged. "Not exactly. My man of business tells me that it will be extremely profitable. Adrian had assembled only the best, and there have already been inquiries from several mare owners who wish to breed to our stallions. The foals that were born last year did extremely well at the sales, and the market for the foal crop next year, so my man tells me, should be even better."

The remainder of the day passed pleasantly, and it was only when she began to dress for dinner that the knot in Sophy's stomach reappeared. Last night had been a revelation to her. With Simon the act of lovemaking had always been a degrading experience, but in Ives's arms she had discovered that it did not have to be so. To her amazement, she had learned that much pleasure could be had from simply touching, that the brush of another's lips could fill one with wild, exciting emotions, and the joining of male and female could arouse powerful sensations, thrilling sensations that had *nothing* to do with degradation and everything to do with pleasure.

Still, Sophy did not trust those stunning and unpredictable emotions. She did not like being out of control.

Though the pleasure had been intense, it had frightened her to be at the mercy of such powerful sensations, sensations that overrode coherent thought, that banished reality and left her awash in a sea of primitive demands—demands that only Ives seemed capable of fulfilling.

To her dismay, a little stab of anticipation went through her at the knowledge that Ives would come to her bed again tonight. Would his lovemaking sweep her away as it had last night? Thinking of last night and of the pleasure that had been hers, an aching warmth suddenly flooded her lower body, and she was astonished. Not once in all the years of her marriage to Simon had she looked forward to his possession with anything but revulsion. Yet in one night Ives seemed to have banished many of those old ugly emotions.

But not all of them, she reminded herself, unable to deny that while one part of her responded uncontrollably to him, there was another part of her that was wary and suspicious, not only of him, but of her own reactions to him. Until she trusted him, she would be on her guard.

Last night, she thought uneasily, could have been a mere aberration. Tonight, she realized, as she prepared to join Ives for dinner, could be vastly different. Tonight he could come to her with the same brutal, careless cruelty that Simon had practiced.

Ives was aware of the change in Sophy's manner the moment she entered the room. The wariness that had been absent for most of the day had returned, and he sighed. He had not expected that one night in his arms would allay all her fears, but he had hoped that he had made some progress. From the way her gaze slid nervously from his and the way she politely avoided his touch, it appeared he was wrong.

She did not deny him, though. Later that night, after they had dined and spent an increasingly tense evening playing a few hands of cards, when Ives came to her, she did not repulse his advances. But he was aware every moment of the need to proceed cautiously. She was like a wary animal ready to burst into flight at the first hint of danger. He wooed her and gentled her as he had the previous evening and their eventual mating was every bit as sweet, as explosively powerful as it had been the first time.

Though it went against his own desires, after several minutes of lazy kissing and lingering caresses, he left her and headed for his own cold, lonely bed. He would have been cheered to know that Sophy watched his departure with mixed emotions, relief and an odd regret that he would not remain with her throughout the night.

On Wednesday, Ives took Sophy to meet several of the tenants and their families. Seeing the neat farms and well-kept cottages, the smiling faces of the residents, the way entire families would rush to envelop their gig when they arrived, laughing and eager to speak and meet with the lord's new lady, she could not help but remember the disgraceful state of Simon's farms and the sour, bitter faces of his tenants. Ives was obviously a good steward of both the land and the people who farmed it. And that night when he came to her, as she lost herself in the dizzying passion he seemed to rouse so easily, she admitted that he seemed to be a good steward to his wife, plowing strongly into her and sowing his seed deeply. . . .

*   *   *

It had been decided that they would return to London on Thursday, and so, the next morning, there was quite a bustle about the house. Early that morning, her trunks were repacked and, along with Ashby and Peggy, sent on their way to London. After a leisurely breakfast, Sophy and Ives set out for London a few hours later.

The return trip to London was very different from the journey out. Sophy was relaxed and, while not comfortable in her marriage, at least not fearful. Her mistrust was still alive, but her fears of the marriage bed had been greatly diminished. In fact, to her growing consternation, she was discovering that she actually looked forward with growing relish to her husband's nightly visits. To her chagrin and no little dismay, memories of their lovemaking had the disconcerting habit of suddenly popping into her mind when she least expected it, making her breasts tingle and a damp heat surge in her loins.

There were many practical things to talk about on their ride to London and by the time the outskirts of the city came into view, they had decided upon several things. It would be simpler and less disruptive if Ives, and those members of his staff he deemed vital to him, removed to the Grayson town house on Grosvenor Square. His own house would be shut up and the staff sent back to Harrington Chase.

Edward's death had changed the entire outlook for Marcus and Phoebe. Ives was confident that he and Sophy would be named trustees of her father's estate, and the problem of Edward's raids on the remaining Grayson fortune would be halted. Marcus, with Ives and Sophy's help, could finally learn how to handle the reins of his vast estate.

Life for Phoebe would continue as it was for now. In

due course she could make her debut into society, and Sophy was quite positive that she would make an excellent match. As she told Ives, Phoebe possessed not only a pretty face and delightful manner, but a huge fortune, even after Edward's depredations were taken into account. It was understood between them that Phoebe would live with them and Anne at Harrington Chase. Marcus, Ives had murmured, would of course, always be welcome to join them.

Arrangements for when they left London, which would be occurring in less than a month, were a bit more tricky. It was unlikely that Marcus would be willing to abandon Gatewood for an indefinite period of time and live with them at Harrington Chase. At nineteen, Ives and Sophy agreed, he was too young to be simply turned loose on the estate with no family or guardian for company.

Ives considered the problem for several miles, then said slowly, "I see that for the next few years, we shall have to divide our time between Harrington Chase and Gatewood. It is the only solution. I cannot abandon my own home, and yet I cannot in fairness expect Marcus to abandon his. What do you think? Will it suffice?"

Her heart full, Sophy had merely nodded, too moved by his thoughtfulness to speak.

Their arrival at Berkeley Square was greeted with great fanfare; the coach had barely halted and Sophy helped down, when the front doors were thrown wide and Marcus, Phoebe, Anne, and even Lady Beckworth tumbled down the steps to greet them like the commonest inhabitants of London.

Laughing at their exuberant greetings, Sophy and Ives were swept into the house, everyone talking at once. Her eyes smiling, Sophy said, "My goodness! If I had known that just a few days' absence would arouse such enthusiasm for my presence, I would have left you more often."

Marcus grinned at her. "We have missed you," he said, "but that is not why we are so relieved that you are home." His eyes suddenly lit with excitement. "Sophy! It is the most famous thing! *A robber broke into the house last night!*"

Chapter Twelve

❧

"*A robber!*" Sophy repeated, aghast, her smile fading. "You must be bamming me."

"Oh, no, he is not," chimed in Lady Beckworth, her plump cheeks quivering with indignation. "A robber *did* break into the house! Only the fact that Marcus was unable to sleep and had gotten up to go to the library for a book saved us, I am sure, from being murdered in our beds."

Frowning, Ives herded everyone out of the main hallway and into the sitting room. "What happened?" he asked Marcus.

His eyes shining, Marcus said excitedly, "I was just going down the hall when I noticed a light coming from beneath Sophy's bedroom door. It was deucedly strange. I could not think of a reason for a candle to have been left burning in her room, but I never suspected a robber, I can tell you! And he never expected me either! I do not know which one of us was astonished when I opened the door—I was simply going to snuff out the candle and go on my way—when I found myself staring at a fellow wearing a black domino and a mask. He was in the act of sweeping some of Sophy's crystal perfume bottles into a sack, and before I had time to think, he had snuffed out the light and flung himself at me, bowling me over."

Marcus unconsciously rubbed his temple, and closer examination revealed a slight bruising. "He swung the sack at my head and hit me so hard, I nearly passed out." Marcus looked crestfallen. "By the time I righted myself and my head cleared, he was gone."

"How very, very interesting," Ives said thoughtfully. "Do you know for certain if anything was stolen?"

"Not very much that we can tell," Marcus replied. "Emerson and the housekeeper had the servants check. They discovered a few things missing—a small pair of silver bowls and a silver candelabra from the dining room, and several of the jeweled snuffboxes from Father's collection in the library." He looked apologetically across at Sophy. "But Sophy, your room is a shambles! We can only guess that I surprised him before he had time to go more thoroughly through the rest of the house."

"Has Sophy's room been straightened already?" Ives asked sharply.

An uncertain expression crossed Marcus's face. "No. The maids were just starting to do that when your man, Ashby, arrived. When he heard the news, he asked me to stop the servants and to lock the doors to Sophy's rooms. Said you would like to see it just as it is."

Ives smiled. "One can tell a great deal by viewing the, er, remains."

"But how did he get in?" Sophy asked, her features still shocked. "Have you been able to discover that?"

It was Lady Beckworth who answered. "Oh, indeed we

have, my dear. The door to the conservatory was found standing wide-open, the key on the ground. One of the servants must have forgotten to lock it last night before we retired for the night, although they have all denied doing it." She shuddered delicately. "To think that we might all have been murdered because of such a little oversight."

"Have you sent word to Bow Street?" Ives inquired.

Marcus shook his head. "No. Again, it was Ashby who suggested we wait until you and Sophy had returned."

Ives nodded. "Very good. I shall see to it, but for now, I suppose we should view the damage."

Flanked by Phoebe and Anne, who each held tightly to one of her hands, Sophy followed Lady Beckworth up the stairs. Ives and Marcus were right behind them.

"Oh, Sophy," Phoebe began in quivering tones, "I am so glad that you are home! When Lady Beckworth woke us and told us what had happened, Anne and I were terrified. To think that a robber was actually in the house!"

Holding on to Sophy's other hand with a death grip, Anne blurted out, "We were so scared! Once your brother had awakened Emerson and the footman, and they had searched the premises to make certain the intruder was gone, I was too frightened to go back to my own room. Phoebe felt the same even after Marcus assured us that we were safe. Lady Beckworth kindly let us sleep with her for the rest of the night."

"Poor darlings," murmured Lady Beckworth as she reached the upper floor. "They were shaking like terrified little birds. I was not hard-hearted enough to send them to their own rooms for what remained of the night."

"I am glad that you did not," Sophy replied warmly. "I can imagine how they felt."

"Which reminds me," Ives asked Marcus, "what time was it that you discovered the intruder?"

Marcus shrugged. "I do not know exactly, but I had heard the clock in my room strike the hour of two o'clock a little while before I decided to go in search of a book."

Ives nodded. "A good hour, if one wanted all the inhabitants asleep."

They reached the entrance to Sophy's rooms, and, throwing wide the door, Lady Beckworth said dramatically, "There! See for yourself the wanton carnage."

Sophy gasped at the sight that met her eyes. It was as if a savage storm had swooped down upon her room. Candleholders, pictures, and various garments were scattered wildly around. Pillows had been cut open, the feather mattress half-torn from the bed, chairs upended and their bottoms slashed open, while every drawer in the room had been flung about and lay on the floor in frantic abandon.

"Oh, my," Sophy said weakly as she stood in the middle of the once-elegant room.

"I agree," said Ives from behind her, one warm hand resting comfortingly on her shoulder. "It is a good thing that we already decided to commandeer another set of rooms for our use, isn't it, sweetheart?"

"You are going to live *here*?" Marcus exclaimed excitedly. "You are not going to take Sophy to live at your house on Bedford Square?"

Ives smiled at him. "Not until next Season, if *you* have no objections. Your sister and I agreed that it would cause less disruption, if I, and some of my staff, simply moved here for the remainder of the Season."

"Oh, I say, that is a capital idea!" Marcus said artlessly. "I did not know what you had planned, but I knew that

Sophy would insist that the girls be with her, and I confess, I did not much like the idea of having such a large house all to myself."

"We will talk about it later," Ives replied easily, "but for now, we have a robbery to solve."

"Do you think that you can?" Phoebe asked doubtfully, her eyes very large.

"Hmm. I certainly hope so," Ives murmured, glancing around at the carnage. "At the moment, I think the best thing would be for the rest of you to go back downstairs and let Sophy and me estimate the damage. We will join you shortly."

The room seemed very quiet once the others had obediently trooped out. Sophy sighed, and said, "I am so thankful that Marcus surprised him so early. Otherwise, I shudder to think what the rest of the house might look like."

"You think that it was just a common thief that your brother interrupted?" Ives asked quietly.

Sophy looked startled. "Of course. Don't you?"

Ives shook his head. "Think about it, my dear. It takes a brazen criminal to break into a house full of people. And instead of quickly and silently ransacking the first floor and making off with what he could, he merely filches a few items and then sneaks up the stairs, where any thief worth his salt has to know the family is sleeping, and proceeds to waste a good deal of time wreaking this sort of havoc." Ives frowned. "No, it was not just any sort of thief who did this. I'll wager whoever broke into the house was after something specific, something he thought would be here in your room." He glanced at Sophy. "Something that he obviously thought you might have gone to great pains to hide, if the condition of this room is anything to go by."

Sophy looked blank. "But what?" she cried agitatedly. "I have nothing to hide."

Ives's frown increased. "He was after something . . . something he did not find." He glanced at Sophy. "Have you purchased anything rare or unusual lately? It is apparent that he was not just after the commonplace."

It was Sophy's turn to frown. "Not that I can think of. It is true that we have spent a great deal of money since we have come to London, but it has been mostly on clothing and silly fripperies. Marcus bought some horses, and we did splurge on a new carriage, but none of those things are what would tempt a thief. At least not a thief bold enough to break into the house while everyone slept!"

Ives sighed. "I agree with you. For the time being we shall just have to assume that it is one of those odd occurrences that has no rational explanation. In the meantime I shall notify Bow Street."

But Ives did not like odd occurrences, and instinct told him that there was something else going on here besides a deucedly peculiar robbery. He said nothing to Sophy, however, and after reporting the robbery to the authorities, spent the next few hours overseeing the settling in of his servants and belongings in the Berkeley Square house.

While one part of his brain was on the mundane and practical, another part was busy with the details of the robbery—and Edward's murder—and the trail of the elusive *Le Renard.* Since those three topics were on his mind and since he and Roxbury had already tentatively agreed that the Fox was the most likely person to have murdered

Edward, it was an easy leap to connect last night's attempted robbery to Edward's murder and the Fox.

Scowling fiercely, Ives watched as Ashby moved about his new quarters. Was it conceivable that the robbery was somehow tied to the Fox? His scowl deepened. But how could that be?

For the life of him, he could think of no earthly reason to connect Edward's murder to the destruction of Sophy's former bedroom. Except that there was the same sort of ruthless efficiency about it. And it took a cool head to break into an occupied house, an even cooler head to think quickly enough to react as the robber had when confronted by Marcus. Which, Ives freely admitted, did not mean it had been the Fox who had knocked Marcus down and struck him, but he had his suspicions.

"That's a right nasty look on your face, m'lord," Ashby said after several sidelong glances at Ives.

"I feel right nasty," Ives confessed. "There is something about this robbery that smells rotten, my man."

Ashby nodded. "My sentiments exactly. Which is why I asked the young master if he would wait to have Lady Harrington's room set to order."

Ives flashed him a smile. "For which I am grateful. Words alone would not have described the chaos." Changing the subject abruptly, he asked, "Any problems settling in here?"

Ashby grinned. "None with me, or most of the others, m'lord, but I think that Ogden and the Grayson cook might be at daggers drawing before too long."

"Oh?"

Ashby's grin widened. "Ogden don't approve of all them fancy sauces that the Grayson cook insists are necessary for a *properly* prepared meal. He made no bones about the fact that he thinks such niffy-naffy stuff is a shameful waste of good ingredients. Of course, she took offense and proceeded to ring a peal over him, telling him that she'll not have him in her kitchen. Ogden replied that since your lordship had ordered him there, that *she* couldn't throw him out. And that he *would* cook for you just as he has these past dozen years or so."

Ives laughed. "I'll have a word with Ogden. Carnes and Williams are staying at the stables, I presume?"

"Yes, m'lord. I am quartered upstairs with the other servants, just down the hall from young Grayson's valet, and Sanderson has ingratiated himself so thoroughly with Emerson that they have agreed to share duties."

Domestic chores taken care of, Ives slowly descended to the first floor in search of his wife. He found her, along with the others, in a comfortable room at the rear of the house sharing some coffee and biscuits. The girls, in gowns of pale blue and pink muslin, were clustered around Sophy where she sat on a sofa of dark green damask. Lady Beckworth, a pile of knitting spilling off her lap, was opposite them, and Marcus was standing in front of the fireplace.

At his entrance, Sophy looked up expectantly, and said, "Marcus has been telling us the most interesting news. Grimshaw and several of his cronies came to call yesterday. They are openly speculating that robbery was the motive for Edward's murder—several items owned by him were found in Etienne Marquette's rooms."

"Marquette?" Ives exclaimed, surprised. "A thief? I doubt that. And it hardly seems a motive for murder." He glanced at Marcus. "Did they tell you how it came about that the items were discovered?"

"Not exactly. None of them seemed to know why it

was that Sir John Matthews decided that all of their rooms should be searched before any of them could leave," Marcus replied. "Grimshaw and Dewhurst seem to think that someone had alerted him to the possibility of a robbery." He grinned. "From what Lord Coleman and Sir Alfred Caldwell indicated yesterday, everyone was highly incensed at the notion that they might be considered thieves. No one really expected anything to be found. They were all stunned when Uncle Edward's watch and a few other items turned up hidden amongst Marquette's clothing. Dewhurst thinks it is all a trick to throw Sir John off the scent of the real murderer. Marquette vehemently denied having any knowledge of how Edward's possessions got into his room—and his valet backs him up, swears he'd never seen those items until they were found in Marquette's clothes."

"I am inclined to agree with Dewhurst's assessment of the situation," Ives said slowly. "The murder of your uncle was too elaborately arranged, especially your sis—" He shut his mouth, remembering that only he and Sophy knew the exact details of what had transpired that night.

"I have never been particularly fond of Monsieur Marquette," Sophy said in troubled tones, "but I cannot picture him a thief. There is no need of it—the extent of his wealth is well-known. His was one of the few émigré families fortunate enough to escape France with the majority of their fortune intact. There is no reason for him to steal."

"Again, I agree. But it *is* interesting," Ives murmured. He looked at the rapt faces of the two young ladies on either side of Sophy and added with a grin, "And certainly not the topic of conversation for such young and pretty ears."

"Oh, but you will not exclude us from the mystery, will you?" Phoebe cried. "It is my uncle who was murdered. Surely that is reason enough for us to know everything." She looked stubborn. "And we are not *children*, you know."

Sophy patted Phoebe's hand. "Of course you are not, and naturally we shall make certain that you know everything that we know." She shot a speaking look at her husband. "Won't we, dear?" she added sweetly.

"Of course. I shall be guided by you in all things, sweetheart," Ives replied with a deep bow in her direction and a twinkle in his green eyes.

Leaning closer to Sophy, Anne muttered, "I did not like Lord Scoville, but it seems so odd to think of him being *murdered*!"

"It wouldn't if you really knew my uncle," Marcus retorted bluntly. "Sophy and I thought often of murdering him."

"I would not," Ives commented dryly, "go about telling that to all and sundry."

Marcus flushed. "I am not a fool, my lord."

"I never thought that you were," Ives said with a smile. "I was, in my ham-fisted fashion, merely warning you to watch what you say. Until Edward's murderer is exposed, we must all guard our tongues."

"But surely no one would suspect one of *you* of murdering Lord Scoville?" Lady Beckworth asked anxiously.

Ives shook his dark head. "Of course not. But the less we comment on the murder, the less the gossips will have to say."

There was a knock at the door, and Emerson entered

the room. Looking at Ives he said, "My lord, you have callers. Lord Grimshaw, Sir Alfred Caldwell, and a Colonel Meade. I took the liberty of putting them in the blue saloon."

It was all Ives could do to keep a pleasant expression on his face. Meeting with those three undesirables was the last thing that he wanted to do at the moment, or any other moment for that matter, and he had a very good idea of why they had come to call. He vaguely remembered having made plans to visit a particularly unsavory hell with them before Edward's murder and his subsequent marriage to Sophy.

Being the type of men they were, not one of them would think it odd to leave a new bride to cool her heels while they followed their usual pursuits. And since he had done his best to ensure that they considered him of the same ilk, he could not change his manner now. Not if he wanted to track down the Fox.

The look Sophy gave him when he took his leave of her and the others made his mouth tighten. She did not trust him, and God help him, until the Fox was snared he was going to be able to do nothing to dispel her mistrust.

His guess for the visit by the three men proved correct and after they had shared a glass of hock and congratulated him in a most unbecoming fashion on his marriage, they bore him off for an afternoon and evening of amusement.

Knowing he was damning himself, Ives sent Sanderson with a message to Sophy that he would not be at home for dinner and would be returning late. She could make her own plans for the evening.

Ice settling in the region of her heart, Sophy listened to Sanderson's words but outwardly she kept a serene expression on her lovely face. When she told the others that Ives would be out that evening, Marcus looked askance, and Phoebe asked with obvious puzzlement, "He is leaving you alone on your first night home?"

Rising with regal grace to her feet, Sophy said carelessly, "Of course. Do not forget we are both sophisticated adults and know the way of the world. It would have been most strange if we sat in each other's pockets. He shall have his amusements, and I shall have mine."

"You do not mind?" Anne asked uncertainly.

"Why should I?" Sophy replied, her heart aching in her breast. "I have his name and his fortune to command, and I am sure that he will do all that is proper to assure the success of our marriage."

"That he will," Lady Beckworth agreed. "Although I must confess that I am most surprised that he would forgo an evening with his bride in order to be with his friends." She sighed. "But then that is the gentlemen. They so often simply please themselves."

Sophy's thoughts were not pleasant as she lay alone later that night in her new bedroom, a bedroom she would share with her husband. A husband of less than four days who had deposited her in her home and then gone blithely off to gamble and drink the night away. She had no doubt Ives was doing precisely that at this very moment. It was bitter knowledge, and she had not even the solace of being certain that he would abstain from sampling the charms of the nearest available wench. Hadn't she seen him less than a week ago leering at one of the Allentons' maids?

A terrible feeling of déjà vu swept through her. So might Marlowe have acted. *He* would never have spared

a second thought for his wife's feelings, not if it con-
flicted with his own desires. Ives seemed cast in the same
mold, and yet the memory of Ives's teasing green eyes,
his many considerate deeds, and his seductive lovemaking drifted through her mind.

She sighed. She was confused. He acted the cad one
minute and the next was everything any woman would
want. Which, she wondered miserably, was the real Ives
Harrington? And how was she going to live with him
when her heart was constantly being torn asunder?

Better than you did married to Simon, she thought
grimly. Simon had *never* shown a softer side. And yet,
she could not deny that there were many incidents that
had revealed Ives was *nothing* like Marlowe. Perhaps she
could coax Ives away from his rakish habits and friends?
She had never wanted to do so with Simon, but with
Ives—with Ives, she realized with a start, she wanted a
real marriage. A marriage with a husband who loved
her . . . as she loved him?

Her breath caught sharply in her throat. Oh good gad!
Never say that she had been so foolish as to fall in love
with him! A man who had compelled her to marry him?
A man she distrusted? A man who seemed at times to be
the very twin of her first husband?

And yet how else could she explain this odd yearning
in her heart? How else could she explain why his very
touch seemed to melt her bones, her very inhibitions?
And how else to explain the existence deep inside her of
the certain knowledge that there *was* an explanation for
his inexplicable acts? She did not trust him, she admitted
poignantly, but she wanted to. Desperately.

Sophy slept badly that night, and she woke with the
uncomfortable awareness that she had missed Ives's big

body pressing into hers. She was also embarrassingly aware of a sweetly throbbing ache between her thighs, an ache she feared only one man could assuage.

Ives would have been delighted to know that Sophy had missed him, especially since the night he had just passed had proven to be a boring repetition of other nights he had already wasted in the company of Meade and the others.

He was, however, able to learn firsthand about the events following his and Sophy's departure from the Allentons', though it was essentially the same information Marcus had imparted earlier.

Marquette was no longer seriously considered a suspect in the murder. The testimony of Edward's own valet to the fact that the stolen objects had been in his lordship's room when he had retired for the night, and the simpering confession of a buxom housemaid who had been with Marquette all evening had done much to lift suspicion from him. But questions lingered, and while Edward's valet had no reason to lie, it was agreed amongst the others that the accommodating maid could have been bribed by Marquette.

"Where is Marquette now?" Ives asked idly as they sat in one of the smoky rooms of the vice-ridden hell Meade had selected for the night's entertainment.

"Went to his family home in the country," replied Dewhurst, his blue eyes half-glazed from the copious amount of liquor they had been consuming all evening.

"Hiding with his tail between his legs," said Grimshaw. "Never liked the damned fellow."

"Oh, he is not such a bad sort," Lord Coleman argued, as he sat across the table from Grimshaw, indifferently tossing some cards from hand to hand. "And you know that you do not really believe that he stole those frippery items from Edward and murdered him."

"Someone did," Ives interjected, his gaze on his half-empty snifter of brandy.

"But *not* Marquette," said Dewhurst, and giggled drunkenly.

"Damme, Dewhurst, you're foxed," exclaimed Grimshaw, laughing. "And the evening only half-gone. 'Tis convenient that you live around the corner from Coleman and me—we may have to carry you home." He wagged a finger at his cousin. "But foxed or not, do not forget that we plan to visit Flora's establishment before we end the night."

"Er, I am afraid that I must forgo that pleasure," Ives said quickly. Drinking and gaming, yes. He could condone those pursuits for the purpose of trapping the Fox, but *not* whoring, not when the only woman he wanted was his bride.

"Under the cat's paw already?" Grimshaw asked nastily, his gray eyes hard as they rested on Ives's face.

The situation between Grimshaw and Ives was complicated at best. Knowing that Grimshaw had been the one to instigate the fatal wager that cost Ives his family and aware that Grimshaw's name was on the very short list of suspects given to Roxbury by his father, Ives had found it difficult from the very beginning to act casual around the man. It didn't help that he simply did not like the man under any circumstances.

Of all the gentlemen who comprised the group around Meade, many of whom had also been boon companions to the late Lord Marlowe, Ives found Grimshaw the most offensive. He was a cold-blooded gambler and thought little of brutally fleecing any poor pigeon who crossed his path. It was usually Grimshaw who committed the worst excesses, whether it was drunkenness or flagrant whoring. The others were hardly any better, but it always seemed to Ives that Grimshaw went just that little bit beyond the line of even the hardened rakes he associated with.

And Grimshaw did not like *him* any better than he did the other men. His marriage to Sophy sat ill with Grimshaw; Ives knew that, and was not surprised by Grimshaw's comment. Grimshaw often seemed to be trying to goad Ives into some foolhardy act, but so far Ives had deftly avoided coming to open conflict with the other man.

Ives smiled into Grimshaw's dissipated features. "If Sophy were your wife, I think that perhaps you might not mind being under her paw. It is *such* a sweet little paw, you know."

"A hit! Definitely a hit!" Meade cried gaily, as he lolled by Ives's side. Meade looked expectantly over at Grimshaw, his heavy features flushed with wine, a sloppy smile on his mouth.

Grimshaw shot him a venomous glance. "You're as drunk as Henry."

"Not drunk," murmured Henry. "Foxed—Grimshaw said so."

Ives laughed, and, getting to his feet, said lightly, "Indeed you are, the lot of you. And before I must be carried home feetfirst to my bride, I shall take my leave of you. Good night, gentlemen."

It might have been unwise to leave then, but Ives could only hope that they would put his lack of enthusiasm for Flora's down to the fact that he did possess a young and very lovely bride. Most of them, at one time or other, had vied for Sophy's charms, and he figured that for at least a few weeks none of them would think it strange that he preferred his own bed to that of one of Flora's doxies.

But it was not Sophy's bed Ives sought out when he returned home. Not even he was bold enough to attempt to gain her good graces after having abandoned her so callously. He spent what remained of the night speculating about what he had learned, or not learned, and he concluded dismally that the entire evening had been a complete waste.

He could have, he admitted unhappily, furthered his cause with his lady and spent a most enjoyable evening sampling her delectable charms instead of rubbing shoulders with the worst set of scoundrels it had ever been his misfortune to meet. It didn't help his state of mind any that he still had no real clue as to the identity of the Fox. Or even the confidence that his efforts would eventually prove fruitful. At the moment, the memorandum and Meade seemed to be the only sure way of flushing out their quarry *if* he took the bait.

Ives brightened slightly. There was also Edward's murder to plumb for clues. If Edward had been murdered because he knew something about the Fox . . . He smiled faintly. Perhaps his cause was not entirely hopeless.

It was well after noon before Ives wandered downstairs. He was not looking forward to the meeting with his wife. By the time he went in search of Sophy, upon finally being informed that she was in the conservatory, he was aware that he had not only alienated his wife but completely ruined his warm rapport with the other members of the household. Marcus gave him a decidedly cool greeting as he had passed him on the stairs, and the stiff reply his aunt gave him when he had inquired of Sophy's whereabouts, as well as the less-than-welcoming expressions on Phoebe's and Anne's faces, confirmed that he had thoroughly offended all of them.

Walking into the conservatory a few minutes later, Ives made a face. He had thousands of ruffled feathers to smooth and he was gloomily aware that he would be unable to begin that gargantuan task for some time yet. The glance Sophy gave him when he came upon her reading a book in the conservatory added to his gloom.

For a long moment Ives just stood there looking at her, a powerful surge of pleasure going through him at that simple act. She looked quite fetching in a simple high-waisted gown of yellow-and-green sprigged muslin. Her hair had been left free to fall in an artful tangle around her shoulders, a green-silk ribbon holding the mass of golden curls off her face.

Having acknowledged his presence, Sophy went back to her book, presenting her husband with a stern profile. It was also an enchanting profile and after several moments of regarding it, Ives said gently, "Will you forgive me, Butterfly? It was not kind of me to desert you so soon after our return to town."

Sophy looked at him, one slim brow haughtily arched. "Forgive you?" she repeated calmly, laying aside her book and staring at him. "For what? Following the pursuits of most gentlemen?"

Ives grimaced, wishing he dared tell her the entire tale. But he could not. Despite their marriage, they did not know each other very well, and while he would swear on his life that anything he told her would go no further, it was not just his life at risk. Entire armies depended upon

his finding the Fox. And stopping him. And just one unwise word . . .

Catching up one of her hands in his, he pressed a kiss
on the back of it. Steadily meeting her unfriendly gaze, he
said simply, "Please believe me, my dear, when I say that
it is my most ardent wish to make you happy." He smiled
crookedly. "At the moment you may find that hard to believe, but it is true. Just trust me, Sophy, and all will be
right."

"It seems as if you are always asking me to trust you—
with little evidence that I should, I might add," she returned sharply. A speculative glint suddenly entered her
golden eyes. "Perhaps," she said slowly, "there is a way
that you can show me that you *are* to be trusted, at least
a little."

Warily, Ives regarded her. "And that is?"

She smiled sweetly. "By returning my pistol to me."

Chapter Thirteen

❧

*I*t was the last request that Ives expected, and the wave of relief that went through him left him almost giddy. He had heard many stories of Sophy's standoffs with her first husband, and Percival had eagerly regaled him with the tale of how Sophy had actually shot at her husband the night Marlowe had died. It showed, he thought whimsically, how thoroughly she had bewitched him that the notion of returning her pistol to her did not alarm him in the least.

Smiling idiotically at her, he said, "Of course. I shall ring for Ashby and he will fetch it from my things."

Suspiciously, Sophy stared at him. "You actually mean it?"

Ives bowed elegantly. "Indeed, I do. If you will view it as a measure of trust between us."

Sophy nodded, hardly daring to believe it. Her eyes narrowed. But why? What was he up to, trying to disarm her in this underhanded fashion? She had never expected him to agree with her request, and the fact that he had left her uncertain what to think.

Ashby appeared in answer to Ives's pull of the bell rope; his features carefully blank, he listened to his master's request and immediately departed on his errand.

There was no conversation between Ives and Sophy while they waited. Sophy's thoughts were busy as she tried to understand the man before her. Why was he doing this? she wondered, greatly perplexed. What did it matter to him if she trusted him or not? If last night was any example, it was obvious that he intended to continue with his rakish ways, despite her wishes. And yet, he had asked her to trust him and was even willing to put a weapon in her hands. She shook her head in utter confusion.

Ashby returned, handed the pistol to Ives, and departed. Smiling at her, Ives held out the pistol. "I believe that this belongs to you, sweetheart."

Sophy slowly rose to her feet, warily closing the short distance that separated them. Her fingers were almost on the pistol, when Ives moved, holding his hand and the pistol in it just out of reach. Her eyes flew to his, disappointment crashing through her. It *had* been a trick.

Almost as if he read her mind, Ives shook his head. "No trick, sweetheart, but I think you need to prove to me that I can trust you not to shoot me at the first opportunity."

"And how do I do that?" Sophy demanded, her gaze full of angry suspicion.

"All I ask," he said slowly, "is one kiss freely given, and the pistol is yours."

Sophy snorted. "And why should I trust you? You have already gone back on your word."

"Not precisely. I have only added a condition." He

smiled wryly. "Is the notion of kissing me so terrible, sweetheart?"

"Oh, very well," Sophy said ungraciously, and lifted her mouth to his.

Ives kissed her a long time, his arms holding her possessively to him, his lips gently and firmly reminding her just how devastating his embrace could be. Without volition, she melted into him, her mouth softening, inviting his deeper exploration, suspicion and mistrust momentarily forgotten.

It was the knowledge that if he did not stop kissing her that very minute, he would be tipping up her skirts and taking her where she stood, that finally forced Ives away from the intoxication of Sophy's lips.

His breathing erratic, a distinctly carnal gleam in his green eyes, he stared down into her flushed features. With great willpower, he carefully set her from him. When he felt he was in command of himself, he bowed once more. Putting the pistol in her hand, he said dryly, "Try not to shoot me when I next come to your bed, sweetheart."

Her gaze desire-clouded, she nodded, hardly aware that she did so. It was a second or two later that she became conscious of the weight in her hand and stupidly she stared at the weapon she held. Oh! The pistol! Ives had actually given it to her. How amazing.

Expertly she checked the weapon and smiled with satisfaction when she identified it as her own and verified that it was loaded. She cast him a slightly apologetic glance.

"I did not expect you to give it to me," she admitted baldly.

He smiled. "I know. I am surprised myself that I did."

"Why did you?"

Ives's face softened. "Because you asked it of me."

Her eyes searched his. "And will you always do as I ask?"

"If it is within my power to do so."

"I do not understand you at all," Sophy answered, partly charmed, partly vexed by his answer. One would think that he would at least have the decency to act in a predictable manner!

"I do not understand myself half the time either," Ives said cheerfully, "so do not bother your head over it. And now, may I ask what your plans are for this afternoon? If you like, I am willing to put myself at your disposal."

"Guilty conscience for deserting me last night, m'lord?" Sophy inquired tartly.

"Er, no," Ives muttered, a faint spot of color burning high on his cheeks, and he cursed again the need for secrecy. "It is a pleasant day and I thought . . ." He stopped and shrugged. "If you find my company unnecessary, I will not, of course, force it upon you."

"That has never prevented you in the past," Sophy replied with a little twinkle. His expression made her laugh, and she added, "There now, I will not tease you further. But if you are serious, I wonder if we might not call upon Miss Weatherby." She arched a brow. "That is if you were also serious about discovering who actually murdered Edward."

"I was, and I think visiting Miss Weatherby is an excellent idea, madam wife—not only because of your uncle's murder, but because of Anne's situation, too. Living in this limbo is not pleasant for any of us, and a prolonged public fight will do none of us any good either. I have been thinking about it and have hit upon a scheme which may help resolve the problem—I intend to offer

Agnes money, in the hopes that she will sign over all rights to Anne. If you will wait long enough for me to send a note to my godfather on another matter, we shall be off to confront the dragon aunt."

Sophy stared at him admiringly. "Money! Now why didn't I think of that? But you should not pay the piper. It was my doing that brought Anne into our lives."

"True, but allow me to do this for you." He grinned. "You may consider it a bridal gift."

Utterly disarmed, Sophy allowed herself to be persuaded.

A short time later, his note to Roxbury on its way, Ives, with Sophy at his side, was knocking on the door of the house on Russell Square. A very correct butler in black-and-white livery answered the door, and, after stating their business, Ives and Sophy were politely ushered into a rather charming room done in shades of pale blue and cream.

Miss Weatherby entered a moment later, garbed in an afternoon dress of green jaconet muslin. Her eyes were rimmed in red and there was a haggard air about her. It occurred belatedly to Sophy that Agnes might have cared deeply for Edward.

Agnes greeted them coolly and began aggressively, "I suppose you have come to gloat. You think you hold all the cards, don't you? Well, let me tell you, I shall fight you for Anne—she is *my* niece, after all." She laughed bitterly. "And I have nothing to lose now."

"Actually, you do," Ives said quietly. "You have a great deal to lose—your reputation for one, and our goodwill for another."

"What do I care about your goodwill?" she asked sneeringly.

Ives looked thoughtful. "I came here today to make you an offer." At Agnes's look, he continued smoothly, "If you would be willing to sign over your rights to Anne and allow us to become her guardians, we will make it worth your while. Are you willing to listen to what I have to say?"

An arrested expression on her face, Agnes said slowly, "You are offering me money?"

Ives nodded. "Yes. I am prepared to settle an income upon you for your lifetime. You will not be wealthy, but you will be able to live comfortably, even elegantly. There is a small property that came to me from my grandmother, an attractive house and several outbuildings on fifty acres situated in Surrey. That, too, I will settle upon you . . . if you agree to release all claim to Anne." Ives paused. "I should warn you," he said gently, "if you do not, I shall bring all my resources and considerable influence to bear against you. You would be wise to take the money."

Agnes stared at him for a long time, her expression hard and calculating. Then she shrugged, and said sourly, "Why not? A bird in the hand . . ."

Ives bowed. "I will have the papers drawn up and sent over to you this afternoon."

She flashed an unfriendly glance at Sophy. "You have won, have you not? I'll not wish you well, but if your husband does as he says he is going to and settles the money and house on me, I shall sign whatever documents are deemed necessary to make it official."

When Sophy started to stammer her thanks, Ives said smoothly, "We thank you. I shall have my solicitor draw up the papers immediately and I, myself, shall call upon the trustees of Grandmother's estate."

Agnes nodded curtly. Still staring at Sophy, she said disagreeably, "You certainly managed to land on your feet. You have Anne, and with his lordship at your side, there is none who would dare question you about Edward's murder."

"I had nothing to do with his death," Sophy said tightly, her fingers digging into Ives's arm when he would have entered the fray in her defense.

Agnes shrugged. "So you say."

"I *do* say!" Sophy snapped. "I cannot deny that I had no affection for my uncle, but I did not murder him!"

Agnes made a silencing gesture with her hand. "It does not matter," she muttered. "He is dead and all my hopes with him."

"It was those, er, hopes that we also wished to speak to you about," Ives interposed deftly.

Agnes looked at him. "What do you mean?"

"You mentioned to my wife the night Edward was murdered that he had given up on the idea of marrying Anne. You said that he had hit upon another scheme to recoup his fortune," Ives said slowly. "Would you tell us what you know about that scheme?"

Something flickered in Agnes's eyes, but she merely hunched a shoulder and turned away, staring out the window. "Why should I? What good would it do?"

Sophy and Ives exchanged looks. Shrugging, Ives murmured, "It might help us discover what really happened that night."

A sly expression in her eyes, Agnes's attention turned back to them where they stood together in the center of the room. "I doubt it," she said, a not-altogether-pleasant smile on her face.

"Did he talk to you about it?" Sophy asked urgently.

"Did he tell you what he planned? Or where the money was going to come from? Agnes, please tell us. What you know may help us identify the man who killed him."

"I am afraid," Agnes said, her face suddenly smooth and bland, "I do not know what you are talking about. You must have misunderstood me."

"Don't be a fool!" Ives said bluntly. "If you know something, tell us. Don't think that you can simply take up the reins Edward dropped. Whoever killed Lord Scoville is dangerous."

"I agree. But how you think that I can help you expose him, I just do not know." Her eyes remained steadily on Ives's frowning features. "I repeat, your wife is mistaken. I do not know what you are talking about."

"You *are* a fool!" Sophy cried passionately, her temper spiking. "I am glad that Anne is well rid of you."

Agnes tipped her hand, a faint smirk on her lips. "The gloves are off, are they not, Lady Mar— Ah, forgive me, Lady Harrington."

Keeping Sophy from storming out of the room by holding firmly onto her arm, Ives looked at Agnes. "You obviously have decided not to share what you know. I would only advise you to use extreme caution with the individual you will be dealing with. Remember, he killed your lover. If at any time you change your mind about talking to us, please do not hesitate to call upon us."

Agnes shrugged and appeared bored. Knowing there was nothing else to be done, Ives and Sophy left the Russell Square house.

"That awful woman!" Sophy exclaimed before the door had hardly shut behind them. "She knows something and means to try to blackmail Edward's murderer."

"I know," Ives replied as he helped her into their carriage. "But there is nothing we can do about it—at the moment."

There was silence for a few minutes as the vehicle moved off. Then Sophy blurted, "Couldn't we set one of our servants to watch her? To see where she goes and whom she meets?"

Ives looked at her, something between admiration and astonishment in his gaze. "You are," he admitted wryly, "quite tenacious about this, are you not?"

"You would be, too," she said glumly, "if everyone thought that you were the murderer."

"Do you count me as everyone?" he asked softly.

"Of course not. You are my husband!"

Ives's shout of laughter rang out and they rode together in perfect charity to the Grayson town house.

It was obvious to both of them that Agnes Weatherby knew a great deal more about Edward's plan than she had let on. It was equally clear she had every intention of attempting to follow through with his original scheme, which they strongly suspected entailed blackmail of some sort. It also had not escaped them that Agnes also was able to point the finger of suspicion at Edward's murderer.

"She is running a terrible risk," Sophy said, as the coach drew up at the house and stopped.

"I know," Ives agreed. "But right now there is nothing that we can do to stop her."

As they entered the house, they were met by Sanderson. Taking Ives's hat and gloves and Sophy's pelisse, he said with a telling glance at Ives, "You have a visitor, m'lord. It is the Duke of Roxbury. He insisted upon waiting for you. I put him in the little room behind the library."

"Will you excuse me, my dear?" Ives asked Sophy.

Her heart sank upon hearing Sanderson's first words, but learning that it was only Ives's godfather, her spirits rose again. She was thankful that it was not Grimshaw or Coleman who awaited her husband.

Ives found his godfather comfortably ensconced in a chair of oxblood leather, his feet propped on a stool of the same material and cup of coffee at his side. "About time you returned," he growled. "What did you mean by sending me that dashed cryptic note and then taking off?"

Ives smiled. "I believe my note said I would call on you this evening, sir."

Roxbury harrumphed and muttered, "Never mind that. Tell me about this robbery."

Succinctly, Ives did so.

Roxbury was frowning when Ives finished speaking. "You really think that this is somehow tied to the Fox?"

Ives grimaced. "I think it is possible. You once said you disliked coincidence—I find that I am of the same mind. It *could* be a coincidence, this peculiar robbery, but I do not think so. I cannot fathom how it is all connected—the Fox, Edward's death, and the assault on Sophy's room—but my instinct tells me that there is a connection."

"You could be right," Roxbury finally admitted reluctantly. "But I will withhold judgment for the time being. Now what about Meade? What have you learned?"

"Well, I think that we can safely eliminate one of the names from the list—Etienne Marquette." Concisely, he brought his godfather up-to-date on the latest events.

"I'm inclined to agree with you," Roxbury said after taking a sip of his coffee. "It is apparent that the Fox was merely trying to confuse the issue and deflect any interest in himself by sacrificing Marquette. Which still leaves us two names, Grimshaw and Coleman."

Ives sighed. "I know, and I am no closer to choosing between them than I was at the beginning. Simply because I dislike him and know he was behind that fatal wager, I want it to be Grimshaw, but I can give you no proof that he is, indeed, the Fox. And it could be argued that Coleman's reticent behavior, his habit of not bringing attention to himself, is merely a facade." He glanced across at Roxbury. "Is there anything new on the memorandum?"

Roxbury shook his head. "No. But if your little plan is going to work, I suspect that something should happen soon. If it does not, then we have to suppose that the Fox was too smart to take the bait."

The Fox was considering the memorandum at that very moment. Instinct told him it was a trap. Ives's sudden affinity for Meade's company, his unexpected desire to consort with the determined roués who surrounded Meade was suspicious in itself, and the coincidence of such an important document surfacing at the same time . . .

It could be coincidence, he admitted. And it was possible that having tasted the bland delights of polite society, Ives Harrington had decided it lacked excitement and spice and had been drawn to the likes of himself and Meade and the others. It *was* possible, but he did not think it was so.

But the memorandum. An avaricious gleam suddenly lit his eyes. He had been toying for several months now with the idea of making the Fox disappear forever. He'd had a good run; why not quit while he was ahead? Besides, the end would come soon enough. Whatever the outcome, the war with Napoléon could only drag on so long. And he had enough money now.

Yet the notion of making the filching of the memorandum his final act of treason filled him with pleasure. The French would pay a bloody *fortune* to know the movements of Wellesley's troops on the Peninsula and while he did not precisely *need* the money, a man could never have too much wealth. And then there was the sheer excitement of thumbing his nose at those clumsy fools at the Horse Guards. It would be a wonderful coup. And if it *was* a trap, how thrilling to elude Roxbury's hungry hounds.

But dared he risk it? He rather thought he did.

He had set up a meeting with his French connection for that night. Once the French learned of the existence of the document and the possibility of his laying his hands on it, the die would be cast. The French would want it at any cost, and if *he* did not supply it, they would find someone who would. He had debated the wisdom of what he was about to do for a few days before finally sending word on Tuesday for the need of a meeting. The memorandum smelled wrong, but the smell of gold was stronger.

The meeting with the Frenchman was disagreeable. The man was an oaf who had no concept of the dangers involved and little sympathy for the perils the Fox might face.

They sat in a dark corner of a dirty little tavern near the banks of the River Thames, the stink of the river permeating even the endemic odors the Fox preferred not to identify. He was, as usual for this type of foray, disguised. His clothing was worn and tattered. A scruffy beard and false eyebrows stolen long ago from an actor acquaintance completely changed his appearance. A battered black hat was pulled low, almost completely obscuring his face.

No one would recognize him. It had just been damned bad luck that he had been unaware of Simon's presence when the other man had followed him home that night long ago. In the intervening years, having learned his lesson well, he had grown quite adept at spotting and throwing off any followers. He was, he thought modestly, quite without parallel.

The Frenchman did not think so, and he growled, "*Mon Dieu!* I do not see what is so difficult. Simply steal the document."

"I've told you," the Fox explained with growing impatience, "that I suspect that the document is being closely watched. A copy would give you the same information, but with very little risk."

The Frenchman glanced at him. "You expect us to pay you for a *copy*?" he asked incredulously. "That is impossible, *monsieur*! *Non.* We must have the original."

"And if you have the original, the British will know of it and change their plans."

The Frenchman looked thoughtful. "What do you propose?"

"I propose that I have my underling bring the memorandum to me. I shall show it to you so that you may assure your superiors of its validity, but it will be a *copy* that actually goes to France. The original document will be returned immediately to the Horse Guards, with no one the wiser."

The Frenchman did not like it, but he could see the

wisdom of the plan. "Very well," he said disagreeably. "When can you have it?"

It was the Fox's turn to look thoughtful. The longer they waited to snatch the document, the less time the French would have to take advantage of the information outlined in it. There was also the fact that with every passing day, there was every possibility that the document would be moved beyond Meade's grasp. But the possibility of a trap worried him a great deal, which was why he had not yet expressed any interest in the memorandum to Meade.

"Well?" demanded the Frenchman. "When?"

The Fox threw him a glance of sheer venom. Did not the fat oaf understand that it was *his* neck he was risking?

"No later than this time next week," he said finally.

"*Sacré bleu!* A week! You expect me to wait a week?"

His mouth tightened. "I said," he gritted out, "no *later* than a week. I may have it for you as early as Monday, but I cannot deny that it may take longer. I must make certain arrangements, and that will take time."

The Frenchman regarded him with open dislike. "See that these *arrangements* of yours do not take too much time, *mon ami,* or we may decide to dispense with your services . . . permanently."

The Fox hid his rage, meekly bowing his head in acknowledgment of the threat. The fool dared to threaten him? Once he had been paid for the document, he might just kill this impudent fellow for the pleasure of it.

"You have," he muttered, no sign of his inner fury apparent, "nothing to fear. The document will be yours."

Leaving the Frenchman, the Fox scurried to one of several safe hiding places he had scattered throughout London. Changing back into his normal clothes, he slipped out into the night and, by a circuitous route, made it to his own home.

Pouring himself a large snifter of brandy, he sat down and savored the bite of the liquor on his tongue and throat as he slowly drank. Contacting Meade, he decided a few minutes later, must be his first step, and there was no time to lose.

Setting aside his brandy, he reached for writing materials. Disguising his hand, he quickly wrote a note that would, no doubt, titillate Meade and bring him salivating for gold to the place the Fox had directed for their meeting. It was too late to find some anonymous urchin to deliver the note tonight, but tomorrow morning, first thing, he would see to it.

Feeling rather satisfied with events, he sat back and took another sip of his brandy. He would meet with Meade tomorrow night and, if things went well, by Monday evening he would have the document and the copy.

There was just one little blot on his rosy horizon—that damned ruby pin! He scowled. It had been, he admitted sourly, a dashed bloody mistake to attempt to rob the Grayson house Wednesday night.

Edward had not said outright that it was Sophy who found the pin, but he suspected that it was so. Who else could it have been? Certainly not Edward. If Edward had found it, he would have attempted to blackmail him years ago. No, it had to have been Sophy who showed it to Edward.

Knowing that Harrington and Sophy were not in residence, it had seemed a propitious time to look for it. He had stolen the conservatory key when he had come to call with his friends earlier in the day, so entering the house that night had occurred without incident. Taking a few items on his way up the stairs had been easy, and he had planned to create more havoc in the remainder of the house on his way out.

Grimly he realized that he had run a terrible risk and all for nothing. Despite the destruction of Sophy's room, he had not found the cravat pin. If only he'd had a little more time. . . .

A thrill of fright ran through him as he relived that terrifying moment when Marcus Grayson opened the door and stared at him in wide-eyed disbelief. If he had hesitated even a moment, the boy would have roused the house. By Jove, but it had been a near thing.

That damned pin. It haunted him. For the time being he had to hope that with Edward dead, no one else would connect it to him. But where, he wondered uneasily, was the damned pin? Who actually possessed it? His mouth thinned. Just because he had not found it in Sophy's room did not mean she did not have it, but the idea that someone else, someone utterly unknown to him, might have it sent a chill down his spine.

He took another swallow of brandy. Only Edward, he told himself reassuringly, had connected him to the pin and from there to the Fox. It was the Fox who was a danger to him, not the pin. He had been, he realized, a fool to lose his head and try to find it. He would forget about the pin and, if it surfaced, act as surprised as anyone else that it had been found after all this time. He had been clever and cautious all these years, and he was *not* going to be undone by something as small and insignificant as a cravat pin!

The Season was nearing its end and in less than a month London would be barren of most of the members of the ton. The frantic rounds of balls, soirees, and routs had increased dramatically in recent days, and the news of Sophy's sudden wedding to such an eligible bachelor as Viscount Harrington only added to the frenzy of activities.

Everyone—having learned of the marriage from the announcement in the *Times* that Roxbury, at Ives's request, had placed the previous Tuesday—seemed determined to be among the first to greet the new couple. That Saturday morning, having learned that the newlyweds were once more in residence, found Sophy flooded with cards and invitations—and callers. In desperation, having waved good-bye to the last of several grandes dames of the ton who had come to call, Sophy ordered Emerson to tell everyone that she was not at home. Ives, the wretch, perhaps guessing how it would be, had escaped earlier in the day with Marcus to look at a new horse her brother was thinking of buying at Tattersall's.

Sinking down onto the sofa, Sophy looked across at Lady Beckworth, and said, "I never thought that my marriage to your nephew would arouse such interest. I must confess that I am not used to being so . . . so popular with the ton. I am certainly grateful you agreed to stay here with us for a few more days. I do not know what I would have done if you had not been here to help deflect some of the attention."

Lady Beckworth, sitting in a delicate chair covered in rose silk, was placidly drinking a cup of tea. Putting down her cup, she beamed at Sophy, and murmured, "You do not have to thank me, my dear; you have handled yourself just as you ought. And I have thoroughly enjoyed myself." Something suspiciously like a giggle came from her. "Oh my, was not Leticia Greenwood put out that Ives had chosen you as his bride, instead of that spotty daughter of hers? I could hardly control myself when she began to sing your praises and pretend she knew right from the first how it would be between the two of you. She is *such* a cat!"

Sophy chuckled and helped herself to a fresh cup of tea. Settling into the sofa, she sipped her tea, and admitted, "I know. I did not know where to look when she began to speak in that disgustingly arch manner of hers."

A little frown creased Sophy's forehead as she took another fortifying sip of her tea. "She seemed to think it was odd though, that Ives had chosen to marry *me*. . . ." A little flush stained her cheeks. "Not because of my reputation," she added hastily. "It wasn't that—although she did allude to it. It was something else, as if there was some reason why a match between a Harrington and a Grayson was quite extraordinary."

Lady Beckworth coughed slightly, and her gaze not quite meeting Sophy's, she said, "Well, you know, dear, there is that old business of Robert. . . ."

"Robert's suicide, you mean?" Sophy asked sharply.

Lady Beckworth nodded, and suddenly seemed to be very busy with her tea cup and saucer.

"But what does his brother's suicide have to do with me?" Sophy demanded, her expression confused.

Her eyes full of pity, Lady Beckworth stared at her for a long moment. Then, giving a heavy sigh, she muttered, "I had hoped that Ives would have explained all to you by now, but I see that he has not."

She hesitated as if, for once, considering the wisdom of her words. Old habits won out, and she said in a confiding rush, "You see, dear, your mother, Jane, was the young woman Robert was in love with. Robert killed himself because she married your father. Everyone knew it. And everyone knew how Ives felt about it. Even as a boy his determination to seek revenge was known amongst friends of the family—Leticia and her family have always been intimate friends of the Harringtons. Ives frequently swore that there would never be anything but enmity between himself and the Grayson family. And *that* is why it is so incomprehensible to the likes of Leticia Greenwood that Ives would have chosen to marry *you*."

Chapter Fourteen

❧

Sophy's face went white and she stared aghast at Lady Beckworth's kind face.

"My *mother*?" she finally managed in a strangled tone. "Ives's brother killed himself over my mother?"

Lady Beckworth nodded sadly. "I am afraid so. It was a terrible tragedy."

Sophy stood up. She took an agitated step around the room. "But why did I never hear of this?" she demanded.

"Well, I don't suppose it was something your mother wanted to talk about, and I am sure it was not a common subject between your parents and their friends. Why should you have known? After all, it happened before you were even born."

"But that fact did not, apparently, matter to Ives," Sophy replied tightly, her hands clasped in front of her. Good gad! she thought despairingly. Had she become so completely mesmerized by Ives that she had forgotten the lessons in deceit that she had learned from Simon? What other secrets, she wondered bitterly, had Ives kept from her? And why? Why had he never mentioned what had happened between his brother and her mother? He should have told her, she thought stubbornly, *especially* the part her mother had played . . . unless there was some sinister reason he had not done so?

She took a shaky breath, not liking the path of her thoughts, hardly aware of Lady Beckworth's concerned gaze resting on her pale face. She did not want to believe ill of her husband, but she could not help believing that she had been utterly misled by his many thoughtful acts. It seemed likely, she admitted bitterly, that she had been deliberately charmed and seduced by him. It was more than possible that there had been a dark and ugly reason behind his determined pursuit of her, his inexplicable rescue of her the night Edward had died. Painfully, reluctantly, she came to the conclusion that Ives could have been plotting some sort of twisted revenge against her right from the very beginning. She did not want to think it, but the notion would not go away.

She had almost come to believe that Ives could be trusted, begun to accept the idea that perhaps their marriage was not a bad thing, but now . . . She swallowed convulsively, finally admitting that she had been unconsciously waiting for his dark side to be exposed. That there had been a part of her that had suspected all along that things were not as they seemed, that it was only a matter of time before he revealed that the black heart of a cad lay beneath his supposedly considerate exterior.

Her mouth twisted. Oh, but he had done his work well. And it had all been for one ugly purpose—to disarm her, to have her trust him and to make her fall in love with him—so that when he finally revealed the truth, that he despised her and her family, that he would *never* love *her,* it would be all the more shattering.

Her marriage to Simon had not imbued Sophy with any strong feelings of high esteem, and since there was not a vain bone in her body, she had always been suspicious of the reasons behind Ives's bold pursuit of her.

In fact, she had never quite understood the fascination she seemed to hold for men in general—Simon, Grimshaw, Dewhurst, and the others. It was incomprehensible to her that she was beautiful, and that her beauty might evoke powerful yearnings and strong emotions in the male breast. The notion that her spirit, loyalty, and determination might cause admiration and respect was equally foreign to her.

The circumstances surrounding her marriage to Ives had been unusual and she had been mistrustful of his motives right from the beginning, and she had—foolishly, it now appeared—allowed herself to be swept along by him. He had not wanted to marry *her.* It had not been chivalry that had prompted his drastic actions, it had been *revenge*!

Why shouldn't she believe this? Simon had certainly shown her that men were cruel, hateful beasts. Her uncle had been little better. Ives's apparent predilection for the company of men like Grimshaw, Coleman, and Marquette only added to the evidence against him.

And now, to learn that her mother had been the cause of his adored brother's death, to hear that Ives had sworn vengeance against the woman who had spurned his beloved older brother . . . Jane was beyond his reach, but her daughter was not.

She gave a mirthless little laugh. Oh, it was all so clear now. She had no doubt that he intended to spurn her, just as her mother had done to his brother.

Aware that Lady Beckworth was looking at her with

alarm, Sophy sent her a taut smile, her eyes glittering like molten gold. "This has been a most instructive morning, has it not?" she said with false calm. "I had wondered why your nephew chose to marry me. Now I know—revenge."

"Oh, my dear," exclaimed Lady Beckworth, appalled, "I am sure that you are mistaken. Why, one has only to see the pair of you together to realize that he is utterly smitten with you. I am positive that he has forgotten all about those immature rantings. He cannot blame you for what Robert did."

"We shall just have to see about that, won't we?" Sophy murmured, the expression in her eyes not at all reassuring.

Ives *had* forgotten all about his fleeting notion of using Sophy to satisfy his once-savage thirst to avenge Robert's death. In fact, in the days since he had first thought of it, he came to realize that it was folly and downright foolish to blame Sophy for something her mother had done. If he had been asked about it, he would have burst out laughing at the nonsensical idea.

Unfortunately, returning home in a jovial frame of mind that afternoon, he discovered that Sophy thought precisely that. Her request for an immediate interview in her bedchamber brought a frankly carnal glow to his eyes, and he had been anticipating a lazy afternoon spent making love to his wife when he entered her room. One look at her stony features made it obvious that he was *not* going to be spending any time in her bed in the near future.

In growing dismay and unease he listened to her measured words, his heart clenching into a painful knot. Finished with her recital of the ugly facts she had just learned and her conclusions, Sophy stood in the middle of the room, regal as a queen, and coldly regarded him. "Do you deny it?" she demanded, her face set and hard.

"By Jove! Sophy, you cannot believe that I married you to wreak some sort of belated revenge. You cannot!" he exclaimed, half-furious, half-appalled. "Sweetheart, you must believe me. Such a thought never entered my—" He stopped, uncomfortably remembering that he *had* considered such an idea, the very first time he laid eyes on her.

"Never?" she asked grimly, having noted with a sinking heart his fatal hesitation. "I find that hard to believe. Why *should* I believe you?"

His own temper sparking, Ives snapped, "Why should you not? When have I ever given you reason to mistrust me?"

Sophy opened her lips to hurl back a stinging retort, only to close them abruptly. When *had* he proven himself unworthy of her trust? Desperately, she sought for some event which proved her point. Surely there was something he had done that revealed his perfidious nature? Almost gratefully she remembered his cool abandonment of her immediately upon their return to the city. "You left me to spend the evening with your friends on our very first night back in London."

"Good gad! What does that have to do with anything?" Ives growled, angry hurt building within him. He did not know when he had been more furious, or wounded. Scowling at her, he added coldly, "Am I to be chained to you like a felon to an iron ball?"

His words were knives in her flesh, and her chin lifted,

her fists clenching at her sides. "No, m'lord, you are not! In fact, I'd lief as not have you at my side at all!"

Fighting an urge to shake her, he snarled softly, "Well, that suits me just fine! Good day, madam! Be assured that I shall take care not to inflict my presence upon you in the future!" Turning on his heel, he stormed out of the room, the door violently slamming shut behind him.

Shaken and trembling, Sophy stared miserably at the door. She should be satisfied. She had confronted him. And he had not denied the truth of her words; he had actually tried to turn them against her.

So now she knew. All of his tender caresses, all of those teasing smiles and thoughtful considerations had been an act. She was married to a man every bit as vile and underhanded as Simon had been.

Furiously, she wiped aside a tear that dared to fall. It was better this way. Let there be nothing but indifferent politeness between them. Let them go their separate ways. She had survived one such marriage; surely, she could survive another? Except. Except, *I love him*!

Biting down hard on her lower lip, she kept the tears at bay, wondering how they had come to this dismal state so suddenly. Only yesterday, he had returned her pistol to her. And she had been warmed by his offer to Agnes Weatherby, beginning to believe that there was some rational explanation for his desire for the company of Grimshaw and Meade. And last night . . .

Her lips softened and her heart beat faster. Last night, there had not been a cloud on the horizon as she had lain in his arms and he made love to her, her body responding wildly to him, ecstasy such as she had never dreamed flooding her. And now. Now, everything was gone. Gone like fallen leaves before the winter gales.

*   *   *

It was not to be expected that their estrangement would go unnoticed. Whenever they were in the same room together, despite their polite words and manners, the air seemed noticeably cooler to anyone in the vicinity. Lady Beckworth's departure that very afternoon left a void, the lack of her amiable chatter making the icy aloofness between the newlyweds all the more apparent. By that evening, almost everyone in the house took to swiftly sidling out of any room occupied by both Lord and Lady Harrington.

After an interminable dinner where Ives and Sophy exchanged only the coolest of conversation, the three younger members of the family were grateful when Ives, abandoning the usual after-dinner brandy with Marcus, immediately departed to join his companions. Sophy watched him leave the dining room with dead eyes and, a second later, without explanation, sailed out of the room, leaving Marcus, Phoebe, and Anne to stare at each other in bewilderment.

"What has happened between them?" Phoebe asked Marcus as they made their way from the dining room a few minutes later. "I thought they were happy together. But now!"

"Is Sophy angry because you and Lord Harrington went to Tattersall's this morning?" inquired Anne timidly. "Could that be the cause?"

Marcus shook his head. "No, Sophy would not cut up rough over something like that! And I know that Ives was in great humor this morning, looking forward to spending the afternoon with Sophy."

"And Sophy was so very cheerful, even after enduring the scrutiny of all those scandal-sipping old cats who came to call this morning." Phoebe stopped and looked thoughtful. "At least she was when Anne and I were excused just after Lady Greenwood arrived. I wonder if Lady Greenwood said something . . . Oh, if only Lady Beckworth had not left!" Phoebe exclaimed despondently. "*She* would know what the problem was, and how best to solve it!"

Marcus made a face. "I would not start meddling if I were you," he warned. "This is between Sophy and Ives. I doubt that either one of them would thank you for interfering."

Both girls sent him a disgusted glance. "Oh, pooh! You simply do not want to be bothered," Phoebe said.

"It ain't that. Sophy and Ives are married, and only a fool puts his head between a warring husband and wife. *I* ain't a fool!"

Having delivered that pithy statement, he turned on his heel and went in search of his own entertainment.

That Ives was in a foul mood did not escape the notice of his companions. A malicious smile on his face, Grimshaw murmured, "Trouble at home, dear fellow? Finding the parson's mousetrap a bit *too* confining?"

Ives sent him a look that would have felled a lesser man. "Of course not. Why do you ask?"

"Well, you *do* seem a trifle, ah, bad-tempered this evening," interposed Dewhurst smoothly, his blue eyes fixed on Ives's face. "Only natural to assume it might be trouble with your wife."

"It's not," Ives snapped, and finished off his glass of hock, motioning impatiently for another.

The gentlemen around him—Grimshaw, Dewhurst, Meade, Coleman, and Caldwell—exchanged glances.

"Just so," said Meade, already half-foxed. "Whatever you say, dear fellow."

With a rare show of tact, the conversation shifted, and Ives tried to make himself agreeable.

The evening passed slowly for Ives. He really did try to throw himself into the spirit of things by drinking heavily and gambling feverishly. He lost a rather large sum to Meade, and even went so far as to encourage the advances of a shapely ladybird who had been hanging over his shoulder all evening.

Ignoring the sly glances of the others, he let her sit in his lap and lean intimately against him as he played hand after hand of cards. However, he was not so far gone as to carry it further; when her fingers began to teasingly explore his hard frame, and she nibbled on his ear, he gently removed her from his lap. "Not tonight, I am afraid," he said with a polite smile, and tossed her a gold coin.

"Can it be," Coleman asked in astonished accents, "that you actually plan on remaining faithful to your wife?"

Grimshaw and Meade and the others snickered. Grimshaw even wagged an admonishing finger at him. "This will not do at all! It is clear," he said, "that your bride is playing her old tricks on you. Often did I see Simon wear that same look of baffled fury." He smiled. Not nicely. "Has she thrown you from her bed and held you at bay with her pistol?"

Ives's jaw tightened. "That is not," he said dangerously, "any of your business."

Something glittered in Grimshaw's eye. "Suppose," he drawled, "that I were to make it my business?"

Ives stilled. His gaze locked with Grimshaw's, he spoke in low tones. "That might be a rather hazardous thing to do, my friend. Unless, of course, you think that you may best me with either the sword or the pistol."

Hastily, Meade said, "Oh, come now. None of that. We are all friends here, are we not?" He smiled with drunken affection from one set face to the other.

It was Grimshaw who broke first. "Of course," he said. "Naturally, we are all friends."

Ives nodded curtly, aware of a stab of disappointment. In the mood he was in tonight he really would have looked forward to meeting Grimshaw on the dueling field. Which was as foolish as it was dangerous. The last thing Roxbury needed was for him to face possible death at Grimshaw's hands.

It was Meade who was the first to rise from the table that evening, which was unusual and made Ives look at him carefully. There had been an air of suppressed excitement about Meade all night, but Ives had put it down to his unexpected luck with the cards. Yet discreetly studying the other man, it dawned on him that Meade was not *quite* as drunk as he pretended and that there was a feverish glow in his eyes.

Following Meade's lead, the party broke up, and, with ever-sharpening interest, Ives watched Meade toddle off with Grimshaw at his side. Coleman and Caldwell followed behind them.

Henry Dewhurst, still sprawled at their table, yawned delicately, and said, "Well, I am for my bed. It appears the others have other plans for the remainder of the evening. Probably Flora's. Although, Meade did seem a bit eager for just a night of . . ." Henry chuckled. "Ah, but then Meade prides himself on being quite a man with the ladies." Smiling at Ives, he said, "Since we seem to be deserted by our friends, shall we walk together part of the way home?"

"You know Meade rather well, don't you?" asked Ives idly.

Henry shrugged. "Yes, but probably not as well as I know Grimshaw. Grimshaw and I have always been very close." He smiled sleepily. "And, of course, to a remarkable degree, we *do* seem to share the same vices."

"And the same taste in women," Ives commented dryly, well aware that Henry had hoped to marry Sophy—which was more than he suspected Grimshaw of wanting to do.

Henry laughed uneasily. "Does it bother you that I wanted to marry Sophy? I did, you know. I courted her for a long time, and I was *not* happy when you stole the march on me and married her out of hand."

Suddenly liking Dewhurst for his honesty, Ives said slowly, "That was a handsome admission. And, no, it does not bother me that you wanted to marry her." Ives grinned at him. "I wanted to marry her myself, and I cannot blame you for feeling the same. She is an extraordinary woman."

"And not very happy with you, if your expression earlier tonight was anything to go by," Henry observed tartly.

Ives grimaced. "Let us talk of more pleasant things, shall we?"

Dewhurst followed his lead, and they walked together amiably for several more minutes, Henry happily prattling on about the latest on-dits while Ives wondered how soon he could decently part from him. Meade's whole demeanor tonight had taken on enormous significance to him, and he wanted to assure himself that Sanderson, or whoever had been assigned to watch Meade that night, was especially diligent.

Parting from Henry a few minutes later, Ives suddenly grinned to himself. The devil! He didn't want to assure himself that Sanderson was doing his job; he wanted to be the one trailing Meade tonight. His grin faded. And there sure as hell was no reason for him to hurry home.

Meade had made enough allusions to Flora's throughout the evening for Ives to decide to begin his quest to find the other man there. Swiftly, he made his way through the murky London streets to Flora's. Intent upon his objective, he nearly stumbled across the man lurking in a darkened alleyway just across from the whorehouse.

They grappled for a second, Ives striking a powerful blow that sent his assailant reeling. He was on him instantly, his fingers closing around the other man's throat.

"M'lord!" the fellow gasped. "Is that you?"

"Williams!" Ives exclaimed, loosening his savage grip with a feeling of chagrin and relief. Of course. One of his own men would be trailing Meade.

In the darkness Williams grinned, his teeth a pale flash. "Thought I recognized your handiwork."

Helping his head groom to his feet, Ives asked, "So which one of our suspects were you watching tonight?"

"The colonel. Sanderson is on Coleman, and Ogden is following Grimshaw." Brushing off his clothes, he continued, "Good thing they went their separate ways tonight, else the three of us would have been falling all over each other. Which," he added wearily, "is what we are generally doing. They are all such boon companions that it seems to me you could have had just one of us watch all three. They generally end up at the same places at the same time."

"But not tonight?" Ives asked.

"No, not tonight," Williams admitted.

"I wonder," Ives mused aloud, "if that is significant?"

It was, *very,* but only the Fox knew it. Having finally shaken free of the last of his companions, he swiftly hurried to his lodgings and, after dismissing his valet for the night, set about preparing himself for the meeting with Meade. A change of clothing and a bit of theatrical flair was definitely in order.

Slipping down the stairs, he made his way to a small room at the rear of the house that possessed all he needed, including its own private entrance into the narrow alley behind the building where he lived. Entering the room, he crossed to a large picture hanging on one wall. He lifted it down, revealing a secret hiding place concealed by a little door with a sturdy lock. Using the key he had brought with him, he opened the lock and, a few minutes later, was competently changing his appearance. In clothing fit for a merchant, a rather handsome drooping mustache and a large-brimmed hat that hid half his face, he soon presented an image completely different from his own.

He would have preferred to change in one of his hiding places, but did not want to waste the time tonight. Meade was already waiting for him at Flora's, and he did not want him to become impatient.

A sly smile curved his mouth as he drifted out of the house and into the dark alley behind it—there was no real danger of Meade leaving Flora's. He would, the Fox suspected, wait a very long time to meet with the man who was going to give him a great deal of gold.

He was still smiling as he crept down the alley, stiffening a second later when he realized he was not alone. Someone else was there . . . watching for him?

A cold feeling settled in his chest. How? How could Roxbury have settled upon him? He had been so careful, and for these past several months he had lived an exemplary life, avoiding everything that might connect him to *Le Renard.*

Telling himself to keep a cool head and not leap to conclusions, he remained motionless, staring at the faint outline of the other man in front of him. It could be coincidence. The fellow lurking ahead of him could have nothing to do with him. He could even be a housebreaker spying out a likely target.

He cautiously backed away from the other man, his mind racing furiously. He did not discount the possibility that the watcher *was* waiting for him, but if his identity was truly known, he realized with a flush of triumph, there would be a damn sight more than just one man after him.

But Roxbury could be suspicious of him. A feeling of invincibility mingled with excitement surged through him. The game had suddenly become even more challenging. He would meet with Meade tonight, he thought, almost giggling in his delight, right under their very noses. And if the fellow obliviously leaning against the side of the building in front of him did discover his presence and try to follow him, he would easily lose the fool.

Darting into another alley, he stopped and glanced back, pleased to see no sign of a follower. Contemptuously, he concluded that the incompetent creature had no idea that he had already left the house and was on the loose. Another giggle rose up within him. He would meet with Meade all right, and the man who was to have watched him would remain right where he was, lurking over an empty den! The Fox had already escaped!

Ives was disappointed when he heard the reports of his men the next morning. Having been with Williams for what had remained of the night, he was already prepared for what they had to say. According to Ogden and Sanderson, neither Grimshaw nor Coleman had left his residence once each retired for the night.

Ogden appeared uncomfortable, and at Ives's raised brow, he added reluctantly, "It is probably nothing, my lord, but there was something strange about last night. There was a few minutes when I felt almost as if someone was watching me. I looked around, but didn't see anything out of the ordinary. It was just odd, and I thought I should mention it."

"Probably nothing to worry over," Ives said slowly, "but if it happens again, tell me, and we'll take steps to find out if there is something to it."

Williams had little to add that Ives didn't already know; he had been with him until Meade left Flora's a few hours later and stumbled to his lodgings. Meade had remained there until Ives had given up in disgust and returned to Berkeley Square just as dawn was breaking over the city.

Yawning, Williams said, "He is still at his lodgings. He never stirred from the place after you left this morning. That fellow of your godfather's, Hinckley, has taken over watching him for today; Carnes is following Grimshaw; and Ashby is sniffing after Coleman." He yawned again. "And I, m'lord, with your permission, am for my bed."

Ives smiled faintly. His three henchmen did look rather

bleary-eyed. Having managed only a few hours of sleep himself, they had his sympathy.

"Very well," Ives said. "Get some sleep, the lot of you. I have no doubt you will be in for another long night tonight." Wryly he added, "We all will. I am to meet Meade and Grimshaw and the others this evening for another round of gambling and drinking."

After they departed, Ives paced the small room Marcus had arranged to be set aside for his exclusive use. His head ached, and he could have used several more hours of sleep. But it was not his aching head or the lack of sleep that brought such a ferocious scowl to his hard features. It was thoughts of his wife.

Having had time for his temper to cool and to realize, with no little regret, that there was some justification for Sophy's attitude, he had come home in the early hours of the morning determined to confront her and settle things between them. His usually amiable temper had soared when he had discovered the door to their connecting rooms locked. Infuriated all over again, and in no mood to be balked, he had stalked into the main hallway and stormed into her room from the main entrance.

Sophy was ready for him. Not only was he confronted by an icy-eyed wife, but she had the nerve, the utter audacity, to aim at him the very pistol he had given her less than forty-eight hours previously.

"That is far enough," she said coolly. "Come one step nearer, and I shall shoot you, m'lord."

His attempt on the connecting door must have alerted her, because despite the hour, she was obviously wide-awake and standing in the middle of the room, her gown of sheer pale blue silk drifting tantalizingly around her tall, slender form.

A muscle in his jaw worked. "Has it come to this?"

Sophy dipped her head. "Indeed, I am afraid that it has, m'lord."

"Dash it all, Sophy! Quit calling me m'lord in that odious fashion. I am your husband!"

"Unfortunately."

They stood there glaring at each other, and Ives was gallingly aware that Sophy was not going to give an inch. In the mood she was in now, she *would* shoot him.

Snarling something decidedly ungentlemanly under his breath, he stalked from the room.

Reliving that ugly little scene a few hours later did nothing to make him feel any better about it. Somehow, he admitted gloomily, he had to make Sophy realize that she was all wrong in her assumptions. Robert's death, her mother's part in it, had *nothing* to do with them. His face contorted. All he had to do now was prove it to her. A bitter laugh came from him. So simple, and yet so very, very difficult when the lady had a pistol in her hand!

The day did not get any better. He was greeted stiffly by the rest of the family, and, worse, Sophy herself eluded him, disappearing almost immediately after a strained and uncomfortable breakfast for a drive with Dewhurst.

Feeling thwarted and thoroughly out of sorts, Ives withdrew to his bedroom in the hope of gaining a few more hours of sleep, and perhaps discovering a way back into his wife's good graces.

To his surprise, he slept soundly and woke several hours later feeling refreshed. As for the situation with his wife, no solution occurred to him. Not wishing to run the gauntlet of accusatory stares and stiff conversation, he remained in his room, pacing and moodily considering the future.

At present he saw no way out of the situation with Sophy. He realized it would do little good to assure her of his honorable intentions, then immediately go off to consort with the likes of Grimshaw, Marquette, and Meade. Once again, he wished to tell her of the quest for *Le Renard,* but while in his own heart he was certain that Sophy could be trusted, there were too many lives at risk to take a chance.

The rap on the door caught his attention and knowing that Sophy must have returned by now, he flung it open hopefully. He was disappointed to see only Ogden standing there before him. Ushering him into the room, he asked, "Yes? What is it? Have you news?"

Ogden scratched his bald head. "It could be nothing, but as soon as he was relieved by Sanderson, Hinckley came by with a message on his way to report to Roxbury. Said you might be interested to know that Meade spent several hours at the Horse Guards today."

Ives's brows shot up. "On a Sunday afternoon?"

"That's what he said."

"It *is* interesting, and I'll wager a wagonful of gold that I know precisely what our good colonel was doing—he had to be either copying the memorandum or stealing it." A satisfied smile crossed Ives's harsh features. "The Fox has taken the bait!"

The Fox was also feeling rather satisfied with events as he strolled down the street later that Sunday evening. The meeting with Meade last night had gone just as he had assumed it would, and by this time tomorrow night he would be meeting with the Frenchman. A smile lurked at the corner of his mouth. And if his plans unfolded as they should, Roxbury would be left chasing his own tail.

A touch on his arm startled him. Swinging around, he was astonished to see Agnes Weatherby standing beside him. He bowed politely, and murmured, "Miss Weatherby, how pleasant to see you." He glanced around and seeing no sign of carriage or vehicle, or even a maid or footman to give the impression of propriety, he asked, "Is there something I can do for you? Perhaps escort you home?"

Agnes shook her head. Her hard eyes fastened on his, she said smoothly, "I need no escort, but I *do* wish you to call upon me, very late this evening, at my home, after my servants have gone to bed. I shall let you in myself. Use the side door. You know which one—you've used it before when you accompanied Edward. I want, and I'm sure you'll agree, no one to know of our meeting. It shall be our secret."

At his look of astonishment, she smiled maliciously. "In his cups Edward was, as I'm sure you already know, quite talkative. After you hear what I have to say, I think you will agree that we have much to consider, you and I."

Chapter Fifteen

✌

*B*efore joining the others for another long evening wasted in gaming and other vices, Ives arranged a meeting with his godfather. They met at a small tavern.

Entering the private room Roxbury had procured for their meeting, Ives said, "Well, my lord, it appears that we finally have some progress."

Roxbury nodded. "Indeed, I am inclined to agree with you, my boy. I've had the files checked and the document is still there, but that does not mean that Meade is not carrying a copy around with him at this very moment."

Ives frowned. "My conclusion precisely, but I cannot believe that the French would pay very much for simply a copy. How could they be certain that the information was authentic? I suspect that at some point, the original document is going to have to disappear, at least temporarily, so that whoever the Fox or Meade is selling the information to can assure themselves that what they are buying is genuine."

"I concur, but for now the memorandum is still safely

at the Horse Guards." Roxbury took a sip of the rum punch he had ordered prepared for them.

Ives made a face. "For now."

He took a swallow of the punch and, frowning slightly, said slowly, "I know that in the beginning I wanted as few people to know about this endeavor as possible, but I think the time has come to bolster our troops. My men can only do so much, and they are stretched thin, thinner than I like, and if we were to lose Meade . . ."

He sighed. "At present any chance of success rests solely with the colonel leading us to the Fox, and while I do not want our men tripping over each other, I would feel better if two men were assigned to watch Meade at all times, with a few more held ready in case of need. Could you arrange it?"

Roxbury nodded. "With little effort. What about Grimshaw and Coleman?"

"I don't know," Ives replied moodily. "If there are too many people following our suspects about they are bound to be noticed. I think for now that we had better continue as we are. Meade, however, is the key. We cannot lose him."

"Very well," said Roxbury, rising to his feet. "I shall have two more of my best fellows to help you. When do you want them to start?"

"Immediately."

While it seemed that things were finally moving along in connection with the Fox, Ives was still not a very happy man when he left his godfather a few minutes later and set out to meet with Meade and his friends to dine at Stephens's. Joining the others at their table, he could not help but remember the night he had brought Sophy here with the Offingtons . . . and that passionate kiss in his coach. He scowled fiercely at his claret glass. If things continued as they were, all he was going to have were memories.

That notion did not sit well, and though he tried to pay attention to what was going on around him, the moment he let his guard down his thoughts turned inevitably to his wife. And as the evening progressed and he drank glass after glass of liquor, a strong sense of ill usage sprang up within him.

The little baggage had feathers in her brain if she thought for one moment that he would be so stupid as to marry her simply because of a desire for revenge for some long-ago tragedy. It was true he had sworn vengeance, but dash it all, he had not meant it! At least not recently.

He glared at his glass, his feeling of betrayal and of being poorly used growing with every minute. How dare she aim that dashed pistol at him! He had done nothing wrong. Bloody hell! She was his wife! And she had as good as thrown him out of her room.

By the time the evening ended, half-drunk and feeling that Sophy had served him a great injustice, Ives departed from the other gentlemen. As he walked home, a hazy determination to set her right began to build within him. He was *not* Marlowe! And she had no cause to treat him in this fashion. No cause at all!

Arriving home, he entered the house. Moving with the extreme care of a man who has imbibed too freely, Ives shut the door, locking it behind him, and walked up the stairs to his room.

Shedding his clothes, he shrugged into a robe of maroon silk with tiny golden dragons scattered across it. He poured himself a snifter of brandy and drank it slowly, glaring at the door which separated him from his wife.

She was, he knew, no doubt sleeping sweetly in her bed. The bed in which he should be at this very moment. . . .

The thought of Sophy's soft curves and the pleasure they had shared sent a shaft of longing through him. And the idea of spending the rest of his life this way suddenly became insupportable.

Not precisely drunk, not precisely angry, but stubbornly determined, Ives carefully set down his snifter and walked to the door that kept him from what he wanted most in the world. He tried the door and was not surprised to find it still locked.

Did she really, he wondered with a half smile, think that he would allow a mere partition of wood to separate them? Not giving himself time to consider the consequences, he aimed one big shoulder at the offending barrier and, with one powerful lunge, smashed the door.

As arrogant and unruffled as a jungle cat, he stepped into the room. Sophy had not been asleep. Sleep did not come easily to her since their confrontation. She could tell herself that Ives was a deceiving libertine, a mendacious beast, a vile knave, but somehow that knowledge did nothing to stop the ache to feel his arms around her.

She had never longed for a man before, had never known the frank hunger that could build within one for the touch of one certain man, and she was aghast at the way not only her body but her thoughts had begun to betray her. Her initial fury had faded, and she found herself making excuses for him and wondering if perhaps she had judged him too hastily. Or if she wouldn't have been wiser to let him explain. . . . Her mouth twisted. Attempt to explain.

Restlessly she tossed and turned in her bed, aware of her body in a way that was queer and unnerving. Her breasts seemed unusually sensitive; just the brush of her delicate gown made her nipples swell and an odd sensation flow through her. And low in her belly, she was uncomfortably conscious of a hot ache, not exactly unpleasant, but markedly persistent.

She was not stupid. She knew what her body was telling her, but she pushed that knowledge away. She was *not* going to allow herself to be dominated by simple carnal desire.

Except in her heart she knew that it was not simple, and it was not just the desire to have Ives in her arms again. She missed his teasing eyes and laughing mouth, and perhaps most of all, the comforting sensation of not having to face the future completely alone.

She not only wanted him in a purely physical sense, but in a distinctly intangible way, too. Miserably, she admitted that she loved the wicked rogue, and that made everything all the more complicated. If she could hate him, despise him as she had Simon, nothing he did would matter to her. She could sleep alone a thousand nights and never give him a single thought. But with Ives . . .

A lump grew in her throat. Oh, damn and blast! she thought furiously. How am I to get through the rest of my life, loving him so desperately with all this ugliness between us?

Though the hour was very late, neither sleep nor answers came to her, and she lay there staring blindly at the silken canopy of her bed, alternately damning Ives and longing for him. She was still awake when he returned home, and she heard his steps in the hall as he passed her door. Her heart had thudded painfully.

The soft click of his bedroom door shutting firmly behind him came to her, and though she listened intently, the thickness of the walls prevented any other sound reaching her. After straining to hear sounds of him for several minutes, she gave it up and tried to go sleep. It proved useless. Thoughts of Ives kept drifting through her brain. It was sheer torture, she finally admitted bitterly, to know he was so close and yet so very far away.

At his sudden explosion through her shattered door, Sophy jerked upright in her bed, hardly daring to believe that he had the audacity to break down her door. Not even Simon at his worst had behaved so outrageously. Instinctively, she reached for the pistol and, slipping from her bed, faced him.

The room was in near darkness. Only the light from his room filtered into hers, yet Ives had no trouble discerning her slim form near the bed. It was obvious from her stance that she held the pistol, and he wondered, half-amused, half-regretful, if these would be his last moments of life. If his last memory would be of Sophy firing her damned bloody pistol at him.

He stopped where he was, the candlelight behind him outlining his tall form and broad shoulders, the golden dragons on his robe winking brightly against the maroon silk.

"Are you really going to shoot me?" he asked, as he stared at her across the distance which separated them.

Sophy's mouth went dry, and she was conscious that the pistol suddenly felt slippery in her hand. "I will," she said stoutly, "if you come any nearer." She was dismayed at the lack of conviction in her own voice, shocked to feel her entire body start to tremble, and not with fear or anger.

Ives smiled crookedly, and took a step in her direction. Sophy backed up slightly, but could not go far; the bed was blocking her retreat.

"Stay where you are," she said desperately.

His heart beating like a war drum, Ives shook his head slowly, a lock of gleaming, raven black hair falling down across his forehead.

"I cannot," he said huskily. "I am under your spell, sweetheart, drawn to you like steel to magnet, like blossoms to sunlight. I can*not* stay away from you. So if you are going to shoot me, go ahead. That, and only that, will stop me from making love to you tonight."

The pistol wavered, but she did not drop it. The light from his room suddenly illuminated his face, and seeing his devil green eyes fixed warmly on her, seeing that unbearably attractive brigand's smile on his mouth, something inside of her splintered.

"Damn you!" she whispered helplessly, the pistol falling uselessly to her side.

Ives closed the distance between them, dragging her unresisting form into his strong embrace. He kissed her roughly, all his despair and fear, his pent-up passion in that one kiss.

"We are, it seems," he said thickly, when he finally raised his lips from hers, "damned together."

Sophy did not argue with him. Her blood was singing, her body wildly rejoicing to feel his touch once more. Lifting her mouth to his, she said crossly, "Oh, shut up and kiss me again!"

Ives chuckled and, swinging her up into his arms, said, "Oh, that I shall, sweetheart. That and more."

Laying her on the bed, he gently removed the pistol from her slackened grip and shrugged impatiently out of his robe. Ives joined her immediately on the bed, his big body pressing intimately into hers. He was hard and warm on her, the shaft between his legs thick and solid, its weight seeming to sear right through the thin material separating them. The desperate hunger between them exploded, and Ives's mouth crushed hers. His hands made short, violent work of her delicate gown.

Sophy moaned as she felt his hot skin against hers, the muscles of his broad back beneath her questing fingertips. His mouth was magic as it tasted and ravaged her own, his mere touch blatant sorcery as his hands shaped and explored her body. She was ready for him in an instant, damp heat flooding between her thighs, the primitive need to have him banishing every thought but that one. She wanted him. *Now.*

But Ives had other ideas, and though Sophy twisted up enticingly against him, he ignored the unmistakable invitation and continued to kiss and fondle her. When his lips finally left her mouth and traveled in stinging little bites to her breasts, she was certain she would go mad if he did not soothe the demanding ache which consumed her. But he did not, his dark head sliding lower, his hot mouth touching her in places that astonished her, sliding down low across her belly until he reached the juncture of her thighs.

Blood pounding feverishly, her heart beating as if it would leap from her breast, she cried out in shocked pleasure when he kissed her there between her legs, his tongue seeking that most intimate of all places. He held her prisoner beneath his teasing mouth, his thumbs holding the tender flesh apart as he feasted, long and with great hunger. At that first probing kiss, Sophy's entire body clenched, fire streaking up through her. The maddeningly sweet sensations wreaked by his famished mouth only incited her more, making the demanding ache within her stronger, more intense . . . unendurable.

She thought she was going to die of pleasure. Her fingers fiercely gripped his dark hair, and she was uncertain whether she was trying to pull him away or guide his warm mouth to where the ache was worst. His tongue suddenly stabbed just where she wanted it, and a soft scream was torn from her as sharp, powerful pleasure erupted through her. She shuddered wildly as her entire body seemed to explode into a thousand splinters of sweet ecstasy.

Sophy's reaction was everything Ives could have wished for. The tremors that shook her body revealed more potently than words just how powerfully he had affected her.

The clawing demands of his own body became paramount. Sliding up over her passion-slick body, he found her mouth, kissing her hungrily as he captured her hips and lifted her to him. He plunged into her silken heat.

With swift, powerful strokes he swept Sophy along with him, stoking the fire which burned within each of them to new heights, deliberately prolonging the heavenly torture until there was only the frantic race to reach paradise. When Sophy suddenly cried out and convulsed around him, the sensation was so sweet, so desperately yearned for that Ives could only groan as he exploded deep within her satiny warmth.

They lay locked together for one long moment, neither one wanting to be the one to end it, but eventually Ives slid reluctantly from her body. They were both breathing heavily, aware that nothing had been settled between them. In the faint flickering light from his room, they regarded each other warily.

Sophy tried to think of something to say, some way of prolonging this moment, some way of closing the chasm between them. She could not deny that what had just happened between them changed nothing, she still did not trust him. Helplessly, she stared at him, uncertainty and mistrust evident in her lovely eyes.

Ives's mouth twisted, knowing there was no way he could put her suspicions about him to rest, not as long as the Fox ran free. But there was one area he could talk of openly. His eyes locked on hers, he said grimly, "I did not marry you from some misguided need to seek revenge, and you are a fool if you continue to think so."

Sophy swallowed, tears springing to her eyes. She wanted to believe him, but mistrust died hard. Wretchedly, she said, "Which is exactly what you would say if you *did* marry me for those reasons."

His mouth tightened. "Very well, madam, believe what you will." He suddenly bent down and kissed her almost brutally. "At least, if we have nothing else between us," he said thickly, when he finally lifted his lips, "we have *this*." He stalked from the room.

In utter despair Sophy stared after him, the instinct to call him back very strong. But she did not. Marlowe had taught her well, and the lessons she learned from him were deeply ingrained. Men lied. They went to incredible lengths to gain what they wanted, and tonight, Ives had wanted her.

Sophy rose the next morning, heavy-eyed and not certain how to greet her husband. It was folly, after what had taken place between them last night, to think that she could treat him as she had the past few days—or that she would refuse him her bed. As he had said, at least they had that between them.

The shattered door between their rooms raised some eyebrows and Sophy knew that news of its ruined condition would be common knowledge before long. Sighing unhappily, she left her room, wondering how to explain its destruction.

With relief, she discovered that her husband had already offered an explanation. It seemed, he glibly told Marcus, Sophy had suffered a terrifying nightmare and hearing her cry out, he had rushed to her side, smashing the door down in haste to reach his wife. No one, of course, was brazen enough to comment on the intriguing fact that the door had been locked against him in the first place.

Breakfast was awkward, Sophy so aware of Ives and what they had shared together during the night that she could hardly think of anything else. Ives was little better, his brooding gaze fixed on his lovely wife as she tried to pretend she was perfectly at ease with his presence.

Fortunately, Marcus, Phoebe, and Anne chatted happily, and the constraint between the other two occupants of the room went largely unnoticed. It was apparent to the others that some sort of change had occurred, simply because Sophy joined them for breakfast instead of taking a tray in her room, which she had been wont to do of late. She actually replied almost naturally to Ives's halfhearted conversation, making the other three exchange questioning glances. Were they at peace with each other? It appeared so.

Rising from the table, Ives asked, "I wonder if you

ladies would like to join me for a drive through Hyde Park this afternoon?" He grinned at Marcus. "Perhaps you would like to accompany the carriage on that showy hack you just purchased?"

"Certainly, sir," Marcus answered quickly, relieved to be on more normal terms with his brother-in-law.

The two girls looked expectantly at Sophy, relaxing slightly when she smiled at Ives, albeit uncertainly, and replied, "Thank you, my lord. I think we would all enjoy it immensely."

Emerson entered the room at that moment and, bending down next to Ives, murmured in his ear. Ives's brows shot up, but he said calmly enough, "Thank you, Emerson, that will be all."

Rising to his feet, he said to Sophy, "It seems that we have a, er, caller. He wishes to see both of us and is presently awaiting us in the library. If you will accompany me, madam?"

Obviously puzzled, Sophy stared at him. Why hadn't Emerson simply announced the caller? But following Ives's lead, she rose from her chair and replied, "Of course."

Aware of the younger three watching them perplexedly, she smiled at Phoebe and Anne, and said, "Finish your breakfast, and I shall join you shortly in the blue saloon. You may work on your embroidery until then."

In the hall, Ives said softly, "Do not be alarmed, my dear, but there is a Constable Clarke waiting to see us."

"A constable!" Sophy exclaimed, her eyes widening. "Why ever would a constable come to call on us?"

There was no time for further private conversation between them before they reached the library, but Ives's thoughts were racing. There was only one reason he could conceive of for a morning visit, *any* visit for that matter, from an officer of the law. It had to be connected with Edward's murder, but how?

The constable, a heavyset, grizzle-haired man of middle age, appeared to be clearly ill at ease. When they entered the library, he was pacing the floor and tugging at his stock. He started visibly at their entrance and after introducing himself, said unhappily, "I beg that you will forgive the intrusion, my lord, my lady, but Magistrate Harris felt—once we learned that Miss Anne Richmond was staying with you—that you were the proper people to be apprised of the situation." He shook his grizzled head. "Most unfortunate affair. Most unfortunate."

At his words, Sophy stiffened, her fingers digging into Ives's arm. He spared a moment to smile reassuringly at her, then asked, "It is about Miss Anne Richmond that you wished to see us?"

"Er, not precisely, my lord. . . ." The constable took a deep breath, and said in a rush, "It is about her aunt, Miss Agnes Weatherby. She is dead."

"Dead!" Sophy gasped. "But how can this be? We just saw her on Friday, not three days ago."

"So her butler informed us this very morning," Clarke said, looking extremely unhappy. "It is my unpleasant duty to inform you that not only is Miss Weatherby dead, but that she was murdered—most foully."

"How shocking," murmured Ives, hoping that Sophy, who had blanched at Clarke's news, was not going to faint. Easing her down into a chair of green damask, Ives glanced at Clarke. "Please, tell us what you can."

There was not a great deal to tell. When Miss Weatherby's butler entered the drawing room that morning to open the curtains, he discovered the body of his employer sprawled across a sofa. Miss Weatherby was quite dead. Her throat had been slashed, and from the profusion of blood, it was apparent that she had died almost instantly. Other than Miss Weatherby's body, there was no sign of violence. The house had not been broken into, and all of the servants could account for their time the previous evening.

In fact, Constable Clarke stated grimly, there was nothing out of the ordinary about the previous evening. Their mistress had returned late from an outing and retired as usual. None of the servants had any explanation for the tragedy.

Ives and Sophy carefully avoided glancing at each other. In spite of Ives's generous settlement, Agnes had apparently let greed rule her and approached Edward's murderer—and now she shared the fate of her lover. The conclusion was inevitable.

It had been Miss Weatherby's butler who informed the authorities of Miss Richmond's whereabouts. Clarke cleared his throat. "It was thought best that we tell you of the tragedy and allow you the opportunity to tell the young lady yourself, my lord. It is our understanding that you are in the process of being proclaimed her guardian."

Ives nodded absently, his thoughts on that last interview with Agnes Weatherby. "Yes, yes, of course. I understand."

"Terrible thing," Clarke said. "Respectable woman like Miss Weatherby to be killed like that in her own home." He shook his head. " 'Tis an evil world we live in these days."

After the constable left, Ives and Sophy stared at each other for a long moment.

"She must have talked to Edward's murderer," Sophy

said sadly. "Even after you offered her a comfortable fortune and we warned her that it was dangerous, she went ahead with it."

"So it would appear—assuming that the same person who murdered her, murdered Edward."

"Do you doubt it?" Sophy asked, astonished.

Ives shook his head. "No. I am quite certain that the same person killed both of them."

"I wonder how much Agnes knew. Oh, if only she had spoken honestly with us!" Sophy's expressive face twisted. "And dear heavens, what shall we tell Anne?"

"As little as possible," Ives replied levelly. "She will have to know that her aunt has been murdered, but that is all."

Sophy looked distressed. "It is a nightmare. First Edward's murder, and now poor Agnes. Whoever murdered them must be entirely without conscience."

Ives nodded. Thoughtfully, he added, "And rather desperate to take such chances."

"Do you think the authorities will connect the two murders?" Sophy asked anxiously. She looked down at her hands, a faint flush burning across her cheeks. "At least no one can suspect me of murdering Agnes."

"I wouldn't be too sure of that," Ives said slowly. "Quite a few people know the circumstances surrounding Anne's, er, visit with you. I shouldn't wonder if that fact isn't discovered by Clarke soon enough. And unless the good constable is utterly incompetent, and I do not believe that he is, I do not think it will be very many days before he learns of Edward's murder—and that you and I were found standing over his body."

The color drained from Sophy's face, and Ives cursed his blunt tongue. "Sweetheart," he said softly, dropping to one knee in front of her, "do not be alarmed. No one will seriously consider you a murderess, but you have to realize that it is going to be unpleasant for all of us for the next several days. There is bound to be all sorts of wild conjecture bandied about, and the circumstances surrounding Anne's being under your care are only going to add to that conjecture."

His mouth pulled. "I have little doubt that our visit with Agnes on Friday will be painted in the most sinister of colors." He grinned crookedly at her. "We are going to have the most shocking reputation, my dear."

Sophy smiled faintly. "I suspect you are right. But, Ives, what *are* we going to do?"

He rose to his feet and helping her up from the chair, said simply, "We, sweetheart, are going to do what we originally set out to do—find Edward's murderer."

"But *how*?"

"At the moment, I haven't the faintest idea," Ives admitted cheerfully. A glint entered his green eyes. "Of course, you should know by now that I shan't let such a trifling matter as that deter me!"

Despite the gravity of the situation, Ives's words lifted Sophy's gloom. He was right. Nothing would stand in his way, and they *would* find the man who had murdered Edward and Agnes.

Sophy and Ives saw no reason not to tell the rest of the family at once, particularly since the three younger members of the family were all waiting in the blue saloon, impatient to learn the outcome of the meeting with the mysterious caller.

Anne had not been close to her aunt, but she was understandably shocked and distressed to hear of her death, especially the manner of it. She could not help but grieve;

Agnes, despite her faults, had been kind upon occasion, and she was Anne's last living relative.

"Do not fear that you are alone in the world, my dear," Sophy said kindly, once Anne's first storm of tears had passed. "We are your family now and you will never be alone again."

"By Jove! Sophy is right," said Marcus warmly. "You are our sister now. We shall look after you."

Since Marcus had largely ignored Anne up until then, Sophy was pleased with his reaction. Phoebe, of course, was quick to asseverate her deep affection for Anne, and holding Anne's hand tight, she exclaimed, "Oh, Marcus is right! It will be splendid, you will see! We shall be sisters!"

Uncertainly Anne looked at Ives, who had been mostly silent. Crossing to where she sat, he smiled down at her. "Do not worry, little one. You have nothing to fear. Sophy and I shall be pleased to call you our own."

It was all very affecting, and Sophy was aware of a strong tendency to burst into tears herself. How could he be so kind, so caring, and yet follow so eagerly in the footsteps of blatant libertines like Grimshaw and Coleman?

In view of Agnes's death, any notion of driving in the park was abandoned. Leaving Sophy with the girls, Ives retreated temporarily to his study, where he penned a short note to Roxbury, apprising him of Agnes's murder. With the note to Roxbury sent on its way, after discussing it with Sophy, he went round to see his solicitor to inform him of Anne's change in circumstances and to press for swift action in the court.

At the moment there was little else he could do except wait and speculate about the murder. Deciding he could do that at Berkeley Square as well as anywhere, he returned home.

It was a very quiet afternoon, and Sophy spent most of it with Anne and Phoebe, Agnes's brutal murder diminishing her own problems for the moment. Since Agnes had not been related to the family, there was no need of them going into mourning.

As for Anne, she was not out yet and since they would all be removing to the country within the next few weeks, she needed only to curtail the most frivolous entertainments for the time being. Sophy would see to it that a few gowns in a suitably somber hue were purchased for Anne's use, but it was decided that little more would be done to mourn Agnes.

Dinner that evening was rather subdued, and while no one had been particularly fond of Agnes, her death and the manner of it certainly cast a pall over the household. Sophy was touched that Ives remained home nearly the entire day, and watching him as he teased first a smile and then a laugh out of Anne and Phoebe, she wondered again if she had misjudged him. There was such gentleness in him, such understanding.

Marcus, having a long-standing engagement, had gone out for the evening, but the remainder of the household settled down for a quiet time at home. The girls prevailed upon Ives and Sophy to teach them to play whist, and time passed pleasantly as Anne and Phoebe concentrated on the intricacies of the game.

It was nearly ten o'clock, and the cards had just been put away when Emerson entered the room. Approaching Ives with a silver salver in his hand, he said, "My lord, this just arrived for you."

Ives picked up the note, broke the seal, and read the contents. It was from Roxbury and it was brief.

The game's afoot. Meade has taken the memorandum from the files at the Horse Guards. Meet me immediately at the Green Boar.

Chapter Sixteen

❧

*R*ising to his feet, Ives met Sophy's unblinking gaze. She was not, he realized unhappily, going to be very pleased with him. He grimaced, and said, "I hope that you ladies will forgive me, but I find that I, uh, have a previous demand on my time and must leave you now."

Sophy stiffened. The warmth which had been building in her breast vanished.

"Of course, my lord," she said coolly, her eyes blazing with contempt. "We understand that other amusements call."

The accusing looks Anne and Phoebe flashed his way did not help his frame of mind, and, smothering a curse, Ives bowed and quickly left the room. At least one good thing might come of this, he thought grimly, as he picked up his malacca cane and left the house. With the document gone, there was every chance that tonight would see the capture of the Fox. And if that happened, he admitted more cheerfully, he would be able to tell Sophy all and redeem himself in her eyes—he hoped.

Buoyed by these pleasant thoughts, he swiftly covered

the distance to the Green Boar. Finding Roxbury waiting for him in a private room, he entered, and asked, "When was the document discovered missing?"

Roxbury, who had been pacing impatiently about the small room, looked over at him. "Less than a half hour ago—immediately after Meade left his office."

"The colonel does seem to be working extremely odd hours of late, does he not?"

Roxbury snorted. "Once we knew that the memorandum was gone," he said testily, "I put two more men on Meade in addition to your men. They're working in relays and as soon as they have an idea of his direction or he reaches his destination, one of them will come here and tell us." He raised a brow. "There are another half dozen men waiting outside this tavern to accompany you when word reaches us of Meade's whereabouts. I assumed that you wanted to be in on the kill."

Ives smiled, his eyes very bright. "I look forward to it. The important thing, however, is that we don't lose Meade. Once he's given the document to his buyer, if his buyer *is* the Fox, any hope of catching the elusive *Le Renard* will have disappeared."

"At least the damned information is incorrect," Roxbury muttered, his worry evident. "Nothing must jeopardize Wellesley's plans. Nothing."

Ives smiled. "Do not worry, sir. We will catch him."

"I bloody hope so!"

Ten minutes later, a nondescript man sidled into the room. Meade, he informed them in breathless accents, was headed to one of the hells he was known to frequent. They'd best hurry, if they were to pick up the trail.

Leaving his godfather behind, Ives plunged into the darkness behind Hinckley, as the fellow had been identified. The other waiting men followed quickly on their heels. The distance was traversed swiftly, and Ives was not surprised that the trail led to St. James's Square and a notorious hell aptly named the Pigeon Hole. It was a particular favorite of Meade and Grimshaw's, where they frequently amused themselves fleecing the unwary and green lads up from the country. Ives thought it highly unlikely that Meade had gone directly to his buyer.

The Pigeon Hole was crowded at this time of night and, while most respectable gentlemen avoided it, from time to time the more adventuresome members of the gaming fraternity came to try their luck. Another reason for its lure was the fact that the owner of the hell ran a stable of some of the most attractive ladybirds in London; their much-vaunted charms accounted for a great deal of the fashionable traffic in and out of the hell. Meade was probably simply whiling away a few hours until his appointment.

After spreading his men out in all directions around the hell, Ives reflected that it would not be suspicious if he wandered into the Pigeon Hole himself. He had met Meade here more than once, and his presence would not arouse comment.

A suitably bored expression on his bold features, Ives strolled into the Pigeon Hole and after a discreet glance around spotted Meade, Grimshaw, Dewhurst, and Coleman gathered at the hazard table. He joined them and was greeted as a long-lost brother by Meade.

"I was hoping you would find us this evening," exclaimed Meade, his features already flushed with liquor. "I hear that there is a new ladybird in the flock, and I, for one, want to discover if she is as, er, talented as touted. What about you?"

Ives shrugged. "I have never found buttered buns to my taste. Perhaps another time."

"It seems to me," drawled Grimshaw, "that you are very nice in your requirements, Harrington."

"How very astute of you to have noticed," Ives said sweetly. "And I find it very strange that my habits hold such interest for you. Can it be that you are thinking of emulating my restraint?"

Grimshaw snorted and flashed him a look of dislike before turning back to the hazard table.

No one else paid him any undue attention, and he settled down to wait and see what transpired. Time passed very slowly for him, and by the time Meade and the others were ready to leave several hours later, he was heartily sick of the Pigeon Hole, Meade, and the entire situation.

Despite his avowed purpose for being at the Pigeon Hole, at no time did Meade disappear to sample the charms of the latest addition to the hell's stable of expensive whores, and Ives was heartily grateful. It had occurred to him that the document could be authenticated or transferred while Meade supposedly visited with the new ladybird. He had not been certain what he would have done if Meade had ambled off in search of feminine company.

Sir Alfred Caldwell and a few others had joined them shortly after Ives had entered the hell, and it was a fairly large group of gentlemen who exited the Pigeon Hole at the end of the night. It was by now well after two o'clock in the morning, and most of the gentlemen in the group were either thoroughly foxed or nearly so, Meade in particular.

Frowning slightly, Ives watched as Meade motioned to

a sedan chair and crawled clumsily inside. As the sedan
chair moved off, Ives could hear Meade singing a bawdy
little ditty.

At his side, Dewhurst, not in much better condition,
chuckled, and murmured, "He is quite, quite bosky, is he
not?"

"Very," Ives said dryly, wondering how soon he could
get rid of Dewhurst. The other men had already tottered
off in the direction of their homes, and a few had taken
sedan chairs as had Meade. Somehow, Ives was not surprised that Grimshaw and Coleman were still with him.
Which one, he wondered, which one of you is the Fox?

"Noticed you didn't seem to partake of the wine very
liberally tonight," Grimshaw said almost accusingly, his
gray eyes fixed on Ives's dark face. "Except for gaming—and you're bloody cautious about that, too—I notice you don't participate very much in any of our
amusements. Curious why you seem to like our company."

"I think, my friend, that you are as bosky as Meade,"
Ives said lightly. "And I am rather puzzled why you suddenly seem so very interested in my habits."

"Nosy," said Dewhurst with a giggle, his blue eyes
very bright. "Always has been—even when we were children."

"And at the moment," Coleman interposed firmly,
"badly in need of his bed. Come along, my friend. You
can worry about Harrington's lack of vice some other
time."

Grumbling, Grimshaw allowed himself to be led off by
a surprisingly sober Coleman. Had Coleman abstained
tonight because he knew he would have business to trans-

act later? Or was Grimshaw running a sham and not quite as foxed as he appeared?

A tap on his shoulder distracted his thoughts from the other two men, and he turned to look at Dewhurst. "Think I'll sample the charms of Meade's ladybird since it doesn't appear he is going to do so. Good evening."

Dewhurst disappeared back inside the hell, leaving Ives standing alone. Nonchalantly, he set out in the direction taken by Meade's sedan chair. Almost immediately, he had caught up with the last of his men, who were discreetly keeping Meade in sight.

Knowing that Meade had rooms on Half Moon Street, it did not take Ives long to realize that wherever Meade was going, it was not to his lodgings. And since the sedan chair seemed to be traveling rather erratically, turning first down this street and then that street, it was obvious Meade was either attempting to throw off any followers, or he was too drunk to know where he was going.

Ives and his men were strung out in a long, crooked line behind the sedan chair as they kept to the shadows and moved forward with extreme caution. The streets were nearly deserted at this time, and, as the minutes passed, it became harder and harder to conceal the fact that several men were discreetly following him. Ives began to feel decidedly uneasy. There were too many of them, and he pondered the wisdom of having agreed to the extra men.

When Meade finally emerged from the sedan chair and dismissed it, they were deep in an old part of the city near the Thames. Ives felt his senses quicken. They must be near the meeting place . . . and the Fox?

The sedan chair gone, Meade strolled aimlessly down the narrow, dank streets, apparently without a destination in mind. He seemed in no hurry, and only by the surreptitious glances he occasionally cast over his shoulder was it evident that he was being watchful. Ives noted that any signs of inebriation had disappeared, and he smiled grimly. Meade had obviously not been as drunk as he pretended.

At present there was only one man in front of Ives; the rest were well behind him, ready to spring forward at his signal. It was difficult following Meade. There were too many shadows, too many little black alleys down which he could disappear. The light was murky, fitful, and interspersed with long stretches of darkness.

But it wasn't in one of those stretches of darkness where Meade lost them; it was down a narrow, meandering alley, almost totally cloaked in blackness. By the time the lead man felt it was safe to follow, Meade had disappeared, vanished into the night.

It took Ives and his men several frantic minutes to realize that their quarry had eluded them. When no sign of Meade could be found anywhere along the alley, Ives disgustedly ordered lanterns lit and they scoured the area. Nothing.

The other end of the alley opened onto a wide, surprisingly well-lit thoroughfare, and if he had been there, Meade would have been spotted.

His expression hangdog, Jennings muttered, "I'm sorry, my lord. I should not have waited to go after him. I should have been right on his heels."

"And if you had been," Ives said tiredly, "you would have alerted him to our presence, and he would have immediately sheared off." He smiled wryly. "We would have lost him either way."

Ives assigned some of the men to watch the buildings

on either side of the alley, and sent a couple to watch Meade's lodgings for his return. He dismissed the rest and returned wearily to the Green Boar.

The meeting with Roxbury was not pleasant, but in the end, both men took comfort from the knowledge that the information contained in the document could not harm Wellesley and would only confuse the French troops.

"It was a good plan," Roxbury said sympathetically, as they prepared to leave the tavern.

"If it had worked," Ives replied acidly. "But we are not totally at a standstill. Once we find out who owns those buildings and gain entrance, it is possible we will find some clue to where Meade may have gone."

Despite the hour, through Roxbury's connections, the owner was soon identified, and shortly thereafter, Ives was on his way to see him. All buildings which flanked the alley were owned by an elderly wool merchant, who was incensed at being rousted out of his bed at the unreasonable hour of five o'clock in the morning, even if it was done by a member of the aristocracy. Ives plied his not-inconsiderable charm and by the time they had shared a cup of coffee, the owner had calmed down enough to agree to allow Ives and his men free access to the buildings. As for any clues pointing to the identity of the Fox or where Meade might have gone, the search proved futile.

They were, however, able to discover how Meade had disappeared—a secret door in the side of one of the buildings. Meade had simply pushed the hidden catch and slid the door aside. Stepping inside the warehouse, Meade had likely closed the door softly behind him and vanished. It would have taken only a matter of seconds as Ogden unhappily demonstrated. The runners were well

oiled, and from the outside of the building there was absolutely no trace of the door.

Further investigation revealed how Meade had slipped
by them. There was a secret underground passage connecting several of the buildings, built during the reign of
Bloody Mary, the owner disclosed proudly. The narrow,
damp tunnel exited a half dozen buildings away near the
river, right next to a small tavern. While they had been
desperately scurrying around looking for him, Ives
thought grimly, Meade had been, no doubt, enjoying himself inside the tavern and meeting with the Fox. Damn
him!

Any hope to catch Meade red-handed in an attempt to
return the document to its file at the Horse Guards was
dashed when the memorandum unexpectedly turned up,
that very morning, on the desk of a Captain Brownwell
whose office was several doors away from Meade's. That
unpleasant news was brought to Ives while he was still
examining the warehouse where Meade had disappeared.

The captain had been astonished to find such an important document mixed in with the papers on his desk,
and he had immediately alerted his superior officer. Since
only a few select people had known about the document,
there was quite an uproar before one of Roxbury's men,
in the guise of an officer assigned to Meade's division,
had swiftly stepped in and delicately defused the situation.

Having now gone without sleep for over twenty-four
hours, Ives was not in an amiable frame of mind when he
met once again with his godfather that morning at the
Green Boar. Before Roxbury could be seated, his face
showing the signs of lack of sleep, Ives asked harshly,
"So who returned the document?"

"I do not know," Roxbury replied grumpily, looking as weary as his tall godson as he settled gingerly into a worn leather chair across from Ives. It had been a long disappointing night for both of them.

Glancing at Ives, he asked, "And Meade? Has he returned to his lodgings?"

Ives shook his head. "Not yet. And it worries me—he should have returned to Half Moon Street by now. Was he expected at the Horse Guards this morning, do you know?"

"As a matter of fact, he wasn't. Took a fortnight of leave. Said he was going to Brighton."

"And when did you learn this interesting bit of news?" Ives asked sourly.

Roxbury sighed and pinched the bridge of his nose. "Just before I came here to meet you. It seems that the good colonel arranged it with his superior officer only yesterday, *late* in the afternoon, I might add. And there is no use firing up because we just found out about it— Meade's superior officer was *not* in on our little plan or even aware of our suspicions. I intend to keep him that way."

Moodily, Roxbury admitted, "We cannot let all and sundry know what is happening. I have deliberately kept the number of people who know about Meade to a minimum—there are only four people in the entire Horse Guards who know of our suspicions."

"But if Meade was going to Brighton," Ives said slowly, a frown wrinkling his forehead, "why didn't he return to his lodgings before departing? Assuming he is actually going to Brighton."

"You tell me."

Ives rose from the chair in which he had been sitting.

Stalking restlessly around the room, he said meditatively, "I do not think he went to Brighton at all. I'll wager a monkey he is already dead. And I'll wager two monkeys that our friend, the Fox, convinced him to put in for that leave, knowing that Meade was never going to arrive in Brighton. No one is going to be very concerned about Colonel Meade's absence for at least a fortnight."

"And the document? How did it get on Captain Brownwell's desk? Fairies?"

Ives smiled slightly. "That is probably simplest of all—a straightforward bribe to some underling. There is, in all likelihood, someone at the Horse Guards this very moment who was paid to return the document—either by Meade, who concocted a believable story to explain why he had it in the first place, or by the Fox, and we both know how clever he is! My money is on the Fox."

"And of course, without exposing our game, we cannot question anyone about it," Roxbury said wearily.

"Exactly."

It was silent in the room for a few minutes, Ives staring blindly at the floor, Roxbury gazing into space.

It was Ives who broke the quiet. "It seems to be our morning for bad news, sir," he said abruptly. At Roxbury's wary glance, he made a face and added, "The men assigned to watch Grimshaw and Coleman reported that both men returned directly to their lodgings after they left the Pigeon Hole last night, and neither one ventured forth until this morning."

"Damme! If the Fox is not one of those two, who the hell is he?" burst out Roxbury, banging his fist on the table.

Thoughtfully, Ives said, "I would not exonerate them yet, sir. It *is* possible that one of them left his lodgings and was not seen by my men. Don't forget, we have just learned, to our cost, about secret passageways." Ives paused, then added, "There is something else, too, that I have not mentioned before because I thought it meant nothing, but I think it might be pertinent now." Reluctantly, he went on to explain Ogden's odd feeling of being watched that one night.

Roxbury stared fixedly at him. "I cannot tell you," he said hollowly, "how reassuring I find this new information. Do you mean to tell me," he went on with growing anger, "that your men may have missed him? That the Fox has been slipping in and out of our net at will? Scampering about right under our very noses?"

Ives grimaced. "I don't like it any better than you do, sir, but it is possible, especially in view of Ogden's report. And I would prefer to know that we have been, er, outfoxed, if you will pardon the pun, than to admit that we have been chasing the wrong man all this time, that neither Coleman nor Grimshaw is the Fox."

Roxbury sank back into his chair. "I hope you are right. What do you intend to do now?"

Ives shrugged. "In order to make certain that the Fox *isn't* somehow avoiding detection, I'll have to double the men watching Grimshaw and Coleman. I favor Grimshaw for the Fox rather than Coleman—Ogden was watching Grimshaw the night in question, and Grimshaw seems to be paying an uncomfortable amount of attention to my behavior of late." Ives suddenly grinned. "Besides which, I don't like the fellow. He's too smoky by half."

"Do you think it will do any good?" Roxbury asked, defeat in his gray eyes. "I think we have to face the fact that the Fox has bested us. The contents of the memorandum are no doubt already on their way to France, the Fox has his gold, and Meade is very likely dead. The trap is sprung, my boy, and there is no trail to follow. We are back where we began."

"That may be. But, then again, perhaps not," Ives said slowly. "The trap may have failed, sir, but don't forget there is every possibility that the Fox murdered Edward—and Agnes Weatherby. It may be that in investigating these two crimes we shall pick up a new trail, one that will lead us directly to his den."

Roxbury looked interested. "You may be right." His lips twisted. "And we certainly have no other avenues open to us at present."

There was no denying that Ives was bitterly disappointed at losing Meade and the opportunity of exposing the Fox, but he was in a decidedly better mood when he eventually left his godfather and began to make his way home.

He would have to talk to Sophy, he realized. About her uncle. And about that puzzling robbery. There had to be a connection. All he had to do, he admitted wryly, was to find it, hope it led to the Fox, and use it to fashion a snare that the Fox could not escape!

As luck would have it, Sophy was just descending the main staircase when Ives entered the house. That he had been out all night and was just now returning home was apparent by the dark shadow of beard on his face, and the fact that he was still wearing the same clothes she had seen him in last. Her lip lifted contemptuously, but when she would have brushed past him, Ives caught her arm.

"Take your hand off of me," Sophy said in an arctic voice, her gold eyes as cold and brittle as ice.

His hand dropped as if scorched, but he blocked her

way with his body. "I need to talk to you. Privately. Now."

"I cannot imagine why," she returned acidly, attempting to step around him.

"Sophy," he said in a voice that made her look at him sharply, "this is important. Please."

Not liking the way her heart was fluttering in her breast, she sniffed, and said unenthusiastically, "Oh, very well, my lord. Shall we use your office?"

He smiled at her, such a tender and charming smile that, in spite of herself, Sophy felt herself melting. "Thank you, sweetheart," Ives said softly. "You will not regret it. I swear to you."

Sophy snorted, but she meekly accompanied him to the small room at the rear of the house. When the door closed behind them, Sophy took another look at his haggard features and rumpled clothing, and marched over to the bell rope in one corner. Giving it a yank, she said firmly, "I think you will feel better if you have something to eat and drink."

He smiled gratefully at her. Shrugging out of his jacket and tossing aside his once-pristine cravat, he said, "Some strong coffee would certainly not be refused."

Emerson answered the summons, and, after hearing Sophy's request, he departed.

Left alone, Sophy and Ives warily regarded each other across the short distance separating them. Sophy held out for as long as she could, and only when the room suddenly seemed claustrophobic did she speak. "Well?" she demanded. "What is it?"

Ives shook his head and sat down with obvious weariness on the small green-leather sofa that sat against one wainscoted wall. "If you do not mind, I would prefer to wait until after Emerson returns. Once we start talking I want no interruptions."

Sophy's heart nearly stopped. Had he decided that their marriage was a mistake? Was he . . . ? Good gad! Could he possibly be considering divorcing her? Chilled as never before, Sophy stared at him, realizing sickly that she wanted no life without Ives Harrington in it.

Emerson's return with a tray laden with food and drink broke into her unhappy thoughts, and she waited with impatience for the butler to cease serving Ives and leave the room. The door had barely shut behind him before she asked, "And now, my lord, perhaps you could tell me the reason for this meeting?"

Carefully setting down his cup of very hot, very black coffee, Ives nodded. "It is about your uncle—his murder." He frowned. "And to a lesser extent, about Agnes Weatherby's murder."

Sophy almost sighed aloud with relief, the dreadful specter of divorce vanishing from her mind. Weakly she sank down in a comfortable leather chair near where he sat.

But she was also puzzled. What had happened last night that had brought him home to immediately seek out an interview with her about Edward? Despite believing she knew *precisely* what he had been doing all night long, an unexpected thought occurred to her: was it possible that he had *not* been out whoring and gambling last night? Could his abrupt disappearance from home and his weary-eyed return this morning have something to do with Edward's murder? She preferred for such to be the case, but having been previously married for several years to a rakish scoundrel did not engender her with much optimism.

However, she could not help asking carefully, "Does Edward's murder have anything to do with your, er, reasons for being gone all night?"

Ives smiled tiredly. "I do not know. That is why we are having this conversation."

Sophy frowned and ignored the little bud of hope that curled in her breast. She would not be fooled by him. Simon had played tricks on her too often for her to simply take Ives's words at face value.

"Very well," she said prosaically, curious in spite of herself. "What is it you wish to know?"

"Just like that? No further questions? You are going to trust me?"

Seeming quite fascinated by the fold of her pale pink gown, Sophy did not look at him as she said, "I doubt you would answer any of my questions if I were foolish enough to ask them. And as for trusting you"—she glanced up and steadily met his gaze—"no, my lord, I do not trust you. But I will play your game until I satisfy myself that it *is* a game."

He smiled crookedly. "I cannot fault you for plain speaking, can I, my dear?"

"Would you prefer that I pretend otherwise?" she asked coolly. "I can, if you like."

"No, I admire your honesty, I only wish you would learn to trust me a little." He smiled whimsically at her. "I am not a bad man, you know."

Wishing he did not look quite so attractively dissipated sprawled on the sofa before her, Sophy stifled a sigh as she stared at him. His face was worn and creased from his long night, but the weariness sat well on his craggy features, enhancing them rather than taking away from their impact. There was an expression in his bright green eyes that she found far too compelling for her own good. His long legs were stretched out in front of him, his rumpled shirt partially open, revealing the strong column of his neck and a few tufts of springy black hair. She was appalled at how vastly appealing she found him at this very moment.

Agitatedly she rose to her feet. Looking anywhere but at him, she began to pace the small room. "I never said you were a bad man. Simon was not a *bad* man, just a selfish scoundrel who put his own comfort and desires first. I will grant you that you have treated me and my family quite wonderfully. There are times when I believe you are nothing like Simon, but then . . ." She stopped squarely in front of him and her lovely golden eyes fixed on his, she said bluntly, "There are times that I think you are precisely like him."

Ives winced, and leaning his head back against the sofa, closed his eyes. "I probably deserved that," he said, "but I do not want to discuss my character at the moment." His mouth twisted. "Or Simon's. In fact," he said grimly, sitting up and opening his eyes to glare at her, "I would prefer not even to hear his name."

She dipped her head. "Very well, my lord. We shall not discuss him." She sat back down and said, "Now, what is it about Edward that you wish to know?"

Ives rubbed his aching head, aware that he should have taken the time to sleep before starting this interview. However, he was conscious of a gnawing need to discover some clue, no matter how small, that would point him in a fresh direction—*then* he would sleep.

Dropping his hand from his forehead, he asked abruptly, "I know you and your uncle were not close, and that you were seldom in each other's company, so this is not exactly a fair question, but did he seem different to you any time prior to your meeting at Allenton's house party? Had your paths crossed any time just before the night he was murdered? Did you notice if there was something odd about him? I know you saw him about Anne, but was there any other time? Do you recall anything at all—no matter how minor an occurrence you think it might be—anything, dear Butterfly, that might give us a clue why he was murdered?"

Sophy stared at him for several minutes, thinking back over her few interviews with her uncle prior to the night he died. At first she was certain there was nothing. Certainly nothing about the unpleasant interview with Agnes and Edward the morning after Anne had come to stay revealed anything new or strange about him. Suddenly she caught her breath, and a peculiar expression crossed her face.

"How very odd—and I wonder that I did not think of it before. Of course! It explains everything!"

Her face blazing with excitement, she bent forward and declared, "I think I know *precisely* why Edward was killed. Even better, I'll wager I know exactly what our housebreaker was looking for and did not find—because I had it with me! It has to be!"

While Ives stared at her in astonishment, she went on excitedly, "Oh, I know I am right. Don't you see—when I showed it to him, Edward recognized it but pretended not to. The rogue! He was probably already planning to blackmail the owner then—even as he was declaring to me that he had never laid eyes on it!" She gave a delighted crow of laughter. "The ruby cravat pin! It has to be what links everything together—Edward's murder *and* the housebreaker!"

Chapter Seventeen

❧

"*W*hat the devil are you talking about?" Ives demanded, the expression in his green eyes suddenly bright and alert. "*What* bloody pin?"

"Let me show you," Sophy said. Springing to her feet and running for the door, she tossed over her shoulder, "I shall be gone but a moment."

Before Ives's startled gaze she darted out of the room, leaving him to sit and stare at the door through which she disappeared. He had not long to wait. Not three minutes later, a breathless Sophy reentered, a small ornate box held in her hands.

"I believe that the reason the house was broken into," she began excitedly, before the door had hardly shut behind her, "was because our housebreaker was searching for what I have in this box. At least, I strongly suspect it was his reason. And if I am right, and he *was* after the cravat pin, it would certainly explain the queerness of the attempt to rob us."

She smiled impishly. "Of course, he did not find what he was looking for because I had taken this little jewelry box with me when we went to Harrington Chase. My mother gave it to me, oh, years ago, and for sentimental reasons, I suppose, I always take it with me wherever I go—I always have. It does not contain anything of importance, just a few trinkets and odds and ends, nothing valuable." She looked rueful. "At least I did not think so until now."

Sitting down across from him once more, she opened the pretty little box, rummaged around for a second, and then, a triumphant expression on her face, brought forth the ruby cravat pin. Handing it to Ives, she said, "I found this near the top of the stairs the night that Simon died."

There was no denying that the square-cut ruby was worth a small fortune, even to Ives's untrained eye. The setting was unusual, the diamonds surrounding it cunningly placed, and the size of the ruby itself made the pin quite distinctive.

"You found it? What, three, four years ago?" he asked slowly, still examining the pin. "And no one has claimed it before now?"

A little flush stained Sophy's cheeks. "Until recently, no one knew I had it."

At Ives's look, she muttered, "I did not intend to keep it, if that is what you are thinking. I had every intention of finding out who owned it, but you have to understand that when Simon died things were, er, chaotic. I did not give the pin any thought. I was too busy burying my husband and removing myself from Marlowe House at all speed to think about a pin, even an expensive one. The night I found it, I simply shoved it into this little jewelry box, meaning to say something about it the next morning. The discovery of Simon's body put it completely from my mind."

She smiled grimly. "At that time, you must remember, it was openly bandied about that I had pushed him down the stairs—murdered him. I had rather a lot on my mind, and I am afraid that the finding of the pin did not take up any of my thoughts during those days."

"You said 'until recently.' Dare I assume that you mentioned it to Edward shortly before his death?" Ives asked, a glitter of excitement in his eyes.

Sophy nodded. "Until Phoebe accidentally spilled the contents of this box one afternoon a short while ago, I had completely forgotten about it." She smiled wryly. "If I can help it, I do not think about the time I was married to Simon."

Ives let that comment pass, wondering wryly about her thoughts on *their* marriage, before probing gently, "But once Phoebe spilled the box and you noticed the pin?"

"Then, of course, I recalled finding it. I was not certain what to do about it after all this time. I *did* think it was odd, however, even suspicious, that no one had ever asked about the pin or mentioned that it had gone missing. I realized that the house was in such an uproar right after Simon died that whoever lost it might not have wanted to mention it just then. But surely, something would have been said a few weeks later, wouldn't you think?"

Ives nodded and Sophy went on, "If the pin were paste, that would be one explanation, so I decided to find out if the ruby was real or paste. It *is* real. Once I knew that, I knew that I should make an effort to find out who owned it." She made a face. "Edward seemed a logical place to start. He denied any knowledge of anyone inquiring after a lost piece of jewelry. I even showed it to him and asked him if he recognized it. He claimed never to have seen it before."

"Did you believe him?"

"At the time, I thought he might be lying, but I could think of no reason *why* he would lie—except, of course, for pure spitefulness."

Ives sat back in his chair and rubbed his jaw thoughtfully, his eyes still on the ruby pin he held in his other hand. "Most interesting, especially in view of Edward's death," he said after a moment. "If Edward recognized the pin and realized there was some desperate reason why the owner had not come forth exclaiming its loss. . . ."

"I think he did precisely that," Sophy interrupted eagerly, "and I think he decided then and there to try to blackmail the owner." She hesitated a moment before saying, "I have come to believe that the pin being found at the top of the staircase is significant." She swallowed and confessed, "It is probably silly, but I have always had the impression that someone else was in the hall the night I confronted Simon. And knowing that Simon had traversed those stairs a hundred times in a far more drunken state, I agree the suspicions surrounding his death were not unwarranted." Her gaze locked with Ives's green eyes. "*I* did not push him, but someone else could have."

"And lost his cravat pin in the process?" Ives asked, his voice giving nothing away.

"It could have happened," Sophy said a little defensively, the color burning in her cheeks.

"Oh, I do not doubt that it could have," Ives said easily. "And from what I know of Simon Marlowe, I'm inclined to think that is exactly what happened."

He paused, scowling. "But even if it were so," he admitted slowly, "the simple fact of the pin being found at the top of the stairs proves nothing. Unless Edward saw Simon being murdered, your having found the pin when and where you did is not reason enough for him to attempt to blackmail the owner. Besides, if he saw the actual murder, why wait all these years?"

It was a reasonable question, but Sophy had no answer for him, and some of her first flush of confidence began to ebb. Perhaps the pin had nothing to do with Edward's murder.

"I think," Ives said slowly, "that the pin plays some sort of pivotal role in the whole affair, but because he did wait all this time, we have to assume that your uncle did not see the murder being done. But he must have had his suspicions—suspicions that remained only that—until you brought forth the pin and told him your story."

"But it still doesn't prove anything, the pin being found at the top of the stairs." She looked doubtful. "I don't think simply its location would be enough for blackmail, do you?"

"I agree. The timing of your finding it and the location alone would not give him a strong enough hand. He had to have known more," Ives replied. "I'll wager your uncle already had his suspicions about Simon's death, perhaps even guessed who the real murderer might be. Your story about the pin only confirmed those suspicions for him, but did not prove them. Yet that does not mean that the pin isn't important. It's possible that its reemergence acted as a catalyst, both for Edward to try his hand at blackmail and his subsequent murder."

Ives stared off into space a moment, frowning. "Edward had to have known something more about his killer. I think it was that something, coupled *with* the rediscovery of the pin, that decided him to approach the person he tried to blackmail *and* got him killed."

"And Agnes Weatherby tried the same thing and suffered the same fate?"

Ives nodded. "I am sure that is how it happened. Edward was well-known to have had a loose tongue—especially in his cups. I suspect that he was so full of himself and how very clever he was being that he could not help, one night when he was half-foxed, bragging to Miss Weatherby. He may not have told her everything, but I'll wager he told her enough for her to try her own hand at blackmail—and suffer Edward's same fate."

Sophy shivered. "And what do we do now?"

Ives's jaw set. "If you do not mind, I would like to show this to my godfather and discuss the situation with him. He may even be able to identify it."

A short time later, Roxbury was rather annoyed at being rousted from his bed by his godson.

Wrapped in a flamboyant robe of crimson silk littered with small black dots, Roxbury entertained Ives in the elegant sitting room that adjoined his bedroom. Stifling a yawn, Roxbury sat down on a chair upholstered in an exquisite shade of puce. The resultant clash of colors made Ives visibly wince.

Roxbury glanced down at the crimson robe pressed against the puce velvet and chuckled. "Tarted up like a whore on Saturday night, wouldn't you say?" he remarked merrily, suddenly in a much more agreeable frame of mind.

Ives grinned and accepted the steaming cup of coffee Roxbury passed to him. "Indeed, sir, I could not have put it better."

Roxbury gave a bark of laughter, and, after taking a sip

of his own coffee, said, "Well, what is it? You didn't forsake your own bed and get me out of mine just for the amusement of it, not after the night we just spent. Tell me."

Ives's grin faded and, reaching into his vest pocket, he brought forth the ruby cravat pin. Handing it to Roxbury, he said, "Sophy and I think that this little trinket might have a great deal of bearing on why Edward was killed. And, more than likely, Agnes Weatherby. I think that I can even link it to the Fox. But first, have you ever seen it before?"

Roxbury leaned forward and took the cravat pin. He turned it this way and that as he examined it in the light streaming in through the bank of tall windows which comprised one wall of the room.

"A gaudy bauble to be sure, and quite out of the ordinary, but I do not recall ever having seen it before." He shot Ives a dark look. "I hope that you have not been so foolish as to discuss the Fox with your bride."

Ives ignored that last statement, and said mildly, "I doubted that you could identify it, but there was always the happy possibility." Rubbing his fingers tiredly against his temple, he said, "Let me tell you what I know about the pin."

Ives proceeded to relate to his godfather all that he had just learned from Sophy.

When he finished, he looked at Roxbury, and said dryly, "To the detriment of my relationship with my wife, Sophy believes that I am a debauched rake much in the manner of her first husband. Aware of the importance of what we are trying to do, I have done nothing to disabuse her of that unpleasant notion. You have no reason to fear that I may have been indiscreet. She thinks, however, as

I do, that the pin is somehow inextricably tied to Edward's murder. If my suspicions prove true, you hold the means to trap the Fox in your hands at this very moment."

When Ives said nothing more and sank wearily back into his chair, Roxbury was quiet for several minutes, his expression reflective.

"So," he said at last, "tell me how you think this helps our cause?"

Restless despite his lack of sleep, Ives stood up and began to pace the room. "Let us suppose," he muttered, "that the expensive trinket you hold in your hand belongs to the Fox."

Roxbury's brow shot up. "Isn't that rather farfetched?"

"It could be," Ives replied equitably, "but I do not believe so." He glanced at Roxbury. "Didn't you tell me once that shortly before Marlowe died, he and Scoville were sailing perilously close to treason by selling their gossip to the Fox?"

At Roxbury's curt nod, he went on, "And I recall hearing that Simon Marlowe was a rather nasty bit of goods who liked to know other people's secrets. That he, in fact, delighted in wielding power over friend and foe alike by using anything disgraceful he could ferret out about them."

Again Roxbury nodded, adding, "There were always rumors to that effect."

"Knowing that, don't you think that Marlowe might have tried to discover the identity of the buyer of his gossip? It sounds to me like something he would do. And if he *had* discovered such information, would he not have attempted to use it? And might he not even have hinted to

Scoville what he had found? They were, after all, intimate cronies."

An arrested look crossed Roxbury's lined features. "It is possible," he muttered. "Entirely possible, all of it."

"So let us assume that Marlowe had discovered the identity of the Fox—and, if my father's suspicions are correct, our leading candidates are Grimshaw and Coleman, well-known to be part of Marlowe's milieu—so we may also assume that the Fox was a guest at the house party the night Marlowe died. . . ."

"And at some point during that house party," Roxbury mused, taking up the tale, "Marlowe hinted at what he knew or even confronted the Fox. And the Fox killed him."

"Inadvertently leaving behind his cravat pin," Ives said quietly. "Sophy found it and put it in her jewelry box, where she forgot about it until just a few weeks ago when she showed it to Scoville and told him how she had found it."

Roxbury took a deep breath. "The entire premise is flimsy, but not without merit. Considering what happened last—er, this morning, your idea looks to be our only hope. How do you plan to proceed?"

"One place to start would be with the guests at that last house party of Marlowe's. If we knew who was there, we might be able to eliminate some suspects," Ives said decisively.

He cast a bland eye at his godfather. "Of course, other than relying on Sophy's memory, you would have no idea where such information could be obtained, would you?"

Roxbury snorted. "You know very well that I kept at least a nominal track of Marlowe and Scoville back then."

A great yawn overtook him, and, delicately covering his mouth, he mumbled, "I shall have someone go over the old reports and see what can be found." He rose to his feet. "And now, if you do not mind, I am going to bed!" He glanced at Ives's obviously exhausted features, and said, "You would be wise to do the same."

For once, Ives was not averse to following directions, and leaving Roxbury, he repaired immediately to Berkeley Square. Discovering that Sophy had kept a previous engagement and had gone out driving with friends, he saw no reason not to seek out his bed. He did so, falling deeply asleep almost the instant his head hit the pillow.

He slept several hours, and it was nearly eight o'clock that evening before he woke and rang for his valet. Despite still feeling a trifle tired, a bath and fresh clothing made him feel as if he just might rejoin the human race. After a hearty meal of rare sirloin and eggs, he was ready to descend the staircase and face the world once more.

From Emerson, he learned that Sophy was again away from the house. She had gone out to dinner with the Offingtons and was expected to attend the theater with them afterward. She would be home late.

Sophy was only following the pursuits and manners of many a fashionable wife, but that did not exactly sit well with Ives as he realized sourly that he wanted far more from his marriage than a charming companion and a sweet armful in bed. He wanted, he concluded firmly, to share his life with Sophy, and to his mind, that did not mean jointly using the same house and only meeting when necessary. He sighed. He was being unreasonable, and he knew it. He had never given her any cause to believe he wanted anything different. As long as he was condemned to playing the role of dissolute libertine, he had scant chance of showing her precisely the sort of marriage he had in mind.

But for the first time since Meade had disappeared so disastrously last night, Ives was hopeful he could still hunt down *Le Renard*. He was not yet certain how he was going to do it, but he was confident that the possession of the ruby cravat pin was a powerful weapon. He just had to figure out the best way to use it.

He had considered various schemes as he bathed and dressed, but had discarded most of them. He could hardly assemble the most likely candidates and simply ask them which one owned the pin. There was no use identifying the owner of the pin if it sent the man scurrying for cover before they could connect the murders of Scoville and Miss Weatherby to him. And as for connecting the pin to the Fox . . . Ives scowled. That was going to be extremely tricky, if he managed to do it at all.

So how was he going to use the pin?

Wearing it himself would be one way of identifying the pin. Someone was bound to recognize it and comment on his possession of it. Which left him where? The pin's owner would be identified, which was vital, but it would be inevitable that word of the pin would come to the wrong ears, and he would be right back where he started.

He was beginning to become quite annoyed. He had the bloody pin. He was confident the pin was the catalyst behind the two murders and the housebreaking incident. He was thoroughly convinced that the pin would lead him to the Fox. Yet he could think of no way to use it without tipping his hand and sending his prey racing for the safety of Napoléon's arms.

A grim look crossed his face. There was one way, he thought slowly, an astounding idea unfolding in his brain.

What if he were to play *Marlowe's* original game? Blackmail. Not for money. It was well-known that he—even at the rate he had been gambling lately—had no need of money, but for power and control. Control such as Marlowe had enjoyed. The power to make someone dance to the tune of one's own making.

The notion was not so far-fetched. Wasn't he currently doing his damnedest to present himself as a man without character? A libertine? A hardened rake? None of his recent London acquaintances knew him very well, so his descent into naked despotism would not necessarily be greeted with astonishment.

And of course, there was Marlowe's example; it had never been money which had driven him into playing traitor nor had money been a factor in his acts of calculated dominance. Going on the assumption that the Fox had been closely acquainted with Marlowe, the man had to have known Marlowe's penchant for getting his own way. So, Ives concluded, if he were to put himself forth as a creature in Marlowe's mold, why wouldn't the fellow believe it?

The more he considered it, the more Ives liked the idea. All he would have to do would be to decide upon the most likely candidate for the Fox and show him the pin. A few well-placed hints, and then he could sit back and see what happened. He smiled. Unpleasantly. One thing was for certain: He did not intend to end up like poor Scoville.

Knowing his absence tonight from his normal haunts might cause speculation, especially in view of Meade's sudden trip to Brighton, he finally left the house in search of his usual companions.

It did not take him long to find them in another disreputable hell off St. James's Square. He wasn't surprised to find them all together—Grimshaw, Coleman, and several more who made up the nucleus of the group—but he *was* a bit taken aback to see a new set of features amongst the other jaded faces, Percival Forrest's. And Percival did not look very happy. He looked in fact somewhere between a man whose dearest friend had just died and a man spoiling for a fight. Having a good idea what had brought him here in this mood, Ives sighed. Things were definitely getting complicated.

Having greeted everyone and once the others had turned back to their gambling, under the cover of a noisy background, Ives stood just a little apart from the group with Forrest, and said quizzically, "I thought you told me that you had given up this sort of thing."

His blue eyes hard and determined, Forrest said almost accusingly, "And I thought I knew you well enough to believe that you wouldn't be fool enough to allow yourself to be drawn into this group of disgusting libertines! What has possessed you? Have you lost your senses? I even warned you about them. Why, for Jupiter's sake, have you allowed yourself to be sucked into their rotten core? I did not believe what I have been hearing lately, and cannot even now credit my own eyes. To think that I find *you* in such a place and on such easy terms with these ugly rogues! Good gad, Ives, what are you thinking of? You are acting in a manner that is totally foreign to the man I gladly served under, and admired and respected as I do few men."

Repressing the urge to shut Percival's mouth in the swiftest possible way, Ives glanced idly around and was greatly relieved to see that no one was paying any attention to them—yet.

Keeping his face bland and his voice low, he murmured. "If you love me, dear fellow, please reassure me that you have not been spouting that point of view to all and sundry."

Percival looked startled before his brows snapped together in a frown. "What sort of rig are you running, man?" he demanded urgently. "Don't you know these fellows are not the type who take being made to look ridiculous lightly?"

Ives sighed, wishing Percival had chosen another setting in which to express his worries. Noticing that Grimshaw was watching them through narrowed eyes, Ives smiled sweetly and with a deceptively light grasp of Percival's arm, inexorably ushered him to a quiet table in one corner.

His eyes meeting Percival's puzzled blue gaze, Ives said, "Dear fellow, I do appreciate your concern, but for the present, could you please forget that you ever knew me that well? Especially do not sing praises of my supposed virtues, hmm? Or if you cannot do that, at least pretend that my actions come as no surprise to you."

Percival's frown only increased. "What the devil are you up to, Ives?"

Keeping a bored smile firmly in place, Ives glanced with apparent disinterest around the room. Grimshaw was still watching them. Damn. He had to think fast and make a decision immediately. He could continue to fend off Percival's concerns or let him in on the chase. It was not a difficult choice.

Looking back at Forrest, he said softly, "I cannot tell you anything right now. It is too dangerous. But if you will call tomorrow morning at Roxbury's town house, I will explain to you what I can. I might even be able to use your, er, talents."

He shot his former lieutenant a commanding look. "In the meantime, keep your mouth shut and forget that I ever possessed any sort of virtue."

Percival's eyes suddenly blazed with excitement. "By God, sir, it will be good working with you again. Does this have something to do with Bony?"

Ives only shook his head and murmured, "I can tell you nothing at present. I would rather you were not here to see me descend once more into my trough of depravity." He smiled crookedly.

Forrest nodded, and, rising to his feet, said, "I understand. I shall see you at Roxbury's tomorrow morning."

Ives watched him go, noting with dismay the jaunty spring to his step. Someone, he felt certain, was going to comment on Percival's sudden change in demeanor. He was not wrong.

Strolling up to join the others a few minutes later, Coleman demanded, "Whatever did you say to Forrest? One minute he looked blue as a dog and the next he was fairly skipping from the room."

Ives shrugged. "A little matter of a debt I owed him. He thought that I was, er, avoiding paying him, but it was merely that I had forgotten about it." He yawned delicately. "These late nights I spend with ruffians like yourselves has had a detrimental effect upon my memory, you know."

"You were in the army with him, weren't you?" asked Grimshaw, his gray eyes fixed on Ives's face. "His commanding officer, if I remember correctly?"

Ives bowed. "Indeed. I had that pleasure."

"Forrest used to be a much more enjoyable fellow.

When he first sold out, he fit right in with us," Coleman said, glancing indifferently at the cards he held in his hand. "Then respectability must have attacked him because he drifted away and became quite, quite dull." Coleman's hazel eyes lifted. "Do you think that will happen with you?"

"Oh, I doubt it very seriously. You may ask anyone who knows me—I am *never* dull," Ives returned sweetly, carelessly motioning for a servant to bring him a glass of wine.

Dewhurst bit back a snort of laughter, as did Coleman himself, before he turned his attention back to his cards. But Grimshaw did not apparently share the general amusement. His unfriendly gaze still fastened on Ives's dark face, he muttered, "A clever turn of phrase, but I wonder if you are not, my lord, too clever for your own good."

Ignoring the antagonism in Grimshaw's voice, Ives shrugged. "We shall just have to wait and see, won't we?" he murmured and smiled challengingly at Grimshaw over the rim of his glass.

Chapter Eighteen

❧

*I*ves remained with the others only long enough to see if Meade's sudden disappearance aroused any comment. He was both relieved and disappointed when someone—Coleman? Caldwell?—made mention of Meade's unexpected decision to visit Brighton and no one seemed the least bit interested or surprised by Meade's defection. Having learned what he had come for, Ives wandered away and slowly strolled back to Berkeley Square.

His return coincided with Sophy's arrival at the Grayson town house from her evening's engagement. The sight of her golden head emerging from the carriage made his pulse leap and, increasing his stride, he arrived in time to escort her up the steps and into the house.

Sophy was surprised, astonished actually, to see him home this early in the evening, but she kept her thoughts to herself. Her lovely features revealed nothing but politeness.

Ives had been right. He might have barreled back into her bed, and though they had collaborated easily enough together this morning in the matter of the cravat pin, there were still large areas in their relationship in which Sophy was quite wary of his motives.

She couldn't help but be pleased to see that, for tonight at least, he had forsaken his debauched companions, but she did not delude herself into believing that this signaled any major change in his behavior. Even Simon had not gambled and whored *every* night.

"Did you enjoy your evening?" Ives asked, as they entered his study, having decided to partake of a cup of tea and some biscuits together before retiring for the night.

Sophy nodded. "Hmm, yes. The aquatic spectacle was particularly entertaining this evening." She cast him a glance from under her curling lashes. "And your evening? It was pleasant?"

Ives shrugged. "Tolerable." He flashed that brigand's smile of his, and murmured, "I would have much preferred to spend the evening in your charming company."

Sophy's brows rose. "Indeed. I find that most interesting since you have shown no predilection for my company recently."

"Ah, now there you are wrong, sweetheart," Ives said with a gleam in his green eyes. "I seem to remember that very recently I displayed a most *determined* predilection for your company."

Sophy blushed, the memory of their lovemaking suddenly vivid in her mind. She was quite thankful that Emerson entered the room almost immediately with a tray of refreshments.

Only after the butler had departed and they had served themselves and were seated comfortably across from each other, did Sophy attempt further conversation. Having taken a fortifying sip of her tea, over the rim of her cup she looked at him, and asked, "Did your godfather recognize the cravat pin?"

"No, he did not. I did not think that he would, but there was always the chance." He hesitated before adding, "I will be frank, I am nearly at a standstill. I do have a glimmer of an idea I might pursue, but I am not precisely pleased with it." The urge to elaborate and more fully explain his plan was almost overpowering, but Ives decided the less Sophy knew the better for her. Not only better, he thought fiercely, but *safer*.

Sophy waited for him to continue and when he did not, she was aware of a stab of disappointment. Despite the promising start earlier in the day, it was obvious he was not going to confide further in her.

Pushing away her hurt, she said coolly, "I do not see why it should be so difficult. I am sure any number of people will recognize it once we, discreetly of course, ask around."

Ives shook his head. "That is not the problem. I am sure you are right—the pin is too unusual not to be easily recognized. The difficulty is that we do not wish to alert the owner of our possession of it until we know who he is. If we make the wrong move, he may vanish without our ever getting our hands on him."

Sophy appeared thoughtful. She took another sip of her tea as she considered the problem. There was much sense in what Ives said, but she did not believe a solution would be so very difficult to discover.

A little frown creased Sophy's forehead, and, setting down her cup, she said, "We assume that Edward and Miss Weatherby both approached their killer and attempted to blackmail him . . . and we assume that their killer also attended the house party the night Simon died and the Allentons' house party. . . . It seems to me that a comparison of the guests who attended each party would at least eliminate anyone who had not attended *both* functions."

Ives nodded uneasily. He was full of grave reservations about Sophy's role in discovering the owner of the pin, especially since he had the unpleasant feeling that the owner of the cravat pin and his own nemesis, the Fox, were one and the same. The Fox was already responsible for several deaths, and Ives was grimly certain that he did not want Sophy even *remotely* involved. The notion of the Fox bringing his attention to bear on her sent a chill down Ives's spine and brought all his protective instincts surging to the fore.

Oblivious to Ives's lack of enthusiasm, she went on briskly, "The easiest way would be to list everyone that we know attended both parties—that would give us several possibilities."

Again Ives nodded, not liking the icy feeling swirling in his belly. She was, he decided bitterly, too bloody clever for her own good.

Sophy rose to her feet, rummaged around in the desk, and found a quill, ink, and a sheet of paper. She sat back down and proceeded to make a list of the gentlemen who had been at Marlowe House the night Simon had died, and right next to it, a list of the guests who had also been at Crestview. When she was finished, she made a face.

"The problem," she said disgustedly, "is that we are dealing with basically the same group of gentlemen, and so we have several suspects: Edward's boon companion, Lord Bellingham—although I cannot imagine 'Belly' killing anyone; Marquette; Grimshaw; Coleman; Dewhurst; Allenton himself; and three or four others who, while unlikely, were in attendance." She brightened. "At least we can eliminate your friend, Percival Forrest. He was at Marlowe House, but not at Crestview."

"Even if Percival had attended both functions," Ives said bluntly, "I would never put him on that list. Having fought beside him, I know the man, and he is no murderer."

"There was a time," Sophy replied softly, her golden eyes steadily meeting his, "that I would have said that you were no libertine either."

Ives sighed. Wouldn't you know she would give him a perfect opportunity to explain himself and he would not be able to take advantage of it? Damn and blast the Fox! And Roxbury, too! But her words warmed him and gave him hope for the future.

Sending her a wry smile, he murmured, "Sweetheart, we are not talking about my behavior. Let us, for now, concentrate on finding out who murdered your uncle and Miss Weatherby, hmm?"

Her chagrin apparent on her expressive face, she replied somewhat stiffly, "Of course."

Her gaze dropped from his, and she asked neutrally, "Is there anyone on the list that you favor above any of the others?"

If he had been able to talk freely, he could have told her to mark off Marquette—Roxbury and he were in agreement that Marquette was not the Fox. In fact, he admitted sourly, if she knew the truth, they could probably dispense with all the names on the list except for Coleman and Grimshaw. But even if he could not fully explain matters to her, he was not going to send her haring after a false scent. There was enough deception between them as it was, and if they were collaborating together, even in a limited manner, she deserved a measure of truth.

"Well, I like Grimshaw for our villain," Ives confessed, before he fully considered what he was saying. The instant the words left his mouth, he cursed himself for a fool. Determined to keep her safe, what did he do but point her in the very direction he most desperately did not want her to go? Bloody hell!

"Oh, I do, too!" Sophy exclaimed, in perfect charity with him once more. "I have *always* thought him a villain."

Ives grimaced and attempting to retrieve the situation, said weakly, "Which does not mean he *is* our quarry. Perhaps we should not neglect to consider someone else first."

"Oh, fiddle-dee-dee! I prefer Grimshaw above all others. Let us put Grimshaw at the top of the list. He shall be the first one that we approach."

"Approach?" Ives asked carefully, a knife blade of unease turning in his gut. "Would you care to explain precisely what you mean?"

Sophy smiled sunnily at him. "I have just thought of a wonderful plan—I know you shall believe it shocking, but I think that we should try to blackmail him! Not for money, of course, he would never believe it."

Ignoring Ives's expression of stunned disbelief, she went on blithely, "Simon, you know, was always attempting to ferret out other people's secrets so he could dangle them over their heads. I think we should try to do the same thing to Grimshaw and see what his reaction is."

As Ives stared at her in thunderstruck panic, she lightly tapped her lips with one slim finger, and added, "Of course, I should be the one to approach him. I found the pin, after all. And it would be perfectly logical that, after Edward's death, I would begin to add things up and connect the pin to his murder."

When her husband remained silent—in fact, he looked and acted as one turned to stone—she went on reasonably, "And Grimshaw wouldn't think it the least strange that I was attempting to blackmail him. He knows that I detest him. Besides, he will probably simply assume that I am following in my husband's and uncle's footsteps." Breezily, she concluded, "It is a very good plan, don't you agree?"

It was all Ives could do to control himself, torn as he was between wildly conflicting urges. He wanted to shake her soundly for terrifying him, and kiss her for simply being the dearest thing in the world to him. His uppermost emotion, however, was one of raw fright at the mere notion of Sophy putting herself in what might very well prove to be mortal danger.

"Are you mad?" he fairly thundered, appalled that she should have so unerringly fastened upon his own plan.

He took a deep breath, forcing himself to act calmly despite his violent inner turmoil. In a quieter tone of voice, though not *much* quieter, he said, "Two people are dead, Sophy! What makes you think *you* shall have any better luck approaching him? I tell you, it is far, *far* too dangerous a plan for you to even consider attempting!"

She smiled impishly, not the least fazed by his unflattering reaction. "But you forget, my lord, I have an advantage that Edward did not—I *know* the man is capable of murder. Besides, I shall not be in this alone; *we* shall be working together. Our murderer will be caught off guard because he will not be aware that there are *two* of us stalking him."

Ives stood up and loomed over her. "I will not even consider you approaching him, do you hear me? It is out of the question." Flatly, he added. "I would be a poor husband, indeed, if I countenanced your taking part in something that could place you in deadly peril."

Sophy stared at him for a long moment. His words and something in his voice made her heart squeeze with delight. But there was something else in his voice that gave her pause and, consideringly, she looked up into his rigid features. One thing was apparent—he had not been surprised by her plan.

On the surface, she thought slowly, his main objection seemed to be that it was dangerous . . . for her. She frowned. In fact, she mused, he had not condemned the plan at all, only her role in it. Comprehension dawned.

"You were already planning to approach Grimshaw!" she said accusingly. Her eyes narrowed. "Without telling me, I'll wager."

A dark flush burned Ives's cheeks. "I am a man," he muttered. "A man, I might remind you, who has faced an enemy determined to kill him."

Sophy looked only politely interested. "And?"

"Dash it all, Sophy! You cannot be that unintelligent! I do not want you in danger. Let me handle this."

"Oh, I see," she said levelly. "You get to risk your life to find our killer, but I am not allowed even when it is far more logical that *I* be the one to approach our suspect."

Ives bit back a curse, undecided whether to throttle her or kiss her. "Why," he asked with an effort, "are you the more logical one of us?"

Since he appeared to be listening to her, she relaxed a trifle, and said coolly, "Because you have been much too busy ingratiating yourself with Grimshaw and Simon's other friends to suddenly turn ugly with them. On the other hand, Grimshaw knows *precisely* how I feel about him. He wouldn't be surprised at all if I tried a spot of blackmail." Her face twisted. "It's in my blood after all, wouldn't you say?"

"Don't," he said softly, reaching out to run a caressing finger down her cheek, "denigrate yourself. Edward was a selfish bastard and your mother may have been a thoughtless, even callous young woman, but you are nothing like either one of them. You are brave, loyal, and caring. To tell the truth, I find it hard to believe that you have Scoville blood coursing your veins."

Sophy's breath caught, thoughts of the ruby cravat pin and catching Edward's murderer vanishing instantly from her mind. It was the first time since she had accused him of marrying her to avenge his brother's death that they had even remotely touched upon the subject, but she knew that it had not been forgotten by either one of them. It lay between them like a festering canker, and she was painfully aware that she would give much to tear down at least one of the barriers that stood between them.

Searchingly, she stared up into his dark, fiercely hewn features, her heart aching and yet hopeful. They had been forced to marry. She knew that he did not love her; his need for an heir had been well-known. But what he felt for her she could not even guess. Kindness, certainly. Passion, definitely. But what of his brother's suicide? And her mother's part in it? *Had* the desire for revenge played a part in his offer of marriage?

Suddenly she had to know, and blurted out, "Did you agree to marry me to extract some sort of revenge for what happened to your brother?"

An infinitely tender smile played at the corners of

Ives's shapely mouth. He shook his head slowly, and said huskily, "I swear to you, sweetheart, on my honor as a gentleman and on everything I hold dear, that neither Robert nor your mother's part in his death had *anything* to do with the reasons I married you."

She should have been satisfied with his answer, but his words left her feeling oddly bereft. Of course his brother's suicide had nothing to do with their marriage, she told herself stoutly. She had been a fool to believe it in the first place. She knew precisely why he had married her—he had, one might almost say gallantly, married her to protect her from scandal and to, in time, gain an heir.

She forced a smile. "Thank you. I would not like to think that I was to be punished for something I did not do."

"Is that how you view our marriage?" Ives asked whimsically. "As punishment?"

A lump grew in Sophy's throat. She shook her golden curls. "No, my lord. Not punishment."

Ives waited a moment longer, wishing she would say more, hoping desperately that she would give him some clue as to what was going on in that lovely head of hers.

Uneasy with his silence, Sophy cleared her throat, and muttered, "You have been very kind to me and my family. I am exceedingly grateful to you."

Ives made a face, disappointment crashing through him. Gratitude was not what he wanted from her. Turning away he said lightly, "Then I must be satisfied. I would not want you to be unhappy."

Miserably Sophy watched him, the urge to demand what he *did* want of her almost painful in its intensity. But she kept her mouth shut. Life with Simon had taught her some bitter truths, and she had learned, to her cost, that sometimes knowing the truth destroyed all illusions and left one with absolutely no hope at all. As it was, she might not know how Ives felt about her and their marriage, but she could still dream that one day he might love her. She could still hope that more bound them together than merely his need for an heir.

Unwilling to dwell upon the state of her marriage, she picked up her cup and took another swallow of tea, wrinkling her nose at its coolness. Setting the cup down decisively, she glanced across at Ives where he had reseated himself, and said determinedly, "I believe that if you think it over you will agree that it would be best for me to be the one to approach Grimshaw."

When Ives scowled at her, she went on hastily, "If you consider it honestly, you will know that I am right. Simon, Edward, and I are all connected, and he *knows* how I feel about him. He won't give my actions a second thought."

There was too much truth in what she said for Ives to brush her words aside, which was exactly what he wanted to do—violently. Though it galled him to admit it, she *was* the far more logical choice to carry out the scheme.

Even admitting that, Ives was still against the idea of her coming anywhere near the man who might be the Fox. "There is much to your argument," he conceded reluctantly, "but dammit, Sophy! There are too many things that could go wrong."

His green eyes full of anxiety, he stared across the brief space that divided them. Huskily, he said, "I would not, for the world, have anything happen to you."

Her heart leaping in her breast, Sophy thought she would melt for love of him. It was not a declaration of love, but it was enough, and it would do for now. Oh, yes, it would do very well for now, she thought mistily.

The future ahead suddenly seemed much brighter, and beaming foolishly across at him, she said softly, "Nothing will happen to me because you will not let it, will you?"

"God, no!" he swore, wanting to catch her up in his arms and whisk her away from even the thought of danger.

"Then we are decided?" she asked carefully. "*I* shall be the one to seek out Grimshaw."

Knowing he had lost the argument, but unwilling to concede defeat, Ives growled, "I must discuss it with my godfather first. We shall see what he has to say."

If Sophy thought it strange that Ives seemed to need his godfather's advice before proceeding, she kept it to herself. But she was very thoughtful when they left Ives's study a few minutes later and walked up the stairs to their bedchambers.

The Duke of Roxbury seemed to frequently intrude into their lives of late, she realized. Ives had never struck her as a man who relied on others to make up his mind for him, and yet, it seemed he was always rushing off to confer with Roxbury—if the duke wasn't appearing on their doorstep.

Of course, Roxbury *was* Ives's godfather, but . . . Now what was it about Roxbury that nagged at her? Some gossip? Some old scandal?

Her thoughts busy with trying to remember what it was she had heard about Roxbury, Sophy absently bid her husband good night and entered her own room. She was very quiet as Peggy helped her undress. Garbed in only her chemise, she dismissed Peggy with a vague smile and slipped out of the chemise before putting on a nightgown of gossamer silk. Unaware of her image in the mirror before her, she brushed out the earlier expert work of Peggy's nimble fingers and very soon her thick, heavy hair was lying in a shining golden mantle around her slim shoulders.

Roxbury, Roxbury. What was it that she had heard about him? Something about, despite his great wealth and position, he dabbled in the government? But how did that affect Ives?

She gasped, sitting up straighter. Roxbury was some sort of master spy, wasn't that what she had overheard Simon say years ago? He had been talking to Edward, she remembered, and when he had finished speaking, he had laughed in that nasty way of his, almost as if he had somehow managed to push Roxbury's nose in a pile of manure. Edward had laughed, too. . . .

Her thoughts went flying when she heard the door open behind her. Spinning around on the green-satin stool of her dressing table, she looked across the width of the room to where Ives stood in the connecting door between their chambers.

He was wearing a black robe and, with a curling twist in her loins, Sophy knew he was naked underneath the garment. He seemed very large, very male, as he stood there regarding her. And very dear.

He said nothing for a moment. Then strolling coolly into the room, he remarked, "The door was unlocked."

Sophy nodded. "I know," she said softly, rising slowly to her feet, excitement coiling almost painfully throughout her body. "I did not wish to overwork the carpenter."

He smiled crookedly as he reached her. Pulling her gently into his arms, he teased both of them by faintly brushing his lips against hers. "And that was the only reason? Consideration for the carpenter?"

Her lips parted invitingly, her eyes luminous pools of pure gold, Sophy shook her head. "Oh, no, not the only reason."

Ives groaned and crushed her to him, his mouth settling hungrily on hers and Sophy gave up coherent thought for a long time, a very long time. . . .

Bright sunlight was streaming into her room and Peggy had just placed a tray of tea and toast on the table beside her bed, when Sophy once more rejoined the world. Pushing back a thick strand of gold hair, she sat up and winced slightly. A dreamy smile curved her full mouth. Ives had been voracious last night. And she had reveled in it, understanding for the first time that sometimes passion was not always gentle. But, oh, always sweet.

As she took a sip of her tea, Peggy said, "The master has already risen and gone out, but he asked that I inquire if you would care to accompany him to visit his godfather this afternoon. He informed me that he will return around two o'clock for your answer."

Sophy smiled to herself. This afternoon, she decided, was going to be most interesting. To Peggy she said, "Of course I shall go with him. In fact, I am looking forward to it."

Ives was *not* looking forward to it at all. He had the uneasy feeling that events were spiraling wildly out of his control—not, he reminded himself savagely, that he had ever *been* in control.

The meeting between Roxbury, Forrest, and himself

had gone rather well this morning, and if Roxbury was annoyed by Ives's abrupt commandeering of his time, he gave no sign of it. Actually, he seemed pleased that Ives had finally brought Forrest into the fold.

At first, Percival had been highly incensed that he had not been included in the chase from the beginning, his bright blue eyes burning with indignation, but he had quickly calmed down and become excited at the prospect of grappling with the elusive Fox.

When shown the ruby cravat pin and enlightened as to its history and what they suspected about it, he had frowned in concentration as he had stared at the sparkling jewel. Shaking his head, he muttered, "I know that I have seen this before, but I cannot tell you where or when." He smiled wryly. "Perhaps I will remember eventually, but for now, I am afraid that I am no help to you."

Ives was disappointed, but not overly so; it had been an outside chance anyway that Forrest would recognize it. The three men continued to discuss the situation for several more minutes before Forrest took his leave. He had left Roxbury's town house full of enthusiasm for the chase and swearing fervently to be of service in any way that he could. He was, he told Ives happily, going to enjoy himself for the first time since he had sold out and returned to England.

After Forrest departed, Roxbury glanced across at Ives. "You do not," he said, "seem to be particularly happy this morning. Surely, you have no doubts about the wisdom of bringing Forrest into our midst?"

Ives shook his head. "No—I trust Percival implicitly, and in a dangerous confrontation, I could not ask for a better man at my side." Ives took a turn around the elegant green-and-gold room, still not convinced that he was doing the wise, *safe* thing by allowing Sophy to take part in the hunt for the Fox.

Aware of Roxbury's eyes upon him, still uncertain of his path, he said carefully, "Sophy has come up with a plan to approach the person she thinks may have been the target of Edward's blackmail."

Roxbury frowned, and his displeasure was evident in his tone of voice. "I realize," he said sharply, "that she was the one who found the cravat pin, but do you think it wise to allow her to continue to meddle in something so fraught with danger? This is *none* of her business, and you should not be discussing it with her."

He shot Ives a black look. "You know that I am adamantly opposed to her involvement in this affair—I have told you so repeatedly. Allowing Forrest to learn of the Fox is one thing, but your wife? Might as well place a notice in the *Times*. It is preposterous."

Ives smiled bleakly. "I know precisely how you feel about her involvement—it is the reason she currently thinks she has married her first husband's twin."

Roxbury had the grace to look uncomfortable. "*I* am sorry, my boy, that this affair has caused you such . . ." he began apologetically, then caught himself up and scowled fiercely. "May I remind you that I was against the marriage right from the beginning? And didn't I warn you that it would be trouble? If you find yourself in difficulties with your wife, it is your own fault, you know. You should not have married the lady while you were in the middle of trying to catch someone like the Fox."

"I agree, but if you remember, I had little choice. She was suspected of murder."

"Piffle! She might have suffered a few unpleasant months and endured some nasty gossip, but once the Fox was caught, you then could have proceeded with your courtship and set wagging tongues to rest." His scowl deepened. "Do not try to make me feel guilty because of something you did. Against my expressed wishes, I might add."

Ives suddenly grinned. "Do you ever feel guilty about anything, my lord?"

Roxbury cast him a baleful look. "Don't be a damned fool! Of course, I do—frequently! Which has nothing to do with what we are discussing."

"Naturally," Ives replied. Leaving the unprofitable subject behind, he proceeded to lay out the various schemes he had concocted to find the owner of the cravat pin, ending with the plan to try his hand at blackmail.

Roxbury mulled over Ives's facts, asking occasionally to have a particular point explained. Slowly nodding, he finally murmured, "Excellent notion—if your assumption is correct and the Fox and Edward's proposed blackmail victim are one and the same. And I agree, if he were to learn that you possessed the pin and were trying to identify the owner, he might very well bolt for the Continent." Roxbury looked thoughtful. "It would have been so much simpler if someone we trusted could identify the pin." He sighed. "Shame that Forrest did not recognize it."

"I agree, but I had not held out much hope for it."

Leaning back in his chair, Roxbury regarded his godson. "So," he asked quietly, "when do you intend to approach Grimshaw?"

Ives hesitated. It was now or never. Logic told him that Sophy was right in her conclusions. He was also painfully aware that if he did *not* consent to her suggestion—if he imposed his will and went ahead as he had originally planned—that something extremely rare and fragile in their relationship would be shattered.

His gaze met Roxbury's, and he realized bleakly that when he had invited her to meet with his godfather this afternoon, he had already made up his mind.

"Actually," he said grimly, "I have decided that it is not I who shall approach Grimshaw, but Sophy."

Chapter Nineteen

❧

*R*oxbury's explosion was every bit as violent as Ives had suspected it would be, but in the end, his godfather, with much dire muttering and fulminating glances, had agreed that Sophy did have the correct reading of the situation: She *should* be the one to approach Grimshaw.

Ives had never won an argument which gave him so little pleasure—or filled him with such stark terror. But while Ives might have won one argument, Roxbury remained determined that Sophy know no more than she needed to, and that included anything about *Le Renard*!

Sophy, of course, was delighted that Ives had shown such excellent sense by agreeing with her, and to Ives's consternation, she seemed not the least fazed by the possible danger she ran. Sitting primly in a green-leather chair near Roxbury's massive rosewood desk, her jonquil-muslin skirts daintily arranged around her slim ankles, she had glanced brightly from one grave male face to the other.

"Oh, good gad!" she finally exclaimed in exasperation after Ives had again reiterated how treacherous their quarry was, how incumbent it was upon her to take the greatest care, and Roxbury had urgently seconded his words.

"I am not a goose!" she said forthrightly. "And it is not as if I am going off alone to some secluded place, where no one knows where I am or what I am doing!" She looked at Ives. "You have already assured me that when I approach Grimshaw it shall be in a public place of our choosing, and that you and Forrest are going to be hovering nearby. If I let out one little squeak, both of you will come thundering to my rescue."

Stiffly Ives said, "I did not say 'hovering.'"

Sophy smiled kindly at him. "Perhaps not, but that is what you meant."

"Lady Harrington," Roxbury began unhappily, having had more than second thoughts about the entire plan, "you *do* understand how dangerous this man is? That he will let nothing stop him? That while we will do all within our power to keep you safe from harm, that plans, er, sometimes go wrong?"

Ives cast him a stony glance. "Nothing," he said in icy accents, "will go wrong."

Sophy beamed at Roxbury. "You see, my lord? My husband shall not let anything happen to me. Besides," she added with an engaging twinkle, "I shall have my pistol with me—I will not be totally at Grimshaw's mercy should something, er, go wrong."

"Nothing," Ives repeated through gritted teeth, "will go *wrong*."

"Of course not," Sophy replied soothingly, lightly patting him on one lean hand. "You shall keep me safe." She was startled when his fingers curled around hers as if he would never let go.

Feeling he was making a fool of himself, Ives tried to relax, gradually lessening the almost brutal grip he had on her fingers. He was overreacting. But damn it all, it was *Sophy* who would be facing the Fox!

Once it was settled that Sophy would indeed be the one to approach Grimshaw, Forrest arrived shortly thereafter, having been summoned by Roxbury, and quite some time was spent by the four of them working out a final plan.

Hugging the sweet knowledge that Ives had trusted in her judgment, Sophy listened with only half an ear to what the gentlemen were discussing. Ives had agreed with her! she thought giddily. And on something that he had clearly not wanted to! It warmed her and brought a glow to her eyes. Despite the gravity of the conversation, a little bubble of delighted laughter kept rising in her throat, and only the certainty that the other three would think her mad if she allowed it to escape, kept it locked inside of her. And of course, she admitted cheerfully, she *was* mad, quite mad, to be so happy about having won the right to risk her neck!

Something Ives said caught her attention and sitting up in her chair, she interrupted, "Do you know, I disagree with that idea. I think that it might be better if we did not actually make a blackmail threat."

Three pairs of male eyes fastened incredulously on her. A little flush stained her cheeks, and she went on doggedly.

"I am quite certain that it would suit our purposes just as well if I were merely to, er, accidentally reveal the pin to Grimshaw, tease him with it as it were, without putting any specific threat into words. He is not *un*intelligent—if the pin is his, he will know what I am about, and if he is *not* our killer, the pin will mean nothing to him. I will not have made a fool of myself by tossing about ridiculous threats that mean nothing to him."

Roxbury looked at her approvingly, reluctant admiration warming his cool gray eyes. "Upon my soul! She is right!"

Ives nodded, a wry smile curving his mouth. "If you will remember, my lord, I told you so."

A laugh sputtered from Roxbury, and, dipping his head in acknowledgment, he admitted, "So you did, my boy. So you did."

Riding home a short while later, Sophy slanted a glance up at Ives, who was seated beside her in their coach, and remarked, "Your godfather is really a very nice man, isn't he?"

Ives grimaced. "*Nice* is not a word I would usually associate with Roxbury, but yes, I suppose in his way, that he is nice, upon occasion." He looked at her, a warning in his gaze. "He is also ruthless, cold-blooded, and single-minded. Remember that, will you?"

She nodded and, dropping her eyes from his, stared at her gloved hands where they rested in her lap. "I want to thank you for what you did today," she said in a low voice. "I know that you did not want me involved."

Ives lifted her hand and pressed a hard kiss upon it.

"I know," she said softly, "you would prefer to keep me wrapped in cotton wool . . . but while it is sometimes very pleasant to be coddled, it can also be stifling and feel like a prison when one is *always* treated so."

Their eyes met, her heart leaping at the expression in his. Pulling her to him, he kissed her passionately. Blissfully, Sophy gave herself up to the magic of his embrace, her lips welcoming his, her arms closing ardently around his neck.

"I would never," he said against her mouth, a dreamy time later, "ever want you to feel as if marriage to me was a prison."

Brushing back a lock of raven black hair from his forehead, she murmured, "Do you know that since we have been married I have felt freer than I ever have in my life?"

"But not too free," Ives said thickly. "Remember always that you belong to me."

His mouth caught hers again and it was very quiet in the coach. If Lord and Lady Harrington looked slightly disheveled and breathless when they emerged from the intimate confines of the vehicle at the Grayson town house, the footman who greeted them was trained well enough to avert his eyes and keep a smooth face.

Not that Ives or Sophy would have noticed since they had eyes only for each other. With hardly an acknowledgment of the footman's presence, Ives blindly followed Sophy up the stairs and into her bedroom, shutting and locking the door behind him with a decisive movement.

Wordlessly, Sophy turned to face him, her pulse thudding, her entire body rejoicing at what she saw in his dark, intent face. There was a distinctly carnal slant to his mouth and his devil green eyes were glittering with suppressed hunger. His strong arms crushed her against him as his lips urgently found hers. Her soft mouth was his to plunder, and he did so boldly, leaving her in no doubt of his intentions. A shudder went through her at the explicit thrust and demand of his tongue, the sweet hunger already simmering between them, suddenly sharp and intense.

Ives's greed for her was uncompromising, his lips hard, almost ruthless against hers, his hands moving with savage need over her as he swiftly walked her backward toward the bed, his intentions plain. He *needed* her. *Now*.

Even through the fabric of her gown and his breeches she could feel his fierce heat and his bulging, powerful shaft as it pressed insistently against her lower belly. She shivered suddenly when he roughly grasped the skirts of her gown and plunged a questing hand underneath to find her buttocks, to fondle and caress the firm flesh.

Progress toward the bed halted momentarily as he pulled her closer to him, making her even more aware of his arousal. Sophy was dizzy with desire, her breasts, her lower body, her entire *being* aching in anticipation of his possession.

She moaned and wriggled with pleasure when his fingers traveled around to her stomach and then lower, to the juncture of her thighs. He stroked the soft, swollen flesh he found there. Now his tongue mimicked the motions of his fingers, and Sophy shuddered as the now-familiar demand, the sheer erotic hunger, flourished. Oh, mercy! She wanted him.

Driven by the most elemental of emotions, Ives was oblivious to anything but the sweet, soft, yielding shape in his arms, and the clothes separating them became intolerable. Heedless of the damage he did, he single-mindedly disposed of every scrap of material preventing him from reaching the one thing he wanted, Sophy's warm, naked body next to his. When the last shred of expensive garments had been mercilessly dispensed with, he gave a groan of pure sensual satisfaction as he crushed his yearning flesh against the welcoming softness of hers.

Her arms wrapped tightly around his neck, her slender

body pressed eagerly next to his, Sophy reveled in the touch of his hair-roughened chest against her tender nipples and the probing jut of his shaft between her legs. Their lips locked together, his tongue filled her mouth, his blunt motions stoking the fire which already raged between them.

Half-cradling her, Ives parted her thighs and deliberately sank two fingers deep within her. She twisted wildly in his embrace, his invading fingers bringing her to the brink of ecstasy.

Sophy's response shattered the last hold Ives had on his emotions. With something between a growl and a groan, he lifted her and almost threw her on the bed. For a moment he stared with frank appreciation at the unknowingly wanton picture she made against the emerald-silk coverlet, her golden hair spread out in wild disarray, her pink nipples taut and tempting, her alabaster skin gleaming against the brilliant fabric.

Her eyes slumbering with passion, their golden depths promising the most exquisite ecstasy, Sophy stared back at him, her breath deepening as her gaze drifted over his big body downward to the bold length of his shaft.

"Come to me," she said softly. "Come to me."

"Oh, I intend to, sweetheart. Believe me, I intend to," he replied thickly.

Bending over, he trailed kisses down the center of her body, caressing and nipping gently at the silky flesh until he found the warm, musky core of her. Nuzzling and tasting, he teased her, tormented her until she was gasping and writhing under his caresses.

It was unbearably sweet, powerfully erotic, and Sophy was completely under his thrall. She *never* imagined such sensations, such intimacy, such *pleasure* could be shared between a man and a woman.

When Ives raised his head, and said huskily, "Touch me, sweetheart. Touch me as I am touching you," she did not hesitate. She *wanted* the power, the joy of exchanging this shockingly intimate caress. Rising to her knees, her lips sliding down his broad chest and across his flat belly, unerringly she found the hot, rigid length of him. Wonderingly she explored him, marveling at the velvety feel of him, reveling in the helpless groans she wrested from him as her tongue and lips tasted him.

"Dear God, *Sophy*!" Ives suddenly ground out in a nearly unrecognizable voice.

Tipping her back onto the bed, he fell upon her, his mouth crushed against hers, his fingers sinking urgently into her yielding flesh. But the time for mere play was past, and, shifting his body, he kneed her thighs apart and sank heavily into her.

Mindless, searing pleasure cascaded over him as he felt her slick heat close around him. Her welcoming flesh clenched him tightly, driving him to the brink of ecstasy as he began to thrust wildly, hurtling them both into the abyss and an explosive climax.

And when the fierce tempest ebbed, when reality gradually intruded, they were still locked together, their lips tenderly touching, their hands moving in lazy pleasure over each other. They remained that way for a long time, until finally, with a regretful sigh, Ives slowly slid from her body and lay beside her on the bed.

Dazed, *stunned* by the power of the pleasure that had stormed through her, Sophy was astonished at what they had just shared. So *this*, she thought languorously, was what it was like to make love to a lover.

Her head twisted slightly, so that she could glance across at Ives, who was lying collapsed by her side, apparently as shaken as she was. She smiled tenderly as she considered his bold profile: the arrogant nose, the aggressive chin, and the hard mouth. He was her lover. The one man who could turn her into a shameless, demanding wanton.

His eyes suddenly met hers and she was convinced that her heart turned right over in her breast. She did not know what she expected him to say, but she was startled when he said tightly, "After this proposed meeting with Grimshaw, do not think that I shall let you risk your neck, or any other part of your delectable little body, in such a fashion again." He gathered her close, almost crushing her against him. "I do not," he muttered, "*ever* want to experience again what I am feeling right now."

It was not precisely what she wanted to hear, but it would do, and she smiled against his shoulder, her heart singing. He had not said that he loved her, but she would have to be a fool not to realize that he cared deeply for her, and Sophy was definitely not a fool.

Sitting up and brushing back her tangled golden hair, she said briskly. "Nothing is going to happen to me. It is a very simple plan. It will proceed just as we discussed. You have nothing to worry about."

As he dressed that evening, Ives tried to tell himself that Sophy had the correct reading of the situation, but it was not easy. A nagging sense of apprehension continued to bedevil him, and he was frowning blackly at his reflection in the mirror as he finished tying his cravat.

Seeing his expression, Ashby asked, "Is something wrong, my lord?"

Ives shook his head. "No. At least I pray not."

There was a knock on the door and Sanderson entered. "A note just arrived for you from Lord Roxbury," he said, offering a silver salver.

Picking up the note, Ives scanned the contents, his mouth tightening. Looking at the two men, he said, "Meade's body has been found—on the waterfront, hidden in a barrel near an alehouse."

Sanderson cocked a brow. "It doesn't come as any surprise, does it, my lord? We were all of a mind that the Fox would get rid of him. He'd served his purpose."

Ives nodded slowly, not liking the sensations knifing through him. If he'd had any doubts about the cold-blooded efficiency of his enemy, they had been put to rest; and the knowledge that Sophy was going to twist the tail of such a murderous creature sent a shaft of pure ice through his insides.

"I have to see Roxbury," he said abruptly. "He will give me all the particulars." Glancing at Sanderson, he added, "If Lady Harrington goes out tonight, I want the two of you to follow her. Discreetly. And until I tell you differently, she is not to leave this house without one of you trailing after her. Do you understand me?"

Both men nodded, their expressions as grim as the one on Ives's dark face.

Roxbury had little to add to what he had written in his note.

"I kept my men looking for him," Roxbury said, when Ives had entered his study and had been seated. "It seemed likely that the body would have been disposed of nearby, but not where it would be discovered for a while.

One of my fellows was poking around a pile of broken, discarded barrels when he found him."

From under his heavy white brows, Roxbury regarded Ives. "Meade's throat had been cut and he had been stripped of his clothes." His mouth twisted. "This time of year, in another few days he would have been swollen beyond recognition—the rats had already been at him—and we never would have identified him."

"I assume," Ives said quietly, "that you do not intend to make Meade's murder public."

Roxbury inclined his head. "It is my intention to let the story stand that he is away visiting in Brighton." He smiled grimly. "There will be time enough to tell the whole tale once we have captured *Le Renard.*" Roxbury glanced down at his desk, his eyes not meeting Ives's. "When," he asked, "do you intend for Sophy to dangle the pin before Grimshaw?"

Ives smiled grimly. "I am joining Grimshaw and his friends this evening. I hope that I will learn something tonight that we can use to our advantage."

Luck was with Ives: He had not been five minutes at the table at the Pigeon Hole where Grimshaw and the others were gathered, when Dewhurst murmured, "We are all going to Vauxhall Gardens tomorrow night. Will you join us?"

He cast a teasing glance at Grimshaw and half giggled. "It seems that William has fallen in love with a coy ladybird. She is currently under the protection of a very jealous lord." He looked sly as he murmured, "But she has given Grimshaw hope that the situation may change, and she has mentioned that she intends to be promenading through the gardens tomorrow night." He giggled again. "It should be diverting to watch him lusting after her."

A few of the other men snickered, and Grimshaw shot Dewhurst an annoyed look. "Do not forget that it was *your* idea that I pursue her. You said I needed a challenge. And as for Harrington joining us," he added snidely, "I've noticed that he ain't in the petticoat line. Perhaps it is pretty boys in breeches who catch his eye."

Ives did not rise to the bait. "Actually," he said coolly, "I may see you there. It so happens that my wife has requested my escort to the gardens tomorrow night, and I have decided to indulge her."

"Is that so?" Grimshaw asked, his gray eyes fixed on Ives's face. "For someone who professes to be an out-and-out rogue like the rest of us, it seems to me that you have shown a decided preference for the parson's mousetrap."

Ives smiled gently. "If you were fortunate enough, my friend, to be caught by a, er, mousetrap as fascinating as the one which snared me, I would wager that you would show the same preference."

There was a general burst of laughter from the others, but Grimshaw only scowled. "Please yourself, my lord."

"Oh, I shall," Ives murmured, his green eyes glinting.

With the exception of Ives, everyone was delighted that they were going to be able to set events in motion so swiftly. Roxbury, especially, was keen.

"We have little time to lose," he told Ives and Forrest when they met Thursday afternoon to discuss the situation. "Remember the information in the memorandum has already fallen into the Fox's hands. Whether he has delivered it to the French already is questionable, but the more time that elapses, the more likely it is that the information will be on its way to France." He fiddled with a quill on his desk. "And Sophy? She is still willing to do her part?"

"Oh, yes," Ives said dryly. "In fact, she is quite looking forward to this evening. She was quite, *quite* thrilled when I told her the news earlier."

Detecting a note in Ives's voice, Forrest asked, "You are not worried, are you?"

"No, why should I be?" Ives snapped. "My wife is only going to confront a cold-blooded villain and bait him with something he has already murdered two people to get! And do not forget—I assure you that I have not—if he is the Fox, he murdered my family, and not two nights ago, confounded us and callously dispatched Meade." His face grim, he muttered, "Of course, Sophy is not to know any of *that* when she gaily shows him the cravat pin."

Roxbury sighed, his eyes troubled. "Do you honestly think it would be to her advantage to know the full extent of his brutal actions? Would it be good for her peace of mind?"

Leaning forward, he added urgently, "She is already forewarned. She knows that he has murdered two people. Wouldn't the knowledge of just how cold-blooded and merciless he is cause her to falter in her task?"

"It might," Ives snarled softly, "make her decide *not* to risk her neck!"

Forrest shook his head. "I do not know your lady well, my lord, but from what I have seen, if she knew what we suspect, it would make her all the more determined to face him."

Ives ran a weary hand over his face. "Of course, you

are right." He smiled tightly. "It would, indeed, make her all the more keen to play her part."

Despite telling herself to act as normally as possible, Sophy was fairly shimmering with excitement when Ives showed her into the supper box reserved for them that night at Vauxhall Gardens. Forrest joined them shortly thereafter, and briefly, in hushed undertones, they went over the plan again. A plan that was less a plan than a hoped-for sequence of events.

The gardens were crowded this evening, the walks filled with elegantly garbed ladies and gentlemen as well as the less richly attired common folk. Gaily colored lanterns were strung along the pathways, strains of Handel permeated the area, and the air was filled with the happy sound of revelers.

The cravat pin rested snugly in her satin-and-beaded reticule, and it seemed to Sophy that she could feel it burning her fingers through the material. Excited and a trifle anxious, she barely tasted the almost transparent slices of ham and the minuscule morsels of chicken for which the gardens were famed.

There was so much that could go wrong, so many things beyond their control, and she alternated between moments of high excitement and dark despair.

Then Ives suddenly stiffened, and murmured, "There they are. Grimshaw and Coleman just came out of the South Walk, heading in our direction."

Sophy cast a discreet glance in that direction, her heart thumping uncomfortably at the sight of Grimshaw's dissolute features. She took a deep breath. She had nothing to fear. She was surrounded by crowds, and Ives and Forrest were going to be nearby.

Despite the awareness of all that could go wrong, in the end, events went as if ordained. Grimshaw and Coleman, joined by Dewhurst and Sir Arthur Bellingham, spied the Harrington party and sauntered over to greet them. All were soon crowded into the supper box.

Sir Arthur, having been out of town the past few days, was one of the last gentlemen to pay his respects to Sophy. He bent over her hand where she remained seated in the far corner of the box, and murmured, "Dreadful about Edward, wasn't it? Can't hardly believe that the old fellow is gone." His brown eyes gleaming with malice, he added, "Of course, my dear, having no love of him, I am sure that you feel quite differently about the matter."

Sophy smiled stiffly. She had always been ambivalent about Sir Arthur, neither liking nor precisely disliking him, and his manner tonight did nothing to change her mind. He might have displayed a bit more tact, but then she could not blame him for voicing what was common knowledge.

"I am sure," she said coolly, "that *you* will miss his company. In fact, I am sure that he will be missed by many people."

"And I'll wager my grays," said Grimshaw, who had followed Sir Arthur over to greet Sophy, "that you nearly choked getting those words out."

Sophy glanced in his direction. "I am afraid that you would lose," she said calmly. "I do not dispute that my uncle could be quite charming and that there were those who held him in great affection. I was simply not one of them."

His gray eyes resting avidly on her elegant features, Grimshaw murmured, "I have always thought it a pity that you were not more like your uncle. We could have had *such* pleasurable times together."

Sir Arthur snickered and turned away in answer to a question from Dewhurst, leaving Grimshaw and Sophy nearly isolated at one end of the small supper box. Grimshaw's tall form almost blocked the others from her sight.

Ordinarily, Sophy felt nothing but disgust for Grimshaw, but tonight, despite knowing Ives was nearby, a shiver of unease went through her. This man, Sophy suddenly reminded herself, might very well have murdered two people, and she was about to place herself between him and something he might have killed for . . . twice. Stilling the panic that rose in her, her fingers closed round her reticule and the ruby cravat pin inside it.

Grimshaw's gaze fell to her bosom. Sophy's stomach roiled at the lascivious expression that leaped to his eyes as they wandered over the tops of her breasts, revealed by the low-cut bodice of her fashionable gown.

"If you *had* been more inclined in Edward's direction," he purred, "we could have become, oh, quite good friends." His eyes lifted to hers. "I would still be very interested in becoming your, ah, friend, my sweet."

Forgetting her fear, she tamped down the outrage flooding her at his words. How dare he! The urge to strike his dissipated features was strong, but her fingers touched the ruby cravat pin once more and she was reminded of her role.

In all of their planning for this moment, none of them had known precisely when or where it would occur. They had all agreed, however, that following his usual wont, it was highly likely that given the opportunity, Grimshaw would attempt to cut Sophy out from the crowd where he could proposition her. All her husband had to do was see that the opportunity arose.

Savagely aware that Grimshaw had Sophy cornered at the other end of the supper box, Ives, ably assisted by Forrest, proceeded to unobtrusively guide the other gentlemen out of the box, ostensibly to ogle any attractive women in the crowds thronging the gardens. Since he had done his best to convince everybody that he was as disreputable a libertine as the rest of them, no one was overly surprised that he practiced such reprehensible behavior with his wife only a few feet away.

Leaving Sophy alone with Grimshaw was one of the most difficult things he had ever done, and he felt not one shred of satisfaction at how easily things had fallen into place as he stood with the others a few feet away from the supper box. His wife was alone with a known womanizer, a man she feared and disliked, and a man who was very likely a ruthless murderer. Everything, Ives told himself viciously, was just dandy!

Seeing the others occupied outside the box, Sophy knew her moment had come. As if aware of their isolation for the first time, she murmured, "Oh! I did not realize that everybody had gone outside. Perhaps we should join them."

"Now why," Grimshaw murmured, "would we want to do that? It is rare that I ever have a moment alone with you. I am sure we can find some way of amusing ourselves." Boldly he reached out and ran a caressing finger across the top of her breasts.

Sophy did not have to pretend the fury that lit her golden eyes. She retained just enough control on her temper as she surged to her feet to make certain that the reticule fell off her lap, spilling its contents. She was unable, however, to prevent herself from striking his hand away and snapping, "Take your hands off me!"

Grimshaw only smiled, an insufferably arrogant smile that made Sophy's teeth ache. Wrenching her thoughts away from the pleasing notion of slapping it off his face, she forced herself to glance down at the floor and cry with apparent dismay, "Oh, *now* look what you've made me do!"

Grimshaw's eyes dropped and his breath sucked in audibly as his gaze fell upon the ruby cravat pin lying on the floor almost at his feet. Like a man in a trance, he bent down and reached for the pin.

Sophy froze, her own gaze locked on the cravat pin. The ruby center seemed to glow in the candlelight like an evil beacon. Feeling unable to move, she watched numbly as Grimshaw's fingers closed around the pin. He remained bent for several agonizing seconds, minutely examining the pin.

It was clear he recognized the pin—his initial reaction had given that much away—but now she could read that knowledge in his eyes as he slowly straightened and looked at her. Holding the pin out toward her, he asked silkily, "And where, my pet, did you get this?"

Chapter Twenty

❧

*A*n icy shiver went through Sophy, but her voice was careless as she said, "Oh, that! I found it . . . the night Simon died."

Pleased that her fingers displayed no sign of trembling, she calmly reached out and plucked the pin from his grasp.

"It was lying on the floor near the top of the stairs at Marlowe House, and I have kept it all these years as a, er, lucky charm. Why? Do you recognize it? I have often wondered who it belonged to and why no one asked after it."

Grimshaw said nothing for a long moment, his gaze locked on the ruby pin held in Sophy's fingers. Then, shrugging and seeming to lose interest in both Sophy and the cravat pin, he glanced away, and murmured, "I thought it looked familiar when I first laid eyes on it, but I realize now that I was mistaken."

He looked around, apparently noticing for the first time that they were alone in the supper box.

"Shall we join the others? It seems that they have deserted us." He smiled nastily. "I am sure that some people might misunderstand my intentions if we were to be found alone in such an intimate setting, and naturally, I would not want to give your husband an excuse to call me out, now would I?"

Her mission accomplished, Sophy slipped the pin back into her reticule, and said crisply, "Of course not. But you have nothing to fear from him even if he were to find us here. He does not leap to silly conclusions!"

She brushed past him and gave an inward sigh of relief when he made no move to stop her. Stepping out of the supper box, she was delighted to find Ives standing not two feet from the box. From the stiff set of his shoulders, despite his air of interest in the events going on in front of him, she knew that all his attention was focused on what had been going on in the supper box behind him.

Ives sensed her presence immediately and swung around to look at her. With deceptive calm, he said, "Ah, there you are, my dear. I wondered what was keeping you."

Sophy flashed him a dazzling smile and placing her hand on his arm, said quite clearly, "Believe me, nothing. Nothing at all."

Behind her, a muscle twitched in Grimshaw's cheek, but he only said, "Your lady's reticule came open and spilled its contents. We were busy picking everything up."

"I see," Ives replied with commendable disinterest, some of the painful tenseness ebbing from him now that Sophy was no longer alone with Grimshaw. He smiled down at her. "Well, shall we stroll through the gardens?"

"Oh, yes, please," Sophy answered instantly. She gave

a polite, dismissing nod to Grimshaw. "Perhaps we shall see you later this evening, my lord."

A sardonic expression on his face, he stared at Sophy as he said, "I doubt it. My plans for the remainder of the evening are not at all honorable—and you, unfortunately, have always yearned for dull respectability."

With an effort, Ives kept himself from making an unwise reply, but he could not help saying coolly, "Respectability is not a trait to be despised in one's wife."

"Of course not," Grimshaw said equitably. Glancing over Ives's shoulder, he murmured, "And now, if you will excuse me, I will rejoin my companions."

Sophy and Ives both nodded politely and watched him saunter over to join the others where they were standing in a group at the edge of the gravel pathway, laughing and talking. Only when it was clear that Grimshaw was occupied in conversation with his companions, did Ives glance down at Sophy and ask quietly, "Well? How did it go? How did he react to the pin?"

Sophy frowned slightly. "He obviously recognized it, but he pretended not to, just as Edward did. But the odd thing is, I think he was *surprised* to see it."

"Why should that be odd? He had no way of knowing positively that you possessed it. We don't know what Edward told him about the pin. There is an excellent chance that Edward must have provided some clue to its whereabouts, however, else we would never have had the housebreaker pay us a visit. He might have strongly suspected that you were the one who had the pin, but he had no way of knowing for certain, especially since he didn't find it during his abortive search of the house."

"I know. I was just hoping for something conclusive," she answered ruefully.

Ives smiled slightly. "What did you expect? For him to gasp, turn white, and blurt out a confession?"

"No," she said with a sigh, "but I wish he had betrayed more. As it is, I feel that we have wasted our time and have learned nothing of importance."

Having taken his leave of the other gentlemen, Forrest rejoined Ives and Sophy near the supper box. At the question obvious in his bright blue eyes, Ives said softly, "He knows that she has the pin. Sophy thinks that he recognized it, but he pretended not to. Other than that, we have nothing new."

A shiver of unease coursed down Sophy's spine. "Except now," she whispered, "he *knows* that I have it."

Ives's arm came around her waist. "And I shall keep you safe."

Her eyes met his. "It wasn't the meeting tonight that had you so worried, was it? It was afterward . . ." She swallowed. "Afterward, when he knows that I possess what he wants, that I hold something he may have murdered to get. It is what he may do now that had you so anxious, wasn't it?"

Ives nodded. "I tried to warn you, sweetheart, but since you have shown him the pin, there is no way to wrap it in clean linen," he said gently. "You have indeed made yourself a target." Gruffly he continued, "But do not fear—if I or Forrest cannot be with you, one of my men will shadow your every move—don't ever forget that fact."

"You may have become a target," Forrest added quickly. "But if so, you will be a target that we shall see he never reaches."

Sophy smiled tremulously, looking from one intent

face to the other. "I know. I think it is only that the full enormity of what I have done is just sinking in."

"The real question," Forrest murmured, "is whether or not Grimshaw is *our* target."

"And that," Ives said grimly, "we will not know until he makes the first move."

His gaze slid over to the group that included Grimshaw. If Grimshaw was their murderer and the Fox, the sight of the ruby cravat pin did not seem to have alarmed him. Ives made a face. What had he expected? That he would react in the manner he had teased Sophy about earlier, blanching and gasping dramatically?

Disgusted with himself, he took a firmer grip on Sophy's arm, and said, "Since we came to stroll, I suggest we do so. The sooner we have traipsed through the bloody gardens, the sooner we can report to Roxbury."

"Should we do that tonight?" Sophy asked uncertainly. "What if someone observes us? Won't they think it strange that we leave the gardens and go immediately to your godfather's house at this hour of the evening? Wouldn't it look suspicious?"

Ives cast her a glance. "Do you know," he said wryly, "for someone very new to subterfuge, you are developing a keen talent for it."

Sophy snorted. "It could also simply be common sense."

"I stand corrected, my dear. And you do not have to fear that we would do something so overt—Forrest and I are fast becoming old hands at subterfuge ourselves." He grinned down at her. "Roxbury is already waiting for us at Forrest's house, where you and I shall stop for some final refreshments before continuing home. Once we have departed and it is ascertained that no one is particularly interested in our destination, Roxbury will slip away and no one will have been the wiser. We have it all planned."

Forrest's town house on Bruton Street was just a few doors down from the residence of George Canning, the Secretary of State for Foreign Affairs, and one of the reasons they had decided it would be safe to meet with Roxbury at Forrest's home. If Roxbury were seen in the vicinity, it would be assumed that he was in the area to meet with Mr. Canning since they were known to be friends.

Upon hearing Sophy's recitation of her encounter with Grimshaw, Roxbury was neither pleased nor displeased. Seated in a black-leather chair in the library of Forrest's house, he regarded Sophy intently for several seconds after she finished speaking.

"You thought he recognized it?" he finally asked.

Sophy nodded. "He certainly seemed very interested in it at first, but then he just shrugged and acted as if it held no meaning for him." She wrinkled her straight little nose. "I knew that if he was Edward's murderer he would be far too clever to betray a great deal, but I had hoped that he would have revealed a little more."

"Do not become too discouraged, my dear," Roxbury said. "These things take time, and the most important thing is that we have dangled the bait in front of him. Now we must sit back and see if he tries to snatch it."

A shiver went down Sophy's spine. "I know," she said in a hollow tone. "All I have to do is wait for him to try to murder me as he did my uncle."

Ives's hand, which had been resting possessively on her shoulder, tightened. "He will never get close enough to you even to try," he said with quiet assurance. "And I suspect that even he will think twice before attempting to strike at you. Remember, he will not want to draw any more attention to the cravat pin, and he certainly will not want anyone to connect it to the other two murders. He is not a stupid man, and he must realize that with every murder he commits, he runs the risk of pointing the finger of guilt directly at himself."

It was cold comfort, but Sophy accepted it gladly. Surely, Ives was right; Edward's murderer must be having second thoughts about his methods of dealing with those who knew about the cravat pin. After all, she told herself uneasily, he could not simply keep murdering people!

Arriving home a short while later and losing herself in Ives's passionate lovemaking, Sophy was able for a time to banish her fears. Ives's almost desperate hunger for her seemed not to have abated one whit, and she happily gave herself up to his distinctly pleasurable assault.

But eventually, as she drifted down from the scarlet heights that they had shared, reality intruded. Lying sated and limp in Ives's arms, she turned her head on his shoulder to look at him, and asked abruptly, "If Grimshaw is the owner of the pin, what do you think he will do now?"

Ives made a face. "If I knew that, sweetheart, I would feel much easier in my mind than I do. Unfortunately, we can only wait and see what he does. And I find that while I consider myself a patient man, when my wife is hung out like a piece of raw meat in front of a very dangerous shark, an exceedingly *vicious* shark, I am not very patient at all."

His arm curved her closer to his big body. "In the meantime, while our shark decides whether to bite or not, you are to be extremely careful where you go, especially at night. I cannot be seen to sit in your pocket if we are to draw him out, and so we shall have to continue with our separate activities—with slight modifications. If I am not with you in public, either Forrest or one of my men will not be far behind you. I think that our time of greatest vulnerability will be at night, but you cannot drop your guard just because the sun is shining. When you do go out during the day, be very careful where you go. Take precautions that you are always with someone you trust."

"I am not going to do anything foolish," she said tartly. "Believe me, I do not want to suffer the same fate as Edward and Miss Weatherby."

"I just wish you were not involved in this whole bloody affair and that it was over and done with—as it should have been!"

He snarled out the words with such explosive violence that Sophy stared at him in astonishment. A little frown marred her forehead. *As it should have been?* Now what, she wondered, did he mean by that? That Grimshaw should have betrayed himself tonight? That Edward's murderer should have been found before now? Or something else?

Idly her fingers played with the crisp hair on his chest, her thoughts on past events. Not just the events of tonight, or even the last week, but all the momentous twists and turns her life had taken since Simon had died, particularly since she had met Ives.

Suddenly several things came together in her mind with startling clarity. Simon's long-ago comment about

Roxbury. Ives's seeming inability to make certain decisions without Roxbury's consent—Ives, the most confident man she had ever met! Even more important, his sudden and inexplicable predilection for the disreputable company of all of Simon's old friends.

It was true that Viscount Harrington had been an utter stranger to her a short while ago, but in the early days of their acquaintance, she had been drawn to him in spite of herself. And in the early days, she reminded herself, there had been no sign of a tendency to follow degenerate pursuits. Despite her unwilling attraction to him, she would have fled far and fast if she had detected even a hint of the libertine about him. In fact, as she considered it, she would have sworn then that Ives would have spurned the company and morals of men like Grimshaw and the others and would have held them in contempt. But, *recently*, he had not.

Why not? Why a sudden and unpredictable affinity for such men? She thought again of Simon's comment: Ives's godfather, a master spy. If Simon knew enough about Roxbury to make that statement, even in jest, then Simon had to have been dealing with men who knew about such things, such as spies.

"Tell me about Roxbury," she said suddenly. "Simon once referred to him as a master spy. Is it true?"

She sensed the wariness in him immediately, and her certainty that she had stumbled upon some inkling of the truth grew.

"Not exactly. And it is not precisely common knowledge, although he has been called by such a title occasionally in certain circles," Ives conceded reluctantly, not liking this sudden turn, but unwilling to lie outright.

When she continued to wait expectantly, he added unwillingly, "It is possible that there may be some truth in it—his devotion to England is legendary, and I am sure that from time to time he has delved into matters that would lead one to, er, connect him to matters of espionage."

Sophy said nothing for a minute and just when Ives thought that they had put the dangerous subject behind them, she observed thoughtfully, "And if he needed help, oh, in say, tracking down a treacherous spy here in London, is it not possible that he would ask for your help?"

Ives forced a laugh. "I am no spy, sweetheart."

"But if your godfather requested your help," she persisted, "you would give it to him, wouldn't you? To catch a spy?"

If they had not been lying naked together, their bodies pressed closely to each other, Sophy might not have been aware of it when Ives stiffened slightly. But she felt it, and knew that she was on the right track.

She sat up and stared down at him. "You're working for your godfather, aren't you? That is why when anything untoward happens you immediately have a conference with Roxbury. And it is the reason that he has been coming here so frequently, isn't it?" Her eyes narrowed and she added slowly, almost to herself, "And that is why you are always running off to join Grimshaw and the others, isn't it? One of them is a spy, and Roxbury wants you to unmask him."

"Don't be ridiculous." Ives growled, cursing her cleverness even as he admired it. "Do you really think Grimshaw, blackguard that he is, is a spy? Why should he stoop to such a level? It would be his life if he were caught. Treason is punished by execution, remember?"

Her eyes locked on his, she said musingly, "Treason

wouldn't have mattered to Simon. He'd have believed that he was too careful, too smart, too *clever* to be caught, and he would have delighted in tweaking the nose of someone like Roxbury. Perhaps your spy is like him, a man who revels in taking risks. In dicing with danger—and, of course, there is always money. Some men are not above avarice. Some men are greedy, like Edward. I could see Edward selling secrets for such a base reason as gold. Gold has corrupted many a man— why not Grimshaw?"

"I see," Ives said. "In addition to being the object of Edward's blackmail and the owner of the cravat pin, Grimshaw is now some sort of spy?"

Sophy's eyes widened. "That's it, isn't it? *That's* why you have been so anxious about my involvement." An expression of pure delight crossed her vivid face. "It isn't just a murderer we are after. We are going to trap a spy, aren't we?"

"*We* are certainly going to do nothing of the sort!" Ives said savagely, cursing her too-quick intelligence.

Sophy cast him a superior smile. "You can deny it all you want—in fact, I imagine Roxbury has sworn you to secrecy, but you will not convince me! It explains too many things. You, my dear, clever, conniving husband, are hunting a spy! And that is why someone like Roxbury is interested in helping me to find my uncle's murderer. You know something that somehow connects the cravat pin with the man you are pursuing and are hoping to use it to draw him out."

Ives shook his head. "No," he said firmly. "We know of no definite connection." And could have ripped his tongue out as soon as the words left his mouth.

"Aha!" she exclaimed delightedly, her golden eyes

sparkling. "You admit that there is a spy and that you are helping·Roxbury catch him!"

"Dash it all, Sophy! Cease this flummery!" Ives said with an edge, vastly annoyed with himself for not having chosen his words more wisely. "I admit nothing. Concentrate on what we are fairly confident of: Edward and Miss Weatherby were murdered because they tried to blackmail the man who *probably* lost the cravat pin."

She stared at him for a long time, her tousled curls framing her lively features, her eyes full of speculation as they rested on his grim face. Finally, she shrugged, and said airily, "Oh, very well, keep your secrets, but you do not fool me. I know we are hunting a spy and you are working for Roxbury. You will not convince me otherwise."

She paused again, obviously hoping he would make another imprudent statement. When he remained stubbornly silent, she dropped her eyes and from beneath her extravagant lashes peeped at him as she said slyly, "And that is why of late you have been so often in the pocket of Grimshaw and Coleman, isn't it?"

His jaw set. Ives scowled at her; but before he could answer—if he had been going to in the first place—she gave a little laugh and kissed his hard mouth.

"Never mind. I expect you will tell me all when you can."

"Has anyone ever told you that you are a witch?" he growled as his arms closed around her. "An aggravating, bewitching little sorceress?"

She dimpled. "No. Do you think I am a witch?"

"I think," he said thickly, "that you have thoroughly bewitched me and that you are utterly adorable!" And proceeded to show her just how very adorable he found her—her and her extremely responsive body.

As they came together this time there was some new element in their lovemaking. The same explosive passion was there, the same wildly exciting race to ecstasy and afterward, the same lazy, bone-melting feeling of completeness, but something was different.

Her heart still thudding madly in her breast, her body still throbbing from Ives's possession, and her lips still tingling from his urgent kisses, Sophy hazily tried to identify what had been different about this time as she floated dreamily in the aftermath of their lovemaking. Tenderness? Trust? A sense of oneness? Something.

And was she the only one who had felt it, or had Ives been aware of it, too? Was it something solely within her that responded differently to him? Or had there been something different about his lovemaking that had brought forth that feeling of uniqueness? Or was it some powerful emotion that emanated from both of them?

When she turned her head slightly to look at him, a wave of such tenderness, such love rushed over her at the sight of his dark, powerful features that the words slipped out before she had time to call them back. "I love you," she murmured involuntarily, one hand unconsciously caressing his cheek.

Embarrassed at what she had revealed, her eyes fell and she snatched her hand away. Oh, God! How could I have said such a thing out loud! How could I have so brazenly revealed what was in my heart?

As the seconds passed, she was unbearably aware of him lying by her side, aware of little else except for the painful hammering of her heart that had nothing to do with the climax they had just shared. Wishing she could just vanish into the air, she lay stiffly by his side, wondering what he was thinking, what he was feeling. When the silence dragged on, and he said nothing, she began to hope that perhaps he had not heard her.

But that hope was short-lived when he turned suddenly and gathered her against him. In the tenderest voice imaginable, he said, "I believe that, by rights, I should have said those words first, my love."

Her eyes flew to his, and the warm glow, the exquisite tenderness she saw there, made her feel as if she were melting in his very arms. "D-do you want to say them?" she stammered. "To m-me?"

He kissed her. "Indeed. I can think of nothing more that I want to say to you—that I have wanted to say to you." He smiled down at her. "I love you, Sophy. I loved you almost from the moment I laid eyes on you."

Sophy stared wordlessly at him. "But you never said anything," she almost wailed. "You never once gave me a hint!"

He laughed, lightly kissing her fingers. "I married you, didn't I?"

"But that was to save my reputation, and because you wanted an heir. *Everybody* knew that!"

He shook his head. "I don't deny that I shamelessly used the events surrounding Edward's murder to get you firmly shackled to me, but as for an heir? Well, there are any number of nubile young ladies who would have, no doubt, done the job ably. But you see, they all had one terrible, unforgivable flaw—they weren't *you*! I am afraid that only you will do for me." He kissed her nerveless fingers.

"Oh," Sophy said breathlessly, stars shining in her

lovely eyes. "That is the most romantic thing I have ever heard."

His mouth settled warmly on hers again as he murmured against her lips, "Oh, I am a most romantic fellow, my dear. *Most* romantic."

It was quite some time before any reasonable conversation took place between them again, lost as they were in the golden world known only to lovers. Each moment of discovery of each other's emotions had to be marveled at and considered, followed by frequent kisses and soft sighs and sometimes, gentle laughter.

"How could you doubt me?" Ives asked sometime later. "I do not think at any time during our, er, courtship that my actions have been other than that of a man irrevocably in love. Dash it all, Sophy, I have openly dangled after you, bluntly pursued you, and even toadied up to your family."

"Not fawned," she said with a little gurgle of laughter, hardly able to contain the joy which consumed her. *Ives loved her!*

He grinned, that wicked brigand's grin that made her heart leap. "Well, perhaps not that. But, sweetheart, you had to have known."

Sophy shook her head. "I did not. I swear it." Some of her happiness dimmed. "I was too afraid that you had married me for the same reason that Simon had—to gain an heir." Her eyes met his. "And you have to admit," she said softly, "that you have certainly been giving an excellent imitation of a man who has a fondness for the same vices."

His lips twisted. "I love you, Sophy. Know that. And know that I would never betray our wedding vows."

Their eyes clung and after a moment, she slowly nodded. "I do."

"And you have no more doubts about why I married you?" he asked gently.

Arms above her head, she stretched luxuriously, smiling foolishly. "No. Oh, Ives! I am so lucky! And to think that I was so afraid that I had broken my vow to myself, that *if* I ever married again, it would be for love alone. Nothing else would matter. Only love."

Bringing her arms back down to her sides, she glanced at him. Her eyes soft and glowing, she murmured, "But in the end, I did keep my vow, didn't I? We *did* marry for love alone, didn't we?"

He bent his head, his lips finding hers. Against her mouth, he said thickly, "Oh, yes. It was the only reason we married—for love alone."

It wasn't to be expected that Ives and Sophy would try to conceal their love, that it could be hidden. Phoebe, Anne, and Marcus watched them covertly all through breakfast the next morning, the scents of May and orange blossoms almost palpable around the table.

It was Marcus who finally put his own thoughts, and those of the other two, into words. Setting down his cup, he said uncertainly, "Er, I take it that you have, ah, settled your differences?"

Ives beamed at him, and the look he sent Sophy, as Phoebe later told Anne in shocked accents, made her feel distinctly flushed!

"Oh, yes," Ives said easily. "You could say that."

Breakfast suddenly became less than ordinary, and there was much laughter and teasing, the feeling that the future was going to be wonderful infusing each one of them.

But eventually, Ives had to tear himself away. Rising to his feet, he said, "I am afraid that I must leave you all now." His eyes met Sophy's across the table. "A word alone with you, my dear?"

Excusing herself from the others, she followed him from the room, shutting the door behind her.

Standing in front of her in the main entryway, Ives said quietly, "I have previous commitments. But perhaps this evening we shall all gather and discuss plans for the summer?"

Sophy nodded, the smile she sent almost making him dizzy with its brilliance. "I shall look forward to it."

"And your plans for today?"

She made a face. "Nothing very exciting. I have promised the girls that we shall go to Hatchard's this morning, and this afternoon, I think I am scheduled to go driving in Hyde Park with Henry—I shall have to check."

"Very well, I shall see you later." He dropped a swift, hard kiss on her lips. "Be careful," he said softly.

She smiled mistily up at him. "I will be," she promised.

It was difficult for Ives to keep with his usual schedule, but he did so, although his thoughts were on Sophy and what she was doing . . . and Grimshaw. He and Forrest attended a sale at Tattersall's, wandered into Manton's Shooting Gallery, and visited their tailor. By late afternoon, feeling that they had acted the part of gentlemen of leisure, they wandered to a small tavern off Bond Street, ostensibly for some refreshment.

A few minutes later, entering into the private room they had requested, they joined Roxbury at a long, sturdy oak table, where he was awaiting them. Refreshments had already been ordered. Pouring them each a tankard of dark ale, Roxbury said, "Anything out of the ordinary to report?"

Both Ives and Percival shook their heads. Ives explained how he and Percival had spent the day. "No one seemed to pay any attention to us, not that we expected they would."

Roxbury nodded, an impatient expression crossing his lined features. "It is the damned waiting that exhausts one," he said with obvious frustration. "And it is worse when we don't even know for certain that our suppositions are correct." He paused, thinking hard, then muttered, "But *Le Renard* has to be Grimshaw! Everything points to him."

Forrest frowned slightly. "I know why you believe that Grimshaw is the Fox, but could you not be mistaken?"

Roxbury flashed him a vexed look. "Of course we could be mistaken, but there is too much evidence for him *not* to be." He started to tick off the various reasons beginning with the death of Ives's father and the other members of the family. "It was Grimshaw who made the fatal wager that sent the Harringtons to their deaths in the yacht. And it was—"

"No, it wasn't," Percival said slowly. "Remember, I was there that night, and while it was Grimshaw who finally struck the terms of the wager, it was Dewhurst who actually suggested the wager."

Roxbury and Ives exchanged stunned glances, everything suddenly falling into place—especially why, in spite of their best efforts, they had never been able to catch Grimshaw in any suspicious activities. They had been watching the wrong man!

"*Dewhurst!*" Ives exclaimed, Sophy's words from that morning flashed terrifyingly through his brain. Surging up from his chair, he snatched out his pocket watch and glanced at the time. "My God!" he said in shaken accents. "Sophy is with him at this very moment!"

Chapter Twenty-one

🌿

Seated beside Henry Dewhurst in his high-perch phaeton, Sophy was enjoying the fine sunny afternoon. As planned, Henry had picked her up at the Berkeley Square town house just a few minutes previously, and they were merrily bowling down the busy London streets.

Because being driven in Hyde Park was more about seeing and being seen, Sophy had dressed accordingly in a striking afternoon gown of lavender-and-white-striped sarsenet trimmed with lace and purple-satin ribbon. Though she was wearing a dashing little hat of chipped straw that fastened underneath her chin with a jaunty bow, she also carried a white parasol lavished with a great deal of delicate lace. She looked utterly charming.

Glancing at her as she sat by his side, Henry complimented her on her looks. "May I say, my dear, that you look especially fetching today?"

Sophy dimpled at him. "You just did, Henry."

"Why, so I did," he replied lightly. He glanced at her again. "I would even go so far as to say that your marriage to Harrington seems to agree quite well with you."

Sophy looked ahead, but Henry could not help noticing the dreamy smile curving her lips. "Indeed, I find it
most agreeable," she said softly.

"Well, then," he responded, "I am very happy for you."

They said nothing for several minutes, as Dewhurst
expertly threaded his horses through the crowded London
traffic. The noise of the grinding wheels and clatter of the
horses' hooves on cobblestones, as well as the cries of the
many street vendors, created a constant racket. Sophy
was looking forward to the relative quiet of the park.

As Berkeley Square was only a short distance from
Hyde Park, it did not take long for her to realize that
Henry was driving in entirely the opposite direction. She
said nothing for a few minutes, thinking that perhaps he
was merely taking a roundabout route; since the day was
very fine, she had no objections. When he guided his
horses across the Vauxhall Bridge, however, she was
moved to question their destination.

Glancing at him, her curiosity evident, she asked, "Do
you have an errand you must take care of before we go to
the park?"

A smile curved his mouth. "Oh, you might say that, my
dear. It is certainly something that must be seen to immediately."

A feeling of unease slid down her spine, Ives's warning ringing in her ears. Oh, fiddle. I am just being silly. It
was broad daylight and this was no clandestine meeting.
Ives knew about it. So did the servants. They all knew
who she was seeing and where she was going . . . except
she was not exactly going to Hyde Park.

She considered the situation, but did not yet see any
reason to be *overly* alarmed, although she was increasingly anxious that they were rapidly leaving the environs

of the city behind them. I have no reason to be worried, she told herself uneasily; Henry is my friend. She had always had a fondness for him, and he was the only one of Simon's disreputable friends who had never put her to the blush, the only one who had ever treated her with kindness and respect.

But he *had* wanted a warmer relationship with her. Had he suddenly gone mad and intended to spirit her away to a secluded love nest and force himself upon her? She shook her head disgustedly. This was ridiculous; there was probably a perfectly innocent explanation for their detour. In a matter of minutes, Henry would discharge his errand and turn the horses around and they would, indeed, go to Hyde Park, just as planned. She was going to feel like a perfect ninny for doubting him.

Of course the other explanation, the one which sent a chill right through her entire body and the one that she was not quite able to banish entirely, was the possibility that it was not Grimshaw who owned the cravat pin, but Henry. Grimshaw and Henry were cousins—if the pin were Henry's, Grimshaw would have recognized it.

Her throat closed up in fright. But Henry, she reminded herself anxiously, was not the man they were after—it was Grimshaw. They were all certain that Grimshaw was the villain. An exceedingly unpleasant notion suddenly struck her.

She sat up straighter and said sharply, "Henry, never tell me that you are helping Grimshaw in some perfidious scheme!"

Henry laughed, never taking his eyes off his horses, which now, as the traffic began to ebb and the buildings began to thin out, he urged into a smart, distance-eating trot. "No, my dear, I am not helping Grimshaw, but you could say that Grimshaw helped *me*!"

Tamping down a rush of pure terror, telling herself that he could not mean what she thought he meant, she said crisply, "Henry, I demand that you turn this vehicle around this instant and tell me precisely what sort of game you are playing."

"It is no game, and I am afraid, my sweet, that you are in no position to tell me to do anything—unless, of course, you wish to leap from the carriage. I should warn you against such precipitous action. It is a long way to the road, and there is every possibility that I might run over you."

"It is a phaeton, not a carriage," she said absently, her thoughts jostling wildly. It was obvious that it was not a seduction she had to fear, and that left only one reason for Henry's actions.

Her fingers tightened on her frivolous parasol and she longed for the comfort of her pistol. Her pistol, which was now resting safely at home under her pillow.

Her spirits sank as several more unpleasant thoughts crossed her mind, and she was miserable until, with a stab of hope, she recalled Ives's having said that he would set one of his men to watch her at all times. Surreptitiously she glanced over her shoulder, praying that she would be able to spot her watcher, but the stretch of road behind her appeared depressingly empty, and she saw no one who looked even remotely familiar. It was possible, she admitted with deepening misgiving, that despite Ives's precautions, Henry had managed to elude the man assigned to watch her.

Her chin lifted, and she sat a little straighter on the seat beside Henry. Well, if she was on her own, so be it. She

would find a way out of this dangerous predicament all
by herself if she had to. Her faith in Ives never wavered.
He *would* come after her; he would destroy England to
find her. A little shudder of fear went through her. But it
would take him time, and time was something she didn't
think she had.

Having concluded that she was probably on her own,
she considered leaping from the phaeton, but Henry was
right. He had given the horses their heads, and they were
now flying down the road, and the ground was dangerously far away. Besides, there had been a note in Henry's
voice that warned her that he had no intention of letting
her escape—he would run her down before he'd let her
get away. A shiver went through her.

Her only hope, she realized, was to attract the attention
of a passerby, but at the moment they were driving
through a particularly sparse area, and there was no one
in sight. This was a busy road, however, and she was confident that any second several more vehicles or pedestri-
ans would come into view.

A farmer's cart suddenly came around a curve a quar-
ter mile down the road, followed by a lumbering freight
wagon, and her heart leaped.

To her dismay, almost instantly, Henry slowed the
horses and expertly swung down a small lane. It was as
he began to guide the horses into an old barn hidden from
the main road by a grove of trees that Sophy gathered the
courage to leap from the vehicle.

But Henry anticipated her move. Holding the reins in
one hand, he pointed a very small, very deadly pistol directly at her.

"Oh, no you don't," he said grimly. "You stay right

where you are. I have no intention of letting you go until it pleases me."

"You don't expect me to believe that you are going to let me go, do you?" she asked scornfully.

Ignoring her, he finished urging the horses into the building. After halting the animals inside the barn and seeing that they were standing quietly, with one hand he tied the reins to the whip socket and then brought forth a length of rope from its resting place beneath the seat. Despite the slight awkwardness of his movements, she noted unhappily that the pistol was always fixed unwaveringly on her.

A large noose had been formed at one of the rope and, mindful of the pistol, Sophy remained unmoving when he flung the noose over her head and shoulders and pulled it tight, securing her arms at her sides. After that, any chance of escape was doomed. Obeying his command to stand, Sophy soon was trussed up like a fowl for market, several coils of the rope wrapped tightly around her body from her shoulders to her ankles.

"You won't get away with this," she said, when he was finished. "My husband will find you and kill you."

"I'm sure that he will try," Henry replied easily as he lifted her down from the phaeton and set her on the ground. "And he might even have succeeded except for one thing. I have something that he wants more than my life—you. And as long as I have you, he will not lift a finger against me. In fact, he shall dance to the tune of my piping."

From her position propped against the wheel of the phaeton, Sophy watched him with great misgiving as he swiftly reharnessed his horses to the lightweight curricle opposite her. Desperately she sought a way of distracting him, some way of slowing him down, turning him from his purpose, anything that would give her time—time in which Ives, by some miracle, might discover her plight and find her before it was too late. They were, at present, not far from London, but once he loaded her into that curricle, and they set off for whatever destination Henry had in mind, any faint hope of Ives finding her vanished.

Finished harnessing the horses, he turned to survey her. "Well, my dear," he said jovially, his blue eyes twinkling, "it is almost time for the next stage of our journey. Once I have put on my disguise, we shall be on our way."

He grinned, and she wondered how she had ever thought him kind. "Unfortunately, you will not find this part of our journey quite so comfortable. I am afraid that the only place for you is under the seat. Any trail your husband may pick up will end here, even if he manages to find this place."

"I don't have the ruby pin with me," she said quietly.

Henry laughed. "That damned pin," he said with no apparent rancor, only rueful amusement. "I knew it was going to cause me trouble someday. I just never realized how much, or that it would take the form of your uncle's bumbling blackmail attempt. And I never thought that he would be such a fool as to reveal his plans to that detestable Agnes Weatherby. What difficulties they caused me."

Since there seemed little reason to hold back, Sophy asked bluntly, "You killed him, didn't you? And Miss Weatherby?"

Henry nodded. "Yes, I am afraid that I did." He gave a theatrical shudder. "It was a nasty moment or two, I can tell you, especially Agnes. In retrospect, I can see that perhaps I should have allowed him to blackmail me for a little while until I could get my hands on the pin. But you see, I had worked out such a tidy little plan—you were supposed to be accused of his murder." He frowned. "That wretched husband of yours ruined everything."

Sophy's lips tightened. "And the robbery? That was you, too?"

Turning away, Henry disappeared from her sight, but she could hear him moving about the barn. "Oh, yes," he replied in muffled tones. "Until Grimshaw told me last night, I did not know for certain that you had the pin; but after Edward's blackmail attempt, I was fairly confident that you did. For years I wondered if it had been well and truly lost, but I always suspected that if anyone had found it, it was you. And I am afraid I made the mistake of thinking that sleeping dogs were going to remain sleeping. Careless of me. And of course, Edward . . . Well, while Edward spouted a great deal of nonsense, he admitted that he did not presently have the pin, but that he could lay his hands on it anytime he chose. He also rather foolishly mentioned that he'd had an interesting conversation with you recently—he thought he was being very clever—and it took no great intellect on my part to connect his conversation with you and the pin."

Coming around the end of the curricle, he startled her by his transformation. Gone was the dapper, foppish Henry Dewhurst and in his place was a stolid, soberly dressed country gentleman of indeterminate age. It was not only his clothes which had been changed: He had added a pair of gold-rimmed spectacles and a neatly trimmed beard. She would not have recognized him if she passed him on the street.

"I see that I have done my work well," he said with satisfaction at the expression on her face. "Over the years I have perfected several different disguises. So useful."

"Why?" Sophy was compelled to ask. "Why are you doing this?"

He eyed her speculatively. "I wonder," he said musingly, "how much you really know." Then he shrugged. "Oh, well, it doesn't matter. You'll serve your purpose, and if you behave yourself, I might satisfy your curiosity. In the meantime, I am afraid that you are going to have to prepare yourself for an uncomfortable ride."

It *was* an uncomfortable ride. Having disposed of her hat and parasol, he wrapped her in a rug and squashed her under the seat of the curricle. Not only was she unable to move, but the ropes bit unmercifully into her arms and legs. It was also dark and stuffy in the small, cramped space where she had been stuffed.

Lying on the floorboards of the curricle, Sophy was subjected to every bump and dip in the road, and she prayed that the miserable journey would end. But where, she wondered bleakly, was Henry taking her? And what, precisely, did he plan?

Ives had a very good idea what Henry planned, and that knowledge did not lessen the icy fist of terror which clamped his heart. It was obvious that the Fox was on the run and bolting for France, and Sophy was his ticket to freedom. Henry would keep her alive until he reached French soil, of that Ives was convinced—he had to be or he would have gone mad. It was once Henry arrived in France that he refused to think about. Once the scoundrel landed in Napoléon's domain, there would be no real reason to keep Sophy alive.

Having sent Forrest to check on Dewhurst's whereabouts, Ives wrenched his mind away from that terrible thought, and bounded up the steps to the Berkeley Square house, hoping frantically that he could intercept Sophy. It was a faint hope, and he was not at all surprised when Emerson, his blue eyes slightly worried at the expression in Ives's face, informed him that Dewhurst had picked up Lady Harrington almost an hour ago. He had, also, Emerson added, left a note for the master.

Ives fairly ripped the note out of Emerson's hand and headed for his rooms, taking the stairs two at a time. He snapped over his shoulder, "Have my horse, the black, saddled and brought 'round immediately—and send Ogden, Ashby, and Sanderson to my rooms!"

"Er, m'lord, Ashby is not in. He said that he had an errand for you."

For a minute, Ives felt a rush of hope. Thank God, he had assigned one of his men to watch Sophy! Perhaps any second now, Ashby would be returning with news of Henry's destination!

Reaching his rooms, he wasted precious time reading Henry's note. The contents told him nothing new. They only confirmed his suspicions: Henry had indeed kidnapped Sophy and would hold her prisoner until he had reached the safety of France. If Ives behaved, Henry's word, Sophy would be returned to England unharmed. If, however, Ives proved to be foolish, again Henry's word, well then, Sophy would die.

His mouth in a grim, thin line, Ives crumpled the note and hurled it onto his bureau. That contemptible little bastard! Tossing aside his fashionable town clothing, he swiftly scrambled into breeches and boots. He was just shrugging into a bottle green jacket when Ogden and Sanderson arrived.

Curtly, Ives explained the situation. Once the shocked exclamations had abated, he said, "I must not linger. I am going to pay a call on Grimshaw. If anybody knows from which port Dewhurst plans to sail for France, it will be Grimshaw. As soon as Ashby returns, and I am sure that he will at any moment, send word to me."

The sound of thudding footsteps outside his room had Ives striding across the room and flinging open the door. It was Ashby, his face white, his breathing labored.

Gasping for breath, he managed, "It is Henry Dewhurst! He was supposed to take the mistress for a drive in Hyde Park, but he headed straightaway for the Dover Road. I followed for as long as I could on foot, but once he cleared the city, it was impossible." His face stricken, he said, "I'm sorry, m'lord. I lost them."

Ives clapped him on the shoulder. "It doesn't matter. You did your best. We will get her back, never fear."

Turning to the others, he said, "Get yourselves mounted and start riding for Dover. I will catch up with you." An inimical gleam lit the devil green eyes. "Grimshaw now has only to tell us precisely *where* in Dover we may find our quarry."

Ives was halfway to Grimshaw's town house when he met Forrest returning from Dewhurst's residence. Turning his horse and joining him, Forrest merely gave a shake of his head to Ives's cocked brow. Swiftly Ives imparted Ashby's report.

It was only when they pulled their horses to a stop in front of the elegant building that comprised Grimshaw's London house, that something occurred to Ives. He looked at Forrest. "Dewhurst lives just around the block, doesn't he?"

Forrest nodded, and Ives muttered, "Well, that explains Ogden's odd feeling. While we were wasting our time watching Grimshaw, Dewhurst was, no doubt, watching us! How that must have amused him."

Fortunately, Grimshaw was at home, although it was obvious he was just on his way out. He did not look pleased to see them, but he also did not seem surprised.

Ushering them into his library, he said mockingly, "This is a pleasure, gentlemen. What can I do for you?"

"You can tell me," Ives ground out, "where Dewhurst has taken my wife!"

A malicious smile curved Grimshaw's mouth. "Oh, dear. Has she run off with Henry? Pity. I always hoped that I would be the one."

Ives was across the room, his fingers locked around Grimshaw's throat before the words had hardly left his mouth. His green eyes nearly black with fury, Ives said softly, "No games. Tell me where Dewhurst has gone."

Grimshaw fought to tear loose Ives's iron grip, but to no avail. Ives let him struggle for a second, then increased his stranglehold. Grimshaw's eyes bulged, and he made a series of cawing noises.

The savage expression on Ives's face did not abate. "Tell me," he said in the same dangerously soft tone. "Tell me, and I will let you live. Otherwise . . ." His fingers tightened.

Grimshaw fought desperately for breath. Reading doom in the dark, savage face in front of him, he finally gasped out, "Folkestone. He keeps a small yacht at Folkestone—the *Vixen*."

"Just the yacht? No house?" Ives questioned swiftly, his fingers not lessening their unrelenting pressure.

"I only know about the yacht," Grimshaw choked out.

"He may have a house there, but I do not know of it. I swear it!"

"And do you know what your dear little cousin has been doing these past few years, hmm?"

Grimshaw hesitated, and Ives's lethal grip tightened. Grimshaw's fingers clawed helplessly at his hand. Desperately, he cried, "Have mercy, m'lord! You're killing me."

"And I shall, if you do not tell me what I want to know." Patiently, he repeated, "Tell me about Henry."

"I don't know anything—" he began, only to add hurriedly at subtle increased pressure of Ives's fingers around his throat, "at least not for certain. But I suspect that he has been in the pay of the French."

"And did you help him?"

"Good gad, no! I am no traitor." Grimshaw was clearly appalled at the idea. It seemed the bastard had his limits.

Ives smiled grimly. "No traitor yourself, but yet you suspected Henry and said nothing to the authorities?"

With as much haughtiness as he could muster under the circumstances, Grimshaw muttered, "Henry is my cousin. I would not betray a member of my family."

"And you are sure, quite sure that you do not know the direction of any dwelling place he may have in Folkestone?"

"I swear to you—on my life! I only know of the *Vixen*. He may have quarters in the village, but I do not know of any."

Ives regarded him for a long minute, and finally deciding that Grimshaw had told him the truth, he flung him aside as contemptuously as a dog would toss a dead rat.

"I think it would be wise," he said with terrifying politeness, "if you retired to the country for a while. And I should warn you that in the future, should you cross my path—or any of my family's"—he smiled a smile that had Grimshaw, from his position on the floor, edging warily away from him—"I am afraid that I shall have to kill you. Do we understand each other?"

Gasping and holding his injured throat, Grimshaw nodded.

"Good!" Ives said cheerfully. "This has been a most informative chat. We shan't keep you any longer."

It was not very many minutes afterward that Ives and Forrest met Ogden and the others. "Folkestone," Ives tossed at them, as his horse swept by. "And don't spare the horses—he has over an hour's head start on us."

There was no hope of catching Dewhurst if they stayed on the roads, and so, following the flight of the crow, Ives led his men in a direct line to the small fishing village of Folkestone, just south of Dover. They rode like madmen, taking fences and creeks and ditches at a breakneck clip, trampling over cropland and tearing through orchards, narrowly avoiding the wide, spreading branches of the trees. Only in order to conserve their mounts did they stop, allowing them to drink and rest briefly, before again taking up the chase. The tired horses sailed valiantly over stone walls and careened down hilly slopes as they neared their destination.

Darkness had fallen by the time they pulled their sweating, heaving horses to a standstill near the sleepy fishing village nestled at the foot of the chalk hills on the shore of the English Channel. Leaving their exhausted horses in an abandoned shed at the edge of the village, they dispersed on foot, drifting like ghosts toward the shabby waterfront.

Ives found the *Vixen* easily amongst the smattering of

fishing boats anchored in the harbor, her gleaming white sides and sleek lines trumpeting her aristocratic heritage. A fishing boat, she was not.

They watched for several minutes, and it soon became plain that they had reached Folkestone in time. There was no sign of activity on board the *Vixen*. But that situation was not likely to remain so for very long. They had, Ives estimated, minutes at most before Dewhurst arrived—with, pray God, Sophy.

There was a hurried exchange between Ives and Forrest as they continued to scan the yacht and surrounding area. "Are you insane?" Forrest hissed, when he heard of Ives's plan to board the yacht. "We outnumber him. We can take him here, before he ever reaches the damned boat."

"And while we are falling upon him," Ives asked levelly, "what do you think he will be doing to Sophy? Don't you think that he is going to have a pistol pointed right at her heart? If we make a move, *any* move, he will kill her."

Forrest hesitated. "We might be able to surprise him and overpower him before he can fire," he offered lamely.

"And we might *not*," Ives retorted. "I am not taking any chances with her life."

"And you think you'll stand a better chance alone at sea with him? Are you daft, man?" William Williams blurted out, anxiety etched on his long face. Appalled, he blushed and muttered, "Beggin' your pardon, m'lord."

In the faint light which came from a nearby ramshackle tavern, Ives grinned at him.

"No, you were right to question my wisdom. But, hear me, we dare not try to attack him as long as he has Sophy. He is going to be prepared for us to try to stop him from reaching his yacht. We will have no element of surprise, no opportunity to prevent him from hurting my wife."

His grin faded, and his eyes moved from face to face as he added fiercely, "And you can be bloody well assured that he will if he is cornered. Our only chance is to let him *think* he has escaped. Once on board the yacht and having put out into the Channel, he will drop his guard, confident that he has slipped past us. He will not be expecting me." Something ugly and deadly moved behind his eyes. "And then I will be upon him."

"I don't like it!" Forrest said vehemently. "It is too dangerous. We may lose both you and your lady. There must be some other way."

"There is not," Ives said flatly, and turned to look back at the yacht.

Despite some low-voiced, almost desperate arguments to the contrary, Ives would not be dissuaded. Unhappily, Forrest and the others kept vigilant watch as he crept aboard the yacht. Only when he gave a wave of his arm and disappeared below did Forrest move.

Sinking deeper into the shadows, he said gruffly, "If he thinks that we are going to let him risk his fool neck like this without doing something about it, he has lost his wits."

"But what are we going to do?" Ashby asked, his brown eyes fixed on Forrest's face.

Forrest cursed and despairingly looked out over the small waterfront. Spying a small, neatly crafted sloop, moored not far from the *Vixen*, his eyes narrowed.

"We," he said slowly, "are going to pirate a boat of our own and follow him—discreetly, of course."

Ogden grinned, his bad teeth glinting in the shadowy light. "Of course."

Chapter Twenty-two

✣

*W*hen Henry finally pulled his pair to a stop, Sophy breathed a fervent sigh of relief. Gagged and bound, she had been in that musty, cramped space for what seemed like forever, and for the last several miles she had been in the grip of a severe case of claustrophobia. Feeling as if she were smothering, as if the rug was pressing down against her nose and face, she had struggled to keep from screaming, terrified that if she started screaming, she would never be able to stop.

She forced herself to take deep, steadying breaths through her nose, to think of something else, to focus on anything but where she was and what was happening. Every part of her body ached—where it wasn't numb. She was certain she would never be able to walk again; her legs had to have become frozen in their bent position.

"Well, my dear," Henry's voice floated to her, as he leaped down from the curricle, "your current ordeal is almost over. Give me a moment to unharness my horses, and I shall let you out of your, er, rug."

The interval seemed to take hours, but true to his

words, Henry eventually returned and dragged her out from her hiding place. A few minutes later, the rug dispensed with, she was blinking owlishly in the light from a small lantern sitting on a rickety wooden bench.

As her eyes adjusted, she looked around and discovered that she was in a building hardly big enough to hold the curricle and the two horses. The place appeared to be seldom used; cobwebs draped the rough beams, and a thick coating of dust and debris lay over the flat surfaces.

"Not precisely what you are used to," said Henry politely. He studied her for a second. "I should tell you that this place is quite isolated. If I were to remove your gag and you were foolish enough to start screaming, it would do you little good. No one would hear you, and it would make me *very* angry. So, would you like your gag undone?" Meekly, Sophy nodded, and he reached down and removed the wad of rags from her mouth.

It was heaven to have her legs stretched out and the rags out of her mouth. For a second, she simply savored the sensations. Glancing up at him, she asked, "Where are we?"

"At Folkestone. I keep a small yacht here and, of course, a rather unpretentious little dwelling. I am sure that you will find its limited accommodations far more appealing than your current place."

Sophy was a little unnerved by Henry's polite, almost teasing manner. He was acting as if this were some sort of social call, as if he found the situation vaguely amusing, and not as if he had kidnapped her and kept her bound and gagged for the past several hours. He was a murderer twice over—and possibly a spy, a traitor who was responsible for the deaths of scores of men fighting against Napoléon. She shuddered, wondering how she could have been so misled, how she could ever have considered him a friend. He was a monster.

Something of what she was feeling must have shown on her face, for Henry smiled, and said bracingly, "Oh, come now, my dear, I am not all bad. And if you are a good little girl and do exactly what I say, you shall be set free to fly to the arms of your rather doltish husband."

Her eyes met his, and what she glimpsed in his was not reassuring. Ignoring the slur against Ives, she said bluntly, "I do not believe you."

Henry shrugged and bent down to drag her upright. "It doesn't matter whether you believe me or not. Behave yourself, and you might just get out of this alive."

It was awkward trying to walk, bound as she was. After a few difficult moments, Henry simply lifted her over his shoulder and traversed the short distance between the shed and the house. Inside, he dropped her into a chair and quickly lit some candles.

The house was no more impressive than the shed, but at least it appeared clean, and there was some degree of comfort. She was in a small room, furnished with a few comfortable leather chairs and some tables; a faded Turkey carpet in crimson and gold covered the floor. A tiny fireplace was against one wall, a pile of neatly stacked kindling lay on the hearth.

As she looked around, considering her chances of escaping, Henry pulled out his pocket watch and, seeing the time, made a clucking noise.

"Our journey took a trifle longer than I expected," he said conversationally. "But never fear, we shall not remain here for very long."

Crossing to her, he stood her up and explained, "Now listen to me, my dear, I must rearrange your ropes. Do not try to do anything stupid. Continue to be your sweet, docile self, and this ordeal will be far less painful than it could be. Do you understand me?"

Sophy was not deceived by his polite words or manner—it was clear that if she tried to escape, he would not hesitate to hurt her, and that he would enjoy doing it.

She remained stiffly upright as he worked, and she wondered why he had even bothered to warn her. He took no chances, and while she was soon no longer trussed up like a fowl at market, she was still just as securely bound. Dispensing with most of the rope, he fashioned a pair of efficient shackles for her ankles out of some of the lengths he had cut, leaving her just enough room to take small, mincing steps, but not enough to allow her any degree of freedom. The rope shackles were hidden beneath her skirts and her hands were resting in her lap, securely tied in front of her. At first sight, the bindings were not visible.

"You will, of course, be wearing a cloak when we leave for the yacht, and I shall have my pistol aimed directly at you," Henry said, as he surveyed his work a few minutes later. "I do not expect that we shall meet anyone, but all you have to do is simply smile and look pretty." His blue eyes hardened, and she wondered how she had ever thought them merry. "I will not hesitate to kill you if the need arises. Remember that, will you?"

Seating himself across from her, he took out his watch again and frowned.

"Are we waiting for someone?" Sophy asked politely.

"Yes, a, er, colleague. He seems to be running a trifle late." Henry smiled. "I suppose he is rather flustered by my unexpected change in plans; he had several arrangements to make. We were not to meet until tomorrow night. But I have complete faith in him—he has never failed me yet. Once he has arrived, we shall board the *Vixen* and be off to France."

"Is he a Frenchman by any chance? The gentleman to whom you have been selling military secrets?" Sophy inquired sweetly.

Henry's face darkened. "So, you know that, do you?" He eyed her narrowly. "I am surprised that your doting husband let you in on the game. I would have thought that Roxbury would want to play everything close to his vest."

Sophy shrugged. It suddenly occurred to her that perhaps it was not wise to reveal what she might or might not know.

Her mouth tightened. What did it matter? Henry was going to kill her. She was convinced of that, despite his assurances to the contrary. Her breath caught on an anguished sob. She would never see Ives again, never again know the sweet magic of his embrace . . . never grow old with him.

A rap on the door broke into her gloomy thoughts, and she glanced curiously at the fat gentleman who entered the room a few seconds later. He was a stranger to her, and from his clothes, though costly, it was immediately apparent that he was no member of the ton; a decidedly slovenly air entered the room with him.

It was also apparent from the ghastly expression on his face that he was horrified to see her.

"Mon Dieu!" he cried, greatly agitated. "What is *she* doing here? Have you gone mad? First you upset all our plans with this wild scheme, and now *this*!"

His speech clearly betrayed his origin, and Sophy's spirits sank lower—the Frenchman. She was running out of time. Once they left England's shore, she knew that there was no escape.

She did not have time to consider that terrible prospect; Henry jerked her to her feet and settled a cloak around her shoulders. Showing her the pistol he kept concealed underneath his jacket, he said, "You worry too much, my friend. Lady Harrington is my voucher for a safe crossing. With her on board the *Vixen*, even if Roxbury or her husband were lucky enough to have found me out, they would be helpless to strike at me." His voice hardened. "If they ever want to see her alive again, they have no choice but to let me go."

Some of the Frenchman's first alarm faded, and a crafty expression entered his eyes. "Perhaps you are right, but I tell you, *mon ami*, I do not like this. And what Paris will have to say, I dare not think."

"Paris," Henry said easily, as he guided Sophy toward the door, making sure she felt the barrel of his pistol in her ribs, "will be too busy crowing over the copy of the memorandum I carry with me to be overly concerned with my defection from England."

"You are probably right," the Frenchman answered resignedly, following close behind as they left the room.

"I usually am," Henry replied. "But of more interest to me is your part of our bargain—did you bring the gold?"

The Frenchman nodded. "*Oui*, it is outside in my carriage."

"Good! Once it is transferred to the *Vixen*, I shall be off for France."

Although it was a goodly distance from Henry's small cottage at the edge of the village to the harbor, to Sophy it seemed like an all-too-brief ride in the Frenchman's carriage. Her plight was hopeless; she knew that. Even if help were to miraculously appear, Henry's pistol jammed against her ribs precluded her from taking any action. But she was not ready to concede defeat. Not yet.

While the Frenchman and his driver unloaded a heavy trunk and placed it on the yacht, Sophy peered intently into the night, urgently looking for something she could use to her advantage. Nothing met her gaze. The streets appeared abandoned and lifeless. Despite the cold knot of fear in her chest, she told herself that she was not going to give up. Not even when Henry bid the Frenchman good-bye and the coach rumbled away did her determination to escape abate.

Looking Henry in the eye, she said levelly, "You will not get away with this. Ives will not let you. He will find me and when he does . . ."

Henry smiled at her. "Such loyalty does you credit, my dear, but I am afraid that your belief in your husband is overrated." He ran a caressing finger down her cheek, and she flinched. "If your husband were foolish enough to follow you to France, it would be too late, my sweet. By then you would be, ah, tarnished goods, and I do not believe that his pride would allow him to take you back. *If* he were to find you. No, I am afraid that you must resign yourself to pleasing me. Allow me to assure you that you shall not find me an ungenerous protector. Now shall we go below?"

"You bastard!" Sophy said forcefully, her eyes glittering like burnished gold.

Henry chuckled, and murmured, "Such passion! Do you know it was all that suppressed vitality I often glimpsed in your eyes when you defied Simon that first aroused my interest in you? I knew then that you were not as cool as you appeared. I suggest, however, that you save some of your righteous passion for when we are alone, my dear—I shall enjoy taming it." And then he forced her below into the galley.

To Sophy's great relief, after seating her on one of the bunks and checking her bonds, he went aloft. She swiftly scanned the small space for something, anything, to use as a weapon, but nothing met her gaze.

Hope that she might escape finally died when the *Vixen* weighed anchor and she felt the rocking motion of the Channel's waters against the hull. Blinking back tears, she stared dismally at the wall opposite her.

She would never, *ever* see Ives again! That thought disturbed her more than the knowledge of her own impending dishonor and probable death. Oh, Henry might keep her alive for a while longer, as long as she was useful to him, but she had no illusions about her fate: He intended to dispose of her at the first convenient opportunity. She had read it in his cold blue eyes.

Angry at herself, she berated herself for giving up so easily. If she believed she was defeated, then she well and truly was.

When Henry had gone up on deck, a small lantern had been left hanging from one of the beams of the yacht, its fitful light dancing and swaying with the motion of the yacht as it sailed deeper into the choppy waters of the Channel. Taking her time, she again looked carefully around the room. At first glance, nothing seemed to have changed. It was a small, simple galley, lined with a pair of bunks attached to each side of the hull: A heavy scrubbed oak table sat between them. A series of narrow cupboards and counters ran the length of one wall and, except for a few odds and ends of a nautical nature, the room was bare.

She would not accept defeat, she told herself stubbornly. There had to be something. The yacht gave a sharp lurch as it was buffeted by a particularly large swell and the lantern swung wildly, shining its light into one of the shadowy corners of the room. Sophy's heart leaped as she caught sight of a stout, long-handled hook. A gaff. Standing in the corner. A large, wickedly curved gaff. . . .

She flew off the bunk, grateful for the whim that had led Henry to tie her hands in front of her. Determinedly, her fingers closed around the handle of the gaff, and a feral smile curved her mouth. When Henry returned, he was going to be *very* surprised.

But Henry was already surprised, and not pleasantly. He had been busy with setting sail for the coast of France and had not been overly attentive to other events. The unexpected sight of a small sloop, her running lights fully lit as she tacked to the starboard side of the *Vixen*, sent a disagreeable chill through him.

He told himself that it was coincidence that the sloop left Folkestone right behind him. Despite his note to Harrington, he could not believe that Ives had found his trail that quickly. Few people knew about the *Vixen*, and the few who did would be unlikely to simply volunteer the information. No, no, it would take Sophy's wretched husband hours to pick up his direction, and by then, it would be too late. He was quite safe. The sloop was, no doubt, on a perfectly innocent journey.

He frowned. It was, however, an odd time of night to be crossing the Channel, and the vessel seemed to be keeping pace with the *Vixen*. The other boat would bear watching, but he was certain its presence had nothing to do with him. Almost certain.

He'd known, once Grimshaw told him about the ruby cravat pin, that he could not afford to linger in London.

Fleeing to France was the only course open to him. It was time. Remaining in England would have left him too vulnerable—once Roxbury and Harrington homed in on him there was no telling what they might discover. Henry sighed. He had enjoyed his run as the Fox, but it was over.

His gaze traveled to the trunk of gold sitting on the deck of the yacht. At least money would not be a problem, and naturally he would offer his services to Napoléon. Perhaps he could be of use ferreting out English spies in France. He smiled. He would like that. It would be a perfect revenge against Roxbury to find the old bastard's men and identify them for the French.

And as for Sophy. A distinctly carnal gleam lit his eyes. Of course, he would have to dispose of her, but not before some, er, time had passed.

All in all, he was not displeased with the circumstances. Grimshaw would help him transfer his assets from England to France, and even if he did not offer his services to Napoléon, he would be quite comfortable. Perhaps he would simply retire to his château in the Loire Valley, purchased some years ago during the Peace of Amiens.

Contemplating his future, Henry's gaze traveled fondly over his yacht. The *Vixen* had always been ready for an exigency such as this one. It was why he had bought and outfitted her in the first place. It was also why he had purchased a French château and maintained a generous sum in French banks. A spy always had to have his escape route planned.

Yes, the *Vixen* was a good little boat, and he was as familiar with her as he would have been with a mistress, which was why when his gaze fell upon the hatch cover of the small cargo hold near the stern of the boat, he stiffened. The cover was slightly askew . . . as if someone had lifted it and put it back carelessly. . . .

He glanced at the sloop, still relentlessly tacking along his starboard side. Henry cursed under his breath. Not only was the boat staying abreast of the *Vixen*, but the distance between the two boats had narrowed.

His gaze went back to the hatch cover. Had it moved? Pulling forth his pistol, he said sharply, "I know you are there! Come out immediately! Show yourself, or I shall shoot!"

Beneath the deck, crouched in the cramped space of the small hold, Ives swore viciously to himself. He'd known he was moving too quickly, known he should have waited until he was certain that Henry had gone below before attempting to leave his hiding place. But knowing Sophy was on board, having heard her voice, knowing she was alone and frightened and thinking herself beyond hope had made him reckless—and careless, he admitted savagely. Now what was he to do? Surrender to the bastard? Join Sophy in confinement?

"Harrington, is that you?" Henry demanded, as the moments passed and nothing happened. "I know it is—it could be no one else. Only a lovesick sapskull would be so foolhardy. Come out. Show yourself, or I shall have to bring that lovely wife of yours on deck and convince her to add her voice to mine." Henry chuckled. "And you won't like what I shall do to her to make her obey me."

That threat decided Ives. Resignedly, he pushed aside the hatch cover and stood up. He had lost the element of surprise, but at least he was on board the yacht with

Sophy. Surely he would be able to overpower Henry before the situation became fatal?

His back to the door leading down to the galley, Henry regarded him almost with amusement. The pistol was aimed at Ives's heart, but Henry's voice was most pleasant as he said, "So good of you to join us. In a way I was hoping for this—I so dislike leaving loose ends."

Ives smiled, forcing himself to adopt the same manner. "Is that what I am? A loose end?"

"Not precisely, but since I managed to rid the world of most of the Harringtons last year, it seems only fitting that I add you to the lot, doesn't it?"

Only by the deepening green of his eyes did Ives betray that the shaft had gone home. "So you admit that you sank their yacht and sent them to their deaths?"

"Oh, yes." Henry smiled. "I admit everything, my dear fellow. Why not? You are not going to live to tell anyone about it."

Peripherally, Ives caught a glimpse of the sloop, although some distance away, still loyally tacking alongside the *Vixen*. Forrest? It had to be! Feeling marginally more confident, Ives coolly climbed the rest of the way out of the cargo hold.

"So what are you going to do now?" Ives asked. "Shoot me?"

"Well, yes, that is precisely what I intend to do," Henry said amiably. "You didn't think I was going to take you to France with me, did you? No, no, dear fellow, I am not such a fool. You, I am afraid, are about to go into the Channel. Such a tragedy! I shall have Grimshaw send me the English papers—they will no doubt be full of the sad story of your demise." Henry glanced in the direction of the sloop. "And as for your friends, I'm afraid that there is little they can do to stop me—"

"But *I* can!" snarled Sophy, hurling herself out of the galley. Almost stumbling in her haste, she swung the gaff with all her might at Henry's pistol arm.

The sharp hook bit gratifyingly into the flesh of Henry's upper arm, and a yowl of shock and rage erupted from him as the pistol went flying. His face contorted by fury, he jerked the gaff free and braced to meet Ives's charge.

Like a jungle cat, Ives sprang across the short distance separating him from Henry. They grappled, Ives's powerful hand locked around Henry's wrist, keeping him from bringing the gaff into play. It was an ugly fight. The rocking of the boat kept both men off-balance, the knowledge that only death would be the final outcome driving both to brutal violence.

Sophy spared only a glance at the struggling figures as she scrambled after the pistol. It took a few minutes to find it, but her heart sang when her questing fingers finally closed around it.

Her bound hands hampered her movements, but not enough to make her helpless. Henry had made several mistakes tonight, Sophy thought fiercely, including leaving her hands tied in *front* of her, which allowed her not only to untie her feet, but to strike him with the gaff.

"Enough!" she cried. "It is over, Henry. I have you in the sights of the pistol."

But Henry was too maddened to pay her any heed. He was also aware that, locked in mortal battle with Ives, if she did fire the pistol there was every chance she might hit her husband instead. He was gambling that she would not risk it.

He was right. In mounting frustration Sophy watched the two men as they lurched and thrashed across the deck in front of her. Once she thought she had a clear shot, but the moment was lost instantaneously. Angrily, she lowered the pistol, still poised, however, to intervene at the first opportunity.

Larger and stronger, Ives had no doubt that he would overcome his opponent, but Henry was like a cat, supple and quick, and the fight went on longer than Ives would have thought possible. But the end came quickly; Ives tightened his hold on the arm which held the gaff and brought it down with one powerful motion against the railing of the boat. The sound of bone snapping hung in the air, and the gaff dropped from Henry's nerveless fingers.

Ives immediately stepped away, watching carefully as Henry stood there swaying near the edge of the boat, his broken arm hanging useless at his side. Sophy moved up to Ives's side, their shoulders almost touching.

"It is over, Henry," Ives said quietly. "You have lost."

Henry flashed them a ghastly smile. "Perhaps, but I'll not give you the satisfaction of taking me alive." He looked at Ives and laughed wildly. "It is fitting, do you not think, that I suffer the same fate as your father and uncle?" And with one last, agile movement, he flung himself over the side into the dark waters of the Channel.

Even as Ives lunged after him, he knew it was futile. He caught a glimpse of Henry's head bobbing in the waves and disappearing beneath the dark waters.

"He's gone," he said softly, turning to look at Sophy.

She flew into his arms. Wrapped protectively in Ives's strong embrace, Sophy's horror of the night faded as their mouths met.

"Take me home," she said breathlessly, several minutes later. "I find that I do not care for yachting in the least!"

It was Forrest's hail as the sloop sailed near that brought Sophy and Ives back to the present. Keeping abreast of the *Vixen*, there was a hurried exchange between Ives and Forrest, and in a matter of minutes Sophy, Ives, and the small chest of gold were standing on the deck of the sloop watching the *Vixen* sink beneath the waves.

Glancing at Ives's impassive face, Forrest remarked, "That was rather a clever idea of yours to sink the yacht. Claiming that Henry went down with his boat is a nice touch, too. It will certainly save his family a great deal of embarrassment and shame."

"It will also," Ives said blandly, looking away from the spot where the yacht had finally disappeared beneath the waters, "save us from having to answer a multitude of questions that I would just as soon avoid. As far as anyone is concerned, we went on a spur-of-the-moment sail and, for reasons we can only guess, the boat began to take on water. A fisherman happened by to save Sophy and me, but poor Henry was not so fortunate and went down with his yacht."

"What about the memorandum?" Forrest asked. "Do you think the French have it?"

Sophy spoke up. "I think I know the answer to that— it went down with Henry. He told a Frenchman that he had it on him."

"Which doesn't mean that the Frenchman doesn't remember some of the information, but since it was all fake anyway, it probably doesn't matter too much," Forrest said.

Ives nodded. "I don't think we have to worry about the memorandum any longer." He looked down at Sophy where she stood by his side on the deck of the sloop. "Can you identify the Frenchman?"

"Oh, yes. But how are we to find him?"

"I suspect from your description that Roxbury will recognize him."

It was not until the next evening that Roxbury heard the entire tale. Their horses worn-out, Ives and Sophy and the others found accommodations in Dover for the remainder of the night. It was late morning before they finally arrived back in London. Another several hours of sleep and a bite of nourishment left everyone feeling almost human.

Ives had written Roxbury a concise report of what had transpired, and though nearing exhaustion themselves, Forrest and William Williams, astride new mounts procured in Dover, had carried it on to London ahead of the others. Consequently, when Roxbury greeted Ives and Sophy the next evening, he was smiling hugely.

Seating himself in one of the chairs in Ives's study, he said jovially, "A most successful ending! Your family avenged, *Le Renard* dead, and the memorandum destroyed. Most successful."

Ives merely smiled and took a sip of his brandy. He and Sophy were sitting side by side on the small sofa, their hands clasped. Roxbury regarded them for a moment and, his eyes meeting Sophy's, he cleared his throat, and murmured, "I believe I owe you an apology, my dear. And an explanation for your husband's recent activities.

He wanted to tell you everything—it was at my insistence that he did not. I am the one with whom you should be angry."

Sophy dimpled. "You do not have to apologize. I had already concluded that you were the reason he was spending so much time with Simon's old friends—and *not* because he found their activities enjoyable, thank goodness! I could not bear it if I had been so foolish as to marry another callous libertine." She glanced at her husband. The look she sent him was so warm and loving that Roxbury decided this was one time that silence was the best course.

The possible identity of the Frenchman was discussed and Ives was correct—from Sophy's description, Roxbury recognized him.

"It sounds very much like the Chevalier Ledoux," said Roxbury with a frown. "He is not a true chevalier—he merely styles himself as such. His name has come up from time to time, but until now we have never seriously considered him a danger. He will bear watching." He suddenly smiled. "Hmm, I think perhaps we will let him run free for a while and see who his friends are. . . ."

After Roxbury left, Ives and Sophy remained in the small study. Having seen his godfather out, Ives returned to his seat beside Sophy. Taking her hand in his, he dropped a kiss on the back of it.

"Happy?" he asked, his green eyes caressing her face.

She looked thoughtful. "I think if you were to put down your brandy snifter . . ." And as Ives followed directions and carefully set down his brandy snifter, she added, "And if you were to put your arm here . . ." She gently placed his newly freed arm around her waist.

"Now then, if you were to put that other arm right here . . ." she murmured. Ives dutifully complied.

Encircled in his strong embrace, she glanced up teasingly at him from beneath her extravagantly long lashes and a tiny smile curved her mouth. "And, now, if you were to kiss me and tell me again how much you love me, I think that I would be, oh, *most* happy."

His arms tightened and his mouth came down on hers. "I am," he said several pleasurable moments later, "a most obedient husband, am I not?"

Sophy gave an enchanting laugh, her golden eyes glinting. "Indeed you are not, but oh, Ives, I *do* love you!"

"And I," he said softly as he enfolded her even nearer to him, "adore you!"

There was no more conversation between them; each knew what was in the other's heart. Except for the soft, inarticulate murmurings of the two lovers, it was quiet in the small room for a *very* long time.

If you enjoyed FOR LOVE ALONE,

don't miss Shirlee Busbee's

LOVERS FOREVER.

Turn the page for a special excerpt.

*"D*id you see that gown? And to wear it to Lady Oak-hurst's charity bazaar of all places! It was a shock, I can tell you, when I first laid eyes on it—cut so low, I didn't know where to look! And the color! As close to orange as I ever hope to see! You'd think at *her* age—why, she must be at *least* five years older than I, and I am not considered a green girl any longer—that she'd know better." Hester Mandeville, her lively face full of outrage, barely paused for breath before she went on in heated accents, "Her brother, Randal, not dead a year and Athena is already flaunting herself in a garment that I would not hesitate to stigmatize as fast!"

It was a summation that would have done a woman twice her age proud, but Hester's comment lost much of its moral-izing impact by being uttered with a note of such open envy that her niece, Tess, had to choke back a gurgle of laughter. While Tess had been startled to see Lady Athena, the earl of Sherbourne's older sister, wearing "colors" before the year of mourning was up, the gown hadn't been quite that bad. It had been cut rather daringly, it was true, but the shade had been more of a rich antique gold than orange!

Sending her pretty aunt, normally the most tolerant of

creatures, a look of affectionate amusement, Tess murmured, "But aren't we also beginning to wear some color again? You can't have forgotten," Tess went on with a sudden catch in her throat, "that Sidney died just eleven days after Lord Sherbourne."

Moral outrage over Athena Talmage's clothes was instantly suspended as both women were assailed by a wave of grief. Each dabbed at the corner of her eye with a handkerchief. Hester said fiercely, "Those wretched Talmages! There was no excuse for that wicked, wicked duel! It was done out of spite! Randal knew that Sidney was no swordsman. . . ." A tight, unhappy smile curved Hester's soft mouth. "It must," she added in a husky voice, "have come as a most unwelcome shock to the great earl of Sherbourne that my brother was not quite the novice with the blade that he had supposed." She took a shaky breath and blurted out, "I'm glad Sidney was able to kill him first. And I don't care if I am being uncharitable!"

For several seconds there was silence in the well-sprung coach as it bowled smoothly along the road toward Mandeville Manor, the home of the two ladies. Ordinarily it was a pleasant, if longish, ride from the small town of Hythe, on the coast of Kent, to the gracious welcome of Mandeville Manor, some twenty miles inland. Ordinarily, too, the women would have enjoyed the lovely October day—the sky was a brilliant blue with only a few clouds on the horizon, the sun still warm, the leaves of the oaks and beeches barely revealing a hint of the brilliant color they would display in another month. But neither lady was aware of the passing countryside—each was remembering the terrible tragedy that had shaken the very foundations of their comfortable life some ten months ago.

Staring blindly out the coach window, Tess felt the tears filling her eyes and she took a deep steadying breath, willing herself not to cry. Oh, but it was hard! She had adored her uncle. Sidney, the fifth Baron Mandeville, had been a high-spirited, sunny-faced individual, a handsome man with a merry charm. He'd always had a smile and a kind word for nearly everyone, and despite the fact that he had been a reckless gambler who had helped bring the family closer to ruin, Tess's deep affection for him had not lessened.

Tess's mother had died a few weeks after her birth some twenty-one years ago, and her father had lost his life in a hunting accident before she was four years old, so she had no clear memory of either of her parents. Before she had even been old enough to realize the tragedy that had struck her at such a young age, her father's sister, Hester, and his brother, Sidney, had ably filled the breach, showering her with warm, unstinting affection. Tess hadn't viewed her late father's siblings as parents precisely. Sidney had been only twelve years her senior, while Hester, seventeen years older than Tess, was a mature thirty-eight. Yet no one seeing her aunt's lovely, laughing face and slim form could possibly think of Hester Mandeville as matronly!

Tess sighed heavily as she continued to stare out the coach window, an errant shaft of sunlight suddenly turning a stray curl of hair from beneath her silk bonnet to flame. The death of her uncle Sidney had been doubly tragic—not only had she lost the nearest thing to a father she had ever possessed, but Sidney's death had brought the despicable Avery Mandeville on the scene and *everything* had changed!

Her generous lips thinned. She didn't really begrudge Avery his inheritance; she didn't mind so very much that Mandeville Manor and its broad acres were now his and that she and her aunt lived in their old home at his sufferance; she didn't even mind that he was constantly in and out of the manor, dividing his time between it and the London town house—they *were* his by law, after all. What she minded, and what brought a militant sparkle to her striking violet eyes, was his persistent and decidedly unwelcome pursuit of her hand!

At twenty-one, Tess Mandeville was an arrestingly beautiful young woman. Her rich red hair and black-lashed violet eyes were a stunning combination, and with her delicately sculpted features and trim, lithe body she was undeniably a tempting bundle of femininity. She was also, from her mother's side of the family, a sizable heiress, and while she suspected that Avery had no objection to her comely form, she was more than certain that it was her fortune that interested him the most!

It was common knowledge these days that the Mandeville fortune was sadly in need of repair and that poor Sidney had been haphazardly looking for an heiress to marry before his untimely death. The Mandevilles were not destitute by any means. They could, with a few economies, easily maintain a comfortable way of life; but they certainly could no longer spend money without thought of the future. Receiving word of Sidney's death, Avery, the newest heir to the barony and a distant cousin, had immediately resigned his captaincy in the infantry and returned to England, eager to claim his title and fortune. Upon his arrival from the continent, where he had been fighting under Sir Arthur Wellesley against Napoleon's troops on the Iberian peninsula, he had been greatly displeased to learn that while he could now style himself Baron Mandeville and claim the elegant rooms of Mandeville Manor and the equally sumptuous rooms of the London town house, there was very little ready money with which to support the luxurious lifestyle he felt was his due. It had been swiftly borne upon the new baron that marriage to an heiress was definitely needed. And who should be there right beneath his nose but Tess . . . lovely, unmarried, and so very suitable for his needs. Tess with her greed-inspiring fortune, at present and until she either married or attained the grand age of twenty-five held in trust for her—and excellently guarded from scheming individuals—by one of her mother's younger brothers, Lord Rockwell.

A little smile suddenly flashed across her expressive face. Tess may have lost her parents at an early age, but happily she had been blessed with caring relatives on both sides of her family. Not only had she enjoyed the unstinting affection of Hester and Sidney, but she was also, albeit carelessly, doted upon by her mother's two brothers. Thomas, the current Lord Rockwell, and Alexander, as handsome and as charming a rogue as one would ever meet. Tess seldom saw either of her maternal uncles, which was hardly surprising since Thomas and Alexander were several years her senior and both were well-known, much-in-demand men about town who seldom strayed from the wickedly exciting environs of London. It was true she was infrequently in their company, but she was always aware of their affectionate concern for her.

Her gaze narrowed. A letter from her, containing just a hint of the new Baron Mandeville's increasingly distasteful wooing, and she knew her tall, broad-shouldered uncles would swoop down from London and with brutal efficiency teach Avery a much needed lesson.

Catching a glimpse of the fierce sparkle in her niece's eyes, Hester asked, "What makes you look so, my dear?"

Smiling across at her aunt, Tess said lightly, "I was just imagining the expression on Avery's face if Thomas and Alexander were to pay him a visit."

A hint of color surged inexplicably into Hester's cheeks, but her voice was determinedly casual as she said, "I'm certain that Alexander wouldn't hesitate a moment to take him to task if you breathed just the merest hint of your difficulties with Avery. Alexander is the kindest, most considerate gentleman I know, and he simply would not allow you to be badgered—especially by the likes of Avery! Both of your uncles are very protective of you and rightly so." She smiled faintly. "Their interest would certainly put Avery on the horns of a dilemma, wouldn't it? He wouldn't know whether to fawn upon them, hoping to gain their good graces, or whether to puff with outrage that they suspect him of ungentlemanly activities." Hester's smile faded and she asked quietly, "Has he been particularly unpleasant? Shall I speak to him?"

Tess shook her head. "No, you know we dare not do anything that might impel Avery to demand that we leave Mandeville Manor—Aunt Meg would be devastated."

Since Sidney's death it was a complicated situation in which Tess found herself. Actually, her situation wasn't terrible at all; she was the possessor of a fortune and two fond uncles who would move heaven and earth to keep her happy—she could escape from Mandeville Manor any time she chose to. It was Hester's fate and that of her great-aunt Margaret that kept Tess chained to the manor house in which she had been born.

It was odd, Tess thought, how many of the troubles of the Mandeville family seemed to go back almost seventy years ago, to the 1740s, to Gregory, her great-grandfather, and his despicable abduction of Benedict Talmage's bride-to-be, the Dalby heiress. Theresa Dalby had possessed the red hair and violet eyes that Tess herself had inherited. A tremor of unease suddenly quivered through her as she wondered if she might share her great-grandmother's fate—marriage to a man she did not love.

It was an old, sad tale. Once upon a time there had lived in amiable harmony, as neighbors and friends, the Talmage family, earls of Sherbourne; the barons of Mandeville; and the Dalbys. While the Dalbys could not style themselves as lords of the realm, they were of aristocratic birth and breeding and possessed an immense fortune. The last holder of the Dalby name had been knighted and so could call himself *Sir* Arthur Dalby. It was Sir Arthur's only child and heiress, she of the flame red hair and dancing violet eyes, who had been Tess's great-grandmother and for whom she had been named. The Dalby lands had been situated between the Sherbourne and Mandeville estates, and when it became obvious that Theresa would be the last Dalby and would inherit everything, it wasn't so surprising that the earl of Sherbourne and Baron Mandeville should cast appraising gazes in that direction. Especially so, since each man had an unmarried son . . . a son who as Theresa's husband would gain all those broad acres and all the immense wealth of the Dalby fortune.

An intense rivalry broke out between the earl of Sherbourne's heir, Benedict, and Baron Mandeville's eldest son, Gregory, as both men competed furiously for the hand of the heiress. It had seemed, when Theresa's betrothal had eventually been announced, that Benedict had won the contest and that Gregory would have to retire gracefully from the fray. Unfortunately, Gregory Mandeville was *not* a gracious loser; barely a week before Theresa Dalby's marriage to Benedict Talmage was to take place, Gregory cravenly abducted her from her home.

Despite the Dalby fortune, it had been a love-match between Benedict and Theresa. By stealing his hated rival's bride-to-be, Gregory had not only struck a powerful blow to Benedict's pride, but he had also grievously wounded his heart. Painfully aware of what means Gregory would use to force Theresa's compliance, Benedict searched frantically from one end of England to the other, knowing that when he found the pair that he would be too late to prevent the unthinkable—Theresa's brutal ravishment by Gregory. Benedict's unceasing, desperate quest came to naught. It was not until nearly a year later that Gregory dared return to Mandeville Manor with his new wife *and* their newborn son.

Gregory certainly hadn't taken any chances, Tess thought with a grimace of distaste. Not only had he abducted another man's bride, but he had kept her well hidden until she was not only pregnant by him, but had borne his child. A wave of pity swept through her as she imagined Theresa's anguish. Abducted, raped, and forced to bear the child of a man she loathed.

"Do you think that Great-Grandmother Theresa ever felt anything but hatred and disgust for him?" Tess suddenly asked Hester.

Understandably confused by the question, Hester blinked at Tess, obviously attempting to gather her thoughts. "Are you referring to Gregory and Theresa?" At Tess's quick nod, Hester shrugged. "I don't know. I mean, it's not as if it were something I could ask her about, was it?"

Tess's mouth twisted. "I suppose not. I've just always wondered how she coped. It must have been horrible for her."

Perfectly willing to discuss the matter, but totally mystified about why Tess should be interested in something that had happened so long ago, Hester said quietly, "Well, she didn't have to cope for very long—remember, she and Benedict disappeared together three or four years later."

A dark look on her face, Tess muttered, "I know, but before *that* she had to endure Great-Grandfather *and,* don't forget, watch the man she really loved marry another. They both must have been utterly miserable—she married to a blackhearted scoundrel and Benedict finally forced to marry for the sake of his title. It must have been bitterly heartrending for her when Benedict's son was born. I don't doubt that every time she looked at her own son she didn't think that, except for dear Gregory's perfidious actions, the baby would have been hers and Benedict's."

"It happened a long time ago, Tess. Why are you brooding on it now?"

"I don't know," Tess answered truthfully. "I suppose it has to do with the fact that everyone says I look so much like her—even *I* can see the resemblance between myself and the portrait of her in the gallery. But it's not just the hair and eyes or even the shape of my face . . . it's something inside of me—there are times I feel such affinity with her—almost as if I can feel every emotion she felt." Her mouth set in grim lines. "And I know she hated my great-grandfather with every bone and fiber of her being! I just hope that she and Benedict had a long happy life together when they finally ran away."

"Well, Gregory certainly had a *long* life after she deserted him—and I find it ironic that he outlived not only their son, Richard, but one of his grandsons as well—your father, Edward. Ninety is a vast age, but I doubt he enjoyed very many of those added years."

"He may not have enjoyed them, but I suspect he was thoroughly enraged when he realized that he was dying." Tess shook her head. "He was such a despotic presence, even though he's been dead for over two years now, that sometimes when I walk into the blue salon, I expect to find him sitting there glaring at me."

Hester's soft mouth thinned. "I know it is unkind to speak poorly of the dead, but he was such a devil! He was most unkind to you, Tess, no doubt because of your resemblance to Theresa."

"Clearly he hadn't the least feeling of affection for any of his family. You'd think he'd have left his own sister better provided for, and as for you . . . well, I think he was still punishing you for not finding a wealthy husband, and that's why he made such a shabby provision for you in his will. He *wanted* you and Margaret to know that he didn't give a farthing about your future!"

Hester averted her face, and Tess could have bitten her tongue off. Hester had never said anything directly, but Tess knew that in the past there was someone her aunt had loved or was still in love with, and that her lack of fortune or his had something to do with Hester's unmarried state.

Tess was frantically seeking some way to change the topic when Hester began to speak. Her voice constricted, she got out, "Grandfather couldn't have known that Sidney would die so young. He knew Sidney would take care of Aunt Meg for the rest of her life. And as for me . . ." She smiled painfully, "I never was a particular favorite of his anyway."

"Are you defending him?" Tess demanded, outraged, her violet eyes nearly purple with anger. "You just said he was a devil! And as for *your* not being a particular favorite of his . . ." Tess suddenly grinned. "Oh, but wasn't he furious that his only great-grandchild should turn out to be a mere girl?"

Hester smiled wryly. "Indeed he was. I can remember the day you were born—he took it as a personal affront that your poor father and mother had produced only a puny female. I can still recall his ranting and raving as he stormed through the manor. He was absolutely livid. Claimed your dear mother had done it on purpose, just to spite him. Swore he'd find a way to prevent your father from inheriting the title if the next child wasn't a boy!" Hester shook her head. "I wonder, when your father died just a few years later, if he didn't regret his hasty words." She grimaced and added, "Probably not. He always seemed to believe that he could arrange things precisely as he wanted."

Everything Hester said was true. Tess had grown up under the malevolent eye of her great-grandfather, and during his lifetime, not a day had gone by that she hadn't been reminded that she should have been a boy or that she looked like the wife who had deserted him and vanished with another man. It hadn't sat well with Gregory, either, that she was an heiress in her own right and her fortune was safely in the hands of her uncle, where he could not get his grasping hands on it.

Gregory might not have known Sidney would die so improvidently, Tess conceded grimly, but he certainly had known that by not setting aside a decent amount in his will for Margaret and Hester, he was condemning them to a miserable existence if something *did* happen to Sidney. She would concede that by the time he died Gregory didn't have a grand fortune to command any longer, but from what remained, he could have settled enough money on each of his female dependents to insure them an independence—even if only a frugal one.

Which brought Tess back to her dilemma. Her own fortune was secure, but Margaret and Hester were at the mercy of the new Baron Mandeville for the roof over their heads and the very food they ate. Tess would have gladly expended a portion of her own impressive fortune on her aunt and great-aunt, but both ladies were loath to take advantage of her sincere offer. Despite several long conversations, usually when Avery had done something especially upsetting, Tess couldn't seem to make them understand that allowing her to provide for them would be no different from allowing Avery to see to their care. But both ladies were horrified at the idea of Tess using her fortune to take care of them—they were Mandevilles! It was up to Avery to see to their care. In some convoluted manner that made absolutely no sense to Tess, they felt that it would be unfair to her, that they would be taking undue advantage of her, if they allowed her to settle a reasonable sum on them.

Tess sighed heavily. Unless or until events became absolutely unbearable at Mandeville Manor, neither of the two women dearest to her in the world was willing even to hear of using Tess's money for their own benefit. In the meantime, in spite of Avery's odious attentions, and the possible danger to herself should he decide to follow Gregory's methods of obtaining a fortune, it was unthinkable that she simply abandon Hester and Aunt Meg to the indifferent care of that smarmy toad Avery! Which meant, Tess admitted uneasily, she had to stay at Mandeville Manor and helplessly watch over Hester and Aunt Meg like a hen with two chicks confronted by a rapacious tomcat!

A few minutes later Hester broke the thick silence by asking curiously, "Why were you thinking about the old scandal? Gregory's abduction of Theresa and her later disappearance with Benedict Talmage occurred decades ago. What made you think of them now?"

Tess shrugged. "I guess I had been thinking about the way things have turned out—Sidney's death and how if Gregory hadn't acted so despicably, there wouldn't be such enmity between ourselves and the earls of Sherbourne. Of course Gregory still would have been a spendthrift and wasted most of the money. So the Mandevilles would still probably have ended up in need of *another* heiress with which to repair their fortunes."

Hester shot her a look. "Are you certain that Avery hasn't been annoying you?"

"Oh, perhaps, a little." She glanced slyly at her aunt. "If you and Auntie Meg would let me set you up in a tidy little house near Hythe, I wouldn't have to endure his company at all!"

Hester looked distressed. "He *has* been pestering you!" Leaning forward, she said earnestly, "You don't have to stay, darling. You know your uncles would be most happy if you went to London or to Lord Rockwell's estate in Cornwall to live. And though we would miss you like the very devil, Meg and I would do fine. . . ." She took a deep breath and blurted out, "And if he decides to cast us out of the house or he becomes too obnoxious for us to bear, we will let you buy us that little house!"

"But not until then?"

"Oh, Tess! You are the sweetest child in nature, but you know that we cannot. It would not be right!"

Seeing the worry in her aunt's eyes, Tess put on a sunny expression and said lightly, "Well, I don't think I'd be happy in London, and as for Cornwall, I'd much rather be right here with you—even if it means putting up with Avery!"

The coach slowed and a moment later they were traveling down the elm-lined drive that led to Mandeville Manor. The manor itself appeared shortly, an elegant half-timbered house built in Elizabethan times. Dark green ivy pressed itself to the sides of the building and softened the outlines of the many dormers in the tiled roof; the lattice-worked windows gleamed in the fading sunlight. With a flourish the carriage swept around the shrub-lined circular drive, and the coachman brought the horses to a stop at the base of the broad steps that led to the massive double entrance doors.

The horses had barely been pulled to a stop before one of the carved oak doors was thrown open and a tall man in buff breeches and a form-fitting coat of bottle green came strolling down the stone steps to meet the ladies. The gentleman, Avery Mandeville, the sixth Baron Mandeville, was without a doubt an attractive male, possessed of a well-made body with broad shoulders and slim hips; and the fact that he had been a military man before inheriting the title was obvious in the way he carried himself, his back ramrod straight, his head high. He far more resembled his third cousin, Gregory, than had any of Gregory's immediate offspring, having inherited Gregory's notable thick blond hair and icy blue eyes as well as the handsomeness that ran in the family.

In fact, watching his approach, Tess thought that he could have been her great-grandfather at the same age. A shiver went through her. The knowledge that she bore a striking resemblance to Theresa and that Avery's features were uncannily those of Gregory's made her distinctly uneasy. While the situation was different, she couldn't help wondering, since fate seemed to have assembled a pair of copies of the original players in herself and Avery, if history wasn't going to repeat itself.

Deliberately she shook off her unpleasant musings. It couldn't happen again—she'd never marry Avery, no matter *what* he did! She was far more likely to take a dagger to him if he ever laid a hand on her. As for her being desperately in love with a descendant of the earl of Sherbourne, the whole idea was ludicrous! She'd never met Randal Talmage's youngest brother, the latest earl of Sherbourne, nor did she even know his name. Love an unknown stranger indeed!

Books by Bestselling Author
Fern Michaels

Romantic Suspense from
Lisa Jackson

More by Bestselling Author
Hannah Howell

__Highland Angel	978-1-4201-0864-4	$6.99US/$8.99CAN
__If He's Sinful	978-1-4201-0461-5	$6.99US/$8.99CAN
__Wild Conquest	978-1-4201-0464-6	$6.99US/$8.99CAN
__If He's Wicked	978-1-4201-0460-8	$6.99US/$8.49CAN
__My Lady Captor	978-0-8217-7430-4	$6.99US/$8.49CAN
__Highland Sinner	978-0-8217-8001-5	$6.99US/$8.49CAN
__Highland Captive	978-0-8217-8003-9	$6.99US/$8.49CAN
__Nature of the Beast	978-1-4201-0435-6	$6.99US/$8.49CAN
__Highland Fire	978-0-8217-7429-8	$6.99US/$8.49CAN
__Silver Flame	978-1-4201-0107-2	$6.99US/$8.49CAN
__Highland Wolf	978-0-8217-8000-8	$6.99US/$9.99CAN
__Highland Wedding	978-0-8217-8002-2	$4.99US/$6.99CAN
__Highland Destiny	978-1-4201-0259-8	$4.99US/$6.99CAN
__Only for You	978-0-8217-8151-7	$6.99US/$8.99CAN
__Highland Promise	978-1-4201-0261-1	$4.99US/$6.99CAN
__Highland Vow	978-1-4201-0260-4	$4.99US/$6.99CAN
__Highland Savage	978-0-8217-7999-6	$6.99US/$9.99CAN
__Beauty and the Beast	978-0-8217-8004-6	$4.99US/$6.99CAN
__Unconquered	978-0-8217-8088-6	$4.99US/$6.99CAN
__Highland Barbarian	978-0-8217-7998-9	$6.99US/$9.99CAN
__Highland Conqueror	978-0-8217-8148-7	$6.99US/$9.99C
__Conqueror's Kiss	978-0-8217-8005-3	$4.99US/$6.99C
__A Stockingful of Joy	978-1-4201-0018-1	$4.99US/$6.99C
__Highland Bride	978-0-8217-7995-8	$4.99US/$6.99C
__Highland Lover	978-0-8217-7759-6	$6.99US/$9.99C

Available Wherever Books Are Sold!

Check out our website at
http://www.kensingtonbooks.com